THE MAN FROM LISBON

He had a plan so simple that only a madman or a genius would have tried it. And its beauty, he knew, lay in the fact that it had never been done before and could never be done again. The absolutely unique crime.

THE MAN FROM LISBON

He dared to love forbidden flesh—the Scandinavian actress who taught him the mysteries of love—though she alone could shatter his empire and explode his foolproof scheme.

THE MAN FROM LISBON

"Thomas Gifford is a great discovery. He is a born writer . . . *The Man From Lisbon* is the contemporary adventure novel at its best."
                                        —C.P. Snow

THE MAN FROM LISBON

THOMAS GIFFORD

PUBLISHED BY POCKET BOOKS NEW YORK

POCKET BOOKS, a Simon & Schuster division of
GULF & WESTERN CORPORATION
1230 Avenue of the Americas, New York, N.Y. 10020

ISBN: 0-671-82070-2

First Pocket Books printing November, 1978

For
Julian Bach

I am not I;
he is not he;
they are not they.

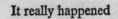

It really happened

PART ONE

THE EDUCATION
OF ALVES REIS

Artur Virgilio Alves Reis. His earliest boyhood memory was as much a recurring dream as it was the recollection of actual events. Yet he supposed, as the years went by and his life took its final shape, that he remembered it pretty much as it had happened. It came often, haunted him like the phrase of an old tune; perhaps because the occasion itself had marked his first venture into the tightly wound complexity of human existence, into the area of refined, obstinate truth where Alves realized for the first time that everyone was not alike.

The year was 1904 and he was eight years old. A Sunday morning in the spring: it seemed to Alves that it was probably Easter. But every Sunday had been a dress-up, go-for-a-walk day. The family, turned out in its only finery, went to the church that morning—the glorious, magical Church of Sao Rocque with its priceless gold altars and tons of brilliant lapis lazuli—and then for a long walk in the feathery weightlessness of the sunshine, through the fragrant streets of Lisbon, a promenade far from the dark, narrow street where his father's mortuary catered to the people who had to scrimp enough together to launch a loved one into the great beyond.

There was Alves' faintly mustachioed mother with her short legs thumping out the pace; his short, stringy father; the older son who was afflicted with a squint; and young Alves with the innocent eyes he would never outgrow. His father had once possessed a similar innocence and a small inheritance, both of which he lost in a slightly shady deal involving inferior cork. With what was left he'd set himself up in the funeral parlor, scraped by with two worn black suits and a shiny pair of black shoes. He lived under a terrible strain that Alves understood only much later, long after his father had died. Having once enjoyed a degree of status however slight, the elder Reis had been forced to accept his own diminution, a particularly galling fate for a Portuguese invested with the customary measure of national and personal pride. Years later he still saw his father cursing impatiently at his fate. By then Alves knew what had really been the trouble: there simply hadn't been enough money. Money, money, money.

There was an air of excitement that Sunday, almost palpable, and a fresh, ceremonial flower bloomed in his father's buttonhole. His mother's flowered shawl fluttered transparently in the breeze. His brother peered anxiously through his thick magnifying spectacles: his eyes floated like dark olives on either side of his broad nose.

Block after block went by, past blue tiled courtyard walls, skipping beneath a glassy pale-blue sky, until finally his father pulled up abruptly, uttered a brief exclamation, and gestured down what seemed to be only another pleasant avenue, tree-lined, coolly shaded, unremarkable He pointed excitedly at the name of the street discreetly lettered on the pink courtyard wall of a large three-story house. Young Alves was at a loss.

"This avenue " his father declaimed, "with all its grand houses and fine trees—" he swept his hand in a broad arc, building the suspense—"Avenue Francisco da Silva Reis, is named in honor of a great man, my sons . . . a man who was an admiral of the Portuguese fleet!" He fixed the boys with a slightly mad gaze as if a candle were flickering in the depths of his dark, onyx eyes. Alves instinctively reached for his mother's warm hand.

His father embarked on another of his frequent disquisitions on the role of the sea and sailors in the life of the Portuguese The sea, he pointed out, was the highway used to establish the most magnificent empire in the history of the world, the most far-flung, the most powerful . . . He summoned up the names of the greatest of all navigators, men like Henry the Navigator and Bartolemeu Diaz Vasco da Gama and the mighty Magellan, who had sailed off from the mouth of the Tagus River to circumnavigate the globe! He may have glossed the surface of history a trifle, but the fact was that little glossing was needed: the two boys

listened, swept on by their father's eloquence. He told
them of how the Portuguese crown had rejected Christopher
Columbus' requests because they had no need of yet another great seaman, sent him packing back to Queen Isa-
bella . . . otherwise, Portugal would have sponsored the
voyage to discover North America.

"And, my sons, Admiral Francisco da Silva Reis was
your great-uncle! Yes, *your great-uncle!* The blood of da
Silva Reis flows in your veins! You must never forget that
—never." He leaned down and placed his arms around
their shoulders. "You are not the sons of an undertaker,
my boys—you are the great-nephews of the great Admiral
da Silva Reis . . . after whom a great avenue of Lisbon is
named." It was a very long time before Alves Reis, a
grown man, realized what a price his father must have
paid as he spoke. Humility, he knew by then, came hard
to a Portuguese.

The blood of da Silva Reis flows in my veins . . . It was
a peculiar idea for little Alves to cope with, an abstraction
that made precious little sense. What did it mean?

He pondered the possible implications of his father's
claim as he and his brother skipped ahead of their parents
on the walk home to the Sao Tiago district. They trampled
the jacaranda leaves on the paving stones and the purple
stains spread, leaving a trail. And Admiral da Silva Reis,
grand as he may well have been, faded from their minds
as they ran, faded as they crumpled the leaves of the orange
and tangerine trees in their tiny fists, inhaling the released
essence, pungent, intense, concentrated. The scents clung
to Alves, like his memory of the day, as the years multi-
plied.

Although the sky was still vividly blue when they turned
toward home, the street itself was engulfed in deep shadow,
the structures on either side seeming to tilt forward, as if
trying to lean against one another for support above the
slippery smooth cobblestones. Alves smelled his grandmother's cooking before he reached the doorstep: fish
stew—and, having gone without lunch, he was ravenous.

Grandmother was a short, stumplike woman with thick
gray hair, shapeless dresses, a deeply lined face the color
of stained oak, and she spoke a dialect he only partly understood. He did not realize then just how primitive her
life had been, how much a product of the Middle Ages she
was; but he knew that her grandmother had survived the

earthquake of 1755 that had destroyed much of Lisbon.
Through her he had glimpsed for the first time his Portuguese past, the days of the limitless empire when Portuguese
seamen ruled so much of the globe. . . . Even as a boy
of eight he had learned those lessons. And such a grandmother made the lessons take on the pulse of life. At times
it seemed that, surely, she must have marched to the Tagus
to watch Henry the Navigator set sail.

The shadowy, narrow house was dark. There was no
electricity anywhere on the block. A skylight provided a
glow and there were lanterns, candles, firelight. His grandmother was humming a tuneless peasant song, her breath
whistling in spaces where there had been no teeth for half
a century. He went to taste the pot of stew, answered her
cursory questions about the afternoon's stroll, stuck his
tongue against the wooden spoon and drew back from the
scorching brew. Climbing up on a stool to watch the old
woman cook, Alves felt secure as only a child can feel in
familiar surroundings, however modest.

His grandmother was stealthily sneaking up behind the
family dog, a spirited, bedraggled specimen who snored
peacefully beneath the scarred kitchen table. Carefully she
took hold of a few strands of flank hair, wrapped it around
her finger and proceeded to saw it clean through with a
kitchen knife Suddenly aware that something out of the
ordinary was being done to his body, the hound awoke
with some alarm, skulled himself on the underside of the
tabletop, staggered dizzily toward the center of the room,
upending his dinner dish, and wobbled yelping down the
hallway toward the front door through which the undertaker and his wife were just now appearing. Their meeting
produced several peculiar sounds as the dog in his confusion mistook them for his attacker. Several minutes were
required to restore the house's normal somber tranquillity.
The dog retired to a safe distance, crawling beneath the
bed shared by the two brothers, and in the meantime Alves
watched his grandmother carry out the errand for which
she had required the dog's hair.

The old woman methodically wrapped the hair in a
triangle of gray cloth. tied it with a piece of greasy string
from the pocket of her apron and with a dozen hearty
whacks of her hammer—adding immeasurably to what
Alves felt was the hugely enjoyable din—nailed the packet
to the plaster wall behind the back door that led to the

alleyway. One of the structure's countless cheaply framed reproductions of Sao Rocque and his dog, the saint for whom their church was named and whose devotion it so sumptuously celebrated, leaped from the wall by the door and clattered to the floor. Alves hugged his knees at the excitement.

When the racket had subsided he took his grandmother's hand and drew her to the packet of hair nailed to the wall.

"Why is this necessary, Grandma? What does it do?"

The old woman gave a snort as if to say that there was obviously little hope for the twentieth century if young men of eight still needed to ask such questions.

"Because," she whistled elaborately, "the dog has been staying out all night, getting into unimaginable mischief . . . bothering our neighbors! I thought even you, a child, knew that the dog's hair behind the door made sure there would be no more such excursions. I *thought* everyone knew that—maybe your father forgot to tell you that. . . . You make sure you remember and when the time comes you tell your children." She waddled back to the woodburning iron stove.

A family of several cousins was expected for dinner that evening, and by chance they brought with them the son of a friend, a boy Alves had met before and to whom he had taken quite a shine. José dos Santos Bandeira, three years older than Alves, was a slender, olive-skinned eleven-year-old with the eyes of an old man, or at least a cynic, punctuating what showed every sign of becoming exceedingly handsome features. The Bandeira family owned land south of Lisbon and maintained residences both in the city and the country. Alves had first encountered José on a visit to these same cousins, had spent a long, grass-stained afternoon of rough-and-tumble on the lawn of the country home, during the course of which he had confided that his father was a mortician and regularly laid hands upon the bodies of the dead! The effect on José had been galvanic: nothing would do but that he visit Alves' father's place of business.

Now, with the chance to impress his new and much older friend both with his grandmother's delicious stew and one of his father's corpses, Alves was quite nearly beside himself with excitement. He took pains to show José the dog hair behind the door and the dog himself beneath the bed. José, whose family was more sophisticated and less saturated with superstition, found the packet of hair most amusing and congratulated Alves on his choice of a grandmother. Alves was enjoying his role of host.

But the evening itself was less than first-rate entertainment for the two boys. The conversation was tedious adult stuff that left José yawning and Alves desperate for diversion. If this were to be the extent of the evening, Alves imagined he'd be lucky even to see José again, let alone become his friend.

Deliverance came in the form of a young doctor knocking at the door with a rather grisly tale. An elderly gentleman a few doors away had passed on and a quick trip to the mortuary was called for, Sunday or not, since death had occurred the previous night and the doctor had not been notified until a few minutes before he appeared at Senhor Reis' door.

"A new client," Alves' father announced with grim solemnity to the guests, vaguely underlining his own indispensability. "I must go when I am called. . . ." He slipped into his black suitcoat, tightened the knot in his tie.

At the door he turned to Alves and José, who had followed him, half afraid to ask if they might accompany him. "Do you want to come with me, boys? My assistant won't be there, not on Sunday night—I might need some help." Alves' heart leaped. He forgot the fear he'd always had, forgot all the times in the past year he and Alfonso had turned down opportunities to go with their father. Tonight was different. José was there, and Alves had bragged about what he could show him.

The mortuary was a few winding streets away, a dark, narrow building, windowless and forbidding. Many of the inhabitants of the Sao Tiago held tight to their old beliefs, the beliefs of their peasant origins. They knew of the dead within and they hurried to pass.

In front was a waiting room for the family of the newly departed; beyond it, through heavy moth-eaten draperies, a chamber for viewing the prepared remains; a catafalque made of rough-hewn beams hidden by a purple velvet cloth; two back rooms with mortuary tables, containers of chemicals, the various gleaming tools of the trade.

While Senhor Reis went to the back door to meet the doctor and take possession of his cumbersome parcel, the boys waited in the front room. José peered cautiously into the viewing chamber. Alves hesitated, his enthusiasm fading fast, riding to extinction on the familiar scent of the rooms. Death had a bad smell, chemical and rotting. It summoned up childhood's horrible images—fears that the back rooms must look like the butcher's work tables, stained and running with blood. . . .

José beckoned him.

"Reis," he whispered urgently. "You promised. There's a box in there." He nodded toward the curtains and beyond. "I'll bet there's a dead one in it." His eyes had grown round. "You promised . . ."

The viewing chamber was lighted by candles that jumped and flickered in a draft. The curtains closed behind him. Ominous muffled thuds came from the rear of the building. Slowly, on tiptoe, they crept toward the coffin, Alves praying that it would be either empty or nailed shut. It was both open and occupied. Sweat broke out like a rash on Alves' face; José exclaimed softly, his hand to his mouth. A fog of sudden fear cloaked Alves' vision, smudged the corners, providing him with a kind of tunnel view that magnified the fear growing in his bowels and spreading through him like a fever. Bogeys from the grave, remembrances of his grandmother's tales of bodies rising from beneath ancient scarred tombstones to snatch small boys who forgot to say their prayers . . . The face before them as they reached the plain wooden coffin was waxen, cheerily cosmeticized, wore a hideous false smile as if he were somehow enjoying the bad joke of his own death. . . .

José leaned over the corpse, unafraid, grinning in amazement. Alves clamped his eyes shut, fighting off a rising tide of nausea. His nostrils filled with the death smell. Eyes closed, he still saw the false face like a feast-day mask. Even at the age of eight he recognized what he had done, that he had impulsively gone too far, begun something without thinking it through or considering the consequences. He had done it before, leaped in without looking and sworn to himself past veils of tears that he would never do it again. He opened his eyes. José was reaching for the face.

"Stop," Alves gurgled. "Don't touch it." His own whisper sounded hollow. "It leaves marks, Papa says!"

"Then you touch," José said. "You know how to do it. Just on the tip of his nose, that won't leave a mark." He was still grinning, sensing Alves' discomfort. "You told me you'd touched lots of dead ones."

Gritting his teeth to keep the stew in his stomach where

it belonged, squinting through shut eyes, Alves extended a small shaking hand and slowly touched the tip of the shiny dead nose.

José leaned forward. "He's breathing!"

Alves screamed, stumbled backward, very nearly upsetting the pedestal bearing the candelabra, darted through the curtain, on through the waiting room, into the street, where his stomach turned itself inside out.

*   *   *

Alves' friendship with José grew during the next few years. José's greater age and experience made him the natural leader, with the younger boy grateful to be included. José's daring, his willingness to sidestep parental commands, the useful ability to make one thing appear something else altogether at just the crucial moment—all this established his superiority.

There was, for instance, the matter of the relics. Now, that struck Alves as a markedly childish prank, even as he willingly engaged in it. However much he had felt his heart pound fit to burst on those occasions the swindle had worked, however much he had sweated out the hours of possible detection, he had always felt that while for José it was a money-making enterprise, for him it was only a lark.

The relics included bits of animal bone from the bins behind the butchery, splinters of old wooden beams the boys scouted out in Lisbon's vacant, sandy, weed-ridden lots. In the name of earning a few extra escudos—José was fifteen, Alves twelve—the two boys met to discuss profitable means of spending the school holidays. There seemed to be vast numbers of foreigners on tour—mostly Germans, Englishmen and Italians—with pronounced interests in the various old and ornately bedecked churches, wealthy foreigners who seemed always on the lookout for bits and pieces to buy, presumably to prove they had been there. José, in the grip of the proclivities which were to give his life its unique texture, leaped on the idea of religious relics and embellished it handsomely.

Their church was Sao Rocque, humble in its exterior views, lavish beyond imagining within. The truly knowledgeable guides made sure it was on their itineraries. The church was blinding with burnished golden altars, columns and altars of lapis lazuli, railings of ebony, bronze and silver work, tons of perfectly matched agate, carloads of amethysts—on and on went the splendors of the small, dowdy church overlooking the dusty plain square well above the bustle of Rossio Square. The paintings of Sao Rocque were everywhere, the saint of the lepers, depicted with his thigh bared to show the mark of leprosy, always accompanied by the monumentally faithful dog who had brought him bread when he was starving. The mosaics that told the saint's story were so detailed and fine that observers could never quite believe they were not oil paintings. All in all, the junior confidence men concluded, what better place could there be to prey on susceptible foreigners with money for appropriate trinkets?

Since the church was renowned for its many reliquaries —Alves had heard his father remark with some cynicism that there were enough pieces of saints' bones in the church to reconstruct an entire saint—relics seemed a good thing to sell. The animal doctors' waste bins were picked over for bits of bone, as were the butchers'. Alves did not find it the most enjoyable of tasks, but the spirit and ingenuity of the moment made up for the nastiness of the job. Shards of bone were then glued onto pieces of cardboard and placed in small boxes acquired by José. Smiling angelically, they waited in the square outside the church of Sao Rocque and chose their victims.

The essential dishonesty of the scheme never really arose as an obstacle in either boy's mind. After all, it was only a matter of a few escudos. José considered the swindle an example of his own sharpness of mind as well as the accepted way in which commerce of any kind was conducted. Alves found it something of an elaborate practical joke— never to be confused with work.

Work, he knew from listening to his father, was long and hard and allowed for no short cuts. Work was what a man did: the harder he worked, the greater his chance of worldly success, money and the esteem of his fellow man. His apprenticeship at the mortuary—that was work. He frequently thanked God for his older brother Alfonso, who bore the brunt of Senhor Reis' teaching methods. Inevitably Alves was cast in the role of observer while his father trained his first son in the various procedures of the mortuarial art. When the lecture grew overly specific, Alves would close his eyes or try mentally to block his ears—

avenues of escape not open to his brother, who might actually be holding something slippery, something sticky, or, worse, something both slippery and sticky. Alves put in his hours among the chemicals and the cadavers and their scent of death. It was a matter of duty. Alves understood duty, the need for honest, determined, unpleasant effort.

Education was something else entirely, something of value, an opportunity to be seized. There was, it occurred to him, no limit but laziness to this business of educating himself. He worked on his English, lost himself in Portuguese history and hammered away at mathematics. He quickly surpassed his fellow students, and it got him through many a long weekend when the mortuary was the only alternative. Senhor Reis applauded his studious son and made do with the squinting Alfonso at the shop. . . .

At the age of eighteen José Bandeira, impatient with the prospects of learning to manage some of his father's land, set off to make his own fortune abroad. His destination, hinted to be Brazil, remained vague, as if his intention was to remain out of touch. Alves trudged down to the quay, weighed down with his friend's bags, bade him farewell and the best of luck, cautioned him to write and returned glumly to his everyday routine. There was schoolwork, which included a course in rudimentary practical engineering, conscientious application to homework and apprenticeship in the mortuary.

There was no word from José for two years. Then the cable arrived: it had originated in Paris and instructed Alves to meet the overnight train at Rossio Station. It was midsummer and José was coming home.

The man who climbed down from the first-class carriage and embraced Alves was even leaner if possible, pale, well dressed, carefully barbered, with white teeth gleaming beneath a pencil-thin mustache, and smelled of a lemonish Parisian cologne. Only traces of the boy were left, in a flashing of his eye, the lilt of the voice, but they were fading fast. It made Alves feel older just being near such an obviously successful gentleman. He was glad that he'd worn his suit.

As they made their way through the hurrying crowds in the vaulting grimy darkness of the station, Alves wondered aloud where José's family was, was he possibly surprising them? The questions, once unloosed, came in a rush, and

as they passed out into the warm late-afternoon shadows
of the square José laughed, held up a manicured hand.

"Stop, stop, we have plenty of time," he chuckled, shaking his narrow, aristocratic head. "First things first, let's
stop for a drink, let me look at Lisbon for a moment . . ."
They found a table outside the Metropole where they could
deposit José's single leather-belted bag on a chair, sit down,
cross their legs, light up cigarettes like careless boulevar-
diers and review the past two years. The streets were full
of beautiful young women, sun splashing them, bathing the
square with the translucent Portuguese brightness. Black
sedans edged against the pedestrians; rich men in black
suits, puffing on cigars, peered from back seats. Lisbon
throbbed in the sunshine. The excitement Alves felt at seeing his friend meshed with the city's great square, so different from the dark, quiet street where the mortuary
slowly crumbled, year after year, like his father's hopes. . . .

"My parents were not at the station," José explained
softly, "because I have returned home in disgrace."

"What do you mean? You arrive in a first-class carriage
from Paris—what is so disgraceful about that?"

"The disgrace," José remarked casually, smiling, "is that
I have spent the better part of the last year in a South
African jail." There was an unmistakable scintilla of pride
in his tone and for Alves, as the story unfolded, an un-
spoken feeling of justification. He had known all along
that José would have to mend his ways—or run the risk
of just such problems. While he had emerged from the
incident of the relics and gone straight to school and the
long hours in the mortuary, José had undoubtedly gone on
to sharper practices. While José wore expensive clothes
and smelled of lemons, he had spent a year in jail; Alves
might still be the poor son of an impoverished undertaker,
dressed in a suit that smelled of embalming chemicals, but
he had most certainly never seen the inside of a jail.

José's story, however, was exciting, and Alves savored
the details, was elaborately seduced by the bizarre tale,
which sounded very much like the plot of a cheap novel.

Although José had set off with the idea of reaching
Brazil, events and some new acquaintances brought him
instead to South Africa, where, in Johannesburg, he had
fallen in with some fleet-footed young rakes who made a
handsome living as burglars. After the first few jobs, which
went off with perfect precision, he presumed that he was

ready to strike out on his own. But on his second solo enterprise he ran afoul of an unforgiving Boer who caught him in the act of rifling the dining-room silver cabinet, tore one of his own candlesticks from the youthful intruder's grasp and skulled him with it. Upon awaking, José found the Boer astride his chest and the Johannesburg police knocking on the door.

The Johannesburg court sentenced José dos Santos Bandeira to three years at hard labor—this brought a gasp of consternation from a stunned Alves—but the wily inmate bribed a guard and escaped after only two months. Undaunted by the side trip to jail, José returned to his wicked ways, and within a few months he played an encore before the same magistrate and was this time sentenced to the remainder of his first sentence as well as four more years on his second offense. But with the help of some newly cultivated jailbird friends the wily Portuguese was once again at large. He turned to selling booze to the natives—illegally, of course. He had a run of nearly three months before he was apprehended and judged an habitual criminal, no longer the responsibility of South Africa. After lengthy negotiations, his father in Lisbon ransomed his wayward son from the Johannesburg authorities, who were fortunately as corrupt as was necessary. José's return to Lisbon and the fortnight in Paris was paid for with what he had been able to squirrel away from his burglaries and bootlegging.

The end of this altogether remarkable recital found Alves caught between admiration for a friend who had experienced such adventures and the inbred righteousness of the moral man who lived a boring existence. José finished his second glass and leaned back, smiling his scoundrel's smile, thumbs hooked into his vest pockets. At twenty he seemed, in Alves' eyes, infinitely grand and sophisticated.

"I know, I know," José said, scraping back his chair and rising, "you disapprove. And you, Alves, will never go to jail." He was laughing.

It was dark. The night had come alive. Shy couples holding hands, rakes dressed to the hilt, handsome men and elegant women were coursing on all sides of the square, and the lanterns glowed like tiny yellow moons. Alves was bereft of ideas to keep the daring magic of José's homecoming alive, but he was absolutely sure he did not want to trudge back to Sao Tiago and spend the weekend in the mortuary with his father and brother.

"I have an idea," José said slyly. "Can you stay out the night?"

"I don't know ... I'm expected—"

"I know, I know. You've been expected all your life. Your father—he's forgotten what it's like to be young and in need of a good time."

"A good time!" Alves said. "Could be he's never had one!" He saw a glimmer of mirth in that and heard José laugh conspiratorily.

Alves hoisted the expensive suitcase. José took his arm. "I'll treat you to dinner—we'll go by hack out to that place on the beach in Cascais. There's a pavilion, there's dancing, we can talk some more, drink wine. . . . Come on, you're only young once."

Alves turned it over cautiously in his mind. After all, there was his brother to help out at the mortuary, and he hadn't heard his father remark on any surplus of business. Yes, it was time he spent a night out. . . . And surely José's homecoming was sufficient excuse. "Why not?" he said.

The evening at Cascais, melting away into the dead of night, fading into the blush of dawn, was the height of sophistication. There was the hack ride through the narrow streets full of shops, on down to the harbor where the moon reflected in the broad, flat river, then past the outskirts of the city, speeding along the riverbed with the lights fading behind them. They ate dinner at an outdoor café with candles winking in the breeze and the mighty Tagus swelling in white furls along the moonlit beach and the cold wine bringing in its wake a new giddiness. He enjoyed everything—the further stories of José's two years at large in an entirely foreign world, the swindles and the little con games, the thrill and stealth of the burglaries, the camaraderie José had found among the criminal class . . . José was utterly unpenitent, obviously a born scalawag.

The wine had made them both a little unsteady; there were wobbles and the odd stagger as they ventured onto the deck where the band played and the dancers slowly swayed to American music. Then, as the moon slid softly among the clouds, the two friends marched off down the beach, singing. José clutched their third bottle of wine. Sand filled their shoes, fingers grappled with knotted ties and

collar studs, and eventually they collapsed laughing, swig-
ging at the bottle.

"And the women," José sighed much later when they
had grown quiet. "The women, Alves . . . Do you know
anything about women? Really?" He was staring off at the
wide river and the ocean beyond. "Do you?"

"No, I don't suppose I do. . . ."

José sighted along his index finger at the disk of the
moon. "I mean, the whole story about women? Do you
think you're ready for it?" He turned to face Alves, grinning wolfishly.

Alves lay on his back, resting his head on a pillow of
sand. "I definitely think I am ready."

"Women are simple creatures—most men make the mistake of thinking they are complex, mysterious, difficult to
cope with. . . . Nothing could be further from the truth—
slaves to their desires, their bodies! And they don't know
for sure what to do about it, you see . . . not and be ladies,
too, that is." José leaned close and whispered a trifle
boozily: "If anything, they think about it more than we
do! *It*—you know. They think about it constantly, and
once a man realizes that, why, all he needs to do is grab
it when he's in the mood and hope she doesn't wear him
out!" He laughed, hiccupping, falling back in the sand.
"There are only three kinds of women. You didn't know
that, eh? Once you master this piece of information—
widely known in parts of Johannesburg as Bandeira's first
law—the battle is won, they'll be knocking themselves out
to get their panties down for you. . . .

"First, there are the sweet little homebodies who make
good wives, love to bear you children as long as you're willing to give them a good poking when they need it and will
never give you cause for jealousy—comforting but not
exactly daring. Second, there are the adventurers, the
beautiful creatures every man lusts for but seldom con-
quers because they inspire fright and timidity . . . yet the
fact is, the world is a highway that leads right between
their legs! Yes, practically for the taking, I guarantee it.
They look at a casual fuck like men—it's fun and good for
the complexion! Yes, by God, give me the adventuresses—
but you've got to remember that the minute you pull yourself out of them they're looking for someone else to stick
it in! And, finally, there are the whores, and they are great
foot soldiers in the sexual struggle. No jealousy here: you

pay for what you get, one way or another, and they know what they're doing, by and large.

"That's it—three types only, no exceptions. Once you grasp this and act on it your prick will never be limp, except from exhaustion!" He collapsed again on the sand, staring at the moon, the wine bottle dropping from his fingers, falling on its side. "Oh, God, the world lost a great teacher when I decided on the life of a ne'er-do-well. . . ." He laughed, rolling over, making a pillow of his arm, staring at Alves.

What an extraordinary world José had lived in: dangerous, of course, but almost glorious. . . . Alves had grown increasingly aware of the terrible, inexplicable gap between the late admiral's glory and dignity and the bleak, penurious world of the mortuary. How could the gap be bridged, what could he do to make that leap? He was nothing, an undertaker's apprentice with a mortuary in his future. . . . Where had the glory and dignity gone? Was it still, somehow, within his grasp? José might be short of dignity, but he'd seen the world, had a taste of adventure and a kind of glory, and what if jail had been the price?

Alves awoke with the sun streaming over the low hills, the sky changing from gray to a pink-tinged blue, and a boot prodding him in the ribs.

"Alves, for God's sake! Are you all right? What's happened to you?"

It was Arnaldo Carvalho. Alves squinted blearily at the silhouette of his school friend. Arnaldo was a solemn, serious fellow with a face to match. Oh, God, Alves reflected, head throbbing, closing his eyes.

"Arnaldo—would you please stop kicking me?" Both his eyes and mouth seemed to have gotten full of sand. He spied an empty wine bottle beyond his outstretched hand. He groaned, closed his eyes again.

"Can you explain what you're doing here? On the beach? Drunk?" Arnaldo kicked the bottle a safe distance away and worked up an expression of dark disapproval.

Alves shook his head. "Can't talk. Mouth is all funny—"

"And this body over here, the great Bandeira?" Arnaldo said, scowling. "I come to the beach to walk by myself as the sun comes up, to read poetry aloud as I leave my footprints in the damp sand—" José belched, half awake from the sounds of Arnaldo's outrage—"and what do I find? My friend, dead drunk like a common tramp!"

José flung back an eyelid and croaked, "Reis, make this man stop screaming. . . ."

Arnaldo pushed his slender volume of poetry into a trouser pocket and shepherded the two disheveled young men across the shingle of sand to the restaurant, where life was slowly stirring. A tired dog lifted its leg against the underpinning of the outdoor dance floor. A woman peered at them from the veranda. Arnaldo arranged for the use of a basin of water and the toilet facilities behind the main building. He sighed at length while Alves and José managed to revive themselves. He prevailed upon the woman's good nature for a simple but recuperative breakfast.

Later, with the sun parching the landscape and the sand burning his bare feet, Alves strolled off by himself, leaving Arnaldo and José to get acquainted. What a pair! He grinned as he moved along the edge of the water. Looking back, he saw José come out onto the empty dance floor and slowly lower himself to a sitting position with his legs dangling in space. He was holding a wine bottle in each hand. Presently Arnaldo joined him. He sat down beside José and took a drink from one of the bottles. Alves peered hard, squinting in the sunlight. He couldn't believe it. Arnaldo . . . Clearly, Bandeira the sophisticate, Bandeira the *criminal* was also a magician!

Alves sat down with his back against the stone wall beneath the roadway, felt the shade bathe him and rested his head on the rolled-up suit coat. He wasn't worrying about the condition of his good suit. He wasn't worrying about what his mother might be thinking or what his father would do without him at the mortuary. He wasn't worrying about anything. He was thinking about José and the stories about the girls, and that was when he looked up at the wide stone steps dropping down from the road, heard the girls laughing and saw her.

*   *   *

A hundred years earlier, perhaps even fifty, Alves Reis, approaching eighteen, would have been most reticent about presenting himself to such a young lady as Maria Luiza Jacobetti d'Azevedo. She came down the steps surrounded by her giggling girlfriends, the ribbon in her long dark hair matching the sky. Her feet were bare beneath layered, billowing skirts, and as she ran, carrying her pale-blue parasol,

her tiny feet kicked up the sand. What made him single her
out for attention? The ribbon? No . . . Perhaps her laugh,
careless and fit for sunshine and the beach, or huge eyes
beneath dark brows, lashes like dainty ferns on her pale
cheek, fawnlike. Yes, he decided, it had something to do
with her eyes. And her nose, which wasn't at all Portuguese
but Roman. He had seen her in profile as she ran past. She
had a certain quality, a style, which he knew placed her
above him. He would have to stretch for this young
lady. . . .

Heat waves shimmered in front of him, and he remembered the taste of last night's wine. He moved away from
the wall, leaning on one elbow, watching the girls at their
silly games, their laughter drifting toward him like the sighing of the surf. In his mind he undressed the girl, fitting
her into José's reminiscences, wondering what her body
might be like. Was she one of José's types? Her voice
reached him: she was much too good for a rake like José,
in any case. He was sure of that, smiling at the thought.

He heard her laugh as she chased the beach ball, which
floated like a balloon on the breeze. She laughed the way
he'd heard other women sing; the mirth attracted him, he
supposed, because he laughed so little himself. He watched
as the girls lost interest in the ball and wandered over toward a large flat-bottomed rowboat. She was shorter than
the others, shapely beneath the yards of clothing. They
struggled with the rowboat, pulling ineffectually on a thick
rope and budging it only a few inches along the wet, dark
sand. Finally he stood up, carrying his badly rumpled suit
coat over his shoulder, and walked across the shining sand.

"Excuse me," he said, "but you seem to need some
help. . . ."

They all chattered shyly, eyes cast down, smiling a trifle
naughtily—all but the tiny one with the Roman nose and
high cheekbones that gave her face a thinner quality than
was common among Portuguese women.

"Yes, please," she said, looking him directly in the eye.
"You might help us get this boat to the water. It's just too
heavy for us . . . but for you . . ." She regarded his broad
shoulders, thick chest, the sleeves rolled up tight on the
bulging biceps. Alves was thinking she was just the right
height.

"Please allow me," he said grandly, heart squirming toward his throat. "Step back, ladies, step back, and I'll

have it in the water in a moment." He took a second look at the craft, which was steel-banded and rather larger than it had appeared from a distance. "Or two." He chuckled feebly, already regretting his offer. Then he caught the girl's eye, figured the effort might be a good investment and put his back into it. A mighty shove.

At first he thought he'd ruptured himself, straightened up very quickly, smiled desperately around the wide-eyed circle of faces. Why had he offered? Why? It was like offering to show José a cadaver and then having to do it. . . .

"Perhaps I'd better pull," he said heartily. "Pushing such a . . . a battleship is no good. A pull—pulling is what it needs, heh, heh."

The rope attached to the front of the boat apparently dated from the maiden voyage of Henry the Navigator. Alves did not trust the rope. Jesus in heaven . . . He wondered if José and Arnaldo, swilling icy wine, were watching.

A tentative tug budged the monstrous thing slightly, and the appreciative cries of the ladies unfortunately gave him confidence. He took the measure of the rope, wrapped it securely around his compact fists, smiled heartily to indicate *savoir faire* and great strength, gave a mighty heave and abruptly threw himself backward into the surf, where for the moment he disappeared.

While the girls bit their knuckles to hold back their laughter, the daring young man struggled to his feet, soaked, grabbing at his back, then glaring in pain and anger at the boat. Finally he made a raging, limping dash at the inanimate object—but she stepped between him and the boat, soothing him, holding him back with her small strong hand.

The flush of that first touch, his blood rising . . .

José and Arnaldo appeared, laughing at his disheveled state, and shoved the rowboat into the water. When they had paddled slowly away, Maria alone had chosen to remain ashore, to massage Alves Reis' poor, wounded back.

*   *   *

As the long afternoon dwindled, patient and nurse sat on the crumbling wall at Cascais watching the traffic at the mouth of the Tagus come and go far out beyond the rowboats. She discovered that this bullish, impetuous young fellow had a famous admiral dangling from his family tree; he learned of her Italian ancestors, prominent among whom was the great playwright Jacobetti . . . and he realized the source of her non-Portuguese physical traits, those cheekbones, that Roman nose. Later, when José and Arnaldo returned with the girls, they ate fresh shrimp with mayonnaise and sipped wine and enjoyed being wonderfully young, careless.

By the time her father, a clerk of some importance in a British-owned firm, arrived in his automobile to take the girls home, Alves Reis was thoroughly in love. As was Maria d'Azevedo. It was something new for each of them.

*   *   *

Portuguese courtships were not unlike the stock exchange —they could be counted on to reflect the slightest seismic changes in the social landscape. Alves plodded along for a year to overcome completely the coolness of his prospective parents-in-law; in their eyes, he realized, Maria was not only failing to move socially upward but was not even verging on marriage with an equal. Times were changing, yes, but this quickly? Alves was a nice boy of course, but . . . Maria gently but accurately conveyed the tone and content of the discreetly discouraging conversations she had with her father. However, Alves persisted from without the d'Azevedo home and Maria from within; he was in love and his wife-to-be was utterly determined. She loved her Alves —he had a future, she sensed it somehow against the force of her father's arguments, was convinced of it, and she was bound to spend it with him.

More practically there was the matter of her dowry, which, though not excessive, would certainly come in handy. He had a plan, a small one but a plan nonetheless, and it required just a bit of ready cash. . . . And a great deal of nerve. The nerve he believed he had.

The formal meetings between the two sets of parents were grotesque, stillborn. They had nothing in common. But whatever the obstacles, the lovers persevered.

*   *   *

Although his father had failed, Alves was a twentieth-century man and defeat was no longer an inherited quality;

Alves did not plan to fail. Hope was in his blood, along with the remnants of the old admiral's accomplishments.

While vigorously pursuing the study of practical engineering, Alves had also continued his voracious reading of Portuguese history, a habit stemming from his father's obsessive interest in the glories of the distant past—and quite possibly the most meaningful legacy he could leave his son. Alves read everything, filling his mind and countless notebooks Inevitably he saw his place in the great scheme accurately, and, unlike less determined students, he knew how he'd gotten there.

The objections of Maria's parents finally worn down, Maria and Alves decided on the late summer of 1916 for their marriage: Alves would by then be twenty years old, Maria nineteen. Although it was a happy time for them both, Alves was discovering throughout the summer that there seemed to be no jobs in Lisbon for young men with not very impressive training in practical engineering regardless of how much everyday know-how they might possess. Day after day he prowled the streets looking for a job with a future, and as the dispiriting results piled up his frustration grew. He still refused to consider the mortuary seriously. In the first place Alfonso was only just now beginning to receive any wages at all, and, in the second, he simply could not face spending the rest of his days there—poor, without hope for advancement, life slowly dwindling away. He deserved better than that. Almost anything was better than that.

As July ran out there was no offer from his future father-in-law of a position in the English-owned firm. Sensing his concern, Maria took his hand in hers one evening as they walked near her parents' solidly respectable, middle-class home. "Perhaps you could at least begin working with your father," she remarked hesitantly. "You could continue looking for a better opportunity." She gestured with a slight toss of her head, left the thought unfinished.

"Try to leave once I'd begun working for him?" He laughed bitterly. "Impossible, my dearest. Once I willingly enter that world of . . . of formaldehyde and tubes and gaping abdominal cavities and loved ones crying in the front room . . . You'd smell death on my clothing and in my hair and when I touched your breast you'd smell it on your own flesh."

"Please, stop!" she cried, holding her hands up to her

ears. "We won't speak of it again." She hugged his arm to her, sighing. "You'll find something."

But the passing weeks, filled with wedding plans and Maria's tea parties with her girlfriends and their mothers, were markedly empty of promising employment for her husband-to-be. He did not stop looking; if he had nothing else, he was blessed—or cursed—with absolute determination. But, by August, less than a week before the wedding, he felt the cutting edge of panic: his resourcefulness was almost at an end.

What saved him at this point was an altogether less personal and therefore less trivial problem brought about two years earlier by the assassination of the Archduke Franz Ferdinand at Sarajevo, an event that served to precipitate the Great War. Two years later Portugal began to feel the waves. While Alves Reis, the twentieth-century man, was readying himself as best he could to benefit from the new spirit of equality, he was not pleased by another kind of equality offered by the war. He wanted no part of it.

In this state of turmoil Alves was driven to act. If he stayed in Lisbon he would almost surely wind up a soldier somewhere in a trench at the front, not an encouraging prospect for an ambitious young man. The week before the wedding he spent busily arranging certain drastic changes in his plans for the future. . . .

The plans were more in José's line, but the fact was that José had once again set sail. Having made amends to his father, he struck a bargain regarding his future. Somehow the elder Bandeira and his first son Antonio, who was a Portuguese diplomat posted to The Hague, prevailed on family friends at Garland, Laidlaw, and Company, a firm of shipping agents doing business with such distinguished groups as Cunard, to take the errant José on as a most junior clerk In Brazil.

Standing before the heavy draperies in the ballroom of the Avenida Palace Hotel, watching the wedding reception swirling about him. Alves felt a trifle remote from the gaiety. It wasn't that he was in any way disappointed; he was in fact more deeply in love than he'd believed possible. His mother stood on tiptoe to kiss him, tears glistening on her plump cheeks, and his father, who resembled his cadaverous clients more each time Alves saw him, hugged his son tightly. Maria's father concluded the festivities tipsy, dancing with Alves' mother, while the bridegroom whirled his new mother-in-law about the slippery dance floor in a cloud of perspiration and champagne fumes.

Flower girls, ring bearers, matrons and maids, unknown relatives, strangers wandering through . . . It was a wedding party slowly sputtering out. The photographer with his endless flashpowder explosions was slowing down, getting just a few final shots. Alves smiled, shook hands, kissed countless cheeks, nodded at remarks he didn't quite hear. But his mind was elsewhere. He missed José, particularly José's devious turn of mind. The plan he'd worked out himself, however, seemed . . . *seemed* a good one, but, God knew, he'd precious little experience of a practical nature. He was worried.

Over a glass of champagne, which he kept dribbling on his fingertips, Alves drew Arnaldo aside and spoke carefully to his best man.

"Tomorrow—you remember what you're to do, what you *must* do, Arnaldo . . . unless, of course, a career in the military appeals to you. We meet at three o'clock. Precisely. Don't disappoint me, Arnaldo." He caught his friend's eye. "You're not drunk, are you?"

"Don't be absurd," Arnaldo snapped. "But why can't this plan of yours wait for even a few days? You'll be, ah, honeymooning—what will Maria say?"

"Look, Arnaldo, we're staying at a hotel in Estoril. And, believe me, the sooner we make arrangements the better off we'll be." He grinned at the solemn, intent face. "Don't worry about Maria. I'll see to it that she's sleeping in the afternoon. . . ."

"Braggart!" Impulsively Arnaldo clapped his arms around Alves and squeezed him tightly. "Congratulations, Alves—may your life be a happy one. Always. For both of you." A tear squeezed out of his eye and hung on his cheek. Champagne spilled.

"For the three of us," Alves corrected him, a hint of emotion catching in his throat. "Three friends—Maria and Alves and Arnaldo. Inseparable . . ." The music was filling the room, and his head, fueled by champagne, threatened to take flight. He wished José were there. That would have made it perfect, absolutely perfect. José . . . wherever he was.

The honeymoon, in the hotel in Estoril overlooking the beach, was a cascade of youthful, playful passion. Both husband and wife were virgins and happily curious, like two dewy-eyed puppies. Their exertions were joyous, unnerving, exhausting, gloriously happy. Maria d'Azevedo Reis was so much more than his imagination had prepared him for—from the moist softness of her body and the shy delight with which she gave herself to him, from the way she whispered in French as he slowly fed her desire, from her constant perusal of the latest novels from Paris with the thick uncut pages as she soaked in the tub, to her habit of buying things her more or less penniless husband could not possibly pay for. . . .

Alves was true to his word the day after the wedding. He met Arnaldo in the city. Together they visited the proper bureaucratic offices, explaining their sincere desire to serve their country in developing the Angolan potential rather than in the trenches. Always persuasive, Alves saw to it that their applications were accepted. Suppose they got to Angola—they were out of the war, but what then? To that question Alves Reis devoted the next several weeks.

The great post-nuptial event of the late summer was a party given by Maria's parents officially celebrating her brother Manuelo's graduation from the University of Coimbra. The young man was full of himself, of course, setting out to make his way in the world of commerce. There had been some talk of his joining the English-based firm through whose ranks his father had risen, but it wasn't set: perhaps, Manuelo suggested, he could do better. . . .

Alves watched from the terrace as Manuelo soaked up the praise, surrounded by his family and college friends in their well-cut suits that were worn with the ease and arrogance of their smiles. His own suit was a boxy affair, the best he could afford, black and pitiful by comparison. He sipped from a cup of punch, watched them roaring at their collegiate jokes, which he could not understand. Several of them actually drove their own automobiles.

Yet he would gladly have pitted his intelligence and knowledge against theirs. He knew he was a quicker thinker, the way he knew his suit was inferior . . . the way he knew his prospects were considerably less hopeful than theirs.

"Well, son, they look a happy bunch, don't they? In one month's time my daughter is married and my son sets out to make his fortune—it does a man good, I tell you." Maria's father had overcome his objections to his son-in-law's humble status, primarily because he had been unable to change his daughter's mind. They got along well enough, except when the subject of Alves' future came up. The older man couldn't quite imagine what Alves was going to do with his life, but the fact was that if worse came to worst Maria could always come home. "Yes," he sighed, "a diploma from Coimbra makes all the difference. . . ."

Alves nodded: what could he say?

"It takes such a load off a man's mind, knowing that his son is a college man . . . the way ahead is smoothed out, doors will open." He sighed contentedly, then turned to face Alves, his face clouding. "By the way, have you made any further plans? You've got to get some work, you know. Life is a serious business, Alves. You can't just slide along and hope for the best."

"I'm well aware, sir," he said solemnly. "I have several inquiries pending. It's only a matter of time, something will break soon. . . ."

"Well, I have faith in you. But it's hard to find a good position these days. . . . Not many jobs. Of course, you could always work with your father. I'm not sure but what that's your best bet. You could get used to it, you know." He was watching his son again, bellowing out some joke or other.

"No, I have other plans," Alves said. "You don't need to worry. I'm going to be fine. . . . Maria will be well taken care of."

"Yes, well," he said, moving away toward the merriment, "I only wish you'd gone to the university. Then everything falls in your lap. . . . But there's no use crying about that, I suppose. It's too late now to spend all those years in Coimbra . . ." He squeezed Alves' arm and went away. Manuelo was waving his diploma over his head while his chums engaged in a rhythmic chant, signifying, no doubt, the great distinction of their education.

Much later, when things had quieted down, a tipsy Manuelo approached him holding a bottle of champagne.

"A final toast," Manuelo said, slurring his words.

"Sure," Alves said. Manuelo poured two glasses brimful, dribbling champagne over his hand.

"To me," Manuelo proclaimed proudly. He drank the champagne off, filled the glass again. He sauntered over to the couch and dropped full length, grinning up at Alves. He took his diploma from the coffee table and held it out to

Alves. "You want to see this? My ticket to success?" He chuckled.

"Oh, Alves, don't be such a drip," he muttered. "You ought to get yourself one of these. . . . Get you out of that damned undertaker's office. That's no life for a newly married man." He coughed, wiped his chin. "My sister deserves more than that. . . ."

"I have plans," Alves said, his face burning.

"He has plans," Manuelo mocked. "You damned well better have some plans. . . ." He laughed, sipping more champagne. "You've got plans and I've got a diploma. I'll take my diploma, thanks."

The only thing left to do with Manuelo was to club him to death with the champagne bottle. Alves decided against that, went and found Maria, left the comfortable house.

"Oh, I had a wonderful time," she said. "I'm so proud of Manuelo. . . ."

Alves nodded. "Yes, he certainly is the college man, isn't he?"

*   *   *

By early autumn the permissions to set sail for Angola came through. And the day was unforgettable for another reason as well. The piano arrived at their tiny flat—a piano, a *grand* piano, for God's sake! "But why, Alves, have I learned to play a piano," Maria had reasoned sweetly, massaging his aching temples, "if I am not allowed to have a piano? You see, don't you, Alves?" He realized early on that, whether or not he understood what Maria had in mind, it was supremely irrelevant. In some things. He was learning with alacrity what other poor men who married above themselves had learned before him.

Maria was engaged in mastering Chopin's etudes that fall evening. Dinner was over, and Arnaldo was staring at Alves across the remains of chicken piccata. Maria's Italian heritage revealed itself most often in the kitchen and at the table. The cigar smoke drifted lazily out the window, port rolled on the tongue. Arnaldo mentioned his official permission to sail for Angola; it was his calling, he reflected happily, to follow Alves. He welcomed his fate. But he was not quite able to grasp what Alves was now suggesting, the next step of the mysterious plan. . . .

"My point," Alves amplified formally, as was the custom

among young men striving to seem older, "is that while the opportunities for advancement may be far greater in Luanda than in Lisbon, we must be realistic—"

"My point as well, exactly," Arnaldo said, perplexed. "And what you suggest bears an unlikely relationship to reality." He relit his cigar from the candle that was guttering in the breeze. They greatly enjoyed the formal speech, managing to seem what they were not but wanted to be.

"An individual without qualifications may be no better off in Luanda than he is in Lisbon."

"A nobody is a nobody, wherever he may be."

A small smile crossed Alves' solemn, perpetually worried face. "While you and I know differently," he went on, "the rest of the world does not yet know that I am anything but a . . . nobody, as you put it. As the key to our plan, we must educate them—we must help them to comprehend what we alone know to be the reality of the situation."

"Double talk!" Arnaldo said bluntly. "The world at large decides what is real and what is not. You are on very treacherous ground, philosophically speaking, my friend—defining reality for yourself. . . ."

"But we are not philosophers," Alves said, as if scoring the climactic point in debate. "We are practical men making our way in the real world. What precisely does our predicament demand from men of ability and ambition?"

"What, Alves?"

"That we be seen by others to be the successful, resourceful fellows we know ourselves to be! We are embarking on the greatest game of all, and our pile of chips would seem to be—well, *low*. What are we to do?" Alves had grown animated, his face working into the slightly crazy expressions Arnaldo recognized.

"Alves, the fact is, we are nobodies! Face it, for God's sake!"

Alves shook his head, drained the last of his port, peered in mock grief into the glass. Arnaldo pressed on, toying with a shred of chicken and sauce.

"We have no credentials, man. We have no cards, no chips. Do you intend to make them up out of thin air?"

"At last," Alves murmured, looking up and into the eyes of his friend. "You see my point. . . . A mere scrap of parchment."

Maria concluded her current etude and leaped merrily to her feet. "I've done it," she cried. "Aren't you proud, dear?" She kissed the top of his head, mussing the neat part. "I've mastered it." She left his spectacles askew.

* * *

The next morning Alves went to a small stationer in one of the shady, narrow streets serving the many businesses located in the Baixa, meandering away from Rossio Square. He purchased four quarto-sized sheets of parchment that he felt were suitably official-looking, a heavy leather folder, three scribe's pens, a bottle of thick India ink and a blotter. Whistling an approximation of a certain Chopin etude, a cigarette dangling from his lips, he strolled back across the warm square with its memorial to Dom Pedro IV, who had made Portugal a parliamentary democracy in 1826, piercing the sunny morning. The crowds were already thickening, chattering, automobiles and horse-drawn carriages clattering past. It was a fine morning, he reflected, to be young, in love and about to begin making his way in the world. For once he ignored the news of the war, which reached the waiting crowds by means of strips of newsprint dripping wet ink suspended from wires above the sidewalk. The eagerness for the dispatches was good for business at the Metropole Hotel, where he stopped for a cold beer.

Halfway through his second glass of beer, Gomes, a boy-hood friend who had gone to the university at Coimbra and was now a secondary-school teacher, arrived, perspiring, with a parcel of his own and a quizzical expression. Alves gestured expansively for a beer for Gomes.

"Alves, it's good to see you!" He wiped a handkerchief across his high forehead, blinked his tiny, shining black eyes. "And I hear you are now a married man! You have my congratulation—lady killer!" He laughed a trifle enviously. "And a wife to be proud of, I'm also told. . . ." Envy was in his nature, like the sweating.

"You have excellent spies, Gomes. And you are on your way to a professorship. I've heard about your great success at Coimbra. You must be very proud, and rightly so, Gomes, rightly so." Together, two young men of the new world, they chuckled. "Now, you have brought the document I requested?"

"Of course," Gomes said, the puzzled expression returning, "but why, I ask myself, why do you want such a thing?" He shrugged. "It is a small favor, happily granted.

. . . But I can't help my curiosity." He smiled, clutching his parcel, awaiting an answer.

"An elaborate joke, nothing more. No one you know, I'm afraid—and I'll have it back to you tomorrow. You have my word, Gomes. But now," he sighed, glancing at his watch in the manner of older, prosperous men of means and affairs, "I'm off for a luncheon engagement—a farewell for a friend who is on his way to naval maneuvers." He held out his hand for Gomes' package as he stood up. "I can't tell you how much I appreciate your meeting me on such short notice . . . and for bringing the item with you. Time, as the philosopher says, is of the essence. Thank you, my friend." The package was handed over at last. Alves smiled. "Enjoy your beer, Gomes. Have another." He dropped a banknote onto the tabletop. "Really you must join my Maria and me for dinner soon. She will play Chopin for you on our grand piano!"

Gomes was suitably impressed by such largess and the grand piano. Alves nodded and strolled away, inordinately pleased by overwhelming even such a negligible fellow.

Twenty minutes later he was back at the flat, already chain smoking the day's second pack of cigarettes, the table covered with the writing materials from the stationer's shop. Maria was visiting her mother at the family cottage near Estoril; she would not be back until the following day. Tomorrow he would have to have the job completed. Now it was time to open Gomes' parcel. Alves had never seen a university diploma at close hand before; he studied it closely in its details, the calligraphy, the wording, the design. A marvelous, almost magical document: a key to opportunity in this new world, the twentieth-century equivalent of just the right nineteenth-century bloodline, just the precise genealogy the old days had required. Squinting, he stared at it through the haze from his cigarette. Insurance for the future, and yet it was only a piece of paper without any worth beyond the few escudos the university had paid their stationer. Quite incredible. But he saw no reason for Manuelo to have such an advantage when he went without. . . .

Six hours later he slumped back in his chair, opened his fourth pack of cigarettes and closed his red-rimmed eyes. Countless sheaves of paper littered the floor, ashtrays overflowed, his eyes were shot through with crimson lightning flashes. But he had mastered the calligraphy on the University of Coimbra diploma. A steady hand, an artistic eye: considering that he had never tried it before, it wasn't a bad job. Now he'd have to produce a final copy, no blotches, no mistakes in spelling. He picked up a sheet containing the fairly lengthy inscription he'd devised. It sounded good, weighty, official, impressive. But would it work?

This was no time to lose faith: it had seemed so simple in the sunshine of Rossio Square, and now here he stood ankle deep in it once again. But still . . . He sighed aloud. . . . There was nothing really dishonest in it. No one would be hurt. Was it his fault that there had been no money to send him to the university, where he would surely have acquired a similar piece of parchment in the normal run of things? He readied himself, picked up his pen, dipped it carefully into the bottle of India ink. . . .

Arnaldo stopped by the flat at midnight. Alves had fallen asleep on the couch and came to groggily. He splashed water over his face while Arnaldo poured two glasses of port. Holding a towel to his streaming head, Alves led the way to the dining table, now free of all the day's remnants.

"Sit down, Arnaldo. I have something to show you that will convince the world of what you and I already know. . . ." Carefully he took the leather folder from the highboy and laid it before his friend. Tired as he was, he couldn't hold back the slow, broad grin.

Arnaldo was silent for thirty seconds or so, then exclaimed with abrupt anxiety, "What in the name of God have you done!"

"Please." Alves closed his eyes peacefully. "Read it aloud."

" 'To Artur Virgilio Alves Reis,' " Arnaldo read somewhat breathlessly, " 'is awarded the degree of Bachelor . . . for his application in the following disciplines. Engineering Science, Geology, Geometry, Physics, Pure Mathematics, Mathematics, Paleography'—Alves, what the hell is paleography?"

"It doesn't matter. I can look it up. . . ."

Arnaldo sighed, read on: " 'Electrical Engineering, Mechanical Engineering, Applied Mathematics, Chemistry, Experimental Physics, Applied Mechanics, Applied Physics . . .' Alves! This is insane, incredible. . . . What do you know about experimental physics?"

"You're missing the point. Anyone can learn these things by reading a book or two. . . ."

" 'General Civil Engineering, Civil and Mechanical Engineering, General Engineering, Mechanical and Civil Design.' Good lord, man . . . civil design? What does it mean, designing civilizations? You have gone too far!"

Alves scraped his chair back and stood up slowly, went to stand in the window bay by the piano. "But," he said modestly, "I must say I've covered matters quite well, don't you think? Read on." He struck a listener's pose, leaning against the piano, stroking his chin.

" 'Bachelor Artur Virgilio Alves Reis is hereby qualified to direct industries referent to the grade in which he has specialized.' My God," Arnaldo groaned. " 'Granted by Oxford University, Oxford, England' . . . signed by the director of the polytechnic, Henry Spooner, and the chancellor of the university, John D. Peel . . . Alves, do these men exist? At all? Anywhere?"

"I really don't know, Arnaldo. How could I?" He pointed to a chair. Arnaldo sat.

"But why Oxford? Do you realize that this document certifies that you have, in effect, studied everything and can do anything?"

"My intent, I assure you. As for Oxford, who knows when one might encounter a disagreeable official, someone who might challenge these most excellent credentials if they were Portuguese?"

"It seems more than likely to me if you're assigned to undertake a little paleography—"

"And if I had a diploma from Coimbra a verification might be easily sought. Oxford, on the other hand, is well beyond reach . . . and, besides, you know that all Portuguese officials are Anglophiles, anything that's English goes unquestioned—who knows why? It is a tradition, a fact of life."

"Alves, it can't possibly—"

"Oh, cheer up, Arnaldo. Remember, I have studied practical engineering. I'm not an untrained dolt. . . ."

"Neither are you an experimental physicist, a civil designer or paleographer." He shook his head despondently.

"It's only a piece of paper," Alves said, yawning. "The world wants such a piece of paper, then it shall have one. But paper is only paper. I know what I'm doing." He crossed the room and clapped Arnaldo's shoulder. Arnaldo nodded, dazed.

* * *

I *think* I know what I'm doing, Alves thought. Every man has his limits. . . . Had he ventured beyond his own? It was such a harmless maneuver, really . . . and surely foolproof. He felt himself nodding off, thinking, oddly enough, of Angola—was that where his life would truly begin?

The vessel of the Portuguese Steamship Lines was crowded. It creaked a good deal, displayed disconcerting amounts of rust in half-hidden places and smelled overwhelmingly of sweat, anxiety and greed. The sweat was inevitable in the heat and humidity; the anxiety was visible in the eyes of those escaping army service; Angola had a way of engendering greed in travelers. There had been a day-long layover at Madeira, then at St. Vincent, then on toward Africa. Maria spent much of the time in the cabin comforting Alves, who was discovering that while the blood of a Portuguese admiral flowed in his veins, he was the inheritor of a landlubber's stomach. Arnaldo paced the deck with nervous concern, checking in several times each day for reports on his friend's condition.

Alves eventually wobbled into view on Maria's arm. Breathing heavily, face moist and ashen, he sagged into a deck chair, grinned faintly at Arnaldo and scanned the horizon for the first blessed sight of land. In the late evening, unable to sleep as the vessel pitched and moaned, he spent hours staring at the Oxford diploma as if it had a life of its own, magical powers, secrets it would divulge if considered in exactly the right way. Maria, trained by culture and tradition to ignore the curlicues of the male existence, paid no attention to the leather folder, never dreamed of inquiring.

The steamer finally slid through the dusk into Luanda harbor, cutting between parallel lines of high cliffs and a long sand pit with the lights of the town glowing through the fog ahead. Hugely relieved, Alves felt himself coming back to life, dined almost normally that night and took pleasure in supervising Arnaldo and Maria as they readied themselves for disembarking the next morning. After a decent sleep in the becalmed harbor waters, the threesome clambered with their steamer trunks and cases into the small craft that ferried them to shore. The cliffs were touched with shades of pastel reds and pinks in the early-morning sun, and at the pinnacle of the cliffline, overlooking the city and guarding the harbor entrance from a jagged crag, Alves picked out the three-hundred-year-old fortress of San Michel. Behind it, sprinkled like an eerie caravan, were the outlines of a church, a convent, a palace, clusters of solid, well-built, timeless buildings. Together they comprised the Upper Town. A shelf of sand separated the rock walls from the sea, creating the Lower Town, which was obviously the commercial section. Shops and houses and warehouses sprawled along the quay and receded back toward the cliffs: the town was bustling, lively. On the waterfront the little sixteenth-century fort of San Francisco welcomed seafarers, harking back to the city's past. There was a railway station, a wireless tower rising from the jumble of low buildings like a jaunty finger pointing to the future.

Within two hours of reaching the dock Alves had recovered his energies and spirits, located the Central Hotel, where he booked a week's accommodation, and engaged an agent to show them houses in the Upper Town. After a hearty lunch he left Maria and Arnaldo to get settled into the hotel and set off through the tattered confusion of dusty streets, through the shouts and smells and sights of the brightly colored markets that offered native goods, pipes, tobacco, snuff, vivid skeins of yarn, large quantities of dried salt fish and tureens of exceedingly messy, oily foodstuffs. But it was all a blur as he quickly marched to the Central Public Works Office. Once past the banging screen door, brushing dust from his coat, he realized that, as usual, he was in up over his chin and had no choice but to act forthrightly, depending on his natural gall, earnest face and forged diploma. The clerk behind the wooden railing looked up inquiringly. It was now or never. . . .

By five o'clock, however, Alves' burden of worry was considerably lightened. Senhor Terreira, a sixtyish bureaucrat who preferred to spend the bulk of his time on expeditions inland hunting sable, took one look at Diploma Number 2148 from the Polytechnic School of Engineering at Oxford and favored the young man before him with a tug of his white mustache and a smile appointed with sparkling gold. "Heaven has intervened in Angola's behalf,

Engineer Reis!" he exclaimed in only partially mock wonderment. "Our director of building and sewerage has just returned to Lisbon, a sick man—after seventeen years of glorious service. And here you are, fully qualified to replace him! It is almost too good to be true." Alves assured him that it was indeed true.

Senhor Terreira hooked his thumbs through his braces, leaned back in the squeaking swivel chair and began enumerating the new director's responsibilities, going over several folders of works in progress and repairs being carried out and determining a salary that turned out to be considerably more than Alves' father had earned in any one year in his entire life. Alves nodded sagely from time to time, made a mental note to cultivate a mustache and buy a pith helmet and drew some satisfaction from the realization that a child could have understood and conquered the challenges of the building and sewerage job. A secretary entered with forms to fill out, thick bitter coffee was served, and he was introduced to several of his perspiring and mustachioed colleagues, none of whom happened, fortunately, to be an Oxford man. A bank draft was issued against his first month's salary, the name of a tailor was provided, his hand was shaken enthusiastically and an invitation was presented for dinner the same evening at the European Club. As Terreira saw him to the door, he remarked, "You know, Reis, I'd wager a sizable batch of escudos that you are the only graduate of Oxford in all Angola!" Behind his voluminous mustache he beamed, relieved at his good fortune in finding such a remarkable young man.

Within a week the newly pregnant Maria had found a large walled-in old house in the Upper Town, whitewashed, tree-shaded, encircling a splashing fountain; the three of them—Alves, Maria and Arnaldo—had moved in, and Alves had hired Arnaldo as his assistant. Together they got off to a good start, mopping up old projects, moving ahead with new ones. After two months of clearing his desk, Alves took a break, gathered up Maria and went off to a dinner party hosted by Terreira. Late in the evening Alves strolled onto the veranda with a sun-blackened man named Chaves, who was a director of Angola Railways.

"So you're the man from Lisbon . . . Terreira speaks well of you, Reis," Chaves growled past the stub of his cigar. "Says you've taken hold remarkably well. Very rare out here, Oxford men. . . ."

"Yes, very rare," Alves said. "Senhor Terreira is very kind, of course. My work here has gone well. My problem is that there is not really enough to do."

"Aha, well then, there is a matter we should discuss." Chaves spit out a tangle of wet tobacco leaf and pointed what was left of the cigar at Alves. He was short, low-browed, with a nose that drooped like an overripe fruit. A gold chain stretched across the expanse of vest. There was a crust of permanent dirt beneath his fingernails: he bore the signs of a man who had worked his way to the top.

"The railway here is in the process of dramatic growth," he rumbled softly. "You've seen the crews out blasting right-of-way, building roadbeds, laying track—they're all convicts. There is no death penalty at home, as you know, but those who deserved it are shipped out here. We put them to work, hard work but better than a firing squad. Eventually, if they behave themselves. they're given their freedom . . . but in the meantime they build the railroads and do a damned fine job of it, all things considered. . . ."

"And the matter we should discuss?"

"Terreira says you're full of mechanical qualifications. Is it true?"

"Not to seem immodest, but he's not entirely wrong." Alves smiled ingenuously, shot his cuffs, noticed that a button was missing.

"Well, then, here is my point. While the track is being put down, we have problems with our locomotives. To give it a name—" his voice dropped to a throaty whisper— "many of them just won't run. . . . There are, you see, very few farm-to-market roads—"

"And," Alves concluded for him, grasping at once what was coming next, "the produce must therefore move to market by rail. So the locomotives must be made to run. Correct?"

Chaves nodded. "Obviously. We have few spare parts, and the ones we have are infrequently the ones we need. The problem is, would you consent to look them over? They are of Belgian manufacture, you may be able to do nothing . . . and, please, I realize that you are not merely a mechanic. I would normally hesitate to apply to a man of your skill and learning for such a practical diagnosis, but quite frankly we are faced with an emergency, Reis. There is only one question left—what to do?" He plunged his stubby-fingered hands into his jacket pockets, worked the cigar into the furthermost corner of his mouth.

"I understand. I sympathize," Alves replied after a thoughtful pause. "I will look at the locomotives. Tomorrow morning." The moon darted from behind the clouds, catching their faces in a bluish light. They smiled.

* * *

When Chaves arrived at the locomotive barns the next morning it was eight-thirty and Alves had already been there, aided by Arnaldo, for three and a half hours. The sound of hammering filled the low, cavernous building with its begrimed windows and hard-packed earth floor. Alves was working on the inside of an engine, freeing up a series of metal plates: he was figuring out how to do it as he went along, and hoped the blacks charged with keeping the trains knew less, wouldn't detect his ignorance. Chaves peered in, shook his head, paced around the huge black piece of machinery for the half hour it took his new adviser to finish, and confronted Reis—who emerged clad in coveralls and generous helpings of thick grease—with an expression mingling shock and pleasure.

"Engineer Reis, one word. You're new here, young and ambitious and capable, but—well, you must understand our ways." He gestured at the filthy coveralls and shook his huge, heavy head, which protruded hornlike from his thick shoulders.

Alves was out of breath from the exertion. Arnaldo threw him a rag to wipe his hands. "I thought you wanted me to—"

"*Look* them over," Chaves said reproachfully. "To *diagnose* the ailment, you might say. But we've got these boys here, these native boys, to do the fixing—the dirty work. That's what we pay them for."

"Well, I certainly had no intention of upsetting the routine. . . ." Alves swallowed hard, looking away from Chaves' suddenly steely eyes. He recognized the key moment: apologize or assert himself. "But there are certain problems that only a trained engineer can possibly master." He turned back, smiling, masking his hesitancy with confidence, relieved at his flanking maneuver. "These fine boys can take care of routine maintenance, I have no doubt, but for sophisticated analysis—well, Director, such matters require a graduate engineer . . . and the adjustments, even on so great a machine, are so fine they must be made by a trained hand." He finished wiping his hands, methodically folded the cloth and thrust it into his side coverall pocket. "All of which undoubtedly explains why these locomotives sit idle and crops rot in the countryside. Technical matters have been either beyond what passed for real engineers here or incomprehensible to blacks, who should never have been expected to handle them. . . .

"I can make these trains run, Director, if you would care to make them my responsibility. I am at your service." He was unable to resist the opportunity, push it for all it was worth.

Director Chaves blinked, swallowed and took this remarkable suggestion back to his suite at the railway office. Alves and Arnaldo reported to the Public Works Office.

Arnaldo followed his friend into his private cubicle and shut the door. "What do you think you're doing, talking to Chaves that way? It's his railroad . . . and you insulted his engineers! You know nothing about trains. . . . Will the great monstrous things run?" Despairing, Arnaldo hurled himself into a spindly wooden chair and began squeezing his temples.

Alves sat down and lit a cigarette. "I think they'll run." He reconsidered: "What am I saying? I'm probably the first person in Angola who's looked at them and had any idea at all what was wrong. . . . His engineers probably spent all their time keeping clean and trying to explain to the native boys what to do. Of course they'll run. They're no different than engines I studied in school . . . just bigger. They'll run, all right." He blew several perfect smoke rings. "Really, it's not difficult. . . ."

Arnaldo gave him a pleading look and went off to visit a sewerage repair site. Alves sat quietly at his desk, reflecting on what a land of opportunity Angola was!

Shortly before noon he was jangled out of his thoughtful reverie by Chaves himself.

"All right, Reis," he said from deep within his thick chest, the stubby, black-haired fingers drumming on Alves' desk, "it's my pleasure to inform you that the locomotive is already in action. I congratulate you, sir!" Abruptly he grabbed Alves' small hand in his own and gave it a single bone-crunching pump of approval. "I have considered your proposal—and I'm now prepared to offer you the position of Acting Chief Engineer of Angola Railways, starting at once!" The room bristled with the man's rough dynamism.

Alves cracked his second pack of cigarettes and slowly lit one, camouflaging his amazement. He hadn't reckoned that this gorilla in a white linen suit was such an impulsive decision maker.

"I'm very pleased, even flattered," he said, once the room had stopped reverberating from Chaves' cries.

"There is a problem, however. . . ."

"Yes?" He felt his heart pounding: the Oxford diploma hissed in his past like something wriggling and poisonous, dangling from a limb in his path.

"What about your present position here? Surely Terreira needs you."

"A mere nothing, Director," Alves said, trying to hide a wheeze of relief. "I can easily manage both sets of responsibilities. You have met my associate, Senhor Carvalho. He is most trustworthy, fully capable of executing my directives. Without disrupting things here at this office, I can report to the locomotive barns at five each morning, clear up any problems there, attend to the daily communiqués to the field . . . and spend the remainder of the day here, always at the ready in case there is a railway emergency. A most excellent arrangement."

"You are," Chaves growled past pursed lips, "a very confident young man."

Alves nodded, losing himself in playing his new role. "May I make a suggestion?"

"Certainly."

"Why not a trial period? A month, say, during which time I will see that all the locomotives capable of running are in fact running. At the end of the month we will discuss permanent appointment. Is that agreeable to Angola Railways?"

Chaves was bobbing his huge head enthusiastically; he liked this man, he liked making a deal. "And your compensation, what of that?" He had a figure in mind, approximately half of what Reis was earning in Public Works. There was no sense in passing up a bargain. Alves could see it in Chaves' eyes.

"No compensation whatsoever for the first month—the period during which you will see if I make the trains run. That way you run no risk whatsoever. . . ."

"And thereafter?" Chaves gazed, perplexed and slightly off balance, into Alves' smile.

"I suggest that a salary comparable exactly to my salary in Public Works—modest in the extreme for the possessor of an Oxford diploma, surely—would be most fitting. In other words, the railway is as important as the sewers. Am I right, Director?"

Chaves knew when he had come up against a sound thinker with a sense of his own worth. He could argue the matter of escudos per hour, of course, but he knew that Reis held the cards. He wiped the sweat from his forehead and fixed on Alves' large brown eyes, which seemed magnified behind his round spectacles. "Right. I agree. The same salary . . . *if* the trains are running in a month." They shook hands again. Alves doubted if his hand could withstand another bargain struck.

The trains ran. Alves decked out in his *macoco,* his monkey suit, became a familiar sight, moving from one locomotive to another, performing prodigies of energy. The local Europeans, who scorned him for getting dirty when he worked, called him "the monkey engineer," but the trains ran. And quite suddenly he was making twice as much money as before, with plenty available for investments, an utterly new experience. Sentimentally, he sunk some of it into railway stock, making him his own employer, at least to a small degree. It was a very good feeling. Chaves and Terreira each claimed credit for discovering the miracle man. Arnaldo wearily shook his head, grinning, encouraging. Maria began to have dinner parties befitting her status as Senhora Miracle Man. Alves grew restless. . . .

*   *   *

He developed a new hobby that he'd never before been able to afford—photography. He bought cameras. He snapped away at Maria, Arnaldo, Chaves, Terreira. He arranged afternoons of family portraiture in Luanda's best photographic studio. He sent copies to his friends at home; he filled photograph albums. He would stand transfixed before the photographer's studio window gazing at the portraits of himself and Maria smiling out at the passers-by, young and successful and full of confidence in the future. He began to see qualities in himself he'd never noticed before: he saw a young man of substance. And what he saw increased his impatience. He wanted to break into a run. He wanted the future now: he was developing some plans. . . .

* * *

The *Official Gazette* in Luanda had organized a small testimonial dinner in honor of Alves Reis. Not only were the trains running; they actually made sense of the new railway timetables. It was an unheard-of phenomenon. A gathering of perhaps two dozen railroad officials and businessmen, drawn from among those most likely to benefit from the new schedule, puffed on cigars and sipped fine port that night in a private room at the Central Hotel. A storm had broken outside, the windows were open to cooling breezes, and Alves, only twenty-three but happily full of himself on this remarkable occasion, acknowledged the chairman's introduction, rose, peered from behind his circular glasses and began to grin. He thanked his hosts, felt a tear building in the corner of his eye and went on in a spasm of emotion to speak of his feelings for this land of opportunity. It was the first official honor of his young life, and he wasn't sure where the effect of the port left off and emotion began. He ought to have felt his nerves fraying, but as he rose he saw in his mind the puffing trains churning along the track, his own face staring confidently from the photographer's windows, the leaders of the community dining at his table. It was all of a piece. No wonder they were all applauding the guest of honor. . . .

"I have sailed along Angola's lengthy coastline," he recalled, nervously rubbing one moist palm against the other, "and I have undertaken many arduous journeys to the interior. I have carefully studied the resources of the country." He paused, swallowing hard, wondering what was coming out of his mouth next. "How to say it, gentlemen, how to make clear my feelings? I am . . ." He heard his voice crack, as if from a great distance. He seemed to be watching the scene, watching this new man emerge from the opportunity Angola had provided, but of course he wasn't watching. He had to say something. "I am lost in wonder at the immensity of the riches in its soil and subsoil. . . . As though Mother Nature in her wisdom had sought a showcase for her might and caprice!" Someone chuckled at the young man's enthusiasm, the flowery turn of phrase.

A rumble of approval drifted toward him, mingling with banks of cigar smoke. The night's breeze carried the wetness and scent of foliage and earth and ocean; he was nearly drunk on it. "Hear, hear!" a banker called from the back of the room. "Viva Angola!" came a cry. Alves sipped the ruby port, rolling it on his tongue, then swept on, carried away by the quality of the moment.

"Gold and silver, copper and tin and iron and . . . diamonds, they all ensure the Angola of tomorrow its place as one of the most prosperous lands not only of the African continent but of the entire globe!" He banged his fist on the table, upsetting the goblet, watching with surprise the stain spreading across the tablecloth, feeling his face go crimson beneath the perspiration. For God's sake, what had he done now?

But drowning out the laughter were more shouts of approval, standing applause, then the presentation of a handsome brass plate bolted to a hardwood plaque with the inscription "Alves Reis . . . who discharges his post with great zeal and competence, thus serving the Colony and the Republic well." Arnaldo led the final round of applause, and, once good nights were said and the group dispersed, the two old friends in their best suits and gleaming shoes strolled the cobbled, glistening streets in the storm's aftermath.

"A satisfying evening," Arnaldo ventured, exhaling a puff of smoke, toying with the gold paper cigar band on his ring finger. "Good humor, your fair share of honor. . . . A kind of pinnacle, to have achieved so much and been recognized for it—"

"And I spilled the bloody port!" Alves interrupted, but his spirits were high. He forced himself to be calm. "A good beginning, yes, but there is so much ahead of us, so much to do, so much world to do it in. . . ." He smiled in the sweet darkness, his ambition and imagination racing before him. Arnaldo seemed always to be satisfied, to accept the way things were as the way they should continue to be. Well, that was Arnaldo, but he was loyal, a man you could count on.

"Dare I ask what next?"

"Now that we are established, this is the time to press our advantage. We must learn what we can in this training ground."

"Training ground? That's not what you called it this

evening. The future lies in Angola, I believe you said." He stopped on the dark street, fixed Alves with a quizzical grin.

"Well, one says what the situation requires." He clasped Arnaldo's arm. "The future awaits us in Lisbon, though, I'm sure of it. The war is over in Lisbon and Europe, and the future is bright! You can hold me to that. . . ." He smiled tiredly, exhausted from the first attempt at speech-making in his life. Frequently in convincing Arnaldo he was able to convince himself. And that was a damned good thing.

* * *

Maria was something else. Arnaldo was a man; you knew what to say to him, and it didn't take a fortuneteller to gauge his response. But a woman! A mystery . . . outwardly so content, so simple, so easily pleased. What Alves missed in her was a sense of sharing his own life. On the one hand, he knew perfectly well that you didn't confide your business to your wife; it was traditionally impossible . . . but, on the other hand, he spent many a night sitting by the fountain in the courtyard, past midnight, smoking, wanting her to know what his life meant. *Really* meant.

But there were the children, the entertaining, her friends, managing the small household staff . . .

Still, once he'd moved on into other fields—discreet moneylending, buying and selling crops, consulting other businessmen on how best to make use of the rail system— he took a tentative step toward increasing communication with Maria. He still retained close ties with both Chaves and Terreira, but increasingly his pursuits took him far afield, into the interior. He took Maria with him, leaving Arnaldo to cope with the office in Luanda.

Maria was more often than not the only white woman the natives had ever seen. She was unafraid, trusting and made friends easily. He found himself enjoying her company—almost as a friend rather than a wife, though he was unable to detect in her manner any awareness of the changing relationship.

Late in the year 1919, having been on his own for six months, he took her with him to visit a tobacco farmer whose crop he was buying. Returning, still on horseback,

with the railway yet another day's ride distant, they sat
by the campfire, alone, the native boys sound asleep.

"You know," Alves said, leaning toward her on one
elbow, searching her face for reaction, "I've put away a
great deal of money. Do you understand what I mean,
Maria?" She watched the flames, hands folded in her lap.
He smelled the leather of her new boots. "Far more money
than your father has. . . ."

She looked up quickly. "You are joking? Aren't you?"
Her voice was soft, startled.

"Not at all."

"I see." She smiled shyly. "I don't know what to say. I
know nothing about money."

"Ah, you know one great thing, my dearest." He took
her hand, tracing the length of her fingers. "How to spend
it."

She nodded, laughing very quietly.

At length she said, "What has this to do with me? Why
are you telling me?" She seemed almost embarrassed by the
subject.

"Because I love you, because our two lives make only
one life, because money makes things change." He lit a
cigarette and looked at the moon. "It cannot buy the moon,
I know, but it is strange and wonderful stuff nonetheless.
You see, I have a knack for making it. . . . It's like a game,
a sport—some people are good at it, others are not. It comes
easily to me. And once you begin playing, there's no
point in stopping. . . ."

"All right," she said. "I'm happy that you are good at
it." She stretched, held his hand to her mouth for a kiss.
Then she cupped his palm around her breast and stopped
his eyes with hers. "You are good at even more important
things. . . ." A giggle barely escaped: she was still so much
a child. He stroked the round, soft breast, feeling her
respond. But he pushed on; he wanted to talk now that he'd
begun.

He wasn't altogether sure she was listening, but he told
her of his recent trip to Europe, the buying and selling he'd
done in what was being called "war surplus" these days.
War surplus—the production overruns left idle in warehouses throughout Europe when the war finally ended. In
France he'd bought an entire trainload of heavy paper sand-
bags that had never reached the trenches. He had shipped
them to Angola, selling them with the guarantee that they

were as strong as jute. Not one complaint! And that was only one of many such business dealings.

Against the background of profit-making, the death of his father had seemed only a moment's interlude. Alves had gone through the photographs he'd saved of his father, trying to fix a happy memory in his mind, but the pictures had been barren of any lightheartedness. It was memory that brought forth the happy moment, the Easter Sunday of his boyhood, his father telling them about the admiral. . . . That had been an exciting day and his father had been part of it. Now his father was dead, saved further grinding down, spared any more humiliation.

"Our future is in Europe," he said. "It is clearer every day."

"But we're so happy here," she protested.

"There's more to life, Maria . . . life is so much bigger than this." He watched her leaning back against the saddle and blanket. He knew when she wanted to make love. He looked away at a night sound. "I'm going back to Lisbon in two weeks."

"Not all of us, not to live?" Her eyes were wide, stricken.

"No, no, my darling. Business. . . . I'm just preparing you for the inevitable."

"Then come to me now," she said. "I know what is inevitable, don't you?" She held out her arms. Shadows flickered across her face, the expression of sudden need.

In the morning he couldn't be sure that she even remembered the conversation. Perhaps it made no difference to her, one way or the other, knowing about his life. Perhaps women thought only of their houses and their children and their sexual needs. It was a mystery. He looked at her out of the corner of his eye as she rode beside him. Not a clue. He'd better forget his idea of sharing that part of his life with her. He'd been wrong. Women were women.

* * *

While picking through a derelict warehouse in Lisbon near the docks, far below the serpentine streets of the ancient Alfama district, he came across two dozen unused tractors left behind from the day the Portuguese government had impounded all German shipping and goods. Despite some surface rust, a cursory inspection convinced Reis that they were in no way permanently damaged. After a morning of poking about in the clammy, filthy warehouse, he offered to buy the lot for one tenth of the original price. The supply chief looked on it as found money; as well, the space would be cleared at no cost to the government.

Having guaranteed to empty the warehouse in fourteen days, Alves found two well-qualified, out-of-work mechanics and hired them to refurbish the tractors. He once again climbed into his monkey suit, and the three of them went to work greasing, sanding, oiling, painting. He made a deal with an Angolan importer based in Lisbon: the price of the tractors, or comparable English-made machines, had risen considerably since the time these had first been manufactured—yet Alves generously offered them, brand new, in mint unused condition, for their original price, a 900 percent profit for himself minus the 4 percent he'd agreed to pay the mechanics. The Angolan importer assumed responsibility in the eyes of his clients, and Alves was well out of it. The deal was signed and the consignment delivered in twelve, not fourteen, days. Money, money, money . . .

Upon his return to Luanda he summoned Arnaldo to a meeting that took place in the handsome beamed study of the ancient walled-in house. He recounted the story of his European adventures and bestowed a substantial raise on his properly impressed associate. Together in their new, elegantly cut dinner clothes and carefully pampered mustaches, the two of them sat in the dim silence and stared at each other from the deep recesses of heavy armchairs. It was one of life's sweet moments when all has been seen to go right in the face of substantial odds.

"Why are you grinning?" Arnaldo inquired, crossing his right leg over his left, pointing the patent-leather toe of his pump.

"What a pair we are!" Alves exclaimed. "We can do anything . . . I'm almost convinced of that."

Together they wandered into the foyer and waited for Maria, who finally bustled in, still instructing the cook about preparations for the late after-theater supper.

Maria clattered down the hall after kissing the children —two by now—good night. She was a determined mother, a natural comforter who gloried in her children, the managing of her home. She was tremendously pleased with her husband's worldly success, both the money and the esteem in which he was held by Luanda's leaders. She found it all particularly satisfying. Socially she made the most of her opportunities. That very night a dozen of Luanda's most prominent figures would dine in her home. And that would make quite a tantalizing subject for a letter home.

The play, *Camille*, was not done well even by Portuguese standards; by Angolan standards, however, it was a treat, and the young company was warmly applauded once the heroine coughed 'her last. The party congregated in the lobby, in the center of the swirling, festive, well-dressed crowd. While the Governor had been unable to attend, both Terreira and Chaves were on hand with their wives, the managing director of the Eastern Telegraph Company, an executive of the steamship company, the importer who had handled the tractor transaction, the editor of Luanda's major newspaper. The women in their jewelry and long dresses glittered and quivered and chattered; the men spoke quietly among themselves and appraised the women.

The newspaper editor's wife, only a few years older than Maria, was the most strikingly attractive woman in the group. For several months Alves had lusted in his mind after her full round breasts, which were much in view that evening, and her quick, intelligent laughter, her pale-blue eyes, her most unusual pale straw-colored hair. She was German, or perhaps Swiss, and he joined her at a small table in the courtyard for dinner.

He leaned over her slightly, peering into the recesses of her low-cut gown, and asked if he might sit with her. There was a knowing smile on her wide mouth.

"Dinner with the famous Senhor Reis, just the two of us," she murmured. "I'm flattered. I hope Director Chaves does not feel slighted . . . you were very intent together during the intermission, you and Director Chaves."

"Business," he said, "mere business. He was seeking my advice about an acquisition—"

"How very interesting," she said. The thick, somewhat coarse Teutonic intonation and pronunciation intrigued him. Everything about her was so different from Maria, including her interest in the business world. "A very large purchase?"

"Extraordinarily," he said, smelling her perfume on the cool breeze. "Several huge American locomotives, machines of the future—we must watch the progressive Americans, learn from them."

"Americans," she repeated tonelessly. "I suppose you are

right, but still, I am a German. . . . I do not find the Americans very sympathetic, you see."

"I apologize," Alves said, reaching across the small table, stroking the soft texture of her hand. "But the fact is their locomotives are of very high quality. I told Director Chaves to buy them at once. They'll never be cheaper." He smiled into the cool eyes.

A stiff, straight-backed figure bowed fractionally over the table. It was a man the editor had brought along for the evening and had introduced briefly to Alves. Leaving such a slight alteration in the dinner plans to Maria, he had failed to remember the man's name. The impression, however, had been dramatic: very close-cropped hair, neck as thick as a tree trunk, with even rolls of hard fat layered down to the back of his collar, flashing monocle, cigarette in an ivory holder—he brought to mind a photograph Alves had seen of a German actor called Von Stroheim.

The woman glanced up. "Herr Hennies," she said, "you've met our host, Senhor Reis?"

"Of course," Hennies said stiffly. "Adolf Hennies." He made it sound like a command, bowed again. "May I join you?"

"Please do," she said. "We were speaking of business."

Seating himself, placing his dinner plate on the table, Hennies nodded stiffly. "I could not help but overhear you in passing—so I stopped, intruding on your *tête-à-tête*, I am afraid." He smiled thinly below the monocle, which gleamed opaquely in the candlelight like a huge Cyclopean eye. "But I could not resist. You have become a famous man in Angola, Senhor Reis . . . famous for your unerring business sense. I hoped for a chance to talk this evening. Tomorrow, you see, I return to the Continent." He chewed a tiny morsel of the excellent stuffed fish.

"You are too kind," Alves said, tearing his eyes away from the woman's pale bosom, confronting the monocle. "You are here on business, Herr Hennies?"

The German nodded. "In a way. Germany must make its way in this new postwar world. There is no time to sit licking our wounds—business is the business of the world, is it not?"

He watched the German, wondering if he was a better bet for the evening than the editor's wife.

"You have done well here, no one can doubt it," Hennies said. "But Africa lacks the stability of Europe. We may

face inflation of the currency in Europe, but there are
alternative currencies—if one doesn't suit you, try another.
Here, where you are also facing inflation, you are locked
to the mother country . . . and business opportunities are
limited. Angola is owned by Portugal, a fact that puts a
finite limit on opportunity. Now—" carefully sipping his
wine, speaking so quietly that the editor's wife was forced
to lean forward—"now is the time for a man of your caliber
to make his move back to Europe. With the way the Angolan economy is developing, well, you must see for yourself what is happening. . . . You have recently been to
France, I understand, and Lisbon. You have undoubtedly
reached these conclusions for yourself. I hope I have not
been presumptuous."

"Not at all," Alves assured him. "Most interesting, in
fact. You are obviously a man who gives such matters
considerable thought."

"Herr Hennies is very deep, very mysterious," the woman
said, smiling at the German. "He is a good man to strike
a bargain with." Her lashes fluttered. "But watch him
closely. Others have not and lived to regret it. I warn you."

"Ah, you defame me," Hennies said, forcing a chuckle.

Alves' attention had swung almost completely away from
the woman to concentrate on Hennies. He had never spoken
at any length with a German before, and he found himself
wondering how the man's mind worked. How much of
what he had always been told about Germans was true? Stiff,
formal, slow-witted, brutal, intransigent? As a Portuguese
he didn't fully trust any German, nor did he pretend to
understand the man's motivation. What did the man
want?

In time the editor came to spirit his wife off to another
cluster of guests, leaving him alone with the German. They
smoked in silence for a moment, listening to the fountain
splashing nearby.

"Seriously, Senhor Reis," Hennies said, "our charming
friend has made a small joke at my expense . . . but let
me say that I hope you recognize it as just that, a joke.
If you decide to return to the Continent I should be most
grateful if you would inform me." He inclined his head on
what seemed to be a ballbearing at the top of his spinal
column, slipped a small white pasteboard from his pocket,
smoothing his waistcoat. "Please accept my card. Men of
vision and ability may often benefit one another. Just pos-

sibly I could put some good things in your way." He stood abruptly, consulted a large gold hunter at the end of a substantial gold link chain and softly brought his heels together. "Good evening, Senhor Reis. My ship embarks at first light."

Alves watched the German move his substantial bulk toward Maria. Alves drained his wine and lit another cigarette.

Director Chaves, as was his custom, was the final guest. Alves found him scraping the sides of the chafing dish.

"What do you know of the German, Herr Hennies?"

Chaves belched appreciatively into his fist. "Seems to me I heard he was a spy. During the war, maybe even now. You know what people say, Alves. Germans are not to be trusted. Now they say that the Germans want to take Angola away from us, that Hennies is here evaluating the situation. . . ." He huffed tiredly. "They say he's passing himself off as a Swiss these days."

"Do you think it's true?" But hadn't he implied he was German?

Chaves shrugged. "Why not? Most of what I hear these days turns out to be true." He put his plate down and yawned. "Can you forgive me? Maria, my dear, I've stayed too long yet again."

"Impossible, Director," she said, taking his hairy hand. "You are always our favorite guest." The cook had come in to clear the buffet. Arnaldo dozed on a bench in the courtyard. His snoring wafted gently on the breeze. Alves walked to the gate with Chaves.

"Hennies thinks I should return to Europe."

"And you, Alves? What do you think?"

"He may be right."

Chaves sighed deeply and nodded. "Sooner or later, I've known it was inevitable—your leaving. I can't say I blame you, if it comes to that. But keep an eye on Hennies. I expect he's a tricky one." He turned in the roadway. "Don't do anything impulsively, Alves. Think it over. But whatever you do, you must make me a promise. . . ."

"And that is?"

"The American locomotives. You must wait for delivery, in case there's a problem. Promise me, Alves."

"Of course I'll wait."

Chaves came forward, squeezed Alves' shoulder. Then he strolled off into the darkness.

That night Alves sat on the bed watching Maria brush her long rich hair, one hundred, two hundred strokes, like a careful, solemn little girl. She was such an innocent, so sheltered: helpless without him. He wanted her. He always wanted her, always enjoyed the yielding softness. Maybe it was better, all things considered, that his little attempt to draw her into his public life had come to nothing. Maybe it was better this way, the old way. . . . Away from the everyday battles, she gave him refuge, a place to forget for a moment. Holding her, watching her tremble, tears on her cheeks as she struggled to reach her climax, he was sure that she was as she should be, complete in her womanhood, innocent of the outside world, devoted solely to the life he made for her. . . . He had been wrong to expect anything else, and only infrequently, when he saw another kind of woman on the street or at dinner, did he wonder what else there was, what secrets might lie within other women.

After they made love, erasing the editor's wife from his mind, he lit a cigarette and told her that they would be returning to Lisbon soon, once the American locomotives arrived.

During the months of waiting for the new locomotives, Alves pursued his various business arrangements with increased fervor. With the decision to return home made he was intent on building up as large a supply of capital as possible. He spent most of his time traveling into the countryside, seeking new and increasingly ingenious ways to make money, and the more he saw the more committed he became in his belief that somehow Angola would play a deciding role in his life. Sooner or later . . .

Traveling alone, by train and horseback, stopping in friendly farmhouses and ramshackle, makeshift inns and outland campsites, he had the time to evaluate his condition, the course his life had taken since that night on the beach with José—that, he felt in his heart, had been the turning point. Late at night he would sit on the plain beneath a shadowy tree, smoke a cigarette, warm his feet by a campfire and consider the moon sliding silently across sleeping Africa. He knew what it took to succeed. He had to ignore his own doubts: doubt yourself, he thought, and the doubts of others would surely follow.

What had always been important to Alves was the country itself, Angola, all 480,000 square miles of Africa's western coast that was fourteen times larger than Portugal

itself. Three and a half million people roamed the vastness
of plain and rain forest and mountainous ridge with areas
larger than all of England, inhabited by only a few thousand blacks. . . . He loved it. He knew he would be
back. . . .

*   *   *

Only a few weeks before the locomotives were scheduled to
arrive from America, Alves received a surprise by post—
a thick envelope, sent from Mozambique. José Bandeira!

He ripped the envelope, a grin spreading across his face.
José—good old José. How often since arriving in Luanda
almost six years before had he longed for word of José. . . .

The letter, which began in a rambling, discursive manner,
laboriously thrashed its way toward the point. Alves
slumped down behind his study desk and read it again
from the beginning, slowly shaking his head.

José was in prison in Mozambique. At least he was
honest about telling his story: he could hardly have fabri-
cated a more depressing tale. First, a year after arriving in
Mozambique, he had stolen two thousand dollars from the
Garland, Laidlaw safe and gone to prison. But his father,
freshly humiliated, had repaid the money and an added
indemnity to the authorities, thereby securing José's release. Then, by pulling additional strings the elder Bandeira had imposed on friends at the Mozambique Railway
to give his son "one last chance, to quote the old boy,"
wrote José, who seemed in remarkably peppy spirits considering his unhappy situation. José went on:

> But I was never meant to be an impoverished clerk.
> I cannot rid myself of the belief that I was born for
> bigger things—you know how I care for good clothes
> and not-so-good women. Temptation is my enemy . . .
> and dealing with these idiots here was too great a
> temptation, I'm afraid. So much money was passing
> through my hands that some found its way into my
> pocket. So, here I am in jail again! Naturally I
> applied to Father for help, but this time he was un-
> forgiving—can you blame him? He compares me with
> Antonio, who has never given him any trouble at all
> and now distinguishes our family in the diplomatic
> world.

The letter continued chattily for another few pages. José, Alves reflected, obviously had plenty of time on his hands. Finally, on the last page, came José's shameless request:

> *Word has reached me of your great successes! You are famous even in Mozambique! Now you have the opportunity to help your oldest friend. From your vast treasury a mere five thousand dollars American will ransom your chum. If you can find it in your heart to aid me at this difficult time I can only give you my frail assurances that you will never regret it.*

The letter concluded with directions as to how the money might be transferred. Alves stubbed out his cigarette. José was José and the loyalty ran deep. There was also much in the letter that Alves understood, much with which he sympathized. Poor José . . . Whatever would become of him? Alves set off for his bank.

*   *   *

Alves hadn't forgotten his origins, but he had just about had it with the mutterings of the rabble. He couldn't see them: they were crowded, hot and dusty, beyond the riveted steel walls of the locomotive boiler inside of which he was stewing in his own fragrant juices. There was a bemused excitement in the native Angolan voices, a counterpoint of irritating jocularity from the Europeans. Patiently he tightened his concentration like palms over his ears and turned his attention back to the recalcitrant damned piece of machinery. There was, he told himself, no point in venting anger on a piece of machinery. Machinery was not constructed haphazardly to confound you; it was predictable and yielded to the man who understood certain basic principles. Basic principles—he wished he knew more about them. His mind wandered as he fussed with the bolts, levers.

As he worked sweat welled up in the transverse crevices of his broad forehead, cascaded down his nose, and when he brushed a grimy hand at the sting he left his face marked like a warrior red Indian. From time to time he changed his crouching stance, groaned and sneaked a look at the circle of glowing, pale-blue sky above him. Why, in the name of God, had he promised Chaves he'd get these damned things going?

He knew perfectly well that the Europeans outside in the shade—including the abominable Englishman Smythe-Hancock with his monocle on a string—were discussing what they'd come to call "Reis' Mistake." Smythe-Hancock of all the Europeans had always bothered him most of all, for a peculiar reason. The man struck Alves as the perfect idea of an Oxford man, seemed always capable of exposing the old diploma fraud. Alves knew it was all in his mind—but he couldn't shake it.

The Angolans in their black cotton robes were judiciously pondering the absurdities of the white man's fascination with large mechanical devices. All of them, the blacks and the whites, were doubtless tanking up on grappa, the native beer.

Well, if all came right with the last series of levers, he'd fix the smug bastards, especially the monocled pudding-faced one.

He was having a hell of a time reading the American repair manual. It was the fact that the huge locomotives were of American manufacture that so amused his fellow Europeans. The locomotives that had always been in use on the Melanje line hadn't been good enough for Transport Engineer Alves Reis, oh no! He had to buy American —and when he got them he couldn't make them run! Smythe-Hancock had haw-hawed his way through many an evening at the Central, verbally sniping at the Portuguese. "Reis, you've been foozled, lumbered, buggered! Most expensive damned pieces of railroad machinery ever brought into Africa, by God, and all they'll do is sit there. . . . What are they, pieces of sculpture?"

Cocktails at the Central Hotel had become something of a trial since the locomotives had arrived. There was nothing to do but fix them, make them run.

The problem with the rabble outside was that its European complement was composed of small, petty men. If Smythe-Hancock was the worst, the margin was a small one. They were still, after all these years, waiting for him to fail. How, he wondered, could they have failed to grasp the one key element in his personality? He knew the answer, of course, down in the core of his soul: it was simply that they wanted him to fail more than they wanted to know why he always succeeded. He didn't like it, but it wasn't something he could change. . . .

He turned away from the repair manual, oil-spotted and folded open to what he suspected was the correct page, and went back to the maze of rods, cogs and levers. Another hour and he'd have it mastered. He was confident of that. He'd make the damn thing work all right. And that was what they didn't understand about Reis, that he never questioned the advisability of trying nor entertained at any length the possibility of failure.

Arnaldo's head appeared upside down over the rim of the boiler funnel, dark and featureless against the still bright medallion of sky.

"My God, you're going to die down there! I'm about to pass out just from waiting. . . . I mean it!"

"I think it's ready." He climbed shakily up the toeholds riveted to the boiler plate and rested his elbows on the rim, the blood draining out of his head, his sight momentarily gone. The soft breeze stroked his face, chilled his soaked jumpsuit against his skin. He breathed deeply, hearing the voices of the onlookers taking notice of his reappearance. It couldn't be more than one hundred degrees now that he was out of the boiler. He took a deep breath and climbed down to the ground slowly, steadying himself.

A few minutes later Arnaldo began to shovel coal into the firebox. Alves manned the controls. Outside the Europeans were laughing at the two of them, sweating, struggling. The fire was roaring. . . .

The locomotive chugged slowly down the spur with Arnaldo gently patting Alves' thick, broad shoulders. As they climbed down in the shade of a grove of tall trees at the end of the spur two hundred yards from the crowd, Arnaldo swore softly in admiration and the two solemnly shook hands.

"Let's get cleaned up," Arnaldo said, "and go get a drink. There's something I've got to tell you. . . ."

The early-evening crowd at the Central Hotel bar was well dressed, smelled of bay rum and perspired elegantly beneath the huge, slowly revolving ceiling fans. The Central's lounge was replete with potted palms, beaded curtains, a long polished zinc bar and a nice haze of cigarette smoke. Ice from a loudly laboring device behind the bar clinked in glasses. It was said that everybody who was anybody in Luanda met for drinks twice a day at the

Central, a broad claim that could be stretched to cover explorers, big-game hunters, traders, English tourists, German spies with hard, expressionless eyes on the riches of the colony, anybody else after the fast killing.

Arnaldo claimed a table against the wall. When the whiskies with soda arrived Alves took a long sip, lit one of his daily hundred cigarettes and leaned back in the cane chair. "And what is it you have to tell me? Some wonderful bit of good news, no doubt?" He leaned forward nervously, resting his elbows on the tabletop. He heard Smythe-Hancock braying in the lobby. The sound made his stomach queasy. He was afraid of Smythe-Hancock, not without reason.

"Not . . . exactly, Alves," Arnaldo said. He recognized the developing situation. He was about to play Sancho Panza to Alves' Don, pointing out still another windmill. Alves was looking around the room, eyes flickering restlessly, as if scouting out a stratagem or an ambush. The next table was occupied by a group of scrupulously groomed young American oil engineers. They were the new breed drawn to Angola, full of non-European optimism and what was generally agreed to be tireless determination, working on the oil concessions. He caught Arnaldo's eye and nodded toward the boisterous table.

"I think I like the Americans," he said. "They're not like our European friends." He gestured minutely, barely fluttering his fingertips at the rest of the room. "The Americans look to the future, you see? Our other friends look backward. . . . It's a new world, I'm convinced of that, full of new ideas, new opportunities." He sipped at the whiskey. "So tell me the news which is not exactly wonderful."

"Well, actually it concerns your backward-looking Europeans and your forward-looking business deals with the Americans—" He stopped his voice on the rise, questioning.

"Their contention is that the locomotives are too heavy for the bridges . . . that the bridges will collapse beneath them! Alves, I've seen their stress tables, which prove conclusively that the bridges absolutely will come crashing down. . . ." Arnaldo shrugged disconsolately, shook his dark, curly head.

"That can't be." Alves stubbed out the cigarette, shook his head. What the hell was a stress table? He couldn't do everything. . . .

"Well, you can't run the risk," Arnaldo said with finality.

"My God, I can see it now, mangled bodies, railway cars broken like toys at the bottom of the ravine . . ."

"Ah, you have an excess of imagination—"

"From you, what a joke!" A rueful smile crossed his dark, smooth, troubled face. "You can't send those locomotives across those bridges," Arnaldo repeated. "Innocent people, unsuspecting—didn't you know the Americans made their trains heavier?"

"Arnaldo, calm yourself." He waited, patting his friend's arm, waiting for his own quiet to come, then engulf Arnaldo. "The problem is not with the locomotives." He sighed, staring at the tip of another cigarette with its beard of gray ash. "The problem is with the bridges. I know nothing of bridges." He shrugged, palms up. "Bridges . . . what to do, what to do . . ." He spoke so softly that Arnaldo lost the words.

"Do you want me to acquire these stress tables they speak of? Perhaps you could interpret them, see that these experts are wrong about these bridges?"

"But what difference would it make?" Alves was striving to conceal his anxiety. "Consider the situation, Arnaldo. The locomotives are useless if they cannot cross the bridges. Am I right? Of course I am. And we cannot accept that. They were purchased on my authorization. I have examined the railway bridges at first hand. I have touched the braces and underpinnings with these callused hands. . . . They seem perfectly solid to me." He pursed his lips, the dark eyes glittering behind his round spectacles. Arnaldo was familiar with the process. Alves was convincing himself, creating confidence out of a very bad situation. Another man would have written it all off, chalked it up to experience. But not Alves.

He stared unblinking at his old friend. "We shall see . . . that the bridges will hold!" He was whispering, emphasizing each word like a canny welterweight punching to the body. The metamorphosis was complete: Alves believed.

"But why will they?" It was Arnaldo's last gesture. "If the mathematics say they won't . . ."

"Because . . ." And Alves searched his friend's eyes for the clincher, turned back within himself, and it came to him, a prideful gesture, an impulse: "Because, my friend, tomorrow Engineer Alves Reis and his wife will take the locomotives across the High Bridge. And the bridge will hold . . . if my life has any meaning, the bridge will hold."

Arnaldo quietly considered his friend, who was hunched forward, hands flat on the table, waiting for his capitulation. Logic told Arnaldo that tomorrow would find Reis a dead man . . . but, then, logic had never had much to do with Alves Reis. Finally, he sighed, surrendering. "Well," he said, "I hope you're right." When they left, Smythe-Hancock was standing in the doorway. He nodded, smirking.

In the street outside the hotel they stood breathing deeply of the cool night air.

"Have the locomotive stoked and ready, Arnaldo. We will begin at ten o'clock. . . . Station Number Two—it's nearest the High Bridge." He shook Arnaldo's hand. "Bring your confidence with you!"

"I know what you are," Arnaldo said. "You are a *confidence* man. . . ."

They laughed at the small joke.

It was well past midnight when he reached his home in the Upper Town. With the sudden, new whiff of danger he saw his house as if for the first, or last, time . . . the sweet-smelling garden and cloistered courtyard surrounded by the customary high whitewashed walls which had long ago been intended to keep the slaves from wandering off. Euphorbia trees cast deep blue shadows in the moonlight, and a nightbird splashed mysteriously in the tiny, decorative pond. Alves stood for a moment in the stillness. When he had such a moment of peace, rare in his hectic, pushing, searching life, Alves could not quite keep from looking back at its remarkable, prospectless beginnings. What would his father have said had he stood beside his son, seen the handsome old house and known young Alves as Engineer Reis? He shook his head. He shrugged his heavy shoulders, took off his spectacles to rub his tired eyes and went inside.

Maria and their sons Virgilio and Guilhermo were sleeping. The baby Antonio was in his crib in the nursery. He bent over his sons' small beds, kissed their cheeks, gently removed a small thumb from between moist lips. In the large bedroom with the massive, rough-hewn, canopied bedstead, Maria slept peacefully, her small dark head resting on a forearm, her tiny hand clenched in a fist. The thin sheet was molded to the soft round contours of her body. On another night he would undoubtedly have fondled her breasts, watching the large, dark-brown nipples swell in her half-sleep, watching her instincts make her body

moist and receptive . . . and then he would have taken her,
leisurely, with maximum pleasure for them both. On
another night, when the morning to come was only another
morning. But not tonight.

That very night, as the patrons of the bar at the Central
Hotel gossiped among themselves, as Arnaldo stopped in
a favorite pub for a nightcap and fell into conversation
with cronies, the news of the coming morning's drama
began to spread. A good deal of the smart money in Luanda
was being wagered against Alves Reis in his match with the
High Bridge. It was, the smart money argued, a golden
opportunity to recoup losses suffered in Engineer Reis's
match with the locomotive that afternoon.

Alves summarily rejected the possibility that he and his
wife would plummet to their deaths with the huge locomotive as their coffin. Still, he slept fitfully, gently haunted
by the caprices of memory, moments of his life thrown up
like targets in a shooting gallery, frozen still, while he
squeezed the trigger of emotion and recollection. He was
not a sentimental man, nor a reflective man. But that night,
as he lay listening to the rhythmic breathing of his dear
Maria next to him, the flood of the past swept across him;
he could not hold it back. . . .

He turned the gilt-framed photograph of the happy
young newlyweds—Alves and Maria, he with a glazed
smile, lips clenched in nervous rigor, face powdered dry
in the intense heat of the photographer's studio, hair
polished ebony and parted in the middle, heavy eyebrows
knitted in unconscious concern; she with glowing embers
in her eyes, an eager tilt to her head as she grasped for the
future, a hint of adolescence as she glanced at her husband.

He wished he weren't in precisely the spot he found himself, but he forced himself to consider it from another angle.
His eyes roved toward the photograph: he was sure as hell
better off now than he had been that day in Lisbon. He had
learned a great deal and accomplished at least as much,
the train and the bridge aside.

The dim light of morning reached the Upper Town first,
turning it slowly from shadowy midnight blue through
shades of gray as the trees and buildings and walls were
revealed bit by bit as if smoke were being blown away.
Alves yawned, stretched, set fire to the morning's first
cigarette.

He soaked awhile in the deep tub and then began ceremoniously to complete his toilet, like a bullfighter readying himself for what could in the nature of things be his last fight. He meticulously clipped his mustache and snipped an errant hair or two from his nostrils, then waxed his mustache until it shone like onyx. Carefully he pomaded his black hair, combed it smooth to his scalp, brushed his even teeth to a new luster, talcumed his body, applied generous ladlings of bay rum to his face and neck.

Engulfed in his robe, he went to the bed and sat down beside Maria, waking her with a gentle touch.

"Maria, my darling wife, wake up. We have much to do this lovely day." Her eyes came sleepily open; her fingers closed like an infant's on his arm. She smiled up at him. Never, he reflected, had there been such trust. . . . "Today, my beloved, we ride the American locomotive across the bridge on the Melanje line." He bent to kiss her cheek. "We have been chosen to inaugurate the service, my dearest, and I want you at my side. . . . And I myself will be at the controls." He smiled, he hoped reassuringly.

"Oh, Alves!" she whispered excitedly. "I know, I will wear my new white dress—the silk shantung. And my white hat with the crimson plume! Will there be a great crowd to see us?"

He nodded. "Quite a large crowd at the bridge, I should think. Everyone will be there, never fear." Smythe-Hancock wagering his packet, no doubt, he reflected.

As he methodically dressed in the fitted white linen suit, he heard her humming gaily to herself, making her own preparations. He was, despite his occasional lecherous impulses, deeply in love with and devoted to his wife. She had never doubted him, never weakened in her support; and for him loyalty was a virtue above all others. Now, this particularly fateful morning, he didn't think twice about deceiving her. She played no part whatsoever in his business life, knew nothing of how he conducted his affairs.

If, he reasoned, as he buttoned up his trousers and bent to tie his shoe laces, if they were going to their deaths on the High Bridge, then it was as it should be: they would die together, still trusting, still in love. She had made her husband her life. If life was to end, so be it.

But, of course, there was no point in morbid thoughts. They were not going to die, he told himself, not today. His hands were shaking badly as he tried to knot his cravat. Quietly he cursed the locomotives. Already they had cost him the better part of a year. It had been nine months since the dinner party, since he had told Chaves to go ahead and buy the American locomotives. It had taken seven months for delivery, another month to make them ready, another month to test them—and now this damned business with the stress tables! Well, the hell with it. . . .

It was time for a grand gesture. Impulsively he'd committed himself to make it. He shrugged. It was José and the cadaver all over again. . . .

If in fact the locomotives were too heavy and therefore useless, Angola Railways was ruined. It was brutally simple. Too large an investment had been made and the responsibility would undoubtedly be laid at Engineer Reis' doorstep. It was the sort of charge that could never be lived down. He would become "the man who bankrupted the Angola Railways." And there would surely be an investigation into his qualifications. The fraudulent Oxford diploma would quickly be revealed for what it was; any official engineering examination would prove insurmountable. Either ride the train to glory, or ride it to the bottom of the chasm. No choice.

"Alves, look—I have a surprise for you." Maria's voice trembled with pride. He knew that she would follow him, insist on accompanying him, even if she knew the risk involved. He composed his face into a mask of contentment and turned. "See, our sons will share today's honor!" On either side of Maria, in the crescents of her arms, stood their white-suited sons, miniatures of Alves, aged five and three, smiling solemnly at their father. The baby would be left behind.

"Maria," he said softly, "we must not . . ."

At once he saw her excitement and happiness begin to fade. The three sets of eyes, the three solemn faces with quivering lips blurred before him; he felt tears pulsing as he tried to hold them back.

"Of course," he said, hugging them, struggling to control himself, "of course, we will all ride the train! It will be a great adventure, a great treat!"

Feeling the warmth of their bodies against him, hearing his children's cries of delight, smelling Maria's perfumed sweetness and kissing her lowered eyelids, Alves bore the brunt of his decision and realized with a chill what it was to be truly alone.

At the office of Director Chaves they met Arnaldo,

whose voice was stuck in a loud, panic-stricken whisper. "Alves, reconsider, for God's sake—"

"Please, Arnaldo, calm yourself. There is nothing, absolutely nothing, that can go wrong." He took his friend by the shoulders, fixed his eyes. "I went over the stress tables last night," he lied, voice at the breaking point. "Why else would I be willing to take Maria and the boys with me? Would I risk their lives?"

"Yes. If you had to," Arnaldo replied numbly. "I don't know . . ."

Alves glared at him and gestured to Chaves' anteroom, where the director was awkwardly making conversation with Maria. "Now get Chaves in here so I can tell him what's going on—that the fears are baseless, that it is a gala occasion and should be treated as such. . . . And get three white horses for us and have them ready at the station. We'll get there in Chaves' limousine. And see that the locomotive is running with a good head of steam." He smiled finally, beginning to be caught up in his own bravado.

The same explanation of the morning's program left Chaves unconvinced but unable to circumvent it. He no longer knew what to believe, but then Reis had never failed him. The three adults and two children settled into the back seat of the Rolls-Royce limousine, the children bouncing on the jump seats, Maria composed and oblivious, Chaves sweating profusely, Alves monitoring his rushing heartbeats.

The word of the run across the High Bridge had spread like a brushfire during the night and early morning. Now, as the dusty black automobile rolled over the cobbled streets, beneath the green sheltering trees, he saw that the regular morning routine of the city had been interrupted; the streets were empty, the vendors were nowhere in sight, all as if a terrible plague had paid Luanda a visit.

The crimson had faded completely from the cliffs, the sun was its customary gold, the sky a brilliant blistered blue.

At the station in the Upper City he fixed a grin in place, shepherded his family to the three white horses Arnaldo had waiting. The crowd of natives seemed to be raising their arms in unison, shaking their fists, cheering loudly. They might as well have stood behind a pane of thick, soundproof glass. He was moving in an almost senseless trance, mechanically, like a man who marches quickly to face the firing squad, already dead.

"The horses, Alves," Arnaldo said.

"Right." He turned to Maria. "Up you go, my dear," and he assisted her into the sidesaddle. She mounted lightly, her elegant hat with its dashing furled brim and rakish plume at just the right tilt. He tried to imprint her forever in his memory as she looked down at him from the great white stallion. "Arnaldo," he said, turning to his friend, "would you be good enough to walk the children's horse? We don't want an accident." Arnaldo nodded and took the reins as Alves lifted his sons onto the broad white back, the huge saddle that comfortably engulfed both boys. "Don't be afraid. While he is a very large horsey, I have looked him in the eye and I know that he is very gentle." He mounted his own white horse and they set off in single file, at a majestic pace, toward the waiting locomotive, crouching like a great steaming weapon where the rise of track met the horizon in a heat haze.

The blacks in their robes and rags grew in numbers as the procession drew closer to the locomotive. The crowd swarmed in behind the children's horse and seemed to sweep the riders inevitably forward toward the train. Alves blinked. Each time he did so the bloody damned thing seemed to leap larger in his view, gargantuan. . . . What kind of bridges must they have in America? My God . . . He turned to Maria and smiled. She was happy, even with the dust caking her new dress; she was radiant, smiling, proud. They were approaching the large knot of onlookers gathered about the train engine, but even then there were few Europeans, just a jostling gaggle of blacks. Then it struck him: the Europeans were all at the bridge . . . waiting. Best seats in the house.

He was vaguely aware of the hissing and clanging of the locomotive. They dismounted at a seemly distance and waited while Director Chaves' limousine slowly parted the crowd. Chaves beckoned to him.

"Do you have any idea what's going on here? Any idea at all?"

"They think it's a celebration," Alves said. "I am in charge of the first ceremonial voyage of the American locomotive. . . . It's an opportunity to get away from work, to get drunk. They don't need a big excuse, Director." He motioned to Chaves' driver. "Go on, my friend, you don't want to miss the show!"

Time was drawing lamentably short. The crowd moved away in the wake of the Rolls-Royce, following it toward the other audience, those in the dress circle at the edge of the chasm. Alves knew what they were doing, how money was being wagered and odds were constantly shifting. When the word reached the bridge that Engineer Reis was to be accompanied by his wife and children, the bookmakers would make a sudden change. Havoc. He caught himself wishing he'd gotten a thousand or so down himself.

He helped Maria into the cab of the locomotive. "Alves," she said, "I had no idea it would be so big!"

He nodded, received the boys handed up by Arnaldo. "Thank you," he said to Arnaldo. "Mark my word, we will drink French champagne at lunch today!" He adjusted the controls, took a long look up the slight incline to the cliff edge. He wanted to be traveling as fast as possible when he reached the bridge. There was no scientific basis involved; it was merely the quickest way to the other side. Or wherever they were going. . . .

The children were settled; Maria had braced herself against them, wedging all three bodies into a corner. They had adjusted their goggles to guard against the flying sparks. Alves looked at them. He felt faint.

Quickly he released the brake and felt the jarring of the three flatbed cars strung out behind him, cables smashing together, grinding. He stripped off his coat, slid his hands into the heavy fireman's gloves and began to pitch wood from the chest into the firebox. Out of the corner of his eye he saw Arnaldo jogging along, shouting.

"I'm coming with you." Arnaldo made a leap and managed to get his foot onto the first step and his fingers hooked around a railing.

Alves moved immediately to the top of the stairs, blocking Maria's view. "No," he shouted into the steam and the wind and the rattle of the wheels on the tracks so close beneath them. "Get off, I cannot allow this."

Arnaldo clung to two rails, peered upward, his black suit dusty brown. "I must," he cried, cords straining in his neck.

"You and I," Alves said, his head leaning close to Arnaldo's, "we're finished if you insist—the risk is too great. . . ." The locomotive was gathering speed, the wind tearing at Arnaldo. "Off," Alves screamed. And with a quick movement of his forearm he planted a fist in Arnaldo's exposed stomach. Arnaldo dropped away and bounced in the dust. Without another look back, Alves turned back to the pressure gauges, which were still below the danger level. The boiler plating was so thick—that must be why it's so godawful heavy. . . . He fed wood into the fire, squinting, feeling the hellish blast of the boiler on his face, feeling his face grow hot, then numb. And he began to smell his own hair singeing, his eyebrows curling and sticking to the back of his hand when he brushed sweat away.

Sparks like fireworks showered past him, blowing wildly from the huge black funnel; soot filled the air like a ghastly exhalation from the nether world; bits of burning ash seared holes in his shirt, trousers, arms. He had imagined it would be different, stately. And he hadn't counted on what the fear would do to him, how it would galvanize and transform him into a creature who was firing himself as well as the locomotive, one who could endure pain and agony rather than a quiet waiting for the end. . . . The pressure gauges had slipped across into the red danger zones. He turned to see Maria. She was shielding herself and the boys. The three-year-old was crying, but she held him with his face to her breast; the older boy was staring out at the world in clear wonder. Maria, though taken aback by the sudden change in her husband's appearance, still regarded it all as an adventure, though quite possibly one that had gotten rather out of hand. Still, it matched so well her picture of Alves: heroic, fearless, undaunted. . . . She smiled at him, an encouraging look. The woman is mad, he thought, devoted but mad. He saw the crowd undulating through the heat waves less than a hundred yards away; he bent to his stoking again.

Meanwhile Arnaldo regained his footing and made a dash for the engine. Legs and heart pumping in a frenzy, the dust choking him, steam burning him, he had almost no breath left. He gave a final surge, hurled himself upward at the back of the locomotive, clung for his life only inches above the coupling. All of his strength concentrated in his arms and hands, he flattened himself against the black steel and desperately raised his legs above the track flashing past below. He was going with Alves; there was no other way.

Inside the cab, Alves had slumped back, his clothing covered with burns and ashes. The throttle was full open, the firebox overloaded; the pressure gauges had gone as far as they could. He recognized the baobabs and euphorbias growing in the distance, craned his neck to see ahead. The fragile structure of the bridge jutted into view, heading off toward space, and as they reached the crowd he picked out familiar faces in the flash and blur, saw banknotes waved in the air, calabashes of grappa tilted over thirsty mouths, heard vague distant shouts. He felt his burn-tightened face crack in a smile.

The locomotive reached the bridge at top speed, in a horrific rush of sound that blended with the shining morning sun, the vast emptiness yawning below the narrow steel thread that seemed so fragile to bear such a cumbersome, hurtling monster. Smoke blackened his view when he sought the sun overhead; the wind grabbed at his hair and twisted it. The bridge gleamed like an assassin's blade.

The moment froze forever in his mind, soundless, like one of his photographs. He was standing outside the event, which now had a life of its own. He saw it whole and it was fine. The exquisite Angolan morning, the grandeur of the two facing cliffs held together by the span of bridgework, the hollow echoing space between and below, the mixture of dense foliage and jagged rocks dropping down to a gently tumbling stream. The train reached the bridge and like a projectile began its steady journey along the line of steel, the smoke curling back like a black aviator's scarf unfurled in the brisk breeze. From a distance there would be an absolute quiet to the scene, a peaceful progress, the machine age making itself felt in Africa.

In the middle of the bridge it became cool in the cabin. The wind coming up the canyon from the ocean freshened, touched their faces. Like the hand of God, Alves thought. At the back of the locomotive Arnaldo still clung, paralyzed by fear. Behind him the crowd was shrinking into a shapeless, mute creature, finally fading into the landscape. Now his eyes were closed, his lips moved, but he could not hear his own prayers.

As Alves listened to the creak and straining of the bridge over the wind, he began to realize that the bridge was indeed going to hold. Maria's eyes were closed behind her goggles. Alves saw that she was praying. He leaned toward her, touched his blistered lips to her smudged forehead.

He could hear the children laughing at last, pointing into space, enjoying the thrill of the ride. "Thank God," he murmured, "thank God. I was right."

Slowly Alves braked the locomotive. The bridge was behind them. The wheels screeched on the track, grinding sparks rolling away like cinders, burning pebbles. They remained in the cab, in the stillness, draped like dolls over railings. He wiped his face with a silk handkerchief and the goggles were stripped away, leaving them all with masks of fresh, clean flesh.

Maria touched his cheek. "My darling, your face . . . oh, my dear." She pressed her face against his chest, only half comprehending the truth of the matter.

"But it was a great honor," he whispered, "to inaugurate this great train, was it not?"

"Yes, yes," she said, her full lips muffled against his shirt. "A great honor." The laughing children struggled down the steps, leaping, tumbling to the ground.

"Uncle! Uncle!" The older boy's voice piped clearly.

Arnaldo, shirt torn, streaks of blood running across his hands and staining his cuffs, staggered into view. "Alves," he croaked, a crooked grin stamped across his ashen face. "Alves, I came anyway . . . on the back of the locomotive." He laughed and shook his head, abashed.

Alves wobbled to the ground, helped Maria down and stared at him for a long time.

Together, like children bound by a blood oath, the three embraced in the shadow of the vast American locomotive. As the tears and laughter slowly subsided, Alves kissed them both and moved off toward the bridge.

He wasn't sure of his legs just yet, but he needed to be alone, to stand by the bridge, to see where he had been. He stood at the precipice, stared down into the void, heard the wind whistling in the steel. Blown toward him from across the vast chasm he heard, faintly, as if in a dream, the cheering of the crowd. . . .

*   *   *

Sitting disconsolately in the deep leather chair in his office, a mere six months after his triumphant return to Lisbon, Alves Reis was not prepared to announce that the European opportunities sketched by Adolf Hennies had been illusory, but he had decided it was not quite the bed of

roses he had foreseen. Primarily he had developed a most
sincere concern: how was he ever going to get rich? It was
a warm, humid day, and he loosened his tie, flipped on the
fan overhead, adjusted the louvers on the window shutters
and fitted a cigarette into a black Dunhill holder. He
leaned back and reflected on the state of things. . . .

To begin with, he'd thought he was rich. With operating
capital of seventy-five thousand dollars—quite a stupen-
dous amount of money for a young Portuguese in 1922—
his return had been gaudy, a masterpiece of the *nouveau
riche* impulse, and he'd enjoyed it enormously. He formed
a corporation, A. V. Alves Reis Lda. (Limitado). For a
luxurious twelve-room flat, including a music room for
a new Steinway and a billiard room where he could enter-
tain his business associates, he paid a veritable king's ran-
som—one thousand escudos per month, or fifty dollars.
The household staff over which Maria presided included a
cook, a maid, a butler and her own private, full-time seam-
stress. Alves indulged in a chauffeur, who drove him
through Lisbon's narrow, winding streets in either of his
two Nash automobiles, Nashes because Alves Reis Lda.
had quickly purchased the Portuguese dealership. He furnished his home and his suite of offices in a baronial manner—brass-studded leather couches, hand-carved break-
fronts twenty feet long, appointments of Carrara marble
and onyx. All in all it was a staggeringly effective front.

But, Alves reflected, wiping sweat from his forehead with
a nicotine-stained forefinger, life can be supported by
either of two contradictory principles—namely, illusion
and reality. He saw it now with frightening clarity and
recognized that it had been with him ever since the day he
created his own Oxford diploma, affixed the fictional signatures and found a gullible notary who gave it his stamp.
He had based his entire Angolan adventure on that diploma
—clearly an illusion. And he had emerged rich, respected
and well launched. No one had been harmed. The illusion,
the appearance, had created the reality because he could
personally back it up. It was the way business was done:
you bet on yourself—and he won, kept winning. He was
good at it. It was a trick.

The problem that confronted him now was that while
the illusion remained, the reality of his situation had gone
straight to hell. He had looked up one day from his ledgers

and with a depressing shock acknowledged to himself what he'd feared. Incredibly, he was going broke.

While it was Angola that had been the making of him, he could ironically look to the African promised land for the wellsprings of his current predicament. His unbridled faith in the future of the colony and in its presumed mineral deposits had led him to invest his cash reserves in the South Angola Mining Corporation. Not a ton of iron ore had yet issued forth, and the prospects were less hopeful by the day.

The financial pages made for grim reading. By late summer of 1923 Angola's economy was approaching the dropping-off place, and daily he read the bad news in the pages of *O Seculo.* He watched with dismay verging on panic as the Ultramarino Bank of Portugal continued issuing specifically Angolan escudos at a rate that finally inflated them to the point where they were almost worthless in Angola and absolutely nonexchangeable anywhere else on earth. Currency could no longer be transferred by individuals or corporations from the colony to the mother country. Taken together, these two turns of events had delivered him to the brink of disaster.

Finally, fed up with the worry, he left the office and went walking along the harbor, watching the great ships riding at anchor. He could almost smell Africa on them. It set him longing. Maybe Maria had been right in the first place. They had always been happy in Angola. . . .

* * *

Director Chaves, his old benefactor from Luanda, had come to Lisbon well aware that history and time had reversed their roles. He still moved with the bullish rush, stared out from beneath the jutting gorillalike brow; he still gestured with thick-fingered, hairy fists. But his voice was that of a supplicant as he arrived unannounced and indifferently barbered at A. V. Alves Reis Lda.'s gleaming, polished, most deceptive office. The flower in his lapel was yesterday's, brown-edged.

He hugged Alves impulsively. The faint aroma of brandy hung about him like shaving lotion. Alves, who practiced his English by reading the exploits of Mr. Sherlock Holmes, decided that Chaves had found himself in need of bottled courage. After a smiling exchange of pleasantries, remembrances from old friends in Luanda and a report that the mighty American locomotives were flourishing atop the bridges, Chaves slumped into a deep leather club chair.

"And now," Alves said from behind his vast tycoon's desk, gently inquisitive, "what has brought you all this way, Director?" Chaves' face drooped glumly. "You've come to buy some new bridges!" Alves' accompanying chuckle went unappreciated.

"Things are not good in Angola, Alves," he growled characteristically, hunching forward in the chair. "It's worse than you may have heard. . . . It touches us all, me and Terreira even, and that speaks for itself." He sighed as if the reality was even now having difficulty sinking in. "And the railway . . ." The thought was too much for him to remain trapped in the chair. He bounded to the window and looked down at the carefully symmetrical pattern of the sidewalk tiles below. Goldsmiths lined the street, and after the openness of Luanda's topography he felt as if he could reach out the window and across the way and steal a watch.

"I've read about that too, of course," Alves said. It was true. The difficulties of his old employer, known officially as the Royal Trans-African Railway Company of Angola, known in the marketplace as Ambaca, had been recounted in tortured detail in the daily press. With the economy in shreds and tatters, Ambaca stock had fallen to a few escudos—literally pennies—per share. The shares he had bought before returning to Lisbon were symptomatic of his current predicament: they were worthless. Foreign investors who owned substantial blocks of stock and held large notes sensed either bankruptcy or a takeover opportunity or both. They were impatiently demanding money —unpaid dividends and interest on the notes.

Chaves ran through the brutal details as quickly as possible, huffing and puffing as if he were fading fast on the uphill slope. "What we need," he concluded abruptly, spinning back from the window, hair on the wild side from anxious wanderings of his sausage-shaped fingers, "is some new blood! New investment, someone with vision and skill in putting off our creditors—someone with capital who can step in, take a firm hand, give us back the confidence we've lost. . . ." His dark eyes seemed to swell, pleading, pathetic.

"It is a difficult situation, Director," Alves allowed sagely. He took a cigarette from an ebony box on his desk,

offered them to Chaves, who was distractedly picking his
large nose. "What's your next step?" Chaves popped a
match on his thumbnail and applied it with some vigor to
the fragile Egyptian smoke.

"My associates and I met just before I left for Lisbon
and we agreed unanimously . . . I have come all the way
from Africa, Alves," he said, his voice growing weighty, as
if he were conferring an honor, "to find help for Ambaca.
We agreed that you are the man to save Ambaca. You
have the resources, the knowledge, the experience. . . ." He
shrugged his huge shoulders.

"My God."

"Aha, you say 'my God,' but what can I say to my
associates?"

"But my capital is . . . well, I have other investments,
you understand."

"You mean to say that it is a matter of liquidity?"
Chaves threw the cigarette at a standing floor ashtray, nar-
rowly missed.

"More or less." Inwardly Alves cringed. Could such an
opportunity be passing him by—the chance to control the
Royal Trans-African Railway, the place he'd gotten his
start? The poetry of it quickened his pulse. But of all
times, why now? Chaves was applying for capital, precisely
the ingredient Alves was searching for himself. The irony
of it was indescribably painful. Only last week the Ultramarino Bank had done everything but laugh aloud at his
loan application.

"You might be well advised to liquidate another investment in order to take advantage of this one. Ambaca is
not all that sick a company. . . . To begin with, there's the
hundred thousand dollars in the treasury—my God, billions
of escudos the way things are going these days!"

"What hundred thousand dollars?" Alves asked. Chaves,
taken by surprise, slid down in the club chair. Alves was
now up and coming around the desk, a gleam in his eye.
This, it occurred to him, must be the way *real* money men
are struck by an idea.

"Why, the hundred thousand lent to Ambaca by the government here in Lisbon . . . to pay off the interest on all
those notes, to keep the creditors from foreclosing. I
thought you'd know of that."

"How would I know about that? Believe me, there's
been nothing in the press about that." Alves smashed out

the cigarette stub and quickly fumbled another into his mouth. Be calm, he told himself, take your time. "Well, then, there is life in the firm. . . . That may change my opinion of it, as an opportunity for sound investment."

"When will you know, Alves?"

"It depends, Director." He forced himself down into a chair that matched Chaves'. He studied his manicured nails for a moment, running over his lines. "One of my guiding principles has been never to entrust my money to the possible mismanagement of others. No offense, Director, but . . . but if I am able *to control* matters, then a situation may look considerably more attractive to me. Just between the two of us, you do see my point?"

"Of course, certainly." Chaves wriggled in discomfort, tried to work up a conspiratorial nod. "You have a plan?"

"Were I to find this opportunity sufficiently tempting, what would be required to gain control of Ambaca? So that I might feel comfortable, you understand. Remembering that I am the fellow who may be throwing the rope to the drowning man." He squinted at Chaves. His ash fell on his very expensive suit.

"Forty thousand dollars," Chaves said.

Alves smiled, rose, consulted his watch.

"Let me sleep on it," he said, enigmatic. "Now I must excuse myself. I've called a meeting of the board of one of my interests." He took Chaves by the elbow and propelled him to the heavy oak door. "Meet me here tomorrow at noon. I expect you to respect our confidences, Director."

"I will speak with no one else before we meet tomorrow, in any case."

Alves slapped Chaves' back. Encouragingly.

*   *   *

That evening the illusion was in full flower though the audience of two knew too much to swallow any of it. The lamp hanging over the billiard table moved in the breeze from the open window; shadows flickered across the green baize; a pale-blond cue drew back from the circle of light, drawing tension with it. Alves miscued. The ball leaped as if victimized by a rude gesture, clattered away on the floor. "Shit!" He slammed his cue into the rack and glared through the darkness surrounding the table like a jungle night. "What do I know about billiards?"

Arnaldo sighed. "Alves, billiards should make you relax —that's the point."

"Why should doing some idiotic thing I know nothing about make me relax?" A match flared in the darkness. "What matters is Chaves' suggestion. I've got to get my hands on that hundred thousand in the Ambaca treasury. . . . It's the answer to all our current problems, the answer to my prayers."

Arnaldo leaned over the table and executed a neat bank shot with the two remaining ivory balls. He watched the slow, steady trajectories. The clear-cut parameters of the game appealed to his conservative nature. "Where can you possibly raise the forty thousand you need to get the hundred thousand? And why in the world do you want to control a nearly bankrupt African railway? You mystify me, Alves."

"For the last time," he croaked, "I do not want to run the railroad! I want the bloody hundred thousand!"

"Please, Alves, the veins in your neck—"

"Well, then, don't excite me! Listen carefully—*I need to control the company to get the money.*"

Alves made a strangled sound, coughed on cigarette smoke. He was finishing the day's fifth pack. Arnaldo made another shot. Alves read his face, knew what it meant. He could always depend on Alves to think of something. . . .

"If—I say *if*—there were some way to use the hundred thousand in the Ambaca treasury to buy Ambaca itself . . . I need forty thousand of it to buy Ambaca."

"That makes no sense. A riddle."

"Sherlock Holmes tells me that if all possibilities are exhausted but one, then that one, however improbable, must be the solution."

"Well, I don't see it." Arnaldo leaned on the upright cue, chin on the backs of his hands, staring at Alves.

"Slow boats, fast checks. *Voilà!* The forty thousand." Alves broke off, chuckling to himself.

"Not with such a large amount, Alves! What if something went wrong?" Arnaldo's shock, mingled with a wise man's trepidation, gleamed in the dark like a warning beacon.

"Wait," Alves cautioned him. "Think. Arrange the perspective. Now, just when things look darkest, along comes salvation by way of Luanda. The money exists. I am being *begged* to take it! But there is one small obstacle, the need for forty thousand dollars . . . and only for a short time, when I will then as the man who controls the railroad have access to the hundred thousand, out of which I can make up the forty thousand I have used to buy the railroad! Do you follow me? Well, then, why not by the means of our special system?" He waited for the logic of it to dawn on Arnaldo. "Chaves would not have been provided in our time of need if we were not meant to use him. *He* has thrown *us* the rope!"

"But such large sums—"

"Has anything ever gone wrong before?"

"No." Arnaldo shrugged, muttering.

"Well, then. There is no time to lose. A bold stroke now will bring it all right. And who will be hurt? Eh, tell me— no one! Listen to me, Arnaldo!" He shook Arnaldo's sleeve. Sweat beaded on Alves' forehead.

"I am listening."

"We are in the materialistic world." Alves spoke very quietly now. "We have chosen it, we are suited to it. And in our world there are neither honest men nor rogues— only victors and vanquished. I know which I choose to be. . . . It's the law of the jungle."

Eventually the faithful Arnaldo saw the light.

Alves was rather pleased with the notion of slow boats and fast checks.

*　　*　　*

Owning a Nash dealership—an American-based operation in a European country—had made it useful for A. V. Alves Reis Lda. to open a checking account at the prestigious National City Bank of New York. Knowing full well the value and protean uses of money, Alves issued checks in special circumstances "on our New York bank." It went down well with provincial creditors who had never dealt with a New World financial firm before. More importantly it allowed him the free use of the National City Bank's money for a week or more at a time, counting for an average eight-day sea crossing, Lisbon to New York. Write a check on a Tuesday, have the money working all week— during which time a killing might wisely be made to cover the check and provide for a generous profit—and cable the appropriate amount to New York the following Monday. And if the plans took longer than anticipated, the bounced check would not reappear in Lisbon until the sixteenth day at the earliest and more likely on, say, the twentieth day. At which time one professed astonishment to the creditor, cursed slovenly American clerical errors and confidently suggested he need only redeposit the check, assuring him the National City Bank would be written a stern letter of reprimand. Another eight days' use of the interest-free money had been granted, a month in all to raise the money to cover the check. Eventually the check was good; it was a foolproof system. He knew that: he'd tested it repeatedly, though not on so grand a scale.

When Director Chaves turned up at the office the next day, a chipper, nattily turned-out Alves greeted him with a broad smile and the news that, having slept on it, he had decided to help his old friends out of their difficulties. The shares of Royal Trans-African Railway stock were already being purchased. Within twenty-four hours Alves Reis would have control and in another few hours would institute the move to vote himself chairman of the company. After all, he voted the majority of the shares himself. Director Chaves was so relieved he nearly collapsed.

Within a month the firm of A. V. Alves Reis Limitado was considerably revived. Unopposed in his lunge at the chairmanship, Alves covered his check and used the remaining sixty thousand dollars in the Ambaca treasury to buy outright control of the South Angola Mining Corporation. Having grown wonderfully adept at touting whatever he was interested in at a given moment, he went to work pushing the mining stock. The shares rose on cue, even in the face of the company's continuing lack of productivity. New investments were lured to both Ambaca and the mining operation. He was diversifying. His next enterprise was the exporting of German beer to Angola. But when he returned to Lisbon from Munich there was a surprise in store for him. He was going to jail. . . .

*   *   *

Alves screamed as if bitten by a rabid dog. "You tell me I am wanted by the police! Have you completely lost your mind? What do the police want with me, Reis of Reis Limitado?"

It was the fifth of July 1924, and the sun was turning the office into an oven even with the windows thrown wide open. Arnaldo stood before him in a shirt that clung wetly to his back, in trousers that had lost their crease, reminding Alves of no one so much as his late undertaker father.

"Let me speak, Alves," he said softly.

"Stop mumbling, then!" Alves paced across the carpet, took a limp cigarette from the ebony box and lit it, inhaling deeply. "All right, all right. I am perfectly calm. See, my hand is like a rock." He held out his right hand. Both men stared at it. It quaked as if the catastrophe of 1755 that destroyed most of Lisbon was repeating itself in the streets outside. Arnaldo looked up from the chair Alves had pushed him into. "Stupid test," Alves declared, jerking his hand away. "It proves nothing." He puffed hard on the cigarette, yanked the silk handkerchief out of his breast pocket and wiped his face. "Why isn't this fan turned on? It just sits there. . . ." He gestured imploringly to an unjust deity and turned the switch on the base of the heavy black oscillating fan, which hummed slowly to life. "That's what fans are for, Arnaldo, they are for when it's hot. Are you going to tell me what's going on here?"

"The Ambaca deal," Arnaldo said, his voice too high, catching in his throat. "Two of the directors, not Chaves, but two here in Portugal, have gone to the police with the charge that you embezzled the Ambaca treasury, one hundred thousand dollars American, for your personal use. . . . The police were here yesterday with a warrant for your arrest." The words came hard, and Alves strained to hear them over the racket of the fan. Impatiently he jabbed at the switch, turning it off.

"I am simply appalled. . . . To be perfectly frank, it smacks of a vendetta. Or jealousy. Or politics." He groaned. "A dastardly attempt to discredit me." He marched to the window and rested his head against the pane of glass, eyes closed, sweat dripping from his face. "Ah, fuck! What do they want from me? I've dealt with their creditors, bought time. . . . The company is better off now than when Chaves came stumbling in here like a lost soul looking for salvation—and now the miserable bastards turn on me! Christ, what am I supposed to do?"

"Alves?"

"Yes, yes, yes. What else? Maria has run off with the butcher? Oh God, poor Maria, she'll die of humiliation. . . ."

"They are coming back today. They'll be taking you to

. . . Oporto." He gripped the arms of the club chair to steady himself.

"Oporto!" Alves shouted, livid again. "Oporto? A city where I am unknown, without friends—"

"The two directors are also directors of an Oporto bank. As far as I can tell they simply pulled some strings to have you brought to the Oporto jail. . . ."

"Oh my God," Alves said mournfully, "I am in the hands of my enemies. . . . Is there no justice, Arnaldo, after all I have done for Portugal?"

Arnaldo blinked helplessly.

A heavy, insistent knock came at the door.

* * *

The Oporto jail was worse than he'd expected.

The cell was small, dank, oppressive. Confinement was a constant, desperate goad. At times he would vomit at the loss of freedom, the inability to move here and there at will. The jailers were an uncongenial lot who looked on him as just another swindler. It rained all the time in Oporto—far to the north of his hospitable Lisbon—and a peculiar fungus grew in the corners of the cell. The toilet was a disgrace. And since no one in the Oporto jail paid much attention to what he had to say by way of an explanation of his unhappy state, he was left with only himself to talk to. Which he did and which inevitably led to rumors that the swindler from Africa had gone mad and frothed at the mouth.

Maria, growing ever larger with her fourth pregnancy, came to visit him, and while he denounced his accusers as political enemies plotting his destruction she dissolved in tears of support and incomprehension. She didn't know what he was talking about, but that didn't matter. She believed him; she believed *in* him. When she took her leave, he frequently was raving, smashing his fists against the walls of his cell.

As time went by, however, Alves grappled with his anxieties, tamed them. There were quiet times, times when he settled back on his board cot and read the newspapers and magazines Arnaldo brought. Not since his student days had he been confronted with enough solitude to take his own measure as an adult, to lose himself in reading about the world—the great world. He read and he analyzed,

page after page, indiscriminately, every word, and he
began to take a broad view of what lay beyond the reach
of his own fingertips. He began to educate himself all
over again, this time widening the scope.

And he learned.

He learned that Lenin was dying just as Great Britain
was recognizing the Union of Soviet Socialist Republics,
that Ramsay MacDonald was forming the first Labour
government in London, that something called Teapot
Dome was causing a great scandal in America, that Greece
had been proclaimed a republic under someone named
Venizelos, that a onetime German corporal called Hitler
had been released from prison after serving only eight
months of a five-year sentence, that the Italians had given
a Fascist called Mussolini 65 percent of their votes, that a
peculiar little Indian called Gandhi had fasted twenty-one
days to protest the religious strife between the Hindus and
the Moslems, that J. Edgar Hoover had been appointed
director of the Bureau of Investigation in Washington,
that Stalin and Zinoviev and Kamenev had allied themselves against Trotsky. . . . And to help with his English,
he read a novel by Michael Arlen called *The Green Hat,*
which Arnaldo told him was all the rage, and another
called *The Inimitable Jeeves* by P. G. Wodehouse, which
he found quite enticing but incomprehensible. All of this
brought him a certain calm, which he needed very badly,
particularly following one of Maria's visitations.

He read that the Ford automobile concern had produced
its ten millionth vehicle, that a novelist named Kafka had
died, that two men in Chicago were sentenced to life
imprisonment for kidnapping and killing a twelve-year-old
boy, that everyone in the world including his wife had gone
wild over a game called mah-jongg, that there were an
incredible two and one half million radios in use in the
United States. . . . My God, it was such a big world, made
even larger by his tiny cell.

It was the great world that occupied his mind between
the frantic, nearly hysterical interludes when he was faced
with the destruction of the life he had built in the years
since they had all set sail in innocence and wonder for
Angola. So long ago . . . And now in Oporto could it all
be ending? Was this the whole story? He shook it off.
Everything he'd been reading indicated that life was a
matter of ups and downs, that a man was defeated only

when he gave up. . . . The thought brought him a night's sleep time and again. As a principle it was not to be despised, and he clung to it as he sought to touch bottom. Once he'd hit bottom he'd think of something. . . .

In the end, with money to raise for his defense and more money required for possible restitution payments to the Ambaca shareholders, he had no choice but to liquidate everything. He took pen and paper and wrote to Maria.

> *My Dear and Holy Little Wife,*
> *Arnaldo, who just left my cell, has spent so much time here of late that he will probably come down with pneumonia, too. My cough is no better, my little flower, but do not concern yourself. I have the constitution of a water buffalo! Well, I have lost all hope of getting out of this dungeon before the trial. But don't worry about money, my love, for soon we won't have any! Ha, ha. Do as I tell you through our faithful Arnaldo about the sale of the house and the jewels, the cars, the furs, the billiard table, the piano—this is no time for sentimental attachments, not while your husband rots in this pit of hell. Everything here indicates that all must be handled urgently. Whatever jewels and silver no one buys bring with you on your next visit and we will decide what to do with them.*
>
> *Don't worry, my little one. I am learning that life is all ups and downs, and there is nothing to do but resign ourselves to it. . . . Your poor husband always helped everyone and now nobody comes to help him. What a great lesson! Life is like the African jungle, my sweet. But we must not be bitter. I am learning my lesson. Kisses for my sons. Remember to bring me some fresh bedsheets. And I shall want to know all about this mah-jongg business.*
> *Millions of kisses*
> *from your loving Alves*

Week after week he languished in the Oporto jail, reading, talking to himself, thinking, writing notes to Maria and Arnaldo. Somehow the money derived from the sale of their effects proved sufficient. Maria and the children retreated to her parents' home, where ranks were loyally closed behind Alves and the blame was agreed to lie with his unscrupulous enemies.

Alves read everything. He read by candlelight late into the night, ignoring the damp walls all around him, spent hours scribbling notes to himself on coarse writing paper. He had, he reasoned patiently, used all his initiative and native shrewdness to advance himself. He had begun with next to nothing, no birthright, and he had improvised, he had dared all when the occasion required, he had conquered Angola by his own sweat and determination. He had risen as far in the world of legitimate business as even the sternest taskmaster might have demanded. He had made money and lost money; he had excluded almost everything but hard work from his life; he had played as fair as any realistic businessman could—and he had landed in the Oporto jail.

Something was wrong.

He had proven that by playing his cards within the rules of the game. He simply couldn't hold it all together. Whether it was the system itself, or the powerful jealously guarding their own preserves, or the pettiness of his enemies, the point was that he was in jail and the bankers who put him there were not.

Why?

The answer that presented itself was too simple; it drove him to seek a more complex and sophisticated explanation. Perhaps it was a question of a flaw in his own character. . . . Or a failure to grasp some elusive philosophical oddment. He poked at the question, worried it like the village idiot tormenting a spider with a sharp stick. But it refused to yield a more complicated answer.

The answer was simply . . . money.

He was in the Oporto jail because he had run out of money. It was a question of insufficient capital, the scourge of hopeful businessmen yesterday, today and inevitably tomorrow.

Money.

And what, he asked himself, was money?

Paper! Absolutely nothing but bits of paper. Oh, yes, once it had merely been the everyday symbol for gold and silver, more convenient to carry in your pocket than great lumps of precious metal. But that was ancient history.

Portugal had long ago abandoned any semblance of a gold standard. And the newspapers and magazines were full of the wildly bloated inflation of Germany, where loaves of bread cost thousands of marks. There was nothing to back up currency in Germany, and, his fitful brain working in nooks and crannies of memory, he recalled the German, or Swiss, Adolf Hennies. What was inflation doing to Hennies' grandiose thoughts of Europe as the hope of the future?

And it wasn't only Germany. Hungary. Italy. Everywhere, it was a matter of simply printing more money. Christ! It was only paper. And he was in jail because he didn't have enough of it. What he was having, he realized by the flickering light of the candle stub, was a revelation. Unable to sleep, he drew up a list of questions he needed to have answered, publications he would need to consult. Arnaldo would have some digging to do.

Mystified but willing, Arnaldo took the list, rounded up the various volumes and deposited them on Alves' bare table. "What," he inquired, "is the point of all this?"

"Our future," Alves answered.

Arnaldo went away shaking his head.

By prolonged study, interrupted only by Maria's visits and brief consultations with his lawyer, Alves learned a great deal about the financial structure of his homeland. There had long ago ceased to be gold or silver to lend the currency that elusive hardness. Yet, that lack never seemed to have the slightest inhibiting effect on the printing of more banknotes. For something as serious as money, something which exercised such brutalizing power over each and every individual citizen of the state, such an attitude struck him as breathtakingly cavalier. *They simply printed it when they needed it!*

Digesting this remarkable nugget of information took some doing; he pushed on with his solitary researches. Next he asked himself who the devil "they" were. Much to his surprise he discovered that "they" were not the government, the state itself, as he had assumed; the state had in fact granted this enormous power to print money, to change paper into something of exceptional value and legal validity, to the Bank of Portugal, a semiprivate institution! "Such an enormous privilege," he jotted down among his notes, "can make the state into the slave of the holders of this great power."

Arnaldo was instructed to bring everything he could lay his hands on relevant to the Bank of Portugal—newspaper clippings, bylaws, history, annual reports.

The bank's stock was divided unequally between private

citizens, who held by far the larger proportion, and the government, which owned the piddling remainder. Ever since 1887 the bank had held the exclusive license to issue banknotes, equal in face value to the amount of twice its paid-up capital. The institution's very substantial annual profits were systematically divided proportionately between the private stockholders and the government according to the stock owned by each faction.

By 1891 the banknotes were no longer convertible to either gold or silver. In other words, ever since 1891 Portuguese money had been worth precisely the cost of the paper and printing bills. . . . It was almost too much for the astounded Reis to countenance. He was the one in jail, but look at what those in positions of great power and respectability had done to the very currency he was charged with embezzling!

As the years passed and the government had found itself hard pressed, the structure relating to twice the bank's paid-up capital was conveniently shunted aside. By 1924 the bank had authorized the issuance of *more than one hundred times the paid-up capital*. He rubbed his eyes and shook his head over that one. Could such things be? According to the figures before him, in the postwar period between 1918 and 1923 alone the number of escudos issued by the Bank of Portugal had undergone a sixfold increase, which logically meant that the value of the escudo had suffered a severe reduction in the face of uninflated, hard foreign currency. In 1918 the British pound sterling was equivalent to eight escudos. Six years later there were one hundred and five escudos in every pound: the escudo was worth less than a nickel!

His interest whetted beyond description, Alves plunged forward into the Bank's by-laws, intent on discovering how an institution with such prerogatives actually functioned. With great care he constructed a chart of the bank's many separate departments. To his amazement he discovered that there was no department that had any means of controlling the possibility of duplicate banknotes. There was no provision for checking the numbers printed on the face of banknotes. Should a second issuance of notes with certain numbers—numbers coinciding with those on notes already in circulation—be printed, there was no conceivable way the bank could know it. Used, soiled banknotes returned from the many bank branches and from private banks underwent a simple process. Whereas in England notes returned to the Bank of England were duly recorded, the numbers retired from any further use and replaced by new notes with new numbers, the Bank of Portugal—ironically, to save the printing expense involved in issuing new notes—washed and pressed the old money, sorted it out by series and number and sent it back once again to the economic battlefield.

These discoveries haunted Alves. Such a careless, slovenly way of handling important matters! Somehow, surely, there was a way to turn this process to his advantage. . . . Working from the official estimates of the amount of money in circulation and from the average size of individual issuances of notes, he concluded that three hundred million escudos, worth three million pounds sterling or about fifteen million dollars, could be inserted into the Portuguese economy without upsetting the official bank machinery. . . .

The mere thought of such a sum left him emotionally and intellectually drained. He sat down on his damp cot, forgetting for the moment the vile cell. His mind was free. What splendid undertakings, he thought as he watched the candle's bright flame, he could initiate for Portugal and Angola with such a sum of money!

And for Alves Reis, too.

By the time he had amassed his voluminous researches and reached his somewhat scarifying conclusions, his case was finally due for trial. It was a brief affair, concluded in less than a single day. Outside the rain dripped steadily from the eaves; the magistrate seemed remarkably disinterested, as if the climate had sapped his spirit. On the major charge of embezzling the contents of the Ambaca treasury, Alves was acquitted. But in the matter of the fraud involving the check written against the National City Bank of New York without adequate covering funds, he was ordered held. With almost the last of the money raised from the sale of their personal effects, Alves managed bail and covered the bad check. His bail was returned, providing the stake he needed to begin the rebuilding of his life. He was free again, a new man with a new view of the world and the beginning of an idea.

Like a monk in a medieval cell, he had applied himself to his studies, to learning the true way, and it was a way that no man had ever quite glimpsed before. The innocent man had let his own peculiar strength—the agility of his uncluttered mind—flex its muscles.

He stood in the courtyard of the Oporto jail, feeling the warm rain sifting down. The humidity had steamed his glasses, but he saw in the distance by the courtyard gate a taxi, Maria's face framed in the side window. He waved. He knew she would be crying.

"You're free!" Arnaldo cried, hurling himself into Alves' embrace. "You look good, considering. Not much color in your cheeks—we'll fix that. . . . A few days walking on the beach, you'll be as good as ever."

Arm in arm they began walking toward the car.

"Maria, is she all right? The trip wasn't too much for her, carrying the baby? How has she taken it all, really? We're poor now, you know. She's never been poor."

"You'll be proud of her." Arnaldo smiled, carrying Alves' suitcase. "She's learning how much backbone she really has. It's an adventure for her. You'll see."

The trees dripped rain. The paving stones glistened.

Alves stared at her flawless face, framed with the thick dark hair, lips parted, her huge brown eyes overflowing. He ran the rest of the way to the taxi.

"Alves, my darling . . ." She choked back a sob and he leaned through the window, pressing his mouth to hers.

"I love you," he whispered against her soft, smooth cheek. Sitting beside her on the ride to the train depot, he held her to him, placed his hand gently on her swollen belly, tapped with his fingertips as if trying to establish communications with the tiny creature within—their fourth child. Maria giggled, hugged him. There was no need to speak.

With Oporto already fading behind him, the rain slackened, dried up, and the sun began to shine, revealing a countryside bedecked with rainbows. Maria dozed with a wet cloth across her forehead. Arnaldo chattered on, but Alves' mind was working quietly, intensely as he nodded at Arnaldo's pauses. His concern for the future was alive, possessed a dynamism of its own. His mind was full of the information gathered during the last few weeks in jail. . . .

But how do you start again, no matter how capable you are, when you've come straight from jail?

Out of touch. That was how he felt. . . . He had responsibilities, Maria, the children, the baby . . . He needed to formulate a new set of rules by which to play the game; the old rules had landed him in the Oporto jail. The point was, it was the petty crimes that were punished— the small crimes, the small men—not the important men who manipulated the large amounts of currency, who toyed with the banking rules and did business as it suited them. All along he had been thinking too small. . . .

"We have a surprise for you in Lisbon, Alves," Arnaldo said. "Something you'd never guess—never." He grinned, barely able to keep the secret. Alves nodded. Fine dust sifted into the car, streaking and caking their perspiring faces. But Alves didn't notice.

Rossio Station was dark, echoing like a giant's cave after the steaming run across the countryside. Alves felt a surge of hope: he was back in Lisbon. Climbing down from the carriage, reaching back up to assist Maria, he heard a familiar voice, couldn't place it, turned slowly, her hand in his. The face of the man next to him was smiling crookedly, wolfishly, mustache sloping like a bandit's, eyes drooping and heavy-lidded.

"José!"

He held Alves at arm's length, sizing him up, brushing dust from the shoulders of his dark, rumpled suit. "A little pale, but . . ." He dropped his voice to a whisper, winked. "Jail does that to a man!"

"You," Alves cried, "should know!"

"Please, no unhappy memories," José replied with mock gravity. "We must both begin anew!" He threw his arms around Maria and exuberantly kissed her cheek. "My dear Maria, you must make Alves retire his African fertility doll!" Maria obligingly blushed, wagging her finger.

"You never change," she said.

"Ah, I do so hope you are mistaken there, my little one. I've changed my ways—now we must reform your husband."

"Nonsense," Alves interrupted. "As the Americans say, I was framed!"

"Me, too," José said, nodding enthusiastically. "The world awaits us both, Alves." Then, watching Arnaldo quietly waiting with Alves' bag, he amended, "All *three* of us."

José was leading the way down to the busy square, Arnaldo struggling with Alves' valise and the extra satchel of reading material. It was early evening. The sky was pink, and in the gentle shadows Lisbon looked like a city made of candy. The breeze was cool and Alves stood for a moment on the sidewalk looking around him.

"Come on, Alves," José called from the other side of the shiny black Nash sedan. "We'll be late. Hurry up! You must ride in my new car!" He jumped in behind the wheel, knocking his beige fedora askew. The hat matched his gloves with the tiny pearl buttons. José Bandeira had always been a snappy dresser. The sight of the car and the expensive clothing reminded Alves of the money he'd sent José in Mozambique. It seemed half a lifetime ago. Perhaps there was a chance of getting it back. . . .

"Late for what?" he asked Arnaldo.

"José has suggested a small party. To celebrate your return—in Cascais. A few friends." He helped Maria into the car and stood aside to make room for Alves. "To welcome you home."

Whatever the cares lurking in their minds, they all receded during the ride through the gathering darkness along the Tagus. Huge commercial ships loomed over a variety of luxury liners that made their way south from England, along the coasts of France and Spain to the great Portuguese harbor. Yachts, smaller still, moved jauntily among them, pennants waving. The Tower of Belem, from which Da Gama had sailed for India around the Cape of Good Hope in 1497, rose familiarly out of the dusk. The smell of the sea lay lightly on the breezes. Maria took Alves' hand as they sped onward.

Later she spoke into his ear: "The beach, do you recognize it?"

"Of course. Once I nearly killed myself there, trying to get a silly girl's boat into the water. . . ."

"And the girl, what of her?"

"Nice enough girl, I suppose. Wound up marrying her and carting her off to Africa." He patted her stomach. "And now she has my children! With great regularity. . . ."

She squeezed his arm, eyes glistening in the dark.

"We're here!" José braked the car abruptly to a halt in front of the restaurant overlooking the beach. The outdoor platform built over sand was strung with brightly colored lanterns, and perhaps twenty couples were standing by the railing calling and waving to Alves.

Alves felt tears well up as he bobbed his head, acknowledging the words of welcome as they climbed the steps and moved slowly among their friends. A small American–

French-type jazz combo played in a corner under a striped canopy: a swarthy guitarist, a violinist with a patch over one eye, a black clarinet player, going through all the hits of the day.

"All Alone."

"Limehouse Blues."

"Somebody Loves Me."

"What'll I Do."

The evening fused together into one continuous blur of music and dancing and broiled shrimps and cold wine from Germany, pretty women in daring dresses and potent perfume, dark men in white shirts and silk ties, faces smiling and congratulating him on his return, as if he had just pulled off a business coup of one kind or another. What mattered, it seemed, was that a previously successful entrepreneur had undergone a dramatic reversal and come through it with flags flying. It was the best construction thus far put on the events of the last few months, at least in Alves' opinion, and caught up in the relief of his restored freedom and the spirit of the moment, he danced and drank and perspired freely and told jokes that everyone seemed to find enormously amusing. The lanterns glowed yellow and red and blue, and balloons attached to the lantern poles were untied and floated romantically out over the beach toward the ocean. He watched them go, remembered the day he'd seen Maria and fallen in love.

Later still the musicians melted away, conversation dropped to hushed whispers, and a red spotlight came on, bathing the tiny bandstand in a rich, shadowy glow. "Fado," someone said, and from nowhere the singer appeared with her two accompanists. Without a word they seated themselves in front of her, one with the *guitarra*, the other with the *viola da Franca*. The *guitarra*, in the hands of a scowling young man with black hair to his shoulders and a cigarette stuck to his lower lip, produced the silvery, minor tune which, in all its variations, was so familiar in Lisbon. The *viola da Franca* propelled the music forward by means of a low throbbing. By now it was so quiet that only the sound of the surf could be heard, and the *fadista* stepped forward, breaking her pose, embarking on the mournful song. Her eyes were almost closed, her wild dark mane, held in check by a band of ribbon, was thrown back, her sinewy body swaying sensually to the demands of the two guitars. Like all *fadista*, her voice was rough, primitive and her manner earthy and unsophisticated. It was impossible to guess her background or where José might have found her. Given his nature, Alves assumed that he was most probably sleeping with her and doubtless living to some extent off her earnings, which could have accounted for the exceptionally melancholy quality of her song. Her golden earrings and a golden necklace flashed in the red glow like a gypsy's jewelry around a campfire.

The *fado* exercised a magical hold on the gathering. It appealed even to Alves, who saw himself as the most businesslike of men. Somewhere in the wild moans of sadness and tragedy, in the cries of self-pity at the turns of capricious Fate, in the sounds of the erotic whorishness that lay in the song's heart, he found the hint of an answer, even a philosophic answer. . . . Life, the singer seemed to say, was a mournful business, only a means of putting off the end.

As Alves listened it was as if he were alone. He recalled all the meanings of the songs as the singer wound her way deeper and deeper, and he felt that he knew, from his own experience, of what she sang. The irony, the despair, the discouragement, the caprices . . . If he had never known true ecstasy, perhaps it wasn't within him to feel it. Surely it was not Maria's fault. Love he had known. Ecstasy was for poets. Was ecstasy forever beyond the son of an impoverished undertaker? Was he simply too common a man?

Eventually the *fado* was done, the party over. He said a few words of thanks to his friends, who could see by the tears on his cheeks that he was moved and grateful. The effect of the wine was wearing off and the night air was restoring his equilibrium. His assumption about José and the *fadista* proved absolutely correct: the girl curled up in the front seat of the Nash for the drive back to Lisbon. Maria and Arnaldo, both quite happily drunk, collapsed beside Alves in the back.

At the flat Maria had rented a few weeks before his return he asked José to wait. He carried Maria up the stairs and quickly undressed her, placed her carefully beneath the coverlet. The children were with her parents. He locked the door and went back to the waiting car. Arnaldo was sleeping soundly. José was kissing the singer. Alves climbed into the front seat. The girl slowly straightened up, then tilted heavily against him. José stepped on the gas, and the Nash slid away into the quiet moonlit streets.

"Where are we going?" Alves finally asked. He felt wide awake and everyone else was sleepy.

"I'm spending the night at the girl's place," José said. "Arnaldo will either sleep it off in the car or manage to get to her couch. How do you like my little *fadista?*"

"She is very good. Admirable."

"Very beautiful, too. Kiss her if you like. You've been in prison, after all, and Maria is pregnant. It's the very least I can offer."

"No, really."

"You may kiss me," the girl said. Her voice was higher and clearer than her singing. She smelled of wine, rather tantalizingly.

"If you don't," José said, "she'll be insulted."

"He's right," the girl said. She lifted her face to him. "I'll stay with you all night, too."

Alves was suddenly very uncomfortable.

"Perfectly all right, old man," José allowed, his diction slightly slurred. "A welcome-home present."

Alves kissed her quickly, felt her tongue dart into his mouth. She held him close, pulled his hand against a rising nipple.

"Really, I'm very sorry," he said. "But not tonight." The girl flung herself away, back toward José. "Another time perhaps. . . . All I want to do is go for a long walk. I've been in a cell for so long."

"Of course, old man," José said. "We understand. Very civilized habit, walking. No doubt about it." He stopped at a corner where several darkish streets converged.

Alves got out of the car.

"José, I can't possibly thank you enough for all you've done for me. You've made me see that all is not lost."

The wolf's grin came and went. "Now, have a nice walk," José said. "And I'll make certain we see each other soon. We may be useful to each other. . . ."

When the car was out of sight he put his hands in his pockets and began walking.

A few minutes later, the night closing around him, he found himself looking up at the long gray facades of the Bank of Portugal and the Ultramarino Bank, iron-grilled, characterless, the two great repositories of money. How fitting, he thought, surveying the two buildings in the cold moonlight: the money itself was without character, gained its meaning and nature from the uses to which it was put.

Where better for it to be kept than in these anonymous, remote, faceless structures? His footsteps echoed on the pavement. He stopped to read a political broadside pasted to one of the bank buildings, lit a cigarette from a wooden match scraped on the gray surface, went along to stand at the black iron grill across one of the entryways. He peered into the darkness. He was alone in the street.

He walked on finally, his thoughts lingering with the banks until he realized that he was approaching the ancient Alfama district where as a child he'd been cautioned never to go alone. His grandmother had called it the Mouraria, had warned him that the Jews and the Moors would catch him, cut him to pieces, boil him for soup.

Slowly he began to climb the narrow streets, where by spreading his arms he could almost touch the walls on either side of him. He smelled the food with its hints of Eastern spices, the pungency of the animals who lived cheek by jowl with their owners; he saw and heard and felt the clothing fluttering from ropes overhead where it had been hung to dry. Above him the ancient crumbling buildings, dwellings of the poor, seemed to lean toward one another, blotting out the starry night. A drunk moaned when Alves trod on his foot. Remembering his grandmother, he leaped back, stifled a cry, saw in his imagination the blade glittering as it came, saw the whisper of his own death. He hurried on up the steep cobbled path.

Old Portugal, he thought, still with us, primitive and uninformed, superstitious. The blood of an admiral, yes, certainly, but also the blood of his grandmother, who had been a child when people could still recall at first hand the French Revolution. The tumbrils rolling, the streets of Paris slippery with fresh blood . . . And his grandmother, who never dreamed of reading or writing, had lived in a home where a carved wooden box had contained the *mano refinada*, the "hand of glory," which was in fact the pickled right hand of a corpse whose identity was lost in the mists of time but probably dated from Napoleon's conquest of Europe. She had believed in witches who took the forms of black sparrows and flew away after sucking the life-blood from young children. And Alves remembered her hiding the hair of the family dog behind the door to keep him from wandering away on his regular nocturnal excursions.

The street doubled back on itself, always inching higher

past the narrow, shadowed doorways where cats and dogs growled in their sleep. Somewhere back in the recesses of the district a woman sang, her voice breaking with some emotional anguish that Alves couldn't even imagine. The voice followed him as he climbed, reminding him ever more of the past. Now, on this peculiarly magical night, he felt curiously in touch with the past and with his heritage. Portuguese had once navigated the world, greatness their destiny, and now he felt a tapping on his shoulder as if the past were reaching for his attention. . . .

Romantic nonsense, obviously. But still, almost unbidden, here he was, drawn into the oldest section of Lisbon, upward toward the ruins of the great castle of San Jorge, which had brooded over the city from the time when the Celts and the Phoenicians and the Greek Odysseus had built their temples and forts on the mighty hill that commanded the harbor of the River Tagus. Somehow Alves had forgotten all this as he'd fought to survive, to make his own life more fruitful than his father's. From now on, he thought as his breath grew short and his legs began to ache, from now on pettiness, small success, a little money to invest—all that was dead, gone, forgotten.

If he truly were a new man in a new age there was nothing to keep him from challenging it as Henry the Navigator or the great Da Gama had challenged the oceans beyond the horizon. He stopped to rest at the gate leading into the grounds of the castle. The way beyond was narrow and steeper yet. Vines and flowers clutched at his face as he entered where the quietness was nearly palpable. He heard the splashing of a fountain, the high wind in the trees, the cooing and clucking of the exotic birds invisible in the night.

He walked past the massive cold cast-iron cannons trained out over the city's tiled rooftops toward the harbor, smelling the limes and the flowers, toward the castle walls rising darkly against the night sky. Up the shallow stairways, across the stone bridges, pushing past the oaken doors two feet thick, hinges creaking with the rust of the ages, past the constantly dripping water, the flat shallow ponds, into the courtyard itself where the Moors had replaced the Romans and had been in turn replaced by the Christian Alfonso Henriques, who had led his knights up the treacherous paths in 1147 with Portugal in the hands of the Christian Lord and His servants. . . .

A peacock flared like an explosion in the yellow moon-light, an insomniac cockatoo strutted past, a Chinese Mandarin duck floated motionless on the water, sleeping. He lit a cigarette, sat on a stone step hollowed out and smoothed two thousand years ago by sentries watching the campfires of the enemy on the plains across the wide, dark Tagus. Across the open square of grass and dust a well with its rope and bucket took on a momentarily ominous shape. He blew smoke rings, sighed. The *mouras encantadas,* the enchanted Moorish princesses who were indescribably beautiful and treacherous and who possessed the serpent's tail where their legs ought to have been—the *mouras encantadas* waited at the bottoms of wells to devour the hapless boy or girl who carelessly leaned too far. . . . My God, it was all so long ago, boyhood and the werewolves and the stories of Henry the Navigator and his father toiling in the undertaker's trade. So long ago . . .

He climbed higher still, up the dangerously narrow steps to the crenelated battlements from where, between the stone pillars, he could see the endless, countless rust-colored tile rooftops of his city with Rossio Square huge and empty and quiet. He leaned forward; as he did so he felt the amulet his grandmother had given him rub against his chest, between him and the stone parapet. Ah, superstition and magic! She had been dying and had pressed it into his small hand, explaining that it should go to him, that it had belonged to his grandfather, who had given it to her on his deathbed. It was a link, a bit of the continuity between the generations—in this case, a *pedra de raio,* the amulet of the thunderbolt. She explained the story, slowly and painstakingly since her breath was very short. The thunderbolt, she said, is the great stone shaft that plummets to the earth at the moment we see the flash of lightning and drives itself seven meters deep into the earth. With each passing year it pushes back upward until in the seventh year it reappears, at which time those with great good luck find it and take it with them, thus protecting their homes and themselves from any future thunderbolts—or strokes of calamitous bad fortune, whatever may be likened to a thunderbolt of fate. He held it in his hand, a tiny prehistoric arrowhead that his grandfather must have come upon sometime in the distant past, since he would have been one hundred years old by then, having been born in the early years of the nineteenth century. A hole had been driven through the broad end of the device and a thin leather thong passed through it, making a necklace, which is how Alves had worn it ever since receiving it. His grandmother had gone to her grave secure in the belief that young Alves had been provided for. He looked at it again, its antiquity and primal grace, the smoothness achieved by the passing centuries. He sighed. Ah, it was a good thing she had not lived to see him flattened by the thunderbolt that landed him in the Oporto jail . . . but that sorry event would hardly have shaken her belief in the *pedra de raio*. No, she would have an excuse. After all, you could hardly maintain a belief in magic if your faith reeled every time it didn't work. . . .

Thunderbolts. You never outlive the past, he thought. Never.

When he looked again at the city he was surprised to see that it had grown more distinct, that the sky was going gray, that the ships on the Tagus had lost their shapelessness. But he was not tired. On the contrary he had never felt more hopeful, more alive and eager.

Staring intensely at the city, he spoke, perhaps to his grandmother, perhaps to himself, palms spread on the stone parapet as if he were addressing the city, the past, the present from the mightiest of balconies.

"I . . . am . . . Alves . . . Reis. . . ." He took a deep breath and the hint of a smile quivered on his lips. "And I have . . . a thunderbolt of my own. . . ."

Then he began the long walk home.

They might as well... stood behind a pane of such smoothness. He was moving in an almost inaudible —

PART TWO

PERIL POINT

Alves began his preparations the evening of the day after the welcome-home party. He had wandered wearily, happily back from the Castle of San Jorge with the sun at his back, watching and listening as the streets came alive and the sounds of the fishermen floated up from the docks on the morning's first breezes. He napped the day away while Maria took the children to market and then to play in the park. Hyperactive, he romped on the floor with the two oldest boys while Maria bathed the youngest, then took the sweet-smelling, freshly powdered bundle in his arms and crooned a medley of the previous night's favorites, concluding with an up-tempo rendition of "Does the Spearmint Lose Its Flavor on the Bedpost Overnight?" Which he understood was very big in America.

Eventually the children were all tucked away and Maria was soaking in the tub surrounded by the children's tiny wooden sailboats bumping against her soft breasts, nestling among the soapsuds. He gazed at her fondly, kissed her moist, thick hair and went to the kitchen table, which was cleared and wiped clean. He set out at once to pull his plans into workable form. It had been a fine first day of freedom, and there would be time to savor that later.

Systematically he composed a series of newspaper vindications, a curiously Portuguese custom that would rehabilitate him in the eyes of others and particularly in the eyes of foreigners. In the newspapers there was no simple way to differentiate between columns of news stories and paid columns of advertisements. He knew that doctors, for instance, commonly paid for the columns used by

patients who were willing to sign letters singing the doctors' praises in the matter of curing one's great uncle of
gout, saving someone else's life at the last moment. Alves
composed a series of "news" stories revealing the truth
behind his imprisonment—namely, that he had been rail-
roaded, victim of a public and financial cabal set on
destroying him.

By the second evening's work at the kitchen table he had
most determinedly set about the outlining of a plan based
on the researches he'd conducted in jail.

The aim was to produce a great deal of money for
himself.

The means grew out of what he'd learned while in
Oporto. And the keys to the plan, at least on paper, were
twofold: first, the Bank of Portugal was entrusted by the
government with the power to print money, and, second,
the Bank of Portugal was unable to check on the existence
of duplicate banknote numbers. *Forgery* leaped to the mind
like the fleet-footed hare. Which was where Alves Reis and
the common criminal parted company. Sleeves rolled up,
eyes burning from the incessant cigarette smoke, he savored
the details, unable to force himself to sleep.

He had turned the procedures of the underworld over
and over in his mind, analyzing, evaluating, fitting them
against the requirements he'd formed. Large-scale crime,
as opposed to the sort carried out by men with pistols in
the dark of night, related primarily to the moving of large
sums of money from the people or institutions to whom
it belonged to the people or institutions with the best conceived schemes to acquire it for themselves. The former
approaches were referred to legalistically, more often than
not, as embezzlements or frauds. Such enterprises, he
learned, were almost always accomplished by individuals
who operated from within the organizations being looted,
men who had achieved positions of responsibility and therefore opportunities to loot that were based on trust. The
forging of banknotes, currency, *money* was performed by
individuals lumped together under the name of counterfeiters. Alves' reading about the art of counterfeiting led
him irrevocably to the conclusion that successful counterfeiting was quite possibly the most difficult and demanding
of all criminal endeavors.

Counterfeiters, it seemed, unlike embezzlers and fraud
merchants, operated from outside the system they intended

to plunder. They must also possess the most sophisticated technical abilities and usually required large amounts of capital to invest in just the right paper, enormously skilled artists and plate engravers, printers, front men. . . . The very thought of the effort and expertise involved in counterfeiting would, quite understandably, be enough to deter the most zealous of criminals.

Alves had quickly grasped the fact that he was neither an insider nor a professional outsider. At precisely this point in his researches he had felt stymied. He was, he feared, about to see his dreams of beating the system go glimmering, out the window. . . . He saw himself and he did not spare himself or flinch from what he saw. He was virtually without funds. He had no connections of any significance in Lisbon.

But he also accurately evaluated his resourcefulness. He was not simply a little man with nothing more than a cracked coffee cup and an oilcloth-covered wooden table. Circumstances could be overcome. . . . Angola had taught him that. Oh, yes, the disadvantages he faced were staggering, apocalyptic—but, he heard himself whispering, *I am Alves Reis and that makes the difference.*

Eventually, after thinking about the entire business night after night for such a long time, he reached certain conclusions that reinforced his belief in the plan. Now that he was free again, in the embrace of his family, in his home with more time to go over his plan again, he was increasingly sure of those conclusions. Standing at the window, wiping his forehead with a towel, listening to the quiet Lisbon night, he felt confidence in his break with the past. He was a new man—that was the center of everything.

Unlike most criminals he was not governed by tradition. He was unencumbered with the old ways of doing things; he could fire his imagination into the air like a holiday rocket at Cascais and let it explode, trailing peculiar and wonderful options. The criminal, he decided, was by nature an imitator. There seemed to be precious little new in the universe of crime but merely the next generation of criminals who were convinced that by doing things the old way, but better, they could master the world.

At the thought of his own plan Alves' eyes would sparkle, the exhaustion would fade away, the energy would flow. . . . Its beauty, he knew, lay in the fact that *it had never been done before and could never, ever be done again.* The absolutely unique crime. Unique! The great crime, the dazzling, absurd, coruscating crystal chandelier of crime. . . . He had come upon the foolproof scheme.

During the first week at home Alves was as loving and attentive as Maria could have hoped for. But his mind was far away. He overheard Maria telling her mother just that, going on about how her husband was planning his return to "the workaday world."

He paced the apartment, walked the banks of the Tagus, sat staring on benches in one park after another, retraced the streets of his boyhood where he had played with his brother. He passed the building, which now stood empty with broken windows and rotted doorframes, where the undertaker's parlor had stood. Alfonso had taken over the business and moved to another location, where prosperity seemed just a bit more likely. All the time, as the past moved fleetingly before his eyes, he was turning the plan over and over in his mind. Was there a flaw he hadn't detected, some obvious connection too weak to support his basic concept?

The plan concerned money.

By the end of the week he was convinced it was the perfect plan. He stood alone. He knew that whatever he had the power to imagine he also had the power to accomplish. . . .

There was, however, one condition.

So daring, so perfect was his plan that he realized a less cunning, less nimble mind could not possibly be asked to cope with it. Therefore the road ahead would be a lonely one. Only he could know the truth. He was entering a world of absolute secrecy. The others, the men he needed to reach his destiny, could be allowed to see only the façade he would construct.

It was then that he telephoned José Bandeira.

*   *   *

He was waiting for them as Alves and Arnaldo stepped away from the ever-present crush of pedestrians in Rossio Square and made their way down the narrow, shadowy street of the goldsmiths with its prettily tiled sidewalks and gleaming, opulent shop windows. José was nattily turned out in a fitted pale-blue suit with wide lapels, a crimson flower pinched into his buttonhole, a cigarette in an amber holder, a Panama hat, patent-leather two-tone shoes with a glassy finish and purple bags under his eyes, this last splash of color the result of a week-long *mano a mano* with his fetching *fadista*. He smiled wearily, drawn by curiosity, and the three men took the short walk to the noble street lift that would transport them up to Largo do Carmo, the next level of the city. It was a masterpiece of baroque ironwork, reminiscent of a large Meccano set much like the Eiffel Tower in construction, not overly surprising since Eiffel himself had designed and built the elevator. Somehow it captured perfectly the nineteenth-century quality that made Lisbon so comfortable, so steadfastly picturesque. Slowly the wheels ground on, lifting them into the sunshine well above the square. On the observation deck Alves insisted on spending several moments looking out across the city, at the undulating hills surrounding its core, at the ruins of the castle through a faint haze, at the broad surface of the Tagus to the south, at the acres of rusty orange tiles laid on top of the white buildings and the thick greenery of the hillsides. . . . He was beginning again. How many times had he begun? How many great chances had he taken? Now he was beginning again. For the last time.

With José popping questions, they walked the narrow cobbled streets winding in the direction of the river but far above it. Finally they came to a beer garden, the outside decorated with blue and white tiles of angels, cherubs and gods. They walked through the jumble of tables and out the back door onto a layered terrace where the sun shone and the breeze fluttered the awnings and pigeons took their ease. Ships moved slowly far below, riding deep in the water. Alves ordered shrimp omelets and beer for their lunch and hunched forward, elbows on the table, white hat on the seat of the fourth chair. He plucked the handkerchief from the breast pocket of his newly pressed white linen suit and began polishing his spectacles, squinting in the sun against the smoke rising from his cigarette. Arnaldo munched on a handful of pale-lavender grapes from a wooden bowl in the center of the table.

José impatiently stubbed his cigarette out and looked frustratedly from one to the other. "All right," he said, "enough of this shilly-shallying. Let's get down to what we're here for. And you'd better be buying this lunch. . . .

I should still be in bed. Asleep, I mean. Now what is this business opportunity I couldn't afford to pass up?" He yawned involuntarily behind a hand bearing two large diamond rings. Alves remembered the five thousand dollars he'd once wired to Mozambique.

"I've been a very busy man since I last saw you," Alves said with conscious deliberation. "Whatever you or others may have thought, I still have weighty connections throughout—"

"Wait a minute," José piped. "I never thought for a minute that you were finished, you're too resourceful . . . always have been." He nodded affirmatively. "Not Alves Reis, no sir!"

"Connections throughout Lisbon's business and financial community," Alves continued, staring at José, the dandy, who seemed to have been tailored by life to serve as a front man while somebody else exercised the brain power. "You would be amazed if I could actually reveal the names of the men in positions of great power with whom I have had discussions this week. . . ."

"I'm sure." José nodded humbly. "Say, does Arnaldo know what you're leading up to?"

Arnaldo swallowed a mouthful of grapes. "I haven't seen Alves since the party. I've been putting up with my mother all week. 'Why aren't you looking for work, Arnaldo? Why don't you forget this deadbeat crook Reis?' " He shrugged helplessly, opened his mouth for another comment.

"Both of you, shut up and listen to me." Alves lost his composure. "This is your entire future I'm talking about, and I'm going to have more to do with it than your whores, José, and your idiotic senile mother, Arnaldo!"

"Be calm, Alves," Arnaldo said softly. "We're listening."

Alves dropped his voice to a whisper, licking his lips, rolling a grape between his fingertips. He jerked a look over his shoulder to see if any waiters were near enough to overhear.

"Now this is absolutely secret—got it?" They nodded. "To begin with I can't even give you the names of the men . . . but—are you listening?"

"For God's sake, yes," José whispered loudly. "Go on." Arnaldo gave him a pitying look and told him to calm himself, people were beginning to look.

"I have been dealing with governors of . . . the Bank

of Portugal!" He eased back in his chair as the omelets and pitchers of beer arrived. His listeners froze at their places until the waiter had fussed and arranged and gone away.

"What do you mean, governors of the Bank of Portugal? Where would you meet such men? Like meeting one of the Pope's cardinals . . . like meeting the Pope!" José poked at a shrimp as if it had told him a lie. Arnaldo stared at him.

"True nevertheless," Alves said. "As well as conducting business with them! In their offices, right down there." He gestured casually over the edge of the terrace where, far below, the long, dull gray building sat impassively at the center of the nation's finances. He speared a triangle of omelet and chewed it slowly, while wishing that eating didn't interfere with smoking. He washed omelet down with cold, cutting beer. "No, you underestimate me—I suppose you haven't read the papers either. Full of the true story of my unjust imprisonment."

"You paid for those," Arnaldo said. "We aren't fools, you know."

"So what?" Alves patted his mouth, licked a morsel of shrimp from the tendrils of his mustache. "To the men at the Bank of Portugal—the governors—I am Senhor Angola. I have distinguished myself in Angola's highest technical post, I have aided the royal railway, I have been selfless at every turn. . . ."

"Senhor Angola?" José wondered solemnly.

"And what is this business they have in mind?" Arnaldo said, cautiously.

"Remember, utter secrecy. No *fadistas,* no curious mothers! Understand? Well, here we are, the fall of nineteen twenty-four, and all over the world one nation after another is facing the problems of inflation—and Angola is far worse off than almost any other. Four hundred years a colony and now the bottom has fallen out. . . ." He squeezed Arnaldo's arm, a crack of sorrow on his lips. "Our beloved Angola, my friend. Trade is down to nothing and bankruptcy an epidemic. Old families with old money, all gone. One catastrophe after another, people we *know.* . . . Angolan currency is no longer convertible into any other European currency—not even Portuguese escudos. Which means that Portuguese settlers out there are trapped. No one will buy their farms or their businesses or even their houses. There's no gold there, no other valuable resources . . . as we have reason to know there is, ahem, no oil." Alves turned his attention to his rapidly cooling lunch, finished half of the omelet and carefully placed the plate on the terrace near his chair. Within seconds the tame pigeons were pecking at the pink-veined shrimps.

"I've heard a joke, come to think of it," José said, remembering with some difficulty. "Let's see . . . if Portugal is the Vatican's poor farm, then Angola is Portugal's poor farm. Good, eh?"

"Fabulous," Arnaldo said grimly.

"The problem is that Angola badly needs bailing out. And I, Alves Reis, am the man the governors have chosen to do it!"

Arnaldo and José turned expectant faces toward him, then followed him toward the railing. An awkward double-winged seaplane skimmed low over the Tagus, past the masts and smokestacks, ever lower, wobbly, the pontoons knifed into the gentle waves, disappeared for an instant into furling foam. Alves shook his head. "We live in an amazing age. Machines drop out of the sky into the water and, lo and behold, they don't sink. . . . What do you say to that, Arnaldo?"

"I say, how are you supposed to save Angola?"

"First there is a little something José may be able to help us with."

"Anything," José said. "Name it."

"Antonio . . ."

José looked blank.

"Antonio," Alves repeated, "your brother—surely the name rings a bell, José."

"Oh, yes." José nodded enthusiastically. "Of course, Antonio. What about him?"

"He engages in commercial enterprises in The Hague, does he not? And he must have connections, men he knows who are involved in financial matters. . . . I need an absolutely trustworthy man, someone your brother will vouch for, someone experienced in international finance. Someone who is infinitely discreet . . . and won't turn up his nose at a handsome profit." Alves cupped his hands around a match and lit a cigarette. The wind moved high up in the palm trees.

"I know such a man," José said, turning back to the cliff, holding onto his Panama hat with its gaily colored band. "A Dutchman, very experienced, respectable, discreet. . . . Sophisticated. The man makes a religion of respectability. Perfect."

"José," Alves said solemnly, "I'm going to trust you in this. Be sure you have the right man."

"Yes," Arnaldo said, frowning. "For God's sake, be sure."

"Trust me," José said. He smiled. "I'll get in touch with him today. By wire."

"And I want a complete dossier, everything you know about him. Use all your sources, Antonio, any of your man's friends or enemies. And call me this evening, tomorrow, as soon as you have the dossier and his answer."

"To what?" José looked at Alves in confusion.

Alves took a small leather notebook from his coat pocket and a stub of wooden pencil from his trouser pocket, carefully printed the message. Pigeons clucked at his feet, a woman laughed as she leaned over the railing and the breeze lifted her skirt.

When José had departed Alves turned to Arnaldo.

"Well, what do you think?"

Arnaldo shrugged. "Too bad he's such an idiot, though. Still, he'll probably find you a good man. . . ."

"Us," Alves corrected him. "Find *us* a good man."

They were walking back toward the elevator. A beggar approached them on all fours, the side of his face eaten away. Alves dropped a coin into the tin cup, hurried past.

"Bad omen," he said, remembering his grandmother, who would surely have had an antidote. Peel a lizard, make soup from the skin, pour it on the dog. Something useful.

"Alves, what did the Bank of Portugal want with you? Did you really meet with the governors?"

"Of course I did. But I cannot disclose their plan yet. More meetings, one tomorrow as a matter of fact, at the bank. But I have a special job for you. Do you remember the German we met at Maria's dinner party in Luanda that night, the man who set me thinking about coming back to Europe?"

"Hennies? That was it, wasn't it? Adolf Hennies. . . . I thought he was supposed to be Swiss."

"German or Swiss, the same." They stopped in front of a small church. "I want you to find him. And build a dossier. You can investigate him, contact our legations, hire a detective if you must. I want to know what kind of man he is, a spy, a soldier of fortune. . . ."

Arnaldo nodded. "I can trace him easily enough. But what should I tell him?"

"Tell him that it is imperative that he meet us at the Palace Hotel in Biarritz one week from today. Tell him that I wouldn't ask him to make the trip unless he'd realize a good profit. And if he doesn't agree with me when we've talked, we'll pick up all of his expenses. That ought to appeal to his German sense of efficiency."

As they descended inside the cage Arnaldo began to chuckle behind a fist.

"Alves," he whispered conspiratorially, "we could pay his expenses in Angolan money!"

"Ah, you're a brilliant man, Arnaldo, a brilliant man." Alves smiled and slapped his friend's back.

*　　*　　*

As the wood-burning engine jostled its way northward, leaving Portugal and pushing on through Spain's Basque country toward Biarritz, Arnaldo and José, their missions accomplished, played cards in the nearly empty coach. Alves, in a compartment of his own, lost himself in the dossiers the two had collected. The air was thick with heavy smoke, and he perspired freely in the dense, humid enclosure, his tie pulled loose and collar undone. Warm rain spattered the windows, smudged the countryside beyond.

Arnaldo had done well in his search for Hennies, turning to a detective in Munich and to a woman called Greta Nordlund, who was, after a dashing series of beaux, newly installed as José's lady. Apparently José had met her in The Hague where he had dined, through Antonio's diplomatic connections, at a dinner honoring her. A woman of the world, a rather famous actress, though Alves knew nothing of such matters, she had attracted José without half trying. His dandy's good looks had been enough to interest her, and much to their mutual surprise a satisfying liaison had ensued. When Arnaldo had mentioned Herr Hennies, José replied that Alves should have asked him since his mistress had once been romantically involved with Herr Hennies, though she had said that their relationship had been short-lived. No, Antonio had never met the man, but José was sure that Greta would prove a font of information. Which, by cable and letter, was indeed the case. By combining her researches with those of the detective in Munich a broad yet remarkably clear picture of Hennies emerged—clearer, by far, than its subject might have wished.

Adolf Gustav Hennies, the entrepreneur who had urged Reis to consider that the real future lay in Europe rather than in an African backwater. Now, scouring the dossier, Alves wondered at fate's intervention, placing Hennies before him as it had. Hennies . . . Neither Miss Nordlund nor the detective knew the man's real name, which was precisely the way Hennies wanted it. He had gone to a great deal of trouble to bury his real name, and by the time he found himself in Senhor Reis's courtyard in Luanda he was well into his *third* complete incarnation. He never talked about the first, which had been almost entirely unsatisfactory, and the second, though shed like a tree's leaves in the autumn, was still fresh in his mind when he encountered Greta and a source of some pleasant if not rapturous reflection.

That second life had begun in 1909 when he was twenty-eight years old. For a raft of delicate personal reasons he had left Germany, changed his name and lit out for the New World. His formal, erect bearing made him much taller than his five feet eight inches, and his somber mien, his orderliness testified to his Germanic efficiency. He went to the famous Singer Sewing Machine Company in New York City and convinced them of his worthiness to acquire a small agency. Of course, the entire contents of his bank account helped persuade these knights of capitalism that he was indeed the man to carry their gospel to yet another outpost in the battle against handstitching. The outpost in Manaos, Brazil, was well up the Amazon and not a location for which they had a deluge of applicants. He felt reasonably certain that no one would come quite so far to find him.

For five years he prospered as something like the sewing-machine god, building a fair amount of capital, particularly for Manaos, which was not, he admitted realistically, a financial hotbed.

Just as he had begun to grow restless in the land of the python and the poison dart, the Portuguese National Assembly declared their intention to join England and France in the war against Germany. Quite naturally he assumed that Brazil, since it was still essentially a Portuguese nation although official colonial status had been renounced almost a century before, might also leap into the war against his homeland. His name at the time wasn't Hennies, but he was known to be a German, his second identity having been based on his first—that is, whoever the hell he claimed to be, he was a German in a country he believed to be on the verge of war with Germany. Time to fly.

As it happened, Brazil held off until 1917, but by then Hennies was long gone. He had scouted out an obliging crook in Rio de Janeiro who fitted him out with a lovely Swiss passport and a third persona—that of Adolf Hennies, an international trader of thirty-three with a Swiss father and a Brazilian mother. In November 1914 he sailed on the ancient S. S. *Principessa Mafalda*, made certain he didn't give his nationality away by uttering even a word of German, and by January he'd made a useful contact in Berlin, secured a position as a member of the wartime German Purchasing Commission and was on his way to his new duties in Amsterdam.

While his position was an official one, Hennies dealt primarily in smuggling through Switzerland items prohibited by the Dutch and Danish governments for export to Germany. At the same time he ingratiated himself with Berlin by operating as an agent for the German Secret Service. Holland was an ideal place to be a spy, since secret agents from all combatant governments chummed about a good deal, lived very nicely on their expense vouchers and fed one another enough information to keep the entire international boondoggle going.

Hennies was wonderfully at home. His close-cropped black hair was already touched with gray, his eyes had a piercing, almost Latin quality, he dressed the part of an impeccable businessman. Due to the fact that he had been born with his right leg shorter than the left, he wore a prosthetic corrective shoe with a built-up sole and walked with a slight limp. At his best he was both extremely dignified and quite sinister. He was frequently at his best in those days, a man of the world, a realist.

By 1917 his realistic approach to life's vagaries told him that Germany was bound to come out of the Great War the biggest loser. He wisely went to a Dutch businessman with whom he had had certain slightly irregular, highly profitable dealings and arranged to have his Deutsche marks converted into Dutch gulden—no less than one hundred thousand dollars' worth.

In the shambles of postwar Europe, while Alves was dealing in phony jute bags and rusty German tractors, Herr Hennies was putting the remains of his Berlin connections into effect, getting himself appointed *Abwicklungskommissar* for East Prussia. It was an enviable post for an enterprising man; he was in charge of German reparations and arms deliveries to Poland, as provided in the Treaty of Versailles. What made the position so attractive was the fact that Poland was in the midst of struggling with Lithuania over the city of Vilna, with the Czechs over Teschen and with the Soviets in general. Hungry for weaponry, Poland had become, in the words of one sagacious observer, "the great arms sink of Europe."

Hennies' greed coincided wonderfully with that of the Poles. He pocketed bribes for hastening shipments of machine guns and grenades, for enlarging shipments and hiding the changes in the tide of paperwork; he arranged private deals with certain privately bankrolled Polish factions; he accepted trainloads of Polish-bound American Quaker relief foodstuffs in exchange for what he knew to be slightly substandard hand grenades. When the grenades turned out to lack the requisite fuses the Polish generals who had arranged the deal were trotted out and shot. Hennies made a profit of more than fifty thousand dollars when he sold the Quakers' food to starving Germans on the black market.

Secure in private business, he made trips abroad, including the journey to Angola, where he also did a couple of small jobs for the German Secret Service, which, undaunted, still had designs on the Portuguese colony. Back in Berlin in 1923, he found a way to beat the disastrous inflation that would find the meaningless paper replaced by new gold-backed Rentenmarks. While it would literally take a basketful of the paper marks to get a new gold one, the German Railway's own gold notes already in circulation would be convertible on a one-to-one basis. Hennies' railway pals cut him in on a deal worth more than a million dollars, a deal to exchange uncirculated, and therefore illegal in terms of their convertibility, Railway notes. He was given a diplomatic passport, always useful, and sent to London, where he converted the uncirculated notes into

Swiss francs and pounds, a simple operation that netted him another hundred thousand. A sixth sense told him not to try it again a month later. In the event, the substitute courier was caught and the entire gang of more or less highly placed officials went to jail, where the ringleader, Postmaster General Dr. Anton Hofle, killed himself. Hennies was merely questioned and released, leaving only a small blot on his copy book.

Which brought Alves up to date. Hennies was perfect for Alves Reis's plan. . . .

As he began to go through the second dossier, he stretched, arched his stiff back, took off his glasses, rubbed his bloodshot eyes. His neck ached with accumulated tension, worry that the next day's meeting might not go well. He wondered at the coincidences that were leaping at him from the collected information. Greta Nordlund, for example. Out of the blue, she turns up not only as José's "true love" but as the main source of information about Adolf Hennies, one of her previous conquests. She was an actress, of course, and that explained her deplorable lack of constancy. But was she a good omen for his scheme? Would there be trouble between José and Hennies? He was not overjoyed when José told him happily that Greta was coming to Biarritz from Paris to sneak a few days' holiday with him. . . . Alves sighed, wishing he had a dossier on her.

Then there was the matter of the Dutchman José had come up with. Antonio Bandeira vouched for him in glowing terms, and José described him as just the man for any serious financial dealings, sober and experienced and extremely ambitious. While those were exactly the qualities required, Alves had his doubts. A prostitute in Paris—a friend of José's—had been one of the major contributors to Karel Marang's dossier, having quite recently given Marang aid and comfort following a particularly severe reversal. The man confided in a Parisian tart! Alves had been mortified at such behavior. José's reassurances that the woman was an old friend of both men and the benchmark of discretion had only partially eased Alves' doubts. . . .

Topping it all was the fact that Marang and Hennies were old business associates! Too many coincidences. It gave him an uneasy stomach. Either they would all work well together or there was too much inbreeding for anyone's good health. . . . But which was it going to be? Replacing his spectacles, he returned to the second dossier.

While Adolf Hennies was privately congratulating himself that he hadn't been caught with his hand in the national till on the Railway note matter and was at the same time restlessly casting about for new opportunities, his old Dutch colleague, Karel Marang, who had helped him change his marks into gulden, was concerned with a particularly intimate matter. Like a social disease, it could not be discussed with anyone, not even so liberal-minded a friend as José Bandeira, the younger brother of the Portuguese Minister to the Netherlands and a dashing fellow whom Marang knew to have been in and out of a scrape or two in his time. On the other hand, had he somehow contracted a social disease, José would have been the first person to whom Marang would have turned.

But the sober Dutchman, a reasonably good-looking man with a tidy little mustache and a tendency toward mousiness as well as a command of proper, academic French, had not come to Paris to sate himself at the Sphinx and other such *bagnias de luxe,* normally the haunts of Bandeira. He was newly arrived from The Hague in search of much headier stuff. Still, it was passion that brought him here, a passion that served as one of the obsessive engines of his life. He was calling on a baron. . . .

Marang's greatest attribute was an advanced degree in practical survival and manipulation. So far as education went, he had but little and that ill-taught. His family background was the sort he chose not to acknowledge, but Antonio had dug it out. Born in 1884 in a tiny suburb of Amsterdam called Dordrecht, he was the son of a strong-arm debt collector. Forever trying to divorce himself from the crumminess of his birthright, he was quick to learn how to make money. Among other lessons he learned was one that La Rochefoucauld put into admirable words— "To establish oneself in the world, one does all one can to seem established there already." It was a postulate that appealed to Alves' own sense of striving.

By 1914 he had put aside enough money to become a war profiteer, selling such items as Dutch chocolate, ham, wheat and oils to the Germans, who were, in his view, sure to win the war. Since Holland was neutral and since the Netherlands Overseas Trust made sure that businessmen sent nothing to the Germans that was on the Allies' prohibited list, Marang came face to face with the world of bribery, crooked customs officials and German agents. He found that he was at home in such improvisational interactions. And his foremost contact with the German Purchasing Commission was, of course, that helpful Swiss with the Brazilian mother, Adolf Hennies, who did well out of their business relationship, receiving a 10 percent rake-off on the gross value of all Marang's shipments to Germany.

But in 1917 the 50 percent profits he'd grown accustomed to were reduced to a maximum of 5 percent by the Netherlands Export Company, which regulated all imports and exports. Until the United States entered the war Marang had been doing a huge business in shipping American coal to Holland and then on to Germany, a scheme that came to grief with the arrival of the American Expeditionary Force and the new profit laws.

By 1920 he was prospering again, supplying coffee to Persia and the Middle East and African vegetable oils to Germany. By 1922 he bought out his partner, used the first floor of his four-story home in The Hague for offices and kept the top three floors as living quarters for his family—a wife and two sons—and several servants.

By 1924, when Alves was verging on his trip to the Oporto jail, the wheel had turned again: Marang had come upon hard times once more. The price of coffee had fallen sharply. He was substantially overextended. The day before he went to Paris, where José had reached him, his bookkeeper told him that, in baldest terms, he was more than a hundred thousand dollars in the hole and the banks holding his notes were growing restless.

His mission was not entirely unrelated to his economic future. For one thing it made him feel good just to stand outside the elegant apartment of Baron Rudolf August Louis Lehman, Minister Plenipotentiary of Liberia to the Third French Republic on the Bois de Boulogne, the most fashionable address in Paris, with a pair of Rothschild mansions nearby.

On the face of it, Marang's errand was simple: he wanted his Liberian diplomatic passport, ten years out of date, renewed. But beneath that simple application lay a tangled, desperate mass of motivations that struck directly to the heart of the man's life. Status, titles, money: an inseparable triumvirate composing all that made his life worth living. In the present instance, having little money, he counted on status—whether in the form of a diplomatic passport or a title or both—to confer that appearance of being well off, which could then lead to the fact itself.

Marang had come by the diplomatic passport in 1914, having paid Count Matzenauer de Matzenau, a Serbian who happened at the time to be Liberian Minister to Imperial Russia, eleven hundred dollars for it. Even then its value was much in doubt, since the count himself had been fired by the Liberian government the year before for abuses of his diplomatic privileges. The mere fact that a Serbian count held a Liberian diplomatic post reflected the confusing nature of international relations carried out in the period by marginally significant and almost always impoverished nations. Liberia, for example, qualified on both these counts. Even by 1923 Liberia's entire annual budget, derived solely from customs duties, totaled three hundred and eighty *thousand* dollars.

But human nature being what it was, there were always those who would gladly pay their own expenses as a Liberian diplomat in, say, Paris, in return for membership in the international community. The privileges were mainly social, but the quick thinker could also turn them into ready cash. Smuggling was a common activity, and so was discreet spying, as was the selling of various nonexistent diplomatic posts to whoever might pay for them—and thereby receive such privileges, on a small scale of course, for himself.

Marang had bought such a nonexistent position, which carried with it the legally useless document naming him representative to a government that Liberia did not even recognize—the Soviet Union. Still, the passport was occasionally useful, and, in any case, the count was supposed to carry out another chore included in the price—that is, he had guaranteed Marang that he would get Marang's name into the *Almanach de Gotha,* the standard and acknowledged listing of nobility.

It was all terribly complicated. In 1915 Marang had gone so far as to buy the title of the Manor of d'Ysselveere-les-Krimpen, which entitled him to call himself Karel Marang van Ysselveere if he thought it would do him any good. Which he not infrequently did; his Dutch passport, however, was still made out to plain old Karel Marang. The Liberian diplomatic passport was to be renewed with the noble *van Ysselveere* appended, exactly as it was written on his other somewhat unusual diplomatic documents, none of which included a passport—he was, oddly, the Consul General of the Central American republic of San Salvador and Consul General of Persia to The Hague.

Thus, according to the report of the grand horizontal Françoise, who comforted him several hours later, he found himself in the baron's anteroom taking in the apparent tons of ormolu, silk, marble and gilt, which made him all the more aware of his penurious arrival by Métro, the dust on his dark suit, the sweat on his forehead. He was counting on the renewal of the passport and the addition of *van Ysselveere* to work certain arcane wonders in terms of attracting new business opportunities, which would enable him to stave off the beastly bankers.

Alas, it was not to be.

The baron—who had himself paid dearly for his post as Liberian Minister to France and was a countryman of Marang's, who was himself as bogus as they came and certainly did not appear in the *Almanach de Gotha*—saw Marang for less than ten minutes. He most rudely told him to get the hell out; he was a busy man!

The joyless walk back to the small hotel just off the Champs-Elysées was an agony of despair for Marang. How to recover from this grievous, unexpected low blow? The automobiles, long and low-slung and elegant, exactly the sort of thing he'd always lusted for, with his initials and crest on the door, seemed to mock him as they swirled about the Arc de Triomphe. . . . Where was he to turn next? Which was when he remembered José's beautiful courtesan, Françoise. Whatever he decided to do with his life, he deserved a final splurge. He would lose himself inside her. . . .

When he returned to his hotel, deliverance was waiting for him at the concierge's desk.

A message had arrived from his friend José, who had traced him through his office in The Hague. There was a big deal in the wind, and dear old José requested his attendance at a meeting in Biarritz. . . .

* * *

The Bay of Biscay had a grayish-green look to Alves, altogether inhospitable, with breakers smashing against the huge boulders in wading reach of the shoreline. There was a brisk wind lacing the windows of the hotel room, shaking them in their frames, and the sun was only a gray blur above long, bleak, deserted beach. Earlier in the morning, rain had sprayed the tilting streets and the paving-brick sidewalks, had darkened the sand, rattled on the window glass. There was something about Biarritz that frightened him. The hotel was flung elegantly out on the end of an arm of land with thousands of miles of ocean beyond. In another week the establishment would be shuttered for the winter; as it was now, the Reis party was alone in the long, silent corridors, the echoing dining room, the gleaming mirrored bar.

The waiter had brought trays of brioches and croissants with butter and preserves, hot coffee and hot milk. The men in the tapestried suite gathered about the table. Alves sucked his cigarette, watched them buttering the rolls, sipping the light-brown coffee. Arnaldo stood talking to Hennies, who wore a black suit, white shirt with a stiff detached collar and a severe black tie, stood stiffly, spoke loudly and formally. José chatted with the Dutchman, Karel Marang, who seemed subdued, remote, cautious, though not precisely timid. His fingernails were bitten down to pink flesh. Everyone was evaluating everyone else, and Alves wanted to get past that opening stage as quickly as possible. These men constituted his team, but they must never be overly aware of their subordinate positions. He wanted a confident team. They would know what he wanted them to know, and they would have no worries.

He looked back out the window. A tall woman in a trenchcoat and broad-brimmed rain hat was walking in the street below, looking out at the sea, at the gnarled wind-swept trees on the huge rock formations. A lavender scarf ruffled in the wind. He watched until she moved on along the seawall. She had arrived alone the night before: José's mistress, Greta Nordlund. But more than a mistress, quite obviously: she did as she pleased. A very attractive woman, fair, Scandinavian. Like Biarritz, she rather frightened him. He nervously wished she had not come. This was business, after all.

"If you please, gentlemen? Perhaps we should begin." Arnaldo got everyone settled. Marang fidgeted in his chair, fussing with the creases of his flannel trousers. He seemed ill at ease, disconcerted by his blazer and ascot, a fling at resort wear that seemed at odds with his personality. His black shoes ruined the ensemble, unpolished and growing cracks. Hennies sat rigidly, licked marmalade from a thick finger.

"In the first place," Alves began, trying to shake the quaver from his voice, "let me thank you again for coming. I know how very busy you are. Before I begin let me place one very solemn stricture on all of us in this room. . . . Nothing said here must go beyond these walls." He cleared his throat and pushed his sweating palms into the pockets of his jacket, hoping his nerves weren't communicating themselves. Was that a sneer playing at Hennies' mouth? "The government of Portugal and the Bank of Portugal are depending on us, trusting to our discretion and absolute silence."

Hennies grunted abruptly. "We are not children here, you know." He glanced at Marang with a broad wink that caused his monocle to drop from his eye, dangle from the black ribbon. "We have kept secrets before, eh, Marang?" Marang nodded, motioned to Reis to continue.

Quickly he ran through what he had told José and Arnaldo a week before.

"Angola desperately needs an injection of money— that's what it comes down to—if it is to survive. Otherwise, anarchy, inevitably war, foreign mercenaries, factions of all kinds, grabbing for power . . ." He shrugged. "The works. . . . And the government in Lisbon has tried everything. Banks all across Europe have been approached for loans in the sum of one million pounds sterling—five million American dollars! And do you know what they said?"

Hennies guffawed. "I know what I'd say. . . . I might *buy* Angola for a million pounds! My God, it's twice the size of Texas. But I wouldn't loan a ha'penny."

"You are indeed well informed, Herr Hennies," Alves said.

"Germany has found Angola of interest for some time. As you Portuguese know." Hennies' voice had gone suddenly cold.

Alves hurried on. "That is precisely what the bankers said. Purchase, yes . . . loan, no. There are no external sources of financing for Angola. None." Alves lit another cigarette and went to the table, where he poured himself coffee and cream.

"You brought us all this way to tell us that?" Hennies sighed heavily. "What have we got to do with Angola's troubles? I thought you were through with Africa, Senhor Reis."

"Portugal has faced financial difficulties before, as has every nation in Europe," Alves said firmly. "As you may or may not know, the Bank of Portugal, which is for the most part in private hands, is empowered to issue bank-notes—that is, the bank rather than the government. Such an enormous power—privilege if you will—can make the state the slave, as it were, of the bank. In the end it all comes down to money, doesn't it? And the bank has the power in Portugal.

"Years ago when the government turned the power over to the bank the license allowed for the issuing of currency in the amount of twice the bank's paid-up capital."

Marang smiled cynically; José looked blank, as if his mind were frolicking with the actress. Hennies snorted. "Twice, ha!"

"Hennies has a point," Alves continued. "As of this past summer the bank, to back up the government in variety of crises, has issued notes equivalent to more than one hundred times the bank's capital. The fact is, secret issues of currency have become habitual, though they have not been convertible to either gold or silver for more than thirty years. However, with each issue, the need for secrecy has increased. Since 1918 the total number of escudos issued by the bank has increased six times, accounting for the present low value of the escudo. . . .

"Which brings us to the point of our meeting. My close friends at the Bank of Portugal, who must for obvious reasons of security remain nameless, have agreed to a further secret issuance of banknotes, this time for Angola."

"Another Germany," Hennies barked, running a finger inside his collar, which had left a red mark against the solid rolls of fat. "They have had plenty of practice at printing money!"

Marang chuckled behind his hand. José yawned. Arnaldo filled his coffee cup. Alves went on, hearing the wind racketing outside.

"But it is a most delicate matter, as you can see. I have been asked by my friends at the bank to consider their predicament and this proposition. They are willing to pay a two percent commission to those who can arrange such a loan for Angola—a loan of one million pounds sterling, five million dollars." He paused and looked at the four faces. "The commission figures out to one hundred thousand dollars."

"Senhor Reis, excuse me," Marang said quietly. "But I am confused. You speak of a new issue of currency in one breath, a mysterious loan in the next. Which is it to be?"

"Both. In reality we are talking about an injection of a million pounds' worth of escudos into Angola to tide the colony over. On the surface of things, we are to present ourselves as a financial syndicate willing to loan the million pounds to the colony—present ourselves to the firm we deal with to print the banknotes, that is. In return for our most substantial 'loan,' we—the financial syndicate—will of course be repaid over a period of five years, plus customary interest, by the Angolan treasury. In addition, we are empowered to print, or cause to be printed, up to one million pounds of Angolan currency. . . . That is how we present ourselves. Do you follow me, gentlemen?"

Blank stares, wheels going around behind vacant eyes. Greed, Alves thought, I am watching greed come to life.

"That is the surface of the matter, then. As far as the printer can see, we stand—possibly—to make back our million-pound investment plus interest: but what matters is the fact that we have been empowered by a sovereign nation to print colonial banknotes . . . to print money. More than payment enough, surely, for such a loan. Thus, the surface of things. . . ." He paused for the description of their task to sink in. He lit another cigarette, coughed.

"Now to reality. If you are with me, that is—and I invite your questions later, of course. We are not, obviously, lending a million pounds to anyone. The Bank of Portugal, at the request of the government, *is* pumping a million pounds into the colony, in escudos of course. We are merely arranging with the greatest possible discretion the actual printing of the money. We will take delivery of the new notes. The High Commissioner to Angola will actually see to the transshipment to Luanda. What could be simpler, really? Our primary responsibility is to find the printer and collect our twenty thousand pounds.

"What are your thoughts, gentlemen?"

Alves finally sat down behind a gold-and-white desk, made a bridge of his fingers. Surprisingly Marang, his torso curling forward over his knees, spoke first.

"Tell me, please, what reputable printer will believe this fairy tale about our heading a syndicate that lends such sums to a colony well known to be nearly bankrupt? And who will believe that sane men would accept payment in worthless Angolan currency that is unwelcome anywhere else in the world?" He looked down at his feet, where a bit of white ankle flashed between a falling sock and a hiked-up flannel pants leg.

"The new Angolan banknotes are not payments," Alves said. "They are a bonus, an added inducement to this syndicate. In addition to our interest and principal, we may be planning investments in Angola, we may know of mineral deposits, there may be any of a thousand reasons . . . because it doesn't make any difference to the printer, it's none of his business. We have the documents from my friends at the bank—that's all any printer will care about. So we're accepting a ton of what he believes to be worthless currency . . . so what? The printer doesn't have to believe we're geniuses!"

Marang nodded, eyes hooded, a faint smile on his pale gray face.

"Well, what I don't understand, Reis," Hennies said, jumping to his feet and stumping back and forth beneath a gilt mirror, "is what the hell all this subterfuge is about. Why the hell doesn't the bank just tell the printer the truth and forget about using you and your phony syndicate? The Bank of Portugal is well versed in dealing with printers— why not just go to the printers they've dealt with before and run off another batch of notes?"

Alves leaned back in his chair, tucked his thumbs into his vest pockets and sighed.

"Let's think about that. Why is the Bank of Portugal going to all this trouble? Arnaldo?"

"Mystery to me," Arnaldo said.

"José? José, for God's sake, pay attention!"

"I am paying attention, Alves," José said, hurt. "It's just that I don't know either. So don't pick on me."

Alves closed his eyes, took a deep breath. "In the first place, Portuguese money is worth considerably less than the great hard currencies, the British pound and the American dollar. In the second place, Angola would be best off with an injection of such a hard, gold- or silver-backed, currency. Well, then, say that news of this matter we're conducting should leak out—such things happen, the Lisbon newspapers love it, as you know. So say the word leaks out—and the word is that a syndicate headed by a Dutch businessman, Herr Marang van Ysselveere here, has lent a million pounds sterling to poor Angola." He caught Marang's eye. Hennies was squinting intently through the glass disk.

"Such a controlled leak," Alves said, "would produce a not entirely unhappy effect. It would appear that a vast amount of hard currency had found its way to Angola and therefore there must be something in Angola worth investing in. And more investments by other speculators might well be forthcoming. . . . Surely this is a clear and valid point. But suppose the same leak occurred and the printer had been told the truth—remember, truth or fabrication, it's all the same to the printer. . . . Well, my friend, we're back to the nub of the entire matter. Portugal does not want to be seen in the act of bailing Angola out yet again . . . and further inflating its own currency in the process. Thus, my friends at the bank have come up with their little fiction . . . which stands to make us twenty thousand pounds. A hundred thousand American." Alves stood up. "If there are no more questions for the moment, I suggest we go downstairs for an early lunch. We've had a busy morning."

Since the meeting was being held in his suite, Alves waited until everyone had left, whispering to Arnaldo to arrange for Hennies and Marang to have a table of their own at lunch. "Give them time to come up with any complaints. We can deal with them this afternoon—better to have them start doubting now instead of later." Alone, he bathed his face with a cold towel, shaved for a second time. He'd been unable to sleep, had risen at five o'clock and gone over his presentation of the plans. He had a headache. He went to the window, pushed it open to air out the room. The tall woman with the trenchcoat had come back, was sitting on a bench facing the sea reading a book, some parcels beside her. Greta Nordlund. One look and you knew she'd cost her man a fortune. He hoped José had done very well indeed in The Hague for his own sake.

He was thinking about Hennies' hefty bankroll and Marang's well-bitten fingernails when he reached the street, which curved slowly past sidewalk cafés with locked doors, then sharply back above the beach toward the casino and the town center. He stood for a moment breathing deeply. The woman was still sitting on the bench, engrossed in

her book. Her blond hair fell softly from beneath the rain
hat, disappeared in the folds of lavender scarf. Finally, he
turned and went right, looking down at the dark-brown,
wet sand stretching in a slight curve all the way to a distant lighthouse.

The morning had gone well. He'd given them something
to think about over lunch. The afternoon would be the test.
As he walked along the seawall he recognized the fact that
he had never felt such anxiety, not even waiting for the
great train ride, not even in the middle of the High Bridge
where he'd felt so alone. This . . . this was the most dangerous ride of all.

He felt it was important that his new colleagues be left
to lunch alone. He did not want to be their friend, at least
not at this early stage. They were businessmen, far more
experienced than he, older and with more money. . . . All
he had to offer was his plan, his friends at the Bank of
Portugal, the commission they promised and the possibility,
however vague, that there might be more where that came
from.

At the tobacconist they spoke only French, and his was
rudimentary at best. He pointed to the cigarettes he wanted,
let the old woman with the bright henna rinse take what
he hoped was the proper number of coins from his palm.
He ripped open the pack and lit one, inhaling the vicious
French tobacco with a vengeance of his own. It tasted fine.
"*Merci, madame,*" he said. She nodded, puffed her cigar.

The wind shifted, he felt the spray on his face. What did
he think about *them?* His dossiers were full: Hennies had
been a spy. Marang had been a war profiteer, but, then,
that was a charge that counted for little these days, not
particularly impressive but conservative and sound. He
should fit nicely as the head of the syndicate; surely he
would stand up to investigation should that time come. And
Hennies, too overt and most decidedly too German to head
the syndicate even if it existed in name only, had the money
necessary to carry the scheme through to success. Arnaldo's
financial report, collected through Lisbon's information-
gathering services, had been optimistic, though vague questions had been raised about his private enterprises. Nobody
was perfect. So far, he believed these men could do the
jobs he had in mind for them.

He crossed the street to a large restaurant, where light
gleamed from beyond a row of heavy colonnades. The

streetside tables were located beneath an overhang, and he sat down in one of the wicker chairs. He ordered a ham-and-cheese sandwich, *jambon et fromage,* which he managed in schoolboy French, and a glass of beer. He was nibbling, not noticing the taste, when he saw the woman in the trenchcoat across the street watching the restaurant. Then she seemed to make up her mind, came toward him with long strides, packages in one hand, her book tucked under her arm. There was something about her, something frightening. She seemed so confident, so tall . . . so fair, so unlike Maria. . . .

"Excuse me, Senhor Reis," she said, towering over him as he struggled out of the tight grip of the wicker chair, "may I join you?" She was already seated by the time he was replying that he found the thought enchanting. She whipped her hat off with a grand gesture, brushed her blond hair, caressing her pale cheek, and placed hat and parcels in another chair. The novel in English was *The Green Hat.* He'd read it in the Oporto jail—it was perfect for such a creature of the great world.

"Mademoiselle Nordlund," the waiter whispered discreetly, "a pleasure to see you again. Pernod?"

"If you please," she said with a smile of practiced condescension. "And the escargot. And following that the sautéed veal and perhaps a beggar's cake to finish. And *café au lait.*" She looked up at the beetle-browed man who seemed about to tilt into Senhor Reis's beer. "Thank you, Maurice, for remembering Pernod. . . ." Maurice sped contentedly away, and she turned lavender eyes behind heavily painted lashes on Alves. "I'm famished—such a huge appetite you're thinking, aren't you? Not at all lady-like. I've been walking for hours, shopping, reading." She had a powerful voice that seemed to come from deep within her chest. When she spoke softly, as she was now, there was a catch in it, a hoarseness, as if she'd strained it shouting.

"I know," he said. "That you've been walking, I mean. I've been watching you this morning."

"I beg your pardon?" Mock surprise. "Spying? Senhor Reis, shame on you!"

"From the window where we're meeting, my suite actually. It looks down on the sea road. Every time I looked out, there you were, walking or reading or looking at the ocean. . . ."

"Well, I hope I didn't distract you from your great business deal. And, please, tell me if I'm intruding on your thoughts. Deep thoughts, I presume. International finance, intrigue." Caprice danced on every word. Was she making sport of him?

He fidgeted in the chair, aware of the way she was smiling at him. Her smiles conveyed a confusing range of attitudes. Alves was disconcerted by her presence. "I'm very glad you're here. A most welcome change from Herr Hennies' monocle and Marang's chewed fingernails, I assure you."

She smiled a new way. "Aha, a wit! José's circle is not known for wit. But you're so clever for a Portuguese. José has told me about your many feats!"

"You've discovered a new side to Alves Reis." He sipped the beer, ignoring the sandwich. He wasn't hungry anymore. He watched her drink the Pernod. She drank like a man, enjoying it. "José tells me that you are an actress."

The escargot arrived in their shells, and she tweezed one free, dipped it in garlic butter, savored it with eyes closed. "I'm a good deal more than 'an actress.' I am a star, Senhor Reis, in four languages, as a matter of fact. The Scandinavian Bernhardt, according to the critics of France, Germany, the Netherlands and Norway. . . ." She winked over another escargot, slid it daintily onto her tongue. "You, Senhor Reis, Portuguese financier—that's how José refers to you—are lunching in fashionable Biarritz with the Scandinavian Bernhardt, Greta Nordlund—an item for the press, don't you think? Portuguese mystery man and so on?"

"You are teasing me," he said anxiously, fumbling for one of his French cigarettes. He wasn't sure he was enjoying this. It was like playing a game.

"Flirting," she said. "Boring you too, no doubt." It was she who sounded suddenly bored.

"Certainly not," he said, added: "I've never met an actress before. I've been in Africa. There weren't many actresses there. I saw *Camille* once . . . on stage." He shrugged. "I am not a sophisticated man. Flirting . . . that is beyond me. I am sorry. Truly, I am." He lit the cigarette. The breeze leaped up, blew out the match.

"You have lied to me. You are obviously an outrageous flirt. I must warn José about you." She admired the newly arrived veal. "He fancies himself the ladies' man in your little group, you know."

"Oh, I wish you wouldn't do that—"

"For heaven's sake, relax," she interrupted impatiently. "I *am* teasing you."

Alves had begun to perspire. He watched her carve a large bite of veal. He'd never seen a woman with such a determined appetite.

"I should have known you were the serious, thoughtful fellow . . . but Adolf says you're an Oxford man. I've known Oxford men. What a bunch. They talk too much about Oxford."

Oh God, he thought. This woman was definitely more than he cared to handle.

"Oxford," he said, "was such a long time ago."

"And it happened in another country, I know, I know. Well, you're to be congratulated on refusing to turn every chance remark to cricket, the High Street, your favorite porter, walnuts and a hearty port by the crackling fire. . . ." She took a deep breath. Alves had not the foggiest notion of what she was talking about. Wisely he remained silent, wondering what time it was.

"I've just finished doing Ibsen in Berlin, can you imagine anything more depressing? Well, let me tell you there is nothing more depressing, unless you should fall prey to a madman and do Strindberg and Ibsen in repertory in Berlin. I'm raving, aren't I? Well, that's what happens to actresses who are recovering from a run." She thoughtfully dispatched another morsel of veal. Her cheekbones were high, her mouth wide and especially sensual. She seemed to wear no makeup other than that which adhered to her lashes. There was the faintest suggestion of pale down on her jawline.

"Soon I begin a run in Paris," she continued after patting her mouth with the pristine napkin. "Cleopatra in Shaw's *Caesar and Cleopatra,* a wonderful role for which I am much too tall and fair. So an absolute giant must be found to do Julius Caesar, and I shall spend the entire run in long black wigs of rope and dark, dark makeup. . . ." She looked into Alves' eyes. "And I can't wait to go into rehearsal."

He knowingly nodded. She might as well have been speaking Chinese for all he knew about the theater. He resolved to read this Cleopatra play. After all, now he knew an actress.

"So I wait," she said hoarsely, a sound a man could grow fond of. "And I come to Biarritz with José. Are you curious about José and me?"

"It's none of my business."

"Well, yes and no, but I sense that you are curious. Let me tell you this, since we may be seeing something of each other in the course of your new project with José. He is not a *great* love, do you understand? We met in The Hague last year. We get on well, we please each other. Something of a dalliance. It won't interfere with your work." She pushed the plate away, and Maurice materialized with the beggar's cake and coffee. "Now, you must return to your associates and leave me to my novel." She smiled, dazzling this time, eyes wide and innocent, her slim fingers on Alves' sleeve. He bowed slightly.

"It has been enchanting." He added, catching her eye quite bravely, "I shall hope we meet again."

"*Moi aussi,*" she said, gently dismissing him.

Mind reeling, Alves Reis, newly anointed wit, walked slowly back to business.

*   *   *

Adolf Hennies greeted him with a hearty belch and a slap on the back. He was unwrapping an Upmann cigar. Marang was seated quietly in the same chair he'd adorned in the morning. José was massaging his temples, trying to dispel the effects of too much luncheon burgundy. Arnaldo was standing at Alves' table, holding Alves' briefcase, waiting patiently. Alves took him by the arm and drew him to the window, where they stood with their backs to the others.

"And what mood are they in?" he asked.

Arnaldo shrugged. "They have some questions about you. I reassured them, but it will come up. They are committed in their minds—it remains to clinch the deal. Don't worry."

"Oh, that's easy for you to say."

"Did you have a pleasant lunch?"

"Why, yes," Alves said. "Yes, I did have quite a pleasant lunch."

"That's good. You didn't drink wine, did you?"

"Arnaldo, am I a child that you ask such questions?"

"You didn't, did you? Look at José."

"No, no, I did not drink wine! My God, call the meeting to order."

"Gentlemen, if you please." Arnaldo waited until they were quiet—no great problem in the case of José—then nodded to Reis and sat.

"I hope you have given the proposition some thought," Alves said, trying to sound remote, unconcerned. "Let me make it clear that I have not reached a final decision myself. I am presenting the possibility for your consideration. Does it seem a favorable position for us, gentlemen?"

Marang spoke first in his shy voice, carefully choosing his words, looking into his lap rather than at Reis.

"There is merit in what you suggest. I speak for myself, but I feel sure that Herr Hennies shares my evaluation. However, there is a point upon which we must be satisfied. I hope you accept our concern and curiosity in a purely business sense—"

"Nothing personal," Hennies interrupted. "A simple question—namely, what is this business about your going to jail in Oporto? We have been led to believe by our sources that you were up on a charge of fraud and embezzlement. . . ." The only sound in the room was José breathing heavily through his mouth. "Now if this is so, why in hell does the Bank of Portugal choose you?"

Arnaldo stood and cleared his throat, fists tightly clenched at his sides.

"There is no need for Senhor Reis to defend himself against such implications. Whatever fraud there may have been, I assure you, was on the side of those who made the accusations against him. Small men motivated by jealousy and heaven only knows what intrigues of their own. As you see, he is here among us today, utterly free and trusted by the Bank in the most delicate matter imaginable." He stopped long enough to flip open the briefcase and extract several sheets of newsprint, which he handed around to José, who didn't really give a damn, and to Hennies and Marang, who did. "These are reprints from the major Lisbon newspapers. Vindicating Senhor Reis. In fact, at this very moment, our attorneys in Lisbon are contemplating lawsuits naming the men who brought this contemptible action. Please, read them."

Alves leaned back in his chair, arms crossed, a faint smile of surprise on his face. Could this be Arnaldo, the faithful aide who always stayed in the background, sought the shadows? The fictional attorneys, that was a lovely touch.

"And while you are reading let me remind you of Senhor Reis' remarkable career." Arnaldo was off again, gathering steam. "He is a graduate of Oxford, a master engineer. He has held two of the highest posts in the colony of Angola, chief engineer of the Royal Angola Railways and Inspector of Public Works. He has been honored by both the railway and the government. In effect, by introducing the most modern American locomotives to Angola, he has delivered the colony into the twentieth century—he is a part of African history, gentlemen. And he has also established himself as a businessman of note, both in Luanda and Lisbon. And while still a young man, not yet thirty! I suggest that you consider your great good fortune at having the opportunity to be associated with him in this venture rather than sitting here carping about his misfortunes, which were demonstrably part of a nefarious plot against him." Arnaldo came up for air, decided that he had said enough and sat down, concluding: "This is not a productive line of inquiry. We might better spend our limited time on substantive matters." Feeling a flood of pride, Alves removed his spectacles, turned to watch the rain on the window. Was she still out there?

Marang, struggling to control his chagrin and smooth matters over, said, "I have no reason to pursue the matter further. Hennies?"

Hennies put the paper aside and puffed the cigar, shook his head without speaking.

"Well," Alves said with the smile still clinging, "let me suggest that you exercise your option to withdraw now. You are my first choices in this matter, but I will understand if you feel you are not prepared to continue. In? Or out?"

"In," Marang whispered so discreetly that Alves barely heard.

"*Ja, ja,* in, in," Hennies barked impatiently. His monocle caught the lamplight, flashed like a jewel. He reached across the table and clapped Arnaldo's knee. Arnaldo nodded self-consciously.

"In any case," Alves said, "the contracts are being prepared in Lisbon now and that is all that matters, isn't it? Now, there are certain other matters to go over if we've put this behind us. . . . There is the matter of finances.

My legal defense was ruinously expensive and my enemies have caused certain business reversals. It is nothing I make a secret of. Which is where our associate Herr Hennies comes in, I'm afraid. . . . There are expenses involved in obtaining such a lucrative contract, a contract for which there is bound to be very high bidding within certain very private circles. My close friendships with those in power gives us the inside track, the first chance—if, however, we fail to satisfy their requirements, well, friendship goes only so far." Alves delivered a worldly shrug, palms up. The wind whistled outside.

"Bribes!" Hennies cried, slapping a heavy fist on the arm of the couch. "This is more like it! Money makes friends, I always say. Buy a friend, keep up the payments, and he is yours forever. . . ."

"There is much in what you say," Alves said.

"I'm not sure I like your *close friends* at the Bank of Portugal." Marang, inexplicably to Alves, seemed vaguely shocked at such goings-on. "Such things are unthinkable in a Dutch bank . . . but, of course—"

"Portugal is another country," Hennies said.

"Full of happy, simple peasants," Marang said sarcastically, nibbling on a moist fingertip.

"How much do they want?" Hennies asked abruptly.

"Initially a thousand pounds," Alves said.

"Good gracious." Marang sighed. "Initially?"

"We are dealing in large figures," Alves said. "And there may well be more opportunities once we have completed this one. There are several people involved. I see no point in making rash promises to you I can't keep—a thousand pounds it is. You, Marang, will serve as the head of our syndicate—a fiction, of course, but your demeanor, your style are perfect. Have you any objections?"

"No, I suppose not."

The afternoon wore on. The rain began again. José yawned. Finally there was nothing more to be said.

"Two weeks from today," Alves said, "I will expect you all to meet with me in Lisbon. I will have all the documents at that time. And I promise better weather." He crushed his last cigarette. "Thank you for your attention and wisdom. Arnaldo, wake José."

Hennies and Marang took the night train to Paris. José and Greta went off together. Arnaldo and Alves dined quietly at a small restaurant overlooking a narrow set of steps that led down to the beach. "Thank God, that's over," Arnaldo said. "We have begun."

Alves was keyed up, and once Arnaldo had padded off yawning to his room he decided to take the night air. The rain had stopped again, but the breeze was heavy, ever moving. His steps echoed as he walked the narrow streets. The same restaurant where he'd lunched was still open. A recording was playing somewhere in its recesses. Several regulars at the bar were drinking silently. He sat down at his same table and ordered a Pernod. He looked at the empty chair where the actress had sat. He could see her face before him, the slender hands, the lavender scarf. The Scandinavian Bernhardt, she'd said. He would have to look into that. He drank the Pernod slowly. Well, if nothing else came of it, at least Hennies' check for a thousand pounds was in his wallet. That would stave off his own bankruptcy for a bit. . . . He thought about José and Greta, doubtless entwined at this moment in the aftermath of passion. He was a handsome fellow, but he seemed hardly a match for such a woman. . . .

In two weeks more bribes would certainly be required. Those bankers were a greedy lot. He smiled to himself. He wondered if Greta would come to Lisbon. . . . He was of two minds about that prospect. What an unusual woman! . . .

*　　*　　*

Maria's pregnancy had progressed more rapidly than expected, and the latest addition to the family seemed imminent when Alves got off the train at Rossio Station. He was met by his father-in-law, who conveyed him somewhat anxiously to the flat, which seemed to be seething with people. There were the children, in various stages of undress, overseen by a very fat woman who was serving as nurse/housekeeper. There were two neighbor women, whose aprons were covered with food, sweating in the heat generated by the spaghetti bubbling in the kitchen. There was a gray-haired, efficient midwife Alves had never met before. There was a youngish doctor who was more concerned with a plate of spaghetti that had been pressed on him by the perspiring twosome. Maria's mother hovered like a tent that had blown loose from its moorings. Maria was propped up in a large chair in the bedroom, oblivious to the buzz around her. "Alves!" she cried, holding out her arms. "You're home, my darling—and I thought the baby might come while you were away!" He knelt beside her chair, taking her hands in his, placing his ear against her belly. "So strong," she sighed. "He'll be a soccer player, he's such a mighty kicker."

Alves whispered, "I love you, little wife." She stroked his black hair, mussing it, cooing to him. "When will it happen?" he whispered.

"Soon, very soon. They come faster each time, easier. . . ." She leaned forward to kiss the top of his head.

The imminence of the birth proved to be somewhat overstated. The day after his return it became apparent that it might be another week. The neighbor ladies relaxed, the midwife went on to other clients. The nurse remained during the days and Maria's mother slept on a couch in the living room. Alves tried to stay well out of the way, play with the children and appear the doting family man. But his mind was racing ahead, fitting the next pieces of his plan into place, and Arnaldo kept dropping by to ask if Alves had yet seen his friends at the bank about the crucial documents.

"What do you think I am?" Alves would say. The conversations were always carried on in tense whispers in the hallway. "Can't you see this madhouse I'm living in? How can I get on with anything? My mother-in-law has turned me into an errand boy! The children cry when I leave. . . . Listen to them, there's never any quiet!"

"You need an office," Arnaldo said. "Leave it to me. Remember, you are Alves Reis."

"Yes, I must not forget who I am and what my mission is. Find the office, somewhere in the Baixa. Near the bank, nothing lavish. But a place where I can be alone."

On his fourth day at home he dressed for business, told Maria he had an important appointment and went to his own bank, the Ultramarino, to deposit Hennies' check. He then visited two particularly anxious creditors and thereby averted being taken to court. And finally he went to the small second-story office Arnaldo had found within a matter of hours.

"Less than five minutes from the bank itself," Arnaldo said proudly. The two desks, the old wooden filing cabinet, the gooseneck lamp, the straight-backed chairs, the two windows encrusted with thick dust, the beat-up 1918 Smith typewriter: indeed, it was all he could have wanted for the exceedingly low price. A return to more luxurious quarters would come later.

"It's exactly right," he said. From his window he could look across the street to the display window of a large stationer, a window bearing the almost unnoticeable official seal. Perfect, absolutely perfect. Before Arnaldo left, Alves gave him a hundred pounds in cash—five hundred dollars American. "For your expenses . . . and your first paycheck from our new enterprise. Treat yourself. You've earned it—and say nothing to José." Impulsively he hugged Arnaldo. "I'll be in touch when I've something to report."

From the fly-specked window he watched Arnaldo stride jauntily down the street. Now it was time for business. He began by making a list of what he needed, laboriously batting it out on the rickety Smith.

It was dark outside by the time he had outlined his requirements.

In the first place, he did not know a single soul at the Bank of Portugal. He'd almost begun believing the story he'd told his new associates in Biarritz.

In the second place, he did know that the Bank of Portugal had the power to issue printing orders for new currency . . . the power to issue contracts for the printing of new money. Whoever carried such a contract carried the power of the Bank of Portugal.

Such a contract was merely a piece of paper, a special kind of paper—*papel selado,* which bore the Portuguese seal and by so doing acquired a solemn dignity and validity that went unchallenged. *Papel selado* automatically transformed all business contracts and all written documents passing between the public and the government into official sanction.

The stamped paper could be purchased by anyone but only at specially licensed outlets, such as the nearby stationer. Applications for a job or a passport, a birth certificate, a death notice or a deed of sale—all required *papel selado.* A simple folded sheet with four lined sides, the words *Imposta do Selo* printed at the top of the first and fourth pages. The tax was less than a dime. Alves bought several sheets the next morning, in addition to sealing wax, and at the goldsmith's a few blocks away a ring bearing the Portuguese seal. He then returned to the office, locked the door, forced one of the windows for ventilation and sat down at the typewriter.

He had already composed several drafts of the contract granted to him by the Bank of Portugal for the printing of money. It was simple, not overly specific, granting him the *power*. Now he carefully rolled the paper into the Smith and began typing. He worked well into the evening with a brief stop back at the flat for dinner—noise, crying children, Maria in discomfort, her mother irritated by his lengthy absence—before returning to his nonstop "meeting."

By midnight he sat back with a sense of satisfaction, peeled off his spectacles, rubbed his eyes. He thought for a moment of the night he'd spent with the Oxford diploma, how Arnaldo had dropped by to see his handiwork. But not even Arnaldo could see this yet. . . . Circles of sweat stained the armpits of his striped shirt. He unsnapped the collar and laid it beside his glasses, yawned, poured coffee from the tin pot on the electric ring. Two ashtrays overflowed with cigarette butts. His shoulders ached from nervous tension and the hours hunched over the typewriter.

He sipped the coffee, stared at the result of his long day. With the contract so close to final form he could very nearly smell and taste the power that would soon be his. Just a piece of paper, just the appearance of reality . . . He remembered the old story of the captain from Koepenich who had been nothing but a beggar until he had clothed himself in the uniform of a Prussian army officer. Magic! Nothing less. Now Alves Reis was the magician.

He was tired and there was a chill in the air with the wind scurrying up the dark, empty streets from the Tagus. He turned the collar of his raincoat up and shivered. He walked past the gray, faceless expanses of the Bank of Portugal. Casually, he blew it a kiss. Passing Eiffel's elevator, he heard the cry of an army sentry from the barracks above: "Twelve o'clock and all is well!" The call came floating in English, a remembrance of Wellington's presence. He smiled in the night as he scuffed along. On the whole he agreed with the sentry.

The children were asleep. His mother-in-law snored on the couch. Maria sighed, turning in her sleep, her bulk in the center of the bed. He took off his shoes, which were small and too tight in the Portuguese fashion, and slid them quietly under the bed, lit the day's last bedraggled cigarette, yawned from his honest labors. He dreamed of Biarritz, sitting among the colonnades. . . .

The morning arrived much too soon, with the shouts of the children and the smells of breakfast. Maria's condition seemed static; he kissed her goodbye and set off for another round of business meetings. The fact was he needed to have his *papel selado* notarized, a government requirement.

Every Portuguese contract, every use of a businessman's signature on a legal document, required by law a notarial seal. When going into business, a Portuguese "opened a signature" with a notary by simply placing his signature on file. Thereafter each contract entered into by the businessman would bear that notary's seal, having been applied once the signature on the contract was checked against the one on file. In return for this simple service the notary was paid a small fee and, more lucratively, 1 percent of the value of the contract—except in the case of government contracts. The notary was charged with reading the contract with great care, ferreting out any illegalities. Being a notary was a gold mine.

That morning Alves went to see his notary, Dr. Avelino de Faria, who was out and thereby missed the chance of playing a part in such a remarkable scheme. His assistant was young and always awed by Senhor Reis' exploits, anxious to help with the hope of hearing more stories of Africa. Certainly in the case of Senhor Reis there was no need to waste time with reading the contract—after all, everyone knew who Reis was. He quickly applied the notary's stamp and signature. Then he wondered, with an excess of courage, if Reis might like to join him later for lunch. But, Alves explained, that would be impossible since he had an important appointment at the British consulate.

Each foreign consulate kept on file signatures of all qualified notaries and could therefore verify the notarized application on any *papel selado*. It was not a necessary addition to the document, but Alves wasn't concerned about the necessities: he liked the majestic, overwhelming appearance of the consular stamps. At the British consul a quick check was made of the records and the handsome stamp affixed. From there he went from one consulate to another, French and German and Spanish and Italian and Swedish and Dutch, having one glorious stamp after an-

other added to his contract. By evening he was carrying
a document of startling magnificence, though it was still
incomplete. Exhausted, tie askew, stomach growling, he
arrived back at the flat. Spaghetti, for God's sake! Apparently that was all the nurse/housekeeper/cook could
cook. . . . Maria was perspiring heavily in the bedroom,
having gone through another false labor alarm. The midwife hovered. Maria slept fitfully. He tried to find a place
to nap but finally gave up. There were hundreds, no, thousands of women milling about the flat. With Maria asleep,
he left, sucking in the cool night air, and walked to his
tiny, quiet office.

As he'd made his rounds during the day he had gone
from good humor to a queasy anxiety now that the fog
had rolled up through the commercial district, floating in
the street beyond his window. The loneliness of his situation was making itself felt in an unpleasant, stomach-
wrenching way. He could confide in no one, not José, not
even Arnaldo. He was bound in silence to his plan, and
there would be no confidants, no one to discuss his feats
with, no one to gain strength from when he doubted his
own ability. . . . He shook his head glumly at the empty
street below. He sat down at the desk and began his night's
work. First he retyped the contract on another sheet of
papel selado, improving as he went, adding a flourish here
and there, bits of official jargon he'd forgotten on the
earlier versions. He typed very slowly, made sure there
were no badly registered keys. Could this self-doubting
wreck, he reflected ruefully, possibly be the same man of
affairs who had conducted business only last week in
Biarritz?

The next step—acquiring the official signatures. Not so
difficult as it might first appear. The signatures appeared
on many official documents and proclamations. Painstakingly, he simply traced them onto the papel selado.

Francisco da Cunha Rego Chaves, the High Commissioner of Angola.

Daniel Rodriguez, the Minister of Finance.

Delfim Costa, a Representative of the Portuguese Government.

With a straight razor he cut off the two full pages of
notarizations from the first document, attaching them with
tape to the second signed contract. Then he struck a match
and melted a large crimson drop of sealing wax at the

bottom of the last page. From his vest pocket he took the signet ring bearing the Portuguese coat of arms and pressed it firmly into the congealing wax. To complete the document he taped two brand-new Portuguese banknotes above the wax—a one-thousand-escudo note, then worth about fifty dollars, and a five-hundred-escudo note. He assumed that these would be the best notes for the syndicate to have the right to print in return for the five-million-dollar loan to impoverished Angola.

On the whole it looked just fine.

The next day Maria was delivered of her fourth son. Caught up in the events surrounding the birth and the beloved mother's recuperation, he found the days flying past. He cabled Hennies and Marang that accommodations had been arranged for them at Lisbon's finest hotel, the Avenida Palace.

That evening he sat beside Maria, holding her hand.

"I am so proud of you, my love," he whispered. "Such a fine new son. . . ."

"I do so wish we had more room, Alves. A nursery, separate bedrooms for the boys . . . room for the nurse to stay with us." She lowered her dark, thick lashes. "I am so weak, Alves . . . and the past months have been so . . . hard. For both of us, I know, but for me here alone without you. . . ." A tiny tear escaped from behind the lashes. "Selling everything, all my little jewels, the silver, the runabout . . . watching as they took it all away. . . ." There was a sob stifled in her throat, and Alves kissed her mouth gently.

"Soon you will have more than you have ever dreamed of, my darling. You will forget what you have been through. My beloved, there are wonders ahead."

"But how, my darling?" It was the first time she had ever asked about his public life.

"All I ask is that you believe me. . . . Have I ever failed you?"

When he gazed up into her glistening eyes all that he saw was a certain understandable confusion. He hugged her, cooing and rocking her in his arms.

* * *

The Avenida Palace, not long before known as The International, had always intimidated Alves on previous visits, which had been confined to the brightly lit, sumptuous public rooms. Now he strode briskly across the gilded lobby, through a bevy of lavishly uniformed attendants, stood waiting for the cagelike lift to hoist him upward to his meeting. The music of the celebrated string band, playing their tea-dancing repertoire, floated toward him, summoning up the memory of a Sunday afternoon years before when he had danced to the same band with Maria's mother and seen across the room Maria gazing adoringly at him as she turned slowly in her father's arms. Now, catching sight of himself in a long mirror, he could not help but reflect on time, the changes it had wrought. He had thickened somewhat but hardened as well, and his face was lined with the years in Africa. There was the marked difference in bearing, the bulk of confidence across his shoulders, the absence of hesitancy. He smiled a trifle grimly at his image, patted the briefcase he carried. Becoming a man was quite a remarkable process.

Hennies opened the door of the suite he and Marang shared. The German smiled, shook his hand. Marang bowed. The large room with the gold brocade fittings glowed from the afternoon sunlight. Greta Nordlund stood with her back to the window, feet apart, tall and imposing in a long white skirt and blue overblouse. She smiled, said nothing, shook his hand like a man. José lounged in a deep chair, legs extended and crossed at the ankles, smoking a pencil-shaped cigar. Arnaldo was arranging chairs at a table. Alves wished the actress hadn't come. She distracted him.

Quickly she made clear her intention of leaving them alone. She turned to Alves, spoke softly with the deep husky voice: "Senhor, might it be possible for your wife to join us for dinner? I would so enjoy meeting her. . . ." She teased him: "The woman who caught such an important man! I've heard so much about your exploits since we met —your famous train ride! What a woman Senhora Reis must be! I am intrigued. . . ."

"On the contrary," he said, surprised, "it was I who caught her and was exceedingly lucky to do so. And dinner, yes, of course, unless she has made other arrangements."

"I'm so glad." She touched his sleeve. He watched her walk down the carpeted hallway. With her long legs she took big strides.

Meticulously, slowly, as the room grew hazy with smoke,

he explained his negotiations of the past two weeks and the document given him by the Bank of Portugal's directors. "Nothing," he concluded, surveying the four heads nodding with satisfaction, "could be more simple and straightforward. We are empowered to have the money printed—we being the syndicate headed by Marang van Ysselveere. Our arrangements are exactly as I described them to you in Biarritz. No changes of any kind. So . . ." He sighed and sat down.

"We Portuguese have a name for such an opportunity." José's eyes moved from face to face behind the drooping lids. "It comes from our old interests in the East. . . . When we ruled most of the world. This is a prime example, gentlemen, of a *negocio da China*—a Chinese deal. Which is one in which you can't lose, something for nothing."

Hennies laughed. "The Americans used to say it in New York—it's like taking candy from a baby. Easy money."

"This dates, I take it, from your days as a purveyor of sewing machines?"

Hennies stopped chuckling abruptly, turned to stare at Alves.

"Perhaps," he said.

"Marang, as head of our syndicate, have you any further thoughts?"

"All seems in order. Normally I distrust this kind of thing. Hard work equals money in my experience." He looked sanctimoniously along the length of his nose.

"Oh, come, come," Alves said, tapping a cigarette on the table. "Let us leave our platitudes behind us for the moment. We are men of the world . . . hard work is whatever a particular situation demands. I am quite sure that our friend Marang would look back on his trade with the Germans during the recent hostilities—the chocolate, the ham, the wheat—as relatively easy work, but because a job does not require physical labor does not mean that it is easy. . . ." Marang had paled slightly; a fingertip flew to his lip. "Believe me, we have all done our share of hard work and in this case it was I who did it—hours of negotiations with the bank's directors, convincing them that we were the perfectly discreet men for the job. . . ."

"All that remains is to decide on the printer, is that not correct?" Marang looked around the room.

"A German firm occurs to me," Alves said. "Good quality, long traditions, sober—"

"Out of the question!" Hennies barked, leaping up. He began to pace, limping slightly with the built-up shoe. Alves had never really noticed the limp before.

"Good Lord, why not?" José asked. "You yourself said how much experience the Huns have had since Versailles. . . ."

"There's no need to use that word," Hennies growled. "Versailles?"

"No, you fool, *Hun!*"

"Gentlemen, please!" Arnaldo held out his hands to quiet them. Bandeira bared his teeth, eyes squinting in an imitation of laughter.

"I take it that your concern," Alves remarked slowly, "stems from your near disaster in the railway banknote imbroglio?"

"How do you . . ." Hennies stopped, stock-still, leaning forward toward Alves, menacing. The monocle dropped like a coin from his flat, cold eye.

"Calm yourself, my friend. Surely you don't believe that I would invite anyone into such a delicate operation without the most detailed private inquiries? Surely not—and the fact that you are here at all indicates at least my understanding of your previous activities." He smiled reassuringly.

"Can't be too careful, Adolf," Marang said maliciously.

"You're quite a little bastard, aren't you, Reis."

"You disappoint me, Hennies," José said. He chuckled.

"Now," Alves said, moving resolutely on, ignoring Hennies, who sat down sulkily by the window. "I do see Hennies' point. . . . I should have seen it myself. Herr Hennies' contribution to our endeavors is financial, not, shall we say, moral. He has undoubtedly been badly wronged in Germany, and any reputable German printer of banknotes would not look with unalloyed favor on his participation . . . so, what remains? Suggestions?"

"Perhaps a Dutch firm," Marang said, having recovered his own composure, apparently by observing Hennies lose his. Alves watched it all closely. Never had he felt quite so completely the master of a difficult, complex situation. "Enschede en Zonen have been the exclusive printers of Dutch banknotes for more than a century."

"They can print these notes? These *exact* notes?" Alves held up the document.

"Well, I don't know as to exactness—"

"They must be the same notes . . . there must be no room for discovery by an outsider of any differences. The notes must be duplicates—the point of the entire process, if you recall, was to hide the fact that new money is being printed. Thus, there must be no differences of any kind. . . . None." Fighting against his impatience, Alves tweezed his lower lip between two fingers and pulled a lengthy, thoughtful face.

"Only the original printer," Hennies said sourly, "can possibly produce the same banknotes. Are you telling us, Reis, that your great chums at the Bank of Portugal didn't tell you that? Incredible!" He snorted. "Did you think these firms just pass the plates around among themselves, like some bloody great club? My God, use your heads, gentlemen." He turned back to gaze out at Rossio Square. The constant rumble of traffic filtered into the room.

In the silence that followed, Alves' mind raced, smashing against the walls of his sudden confidence, demolishing them. *Damn . . . God damn . . .* Master of the situation, he felt sickness growing in his belly. He lit a cigarette. Any printer, any printer at all, but the same one . . . only the same printer, who customarily printed the notes, who had the long standing personal relationship with the bank, might destroy his perfect plan—might purposely, or even casually, check with the bank and expose the entire scheme. . . . What in the name of God to do?

Hennies broke the silence. "Well," he intoned imperiously, "well?"

"Well what, Adolf?" Marang wet his lips, peered at his moist fingertips.

"Well, who in hell printed the bleeding notes?" He stood up, plucked a flower from a vase on the credenza, inserted it in his buttonhole. "Reis?"

"The bank stipulated I must not go to the same printer." His mouth was dry. He felt his heart jump.

"That makes no sense," Hennies said. "They want the same note, they must know that only one printer can do it."

But who was the printer? Alves shrugged, cleared his throat.

"I agree . . . there is obviously some mistake."

"Well, there is nothing to do but go to Waterlow in England. The largest printers in the world. Surely, I have heard that they do some Portuguese notes." Marang was full of surprises, Alves reflected, and now he was rescuing the project, like a messenger from a benevolent deity. "I beg to differ with Hennies here, but I expect that Waterlow and Sons, Limited, does indeed have the facilities and resources to literally duplicate these notes. . . . They are a most remarkable firm, so terribly English, so thorough, absolutely dependable and unimpeachable in every way. And they do a large banknote business. Very aggressive, men in every capital, always looking for the new piece of business."

"How is it you are so well informed?" Arnaldo was jotting down notes on his pad.

"My interests are very diversified. More information than you can imagine passes through The Hague."

"Waterlow it is, then," Alves said.

"What else is there?" José asked brightly. "Looks to me like we're off to London. . . . I was right, *negocio da China!*" He clapped his hands and stood. "Agreed?"

"There is one more point," Alves said. "A small financial consideration. Herr Hennies . . ."

"*Ja.*"

"Another thousand pounds."

"You are joking!"

"No, as it happens, I am not. And it is a very great bargain—after all, your contribution, as we agreed, was to be financial."

"Corrupt! Corrupt and greedy, your friends at the bank. . . ." Hennies stuffed his hands in his pockets, stumped back to the window. "This could never happen in Germany."

Marang laughed. José caught Alves' eye, grinned.

"Don't be absurd," Marang said. "As you perfectly well know, bribes are the lubricant of all great business deals."

"*Ja, ja,*" Hennies groaned. He reached for his checkbook.

Alves slumped back in his chair, removed his spectacles, rubbed his tired eyes. He folded the document and returned it to his briefcase. Hard work was an understatement.

By evening his spirits had recovered from the unexpected shock of the afternoon. All would be well: luck had been with him, as it had so often in the past. At such times you could almost believe you were especially blessed. With Maria, abroad socially for the first time since the birth of the most recent son, he arrived at Silva's for dinner in high spirits, which began to ebb the moment he saw Greta Nordlund at the large table, laughing close to José's ear, candlelight casting shadows across the wall behind them. She was all in white, ghostly with her pale skin and pale hair, breasts low and pointed beneath the clinging gown. Her nipples caught the material, stretched it as she moved. Why did José have to constantly combine business and pleasure?

Arnaldo and José fussed over Maria with countless inquiries as to her health, the new baby's health, the health of her parents.

Alves watched Greta's wide thin mouth as she talked, her eyes flickering across his wife's face, her jewelry, the style of her dress, the color of her nails. She was asking Maria about the children, and Maria immediately began to recount the day's events, animatedly, her smile open and genuine. He watched his little wife from the corner of his eye, loving her, wanting to protect her, somehow, from this curiously unsettling Northern woman.

Hennies provided champagne, and the dinner of *cosido* and roast pork moved slowly ahead. Greta ate ravenously while Maria talked, picked at her food. "I must watch my figure," Alves heard her say, and Greta joked, "I'm sure the men in your life do all the figure watching that is necessary." Maria laughed happily, replied that there were no men in her life, only one man. Greta nodded. "Of course, I understand. This is no place for confidences, is it?" Maria smiled, not understanding. Inexplicably, Greta caught his eye. Did she wink, or was it his imagination?

Later José leaned across the table toward him, the candle guttering between them. "Lovely, isn't she?" He chortled, blowing the candle out. "Delicious, seductive, worldly. A tigress, she claws me. . . ."

"Don't be obscene, José," Alves whispered. "They might hear you."

José leaned sideways, nibbled at Greta's earlobe. She shivered, put her cheek against his. "Behave, my darling." Maria looked away self-consciously. "You see, you are embarrassing Senhora Reis. . . . You should be ashamed." She gently pushed him away.

Marang plucked at his sleeve.

"Yes," Alves said. "I'm sorry, I wasn't listening."

"I was merely telling Arnaldo and Adolf some of what I know about the Waterlow firm. Perhaps you would enjoy hearing it."

When he drank, Marang developed a kind of lisp. It was

vaguely amusing. Alves listened attentively for the next
hour as the dinner moved sluggishly to a close. Maria was
still talking about the children, then he heard Greta ask
about the great adventure at the High Bridge and that story
was told in elaborate detail.

The night outside was unusually balmy. When the taxis
arrived back at the Avenida Palace the intention to have a
nightcap was replaced by the idea for a stroll along the
Avenida da Liberdade. Alves resisted: "Surely, my love,
you are tired from such a long evening. Perhaps we should
say good night . . ."

"Oh, no. Alves, please," she said, taking his hand. "I
don't want it to end yet. I'm fine and Greta is a good friend
. . . let's walk with her. Please."

He shrugged. "Whatever you wish, of course."

"What a lovely avenue," Greta cried as she thrust her
arm through his. Four abreast, with Maria holding Alves'
other arm and José on the far side of Greta, they marched
along beneath the moon and the swaying palms.

"A mile long, a hundred yards wide," José said, gesturing expansively, "Palms, Judas trees . . . Originally the
entire avenue was built with walls sealing it off from the
rest of the city. So the shy ladies of Lisbon could promenade and take the air *and not be seen.* Can you believe it?"
He cackled, stomping his feet.

"José is drunk," Alves said to no one in particular.

"How times change," José cried, gasping. "And the
ladies! How they have changed. . . ."

Alves felt Greta squeeze his arm. Maria hummed happily to herself. His head ached.

*   *   *

In bed that night, long after they had left the merrymakers
at the Avenida Palace and taken a taxi back to their tight-
fitting flat, Alves lay awake, his eyes blinking against the
darkness. Maria had drifted off to sleep, smiling in his
arms, leaving him keyed up, trying to organize his thoughts
and marshal the events of the day. He still shuddered from
the mixup over the printing companies. . . . How could he
have left such a gap, after all the care he'd taken with the
documents, the plan as a whole? He grimaced, swung his
legs out of the bed, straightened his nightshirt and padded
out to the kitchen. He heated the remnants of the coffee,

lit a cigarette and sat down at the table. The printing company—what an insane mistake! But, still, Marang had saved the day and the crisis had passed.

Marang had proved most informative on the subject of the printing firm. He had, Alves supposed, that kind of mind, encyclopedic, orderly. Over the dinner, even with José's shenanigans and the attention he'd paid to Greta and Maria, Alves had absorbed what Marang had been saying.

Waterlow and Sons was the largest single printing company in the world. Central to its existence was the banknote division, which supplied money, meeting the most exacting standards imaginable, to governments of many nations. The first Waterlow—Walran had been his name—had come to Canterbury early in the seventeenth century, a silk weaver. Two centuries later James Waterlow, a scrivener, had revolutionized his trade: a man with a new idea, which involved using lithography and printing to produce the legal documents that had always in the past been copied, laboriously, by hand. James founded the firm in 1811, taking his sons in as partners. Alfred, Walter, Sydney and Albert. Business grew dramatically with the growth of the vast railway system, which required millions of timetables, millions of tickets, millions of stock certificates. . . .

Marang's natural tendency toward gossip exhibited itself when he turned to the personalities that emerged with the firm's prominence among printers.

"The English," he had said, meticulously licking champagne from his mustache, "are even more obsessed with appearances than our good Dutch elders. Just look beneath the smooth surface of the English aristocracy, look past Cambridge and Ascot and the City and cricket at Lords . . . and you find something else, something that gives the lie to that carefully nurtured look of things. The Waterlow family, for example, always had its factions, its rivalries, brother against brother, cousin against cousin. . . ."

The company split into two printing firms, at first dividing the available business, then competing bitterly for it.

"Both firms were doing wonderfully well," Marang continued, malice darting across the words, a smile of ironic observation on his narrow face, "at which time greed appeared on the scene. In this case it was Alfred's grandson William Alfred Waterlow who came to the conclusion that

the printing of currency—or banknotes, paper money—
was too lucrative to be left to the *other* Waterlow firm.

"It was nineteen-fourteen, which would have made
William about forty-two, forty-three. . . . And that was
when he remarked to my friend that, by God, why should
the other Waterlows be printing all the money? Of course
he couldn't have known what a quagmire he was venturing
upon. . . ."

1914. He had been meeting Maria at the beach, a mere
boy with boyhood ending. José was back from his esca-
pades, about to set out on the road to more. . . . Hennies
had just become a Swiss and set sail from Rio on the
S.S. *Principessa Mafaldo,* embarking on his third identity.
Arnaldo, like himself, had been a child with little notion of
the world beyond school, home, the neighborhood in Lisbon.

And Sir William, by then the new president of the Fed-
eration of Master Printers of Great Britain, one of the
eighty-one ancient guilds of the City of London, was bull-
ing his way into the enormously competitive banknote business.

Sir William began by raiding Waterlow and Sons, Ltd.,
and came away with a substantial prize—an order for one
hundred million British Treasury one-pound notes: Waterlow Brothers and Layton was on its way in the banknote
business.

By 1919 it had become apparent to Waterlow and Sons
that Waterlow Brothers and Layton had become a major
force in the field of banknote printing, with their sights set
on acquiring even more international business what with
all the new countries created by the war's end. Therefore
Waterlow and Sons suggested a merger with Waterlow
Brothers and Layton, bringing the family together again
and ending ruinous price-cutting competition. The merger
was announced in January 1921. Sir Philip Waterlow, Sydney's son, became chairman of the new firm, with his son
Edgar and Sir William named managing directors.

The word in the City was that Sir William was out-
gunned on a stock-ownership basis and accepted the subordinate position—with much private bad grace—with the
bleak assumption that his second cousin Edgar was bound
to succeed his father, Sir Philip, in the top spot. "Stiff
upper lip, one of those very, very English things," Marang
said, shaking his head disdainfully. "A bitter and nasty pill

that the right kind of Englishman swallows and ignores. Such absurd pretense! They are more enwrapped in vengeance than any race of people since the Borgias. You know what an English financier once said to me over whisky and soda in his club? I've never forgotten it. He said, 'A gentleman never gets angry. He gets even.' Now that, my friends, is why the sun never sets on the Union Jack!"

But, Marang went on, winding slyly on through the complexities of his story, the slimy underside of the banknote business eventually changed all that, saved Sir William's future.

The facts were that Thomas de la Rue and Waterlow and Son had been in secret agreement to share British government printing projects. To keep the price at a comfortably profitable level, bidding for the jobs had become perfunctory, markedly unenthusiastic. Regardless of the printer, the profits were split two ways.

"The problem arose, you see," Marang said, eyes shining at the small but intrigued audience, "when Sir Philip welshed on his part of the deal—just once. Thomas de la Rue did not receive their cut. And they sued because they didn't get their share of a deal that was utterly unethical in the first place! So English! Righteous indignation among thieves, nothing more nor less!"

Marang leaned forward, eyes glittering. "There was," he whispered eagerly, "more to come. . . ."

Sir William snooped around and discovered two interesting facets of the situation that had not yet come to light. First, many of Sir Philip's directors had had no knowledge of the arrangement, and, second, Sir Philip had been keeping the shared profits for himself personally instead of putting them back into the firm. "These discoveries made for some animated discussions in the board room—legendary in the City," Marang clucked. "Laughter behind their backs . . . but the Waterlow clan is reported to be most decidedly thick when it comes to poking fun at themselves. The results were typically upper class: Sir Philip was allowed to get off by merely retiring to the country, chastened, yes, but very well off. The de la Rue lads were bought off for thirty thousand pounds—and the suit never went to court." He peered at their faces, one by one, enjoying the spotlight. What a mind! Alves reflected. What a resource this Dutchman was!

"Edgar, the heir presumptive, was passed over for the simple reason that he had known of his father's misconduct . . . and had not reported it to his fellow directors. And Sir William, back from beyond, was reborn as chairman and, with Edgar, joint managing director."

Inevitably, the great firm was split, both emotionally and strategically, at the top levels. Sir William knew that Edgar would be ever alert to an opportunity to bring him down. Since he realized he could not trust his cousin, Sir William accepted the inadvisability of confiding in him certain key aspects of the firm's business. The important thing was to keep the other nine Waterlow directors on his side.

Toward the end Sir William acquired the entirety of the Crown's postage-stamp printing business. Shortly thereafter he secured the rights to print all of Latvia's currency. The word in the city was that Waterlow's profits were doubling as 1924 entered its last month.

With his various successes in tow Sir William's ambition had taken wings. Once he'd gained his knighthood, he wanted very badly to become Lord Mayor of London. He had laid the groundwork with considerable care. He served as chairman of the City of London School Committee, then as alderman for the Cornhill Ward of the London Corporation, which made him a Magistrate of the City of London, a post that had traditionally been a steppingstone to the Lord Mayoralty.

The rise of Sir William caused Edgar more irritation than he could rationally describe, though he was reported to have tried to do it justice in the upstairs rooms at the Cheddar Cheese on more than a few occasions. The problem was, as he admitted from behind dark scowls, that there was no arguing with the insufferable, self-righteous prig's success. . . .

* * *

Before breakfast Maria saw to it that Alves' bag, old and with a broken belt that commemorated his travels through Africa, was packed for the long train trip to The Hague. Although he'd managed only a couple hours of sleep, he was buoyant. It was all coming together. Today. He fought the excitement in his breast. But it was there; he couldn't resist it. He had been waiting all these months, all that time in the Oporto jail. And now his plans had gone right.

Men more experienced with sophisticated financial dealings than he had seen the documents and been convinced. It was a wonderful morning. . . .

The children, with their nurse, had already kissed their father goodbye and gone off for the morning. The baby lay in Maria's arms and sucked, gurgling happily, on her dark, swollen nipple. Milk dribbled down his tiny array of chins. "Quite gay, wasn't it?" Her eyes sparkled at him. "And such impressive men—all working for you. Well, I was so proud!"

"Quite gay," Alves said, his smile fading slowly, leaning down to kiss the baby's hair. "José particularly was most gay. . . ."

He sat down to coffee and hot bread. He filled the cup with cream and sugar, sipped slowly, watching his wife quizzically. "What did you think of Greta Nordlund?"

"Oh!" Maria exclaimed. "I adored her. So exciting, yet so interested in the children. . . . Alves, I think she's had a very sad life, working so hard in the theater, never having a husband or children."

"You approve of her relationship with José, then?"

"Oh, Alves, don't be so old-fashioned. This is nineteen twenty-five. Some women behave very differently nowadays. . . . She's a woman of the world, a *femme fatale*. Not like your little wife who stays at home and has babies."

"You object, my darling? To staying at home and bearing our children?" He buttered the bread, ladled jam onto it.

"Alves, I love you, I love my life with you." She adjusted her nipple in the baby's mouth and took a dainty bite of Alves' bread. "You shouldn't hold Greta's way of life against her—she's a dear, sweet person. Give her a chance, my darling." She closed her eyes in thought. Alves took the bread back and crammed most of it into his mouth.

"She's much too tall," he said.

Maria laughed. "Too tall for what?"

"Maria, you're as bad as José!"

"And such a beautiful dress. Parisian. She told me the name of her dressmaker. How I would love visiting Paris! The fashions there . . ."

"But, my darling, do you think such a dress as hers last evening would suit you? She does not dress in happy colors, as you do. Her clothing strikes me as quite somber, almost melancholy."

"It's the woman you're seeing, not her clothing. *She* is somber, melancholy. Clothing takes on the personality of the woman—every intelligent woman knows that. Believe me." She patted his hand consolingly. "Anyway, I would very much enjoy visiting her couturier. . . ." A wistful quality colored her voice. Alves winced inwardly. Such moments almost always cost him money. At the moment he had only the little he had squeezed from Hennies. The wonderful morning was almost slipping away.

"You are surely right, my love," he said. "And when the time comes, all your wishes will be granted. And about that you must believe me, you see? A new home! Dresses from Paris! Whatever you long for. . . ." He stood up, patted her hair. "Very soon now."

"And do be kind to Greta. Please, for my sake."

"I shall try. For your sake."

With a tender embrace once the baby was fed, he took his bag and went down to the street. Arnaldo was waiting for him in a taxi.

The Sud Express, one of the great trains of Europe, fretted and fussed in its berth as harried travelers swarmed through the crowds of porters. The Lisbon–Paris run took thirty-six hours, and the carriages were appointed for maximum comfort. Sweet and brushed and perfumed, provided with fresh stiff linen, fresh flowers in the bud vases, the huge steaming engine seemed to be straining to be gone, like a mastiff on a leash.

José, Greta, Arnaldo, Hennies and Marang: the six of them met, eyes bright and voices brittle; the excitement was contagious.

Alves stood somewhat apart, watching, curiously calm within, at ease with the knowledge that only he possessed. The situation called for confidence on his part. He must almost believe the story himself—that was the key. He caught Arnaldo's eye and smiled. Confidently. It was time to board. They were accommodated in three private compartments—José with Greta, Marang and Hennies together, he with Arnaldo.

By evening he had retired alone to his own compartment. Arnaldo, José, Hennies and Marang had gone off to the club car to play cards. Greta had, he assumed, retired for the evening. He smoked, went over the dossiers again and again, jotted down all that he remembered of Marang's remarks about Sir William Waterlow, studied the forged documents minutely, critically, searching out any deviations from the normal. It was wearying and made him both hungry and thirsty. Finally he washed his face, brushed the cigarette ashes from his coat and made his way through the swaying corridors to the dining car.

He had just ordered a bit of sole and a half bottle of Chablis when she came in, saw him and made her way toward his table. She moved gracefully with the rolling motion of the train, then folded herself into the chair across from him. Her eyes wandered nervously, a smile died at birth, she fumbled with the menu.

"Insomnia . . . I only sleep well when I'm working. The rest of the time there's too much energy. I can't seem to exhaust myself. I make terrible demands on José at times." She shrugged solemnly. "No wonder he plays cards with his friends." She sighed, stared at her reflection in the dark, rushing night, stroked her hair. "On trains . . . it's childish but I keep thinking the bed will fold up with me still in it."

"I sympathize. I have the same affliction—my mind races, sleep won't come. Not more than two hours last night."

"You were excited by our night out. I felt the same way."

"The beginning of a new adventure."

"Like an opening night." She caught his eye, seemed to soften. "I understand. You, your excitement, not the great deal you all seem so self-satisfied about." The waiter appeared, and she ordered a chicken sandwich and tea. "We always seem to be eating together."

"A beautiful woman is always welcome at my table." He averted his eyes. This woman, so forward and daring— Maria had actually called her a *femme fatale*—this woman made him feel shy, boyish. He tried to compensate. "I once knew a man in Africa, a man called Chaves, who looked like a gorilla, who used to tell me, "Reis, give me my pipe, my slippers and a beautiful woman . . . and you can keep the pipe and slippers!"

"You are funny, Senhor, in addition to being a financial wizard."

His sole arrived, followed at once by her sandwich.

"Hardly a financial wizard. Just a Portuguese businessman struggling to get along in the jungles of Europe."

"You have put a spell on these men. . . . You should hear them speak of you. Hushed tones, reverence." Clearly she was teasing him. But he detected respect in her voice, manner.

"Please," he said, returning to his sole, washing it down with the pleasant, chilled Chablis. They were alone in the car by now. The waiters were inconspicuously freshening the tables for the first breakfast traffic. It was almost eleven o'clock. An occasional light flared outside in the night, was swept away.

"I'm quite serious. Anyone who has business with Bill Waterlow is most assuredly playing with the grownups. So the poor little Portuguese doing the best he can is not a line that will work with me. I *know* Bill Waterlow. . . ." She sipped her tea.

"Personally? I had no idea." Another coincidence. Again, he didn't know whether he liked it or not. He kept thinking, the more complex the web—in this case the web of coincidence—the more likely one was to become ensnared. . . . "What sort of man is he?"

"Do you know the work of Shaw?"

"Shaw? No, I can't say I do. What has Shaw to do with Waterlow?"

"Nothing, really. I consider Bernard Shaw the greatest English—I should say Irish, actually—playwright since Shakespeare. You know Shakes—"

"Although only a poor Portuguese, I am not wholly illiterate."

"Forgive my teasing, Senhor." She had relaxed. "Shaw is fond of including in his plays a certain kind of typical Englishman—the large, red-faced, blustering, pompous, self-important, God-was-an-Englishman type. Not overly intelligent, but that doesn't matter—it's a question of the right school, the right family and friends, what they call the 'old boy network.' That's what great success requires, and it is the only thing that can make you truly successful. Although tradesmen, the Waterlows have been hanging about for a long time—money, the good schools, the mansions and summer homes and shooting grouse in Scotland." She cast a slow look at him. "I needn't tell you this. You're an Oxford man, aren't you?"

"I understand the English," he said with quiet confidence. "I have been reading Sherlock Holmes and P. G. Wodehouse. Do you know what the P and the G stand for? Why do you laugh?"

"Holmes and Wodehouse," she repeated. "A heightened realism, I suppose. Maybe not such a bad idea, even for an Oxford man—yes, yes, I do know. It's Pelham for the P and Grenville for the G."

"Pelham," Alves said. "Strange name. I think of Dick and Bertie and Wooster and Nigel and Reggie, not this Pelham you speak of."

"He's called 'Plum' by his friends."

"You are a friend of the immortal Wodehouse as well? You amaze me—but tell me, does Wodehouse make any sense in person? I read his books religiously, but I admit it is a rare day when I can say I understand what is going on. I confess it. . . ."

"I know him, yes. He writes sometimes for the stage. So I know him, though not well. Tall, terribly amiable fellow . . . Whereas Mr. Shaw is stocky and vigorous, full beard, once red and still rather red, wears knickerbocker suits. The knickerbocker suits must be the only thing he and Bill Waterlow have in common—they would naturally hate each other on sight, I'm quite sure. Because, as I was saying, this type of roast-beef-and-Yorkshire-pudding Englishman Shaw does so wonderfully well is precisely what Bill is. . . . And greedy to boot. I've never known anyone more involved in the pursuit of *more*—the word *enough* does not exist in his vocabulary." She leaned back and took a great bite of sandwich.

"How did you come to know him?"

"In the theater you meet scads of people who want to take up actors and actresses, invite them for house parties, long weekends spent with wildly mismatched people. The English have a gift for it. You know, come to think of it, I have known people greedier than Bill . . . but they were Waterlows, too. And they got caught. It's more or less *de rigueur* in the best English families, at least one or two really messy scandals. Money or women, it always comes down to that. And seldom does anyone ever get punished . . . after all, God is an Englishman and money and women were clearly meant to be acquired in God's world. The means of doing so is not of great concern."

"Am I to be frightened of this peculiar race? They are

not, then, as Plum portrays them? Funny and silly?" He smiled. "Pretend I didn't go to Oxford. . . ."

"Oh, yes, there are funny and silly ones, too. Bill Waterlow can be both funny and silly, when he plays tennis . . . on his private court, of course. He plays very hard and wheezes a great deal. At Whyte Ways I saw him cheat his vicar out of a half dozen sets one weekend by simply calling the vicar's best serves out. . . ."

"Whyte Ways," Alves said. "What is that?"

"Waterlow's home. If you're unlucky, he may invite you to visit. Still, you're Portuguese—the Latin races, in Bill's view, are to be plundered, not befriended."

"You *do* frighten one," Alves said slowly.

"Don't be," she said. "Think how much more you now know about him than he does about you. That's an advantage, Senhor."

It was nearly midnight when they passed the card players. They sat at the far end of the car, ordered a brandy nightcap and watched the game. Alves lit a cigarette.

"I feel much better," she said. "Perhaps I can sleep now. Thank you for letting me talk. . . . Remember the day in Biarritz? I always seem to rattle on to you. . . . You're very tolerant and understanding. Even though you don't quite like me or approve of me."

"It is merely that you are new in my experience. You are also very beautiful. That bothers me. May I be so frank?"

"Of course." Slowly, deliberately, she placed her hand on his. He watched her hand with its immensely long, fragile fingers pressing against his. "It pleases me to have you think that of me. May I call you Alves?" She was smiling at him when he shifted his eyes to her face. "Try to forget what I look like and my disreputable profession. And, in any event, you should be accustomed to beautiful women. Look at your wife, Maria. She is lovely, unaffected. And she doesn't frighten you, does she?"

"Not often."

"Well, you see, inside I am no different from your Maria. We are both women, quite simple. . . ."

"You don't believe that any more than I do. Don't pretend that you do." He withdrew his hand and stood.

"Alves, are you angry with me? I'm very sorry, whatever I've done . . ." But she remained seated, calmly regarding him as if he were behaving like nothing so much as an Englishman. Funny and silly.

"I am not accustomed," he said, feeling hot and stuffy, as if his collar were too tight, "to . . . to discussing my wife with . . . with actresses. Now, good night!"

As he turned and left the car he heard her laughter pealing like a tiny, fragile silver bell. Damn her! Who did she think she was, toying with him, teasing him, comparing herself to Maria, who was just a simple, decent Portuguese woman, a Portuguese wife and mother. Damn! He really must warn Maria about her. As he struggled to fall asleep, he thought he heard the woman panting and crying out like an animal in the next compartment, making her terrible demands on José! God, women . . .

The trouble with Greta was still bothering him when he awoke in the pink-and-gray of dawn in France. It made him self-conscious and ill-disposed to see her. Damn it, he knew it would come to this—trouble. He'd known since the first time he'd laid eyes on her. She was an unsettling woman, that was all, and that was enough.

He spent a sour, brooding day. Stepping alone out onto the platform at a brief stop, he was driven back inside by the wintry winds. There was the feel of snow and rain in the air, borne in from the Atlantic. Ducking back, he saw her buying a newspaper in a long black cape with fur at the collar. Her pale hair lay like a mantle of snow. She looked up, saw him, began to smile a greeting before he was gone. Silly ass, he cursed himself. Hide-and-seek with a woman.

Late that night, in the dull, damp station in Paris, with a slashing rain falling in the glow of street lamps beyond, he found himself standing beside her.

"I leave you now," she said.

"I see." He didn't know quite where to look. "We're going on to The Hague."

"It's very restful there. Very gentle." She gestured, about to take his hand, stopped herself. "Look, Alves— whatever I said last night . . . I had no idea. . . ." She shrugged, looked away. "Oh, this is ridiculous. Do you want to make up?"

He stared at her, confused. What to say?

"Well, then," she said quietly, "go ahead, be ridiculous. And childish. *Merde!*" She turned away, leaving him standing alone, feeling remarkably foolish. His head was aching.

Once they had left Paris and headed north for the
Netherlands, the journey seemed to work wonders on
Karel Marang. It was as if, with the smell of the Low
Countries in his nostrils, he sensed the finish line and
lengthened his stride.

Alves, fighting to rid his mind of the persistent images
of Greta Nordlund, noticed Marang as they went in to
dinner, then adjourned to the bar car for cigars and brandy.
He looked taller, as if he'd actually grown inches since
they had entrained in Lisbon. His manner shucked any
vestige of timidity, grew almost pompous. He was wearing a different suit, steamed and pressed: a dark-blue,
virtually black, pinstripe, very subtle but redolent of
power, command. More than anything else, he looked like
a successful banker. Alves was delighted. Fate, he reflected, had sent him not merely an acceptable colleague
but the perfect man for the job of front man.

After their second night on the train it was a relief to
reach The Hague, which was shrouded in a thick yet
refreshing fog. To cap his new persona Marang had wired
ahead to have one of his office staff meet them with his
black, somehow ominous Winton Six. In excellent spirits,
Marang saw them all sumptuously provided for in the
ornate Hotel des Indes, which squatted, newly painted in
shades of green with rich orange trim, at the end of Embassy Row. The great trees were barren now, wet and
black, ghostly, the gutters and streets full of the sodden
auburn and rust-colored leaves. The city was quiet and,
yes, as she had said, comfortable. Gentle. Immediately, he
liked it, far more than he'd thought he would. The Winton
had slid silently along the wide canals. Flowers still bloomed
in window boxes like crimson and ocher explosions. He
realized how tired he was. He had been on a train since
time began.

After a nap he awoke, bathed and looked outside to find
it dark. He threw open the window. The night smelled like
cool, freshly turned earth, sweet, fit to clear your head.

He sat at the small writing desk, arranged the hotel's
thick paper with its watermark before him, filled his thick
red Parker pen with ink and closed his eyes for a moment
to compose his thoughts.

My dearest Maria, he began and went easily onward,
telling her the assorted anecdotes of a long train ride.
Menus, sights, weather, the change in Marang . . . *Your*

*femme fatale left us in Paris. I am sorry but I cannot warm
to her as you did. I'm sure there is no harm in her, but
she is—how to say it?—too much like a man for me, too
hard and unyielding. I miss you so, my love! And I am so
inadequate when I try to buy you presents. So why don't
you and one of your friends go shopping for some new
dresses? For the holidays? And don't worry about money.
Very soon there will be more than you can imagine!*

Smiling to himself, he inquired formally after the condition of the children—odd, he couldn't imagine Greta
Nordlund pregnant or mothering her tiny tots—with special good wishes for the newest one.

By writing to Maria about Greta he felt he had wiped
that particular slate clean. Perhaps he had been too hard
on the woman. Perhaps she had meant nothing with her
remarks about Maria. But she made him nervous, made
him feel as if even by chatting with her he was engaging
in something strangely illicit. She was so easy to talk to, so
straightforward, no demurely lowered eyes, no shyness, and
her history—well, he knew enough of that to last a lifetime. Still, as Maria had said, it was possible that he was
old-fashioned. . . . Ah, well, we are what we are, and
there was no point in worrying about it.

Marang arranged the meeting with Sir William Waterlow
for the sixth of December, three days hence, and in the
meantime Alves retreated into a cocoon of sleep, resting for
what seemed the first time in years. There was nothing
more he could do to further the scheme, and the more he
saw of his companions the greater the chance he might let
slip something that would reveal a corner of the truth. He
took long walks in the afternoons, bought a copy of Shaw's
Caesar and Cleopatra, which he began reading slowly, not
more than two or three pages at a time. He wasn't quite
sure why he bothered. As often as possible he took his
meals alone. When he felt the need to talk he turned to
Arnaldo. He pleaded a headache when Marang had them
all to dinner to meet his wife.

The day before they were to leave for London he put
on his raincoat, knotted a scarf around his throat, pulled
his hat low on his forehead and plunged off into the continuing mist for a long midafternoon walk. He chewed a
digestive biscuit. Already his stomach was growing tense
with anticipation. But the gentle, quiet city, with the water
dripping so calmly from the eaves into the window boxes,

the sounds of traffic muffled by the heavy mist—the city was already working its magic on him, giving him peace.

He walked aimlessly along a narrow canal, away from the shops and churches and large stores and restaurants glowing golden in the fog from the lighting within. Crossing a small bridge, he stopped to stare at a family of ducks, floating like corks on the glassy water that reflected the gray sky above. There were still late-falling golden leaves scattered about the canal like memories of autumn. How did the Dutch train their children not to fall into the canal? That struck him as a real problem, and he was thinking of his own children when he heard her voice behind him.

"I hope you are not still angry with me."

He felt his heart leap. It couldn't be . . . but, of course, he knew it was. She was wearing the Biarritz trenchcoat, lavender scarf, floppy hat. Her face was grave, eyes gray, drawing their color from the sky and the canal. She had the most remarkable eyes. Even as he watched they shaded toward the lavender of her scarf.

"I'm sorry for upsetting you. You must believe it was not my intention." She stood stock-still, watching his face, as if waiting to be released.

"Your apology is accepted, it goes without saying. For the life of me, I can't exactly remember what it was that bothered me." The lie seemed harmless, in light of the long-term view, in light of her eyes. He watched her lean forward on the bridge railing beside him. "Let's forget it. . . ."

"Good," she said, looking like a young girl for the moment. Somehow he had always felt she was older than he, superior to him. "Good," she said again, her shoulder touching his. "Do you like the canals?"

"I like it all." They watched the water in silence. Mist drifted against his spectacles. "We left you in Paris. Now you are here. . . ."

"I had contracts to sign and then I sat in my apartment reading, putting logs on the fire, trying to read. . . . I wrapped myself up and walked in the Luxembourg Gardens, watched the women pushing the baby carriages, dropped in at the Deux Magots, drank coffee with my friends. I went home and I was lonely. I missed all of you, so I packed my bag and came here overnight. I'll return tomorrow night, once you've all gone. Unless, of course, I decide to stay until you return." She winked at him. "I lead a very carefree life when I'm between shows."

"Impulses," he said, nodding. "I never seem to have them. It seems to me I'm always planning." Immediately he saw how foolish that was. He had plenty of impulses, plenty. The business on the High Bridge—that had been an impulse.

"My life is largely a matter of impulses. I trust them. Everything always works out, don't you see? If I had a motto, a coat of arms, that's what it would say—*everything always works out.*" She stood straight. "It's chilly here. Shall we walk?"

"Writers, painters, actors," he said. "I know nothing of such people."

"Maybe you know their names. There's a Canadian named Callaghan, several Americans, most of them writers. Man called Hemingway, very poor, but I think great things will happen to him, we all think so. A newspaperman called Jake Barnes, but I don't suppose anybody will ever hear of him. You have heard of Chevalier, of course."

"I have been in Africa," he muttered.

"Ah, of course. Well, when you come to Paris I will take you around, introduce you."

"But I have nothing to say to any of them."

"Nonsense," she insisted. "The Portuguese are a most romantic, artistic people. You would be much appreciated by these friends of mine—please, promise me when you come to Paris—"

"Yes, yes, of course."

They were passing through a grassy park. Children's swings hung limp; a teeter-totter lay at rest with one end jutting up like the prow of a sinking ship. Deep green moss grew thick on the side of a tree trunk. A squirrel foraged among the leaves. Alves watched her from the corner of his eye, wondering what to make of her.

"So you leave tomorrow," she said.

"Yes, to see Waterlow."

She smiled and he felt himself bristle.

"What amuses you?"

"You all seem to be having such a good time. It reminds me of children playing a game . . . or putting on a play for their parents. Oh, please, don't be angry with me again. . . ." She made a fetching face and reached for his arm, took it. "Please, Alves, there's nothing to insult your

Portuguese honor in saying that you seem to be enjoying yourselves."

"Like children? May I say that you have curious ideas of what is an insult?"

"You search out insults. That is the way I am. I say what I see." She pulled her hand back. "Perhaps we were not meant to be friends."

"Do I tell you that your relations with men are childish, irresponsible?"

"Oh, my, and what do you know of my men?"

"You have been Herr Hennies' lover. And here you are now, in Hennies' presence, but now you are the lover of José. That seems odd to me."

She drew back in mock horror. "Immoral, would that satisfy Senhor Moraliste? And I think how many more there have been than just those two. Next you'll be calling me a *femme fatale.* . . ."

"Aha," he cried. "You take the words from my mouth."

"Well, my darling Alves, you can see for yourself how angry I am." She smiled widely and took his arm again, walking on. "Such names do not offend me. But you should beware of them, because they make you sound all the more childish. You should try to be more tolerant of others. And let your devilishly romantic Portuguese nature show through."

"You are laughing at me."

"I only laugh with someone I'm fond of. José said you were a bit stuffy. I merely decided to unstuff you. But I think there is great hope for you, if you only give me a chance. . . ."

Alves stopped beneath a huge, heavy-limbed tree.

"You confuse me, damn it, and you scare me, and I want to get a few things straight here and now. Just sit down and listen to me." Obediently she sat. "I am a simple businessman. I am not one of your great sophisticates. I am not a childish person. I am at present engaged in serious business. . . . I am not romantic. I am very serious. I have a great deal at stake at the moment. I very much dislike being a source of amusement, to you or anyone else." He paused for breath and stared off down the path, pushed his hands into the pockets of his raincoat. "I am not a great womanizer, undoubtedly the sort of man you are drawn to. José is unquestionably a womanizer in a class very nearly to himself. I am inexperienced with women, but still . . .

I am as I am. You are exceedingly beautiful, you come from a world of which I know nothing, and I am not at all sure I am interested in finding out any more about it." He licked his lips, glanced nervously about him, as if he were afraid of spies in the bushes. "You make me feel most unsure of myself. When you inquire about, or comment on, my wife, you increase my awareness of your beauty, your mysterious past, your extraordinary sexual behavior—and the result is that I feel as if I am betraying my wife by even being in your presence."

"You are afraid I'll seduce you," she said with measured surprise. "You've got it the wrong way around, I assure you."

Alves pushed on, not hearing, "When you call me a child, as frightened of your . . . instincts as I am, you are like a hunter, you know? Then calling me a child is too much, too much! I have nothing more to say. I have said what I had to say. That is all."

She stood up and he trudged off after her, feeling half a fool, but glad he'd had his say. It was astounding, the way she brought out the worst in him. . . . Maria wouldn't recognize him.

"I told you that Maria and I had more in common than you could imagine, that we were both just women. You became hysterical and walked out on me. You should have listened to me. I was right. It is silly and childish for you to be frightened of me any more than you are frightened of your lovely wife. Can't you understand that we are the same, only our manners are different? I don't want you to be frightened of me, Alves. I want to be friends . . . I want you to like me." She was watching the grass ahead of her.

"Why? What difference does it make to you?"

She shook her head, walked on.

Later they stopped at a small bakery for coffee. She ordered a pastry. Alves sipped the scalding coffee. He had never before had such a conversation with a woman. Worn down, his emotions rubbed raw, he also felt as if a crisis had been passed. He had been uneasy about the woman all along. He remembered the day at the outdoor restaurant in Biarritz, with the rain falling out beyond the colonnades.

"Remember what I told you about Bill Waterlow. Whatever your business is with him, remember his greed, his ambition. And one other thing—he will do almost anything to show up the other side of his family. He and his cousin, Edgar, are at each other's throats." It was as if they were suddenly conspirators. He liked the feeling. Incredibly, his fear of her—for whatever reasons—was gone. It was like a pounding headache lifting, leaving him free.

"What you said about Hennies and José," she said, almost whispering. "Do you really hold that against me? My way of life? Remember that such friendships are not great things. José passes the time pleasantly."

"There is no more to be said, then," he said.

This time he covered her hand with his.

"Friends?"

"Of course."

Walking back past the various embassies with the colorful flags hanging wetly from angled poles, he reached into his pocket, took the book out and showed it to her. He said nothing. She took it.

"George Bernard Shaw," she said. *"Caesar and Cleopatra."*

She leaned toward him and kissed his lips, much to his surprise. He saw her face as she pulled away. She was pursing her lips for the instant, her eyes still closed.

A block farther on toward the Hotel des Indes they came upon José, Hennies and Arnaldo.

"Come with us to dinner," José said. He kissed her cheek.

"We must keep up our strength," Hennies said.

Greta nodded. "All right. . . ."

"Alves?" Arnaldo said.

"Perhaps I'll meet you later," he said.

"The Golden Head," Hennies said. "We'll save you a place."

Alves watched them go. Then he turned around and set off for the hotel. He needed time to himself, a chance to think.

The bedroom was dark when he awoke, shaking his head, fumbling for his glasses. He must have dozed off, and now someone was pounding on the door. He opened it and saw Arnaldo anxiously about to rap again.

"What is the crisis?"

"No crisis. I thought I'd come back and talk you into joining us for dinner." He stepped into the room, vaguely wringing his hands. "Last night before we set off for England . . ."

Alves nodded and retired to the washbasin in the bathroom. Arnaldo followed him, stood leaning behind him in the doorway. "I'm very anxious," he said. "Excited. Yes, this is our most exciting adventure since the High Bridge. Of course, there's no risk this time, what with our being emissaries from the Bank of Portugal. . . ."

"There was no risk the other time. You forget—but I knew the bridge would hold." He spoke from behind a towel, rubbing his face dry.

"So you say!" Arnaldo muttered. "In any case, I am most excited. Have you ever been to England?"

"Dunce. I am a graduate of Oxford."

"Ah, of course." Arnaldo toured the room, nervously peering out the window, clasping and unclasping his hands behind his back, whistling tunelessly while Alves put on his shoes and tied his tie.

"What is wrong with you?" Alves was exasperated. "Stop your eternal jiggling and fussing. Do you have to use the bathroom? What is it?"

"The kiss," Arnaldo blurted. "You and Greta Nordlund, we all saw you, right there on the street, not a block away. . . ." The words tumbled out in a rush. "What were you doing?"

"Kissing, as you saw for yourself."

"Kissing! Listen to him so calm, the man says 'kissing, as you saw for yourself.' Why were you kissing?" He wiped perspiration from his forehead.

"Completely innocent, I assure you. We had just decided to be friends rather than enemies. Impulsively she kissed me. . . . I was as surprised as you are."

"No more surprised than José, I expect."

"You don't mean to tell me that José was upset?"

"Indeed I do—most jealous. He has, in fact, been something of a trial about it the past two hours."

"Ridiculous! The man is the greatest lecher in Europe! 'Most jealous'! It is absurd, out of the question. An innocent peck!"

"On the mouth, as José pointed out." Arnaldo flopped down in a chair, stared disconsolately at the pattern in the carpet.

"The man has actually offered me the free use of his women before this—urged me to spend the night with a singer, the *fadista,* you remember?" Alves tripped over an untied shoelace and hopped to the bed, cursed, kicked the

shoe across the room. "Now he plays the jealous suitor.
It is not a role that fits him!"

"The fact of the matter remains," Arnaldo persevered.
"He distrusts her . . . or you. Her, I think. I have the impression she can have any man she wants. It puts him off
balance, makes him want to hold her tight. You see?"

"I suppose," Alves nodded, slumping onto the bed.
"Throw me my shoe, please." He caught it, bent to tie it
properly. "But I think he has a great problem with that one.
She is not the sort of woman you can hold too tightly—
not like Portuguese women. She says to hell with it, leads
her own life. She knows all sorts of people. Barnes and
Hemingway and Chevalier . . ." He recited the names as
if he knew who they were.

"You're joking!" Arnaldo perked up. "*Maurice* Chevalier? She knows Maurice Chevalier?"

"Of course, you fool, do you think she sits home alone
at all times? And Barnes, too, of course, and Hemingway."

"My God, Chevalier. . . . I know someone who knows
Chevalier. Think of it. . . ."

"So, José cannot cage this little bird. Big bird. Eagle . . ."

"And think of your own little bird, Maria, at home,
having your children, caring for them." Arnaldo leaped
up, began to pace. "And you, loose, dashing across the
face of Europe, kissing actresses in Holland! How could
you do this to her?"

"Who? Greta?"

"Maria! Your wife, idiot, your wife Maria!"

"I've done nothing to Maria."

"I am serious, Alves. It is not only José who is bewitched
by a woman he can't handle. . . . It could also happen to
you. And, thus, to Maria. Can you imagine how Maria
would feel if she had seen you with that woman on the
street?" He paused for theatrical emphasis. "It would break
Maria's heart. . . ."

"Don't cry, Arnaldo." Alves felt exceedingly sour. "She
didn't see me. All is well."

"All is well only if the kiss was as innocent as you say.
This woman, this actress, she is more dangerous than anyone or anything in your past, more dangerous than . . ."
He groped for the most imposing comparison: "More
dangerous than the High Bridge. . . . Truly. She could
destroy the foundations of your life, your marriage. . . ."
He went to the door and opened it, the yellow light from

the hallway wedging into the room. "I have nothing more to say about it. Are you coming to dinner?"

Suddenly Alves felt a chill, wanted more than anything not to be alone. Tomorrow Sir William Waterlow would examine the false documents and would look into Alves' face. . . . And who would stand by him if worse came to worst? Not Greta . . . but Maria. And Arnaldo. There was much in what Arnaldo said. A momentary kiss, was that such a crisis? He really didn't want to think about it. There was, at just this moment, almost nothing in his life that he did want to think about. *He wanted it to happen.*

The taxi drifted slowly through the clinging fog banks, Arnaldo and Alves quiet in the back, each staring out his own draped window. The restaurant presented a facade of multipaned windows. In the penumbra of street lamps, there was a golden bust, a head, in the cupola high above. Wisps of fog slid past, obscuring the head. Arnaldo paid the driver and held Alves back before entering; they could hear the sounds of a crowd as the door swung open and shut.

"Be prepared," Arnaldo said. "José is, you understand, touchy."

"No, I don't understand, but I accept his state of mind. Come, let's get it over with. . . ."

The restaurant spread off toward dim corners, huge and bustling and full of smoke, loud voices. Waiters pushed their way through the close-grouped tables, platters high. Alves followed Arnaldo, already feeling himself begin to sweat in the hot, stuffy room.

When they reached the table there was a flurry of activity. Greta, in a low-cut white dress he hadn't seen before, was standing up, her face even paler than normal. Her mouth was clamped tight, deep carmine. Hennies was fighting back a smile, soup spoon halfway to his mouth. Marang was gazing off into space. José's eyes were squinting, watching Greta.

"Where do you think you're going?" José said loudly.

She said nothing, clutching her purse. A waiter brought her fur wrap, placed it around her white shoulders. She drew it around her, held it at her breasts.

"Answer me," José said, standing abruptly, knocking over his chair. He grabbed at the fur, but she was gone. She moved past Arnaldo, paused beside Alves and inclined her head.

"I'm sorry, Alves. José is behaving stupidly. Don't argue with him—he won't listen." He felt her hand touch his arm. "Good luck in London." He watched her move away through the smoke. She seemed to glide.

"Arnaldo," he said. "Go get her a taxi." Alves turned to José. "Sit down and shut up. *Sit down*." Marang looked up, surprised. Hennies watched José, who glared at Alves, his face visibly darkening. Slowly, while Alves stared at him, he sank into his chair, as if a heavy hand were pressing on him. "Now, what is going on here?" He took the chair next to José.

"A lovers' quarrel," José said, glowering.

"Can't you keep your troubles out of public restaurants?"

"Can't you refrain from kissing my mistress in the streets?"

José spit the words out, one at a time, a vein pulsing in his forehead.

"Are you so unsure of her? Or yourself? That an impulsive peck between friends can put you in such a disgusting state?" Alves softened, taking José by surprise. He smiled. "Is this the Bandeira I've known all my life? Shaken by a woman? Is this the Bandeira whose conquests are known over half the world?"

"I don't know," José sulked.

Alves leaned toward José, put a firm hand on his shoulder. "You have nothing to worry about, my friend." Hennies leaned forward, trying to catch a word. "Trust me."

"She likes you," José said, looking at his plate. "She told me."

Alves forced a chuckle. "Trust me. I am no ladies' man. You'll make up with her tonight."

"Mmm. Possibly." José shrugged, stroked his mustache. He was calming down.

"But you're only human, Alves."

"Stop worrying. Eat your dinner."

José grudgingly nodded. Hennies and Marang began reminiscing about previous visits to London. Arnaldo returned, consulted the bill of fare. Alves sighed. If this kept on, he'd have a bad stomach. José sat morosely, sipped his wine, stared into space. Alves tried to clear Greta from his mind. He failed.

Morning came too quickly. In the bathroom mirror his burning eyes presented jagged red slashes. He dressed quickly, packed his bag and met Arnaldo for an early breakfast in the deserted dining room. Arnaldo was waiting, trying to decipher a morning paper, blowing on hot coffee. Alves nodded and sat down, trying to move his chair without scraping it.

"We leave for the Hook of Holland in an hour," Arnaldo said matter-of-factly. "Perhaps I should warn you—the crossing may be rough. Marang tells me the Channel has a tendency to choppiness in the winter."

"Always a treat to begin a gray day with a tidbit of good news. Should I wear a bib or lean over the side? Did you speak any more with José last night?"

"Ah, yes, most unfortunate, I must say."

"Unfortunate in just what way?"

"Well, he slept on the couch in my room. She wouldn't allow him in the room. He complained this morning of a crick in his back. Poor fellow. Mixing with a woman like that often produces explosive results."

"Stop playing a Chinese sage." The waiter left a tray of hot rolls, assorted meats, cheese and marmalade on the table, provided a silver coffee server and a cup for Alves, went away yawning. "It serves José right. He behaved like a savage. I admit, he surprised me. And disappointed me, too. I assumed he was above such antics."

"You surprise him. He said he'd never heard you speak so sternly to anyone. I think he had, at least until now, a slightly frivolous view of you. He saw himself as the elder, the worldly one, and you as an amusing *arriviste.*"

"That's why I spoke to him as I did."

"Well, you made your point." He carefully placed his cup in the saucer, wiped a crumb of bun from his mouth. "I must say, Alves, that you have handled yourself very well with these men. They all seem to be much aware of your dominance. Marang and Hennies were not prepared for the research you did into their past careers. . . . I've heard them talking. They've even asked me where you get your information." Arnaldo flashed an impish grin. "I tell them that you have many sources known only to yourself. They frown and fall silent. I find it quite amusing."

Alves chuckled. "Yes. Keep them confident of our enterprise but a little off balance."

Old comrades, they chortled for the moment. As they fell silent, Arnaldo's face went solemn.

"Did you take to heart what I said to you about Maria and Greta?"

"Of course. No one could supplant Maria in my affections. You know that."

"Then I must carry out my trust. Greta was waiting for me when I came down this morning. She gave me this envelope for you. . . . I don't like it, carrying notes to you from another woman, when little Maria sits patiently at home—"

"Don't start, please." Alves held out his hand. "Give me the envelope, not the moral lesson."

Stifling his curiosity, Alves put the hotel envelope in his inside jacket pocket, casually munched on a thick crusty piece of toast, covered edge to edge with cold meat, a slab of cheese, marmalade. Finally, with the appearance of Marang and Hennies and a weary José, Alves rose, wished them all a good morning, suggested that Hennies settle the bill and went alone into the street and sat down on a black bench. He opened the envelope and read.

My dear Alves

Please forgive me for whatever inconvenience I have caused you. José's behavior is atrocious, but I cannot but feel that I might have had the foresight to avoid the situation entirely. After all, you and I have just become friends. Let us give our friendship the opportunity to ripen.

Until we meet again, let me wish you Godspeed on your journey.
Affectionately
G. N.
4.12.24

The Channel crossing lived up to Arnaldo's warnings. Alves and José arrived at Harwick with a touch of chartreuse around the gills and a conviction that only divine intervention could see them safely to London. The boat train rattled and banged through the gloom toward the great metropolitan sprawl on the Thames. It was dark, and Alves felt grease-covered by the time their cab deposited them at that squatting Victorian pile, the Great Eastern Hotel, deep in the bowels of the fabled City, near to the centers of finance. Alves' first impression of England was of a cold, wet wind, dark, low buildings, cabs beetling past in the narrow streets, a sea of black umbrellas, intent wool-suited traveling salesmen clogging the Great Eastern's dim, smoky public rooms. After a light dinner of mutton and warm stout, Alves retired with a packet of digestive biscuits.

Propped up in his bed, with a thousand stags peering down at him from the patterned beige wallpaper, he withdrew his documents again, gazed at them in an attempt to see them as Sir William Waterlow would see them in the morning. He read through the typed words, examined the handsome seals, the attached banknotes, the crucial forged signatures. . . . What more could he do? Nothing, obviously. He remembered the High Bridge, his mind slowing, dissolving at last into a restless sleep.

Midmorning brought a golden haze that hung like festive netting from the chimney tops and steeples of the city. There were those who said that England's power was finally beginning to ebb, that America was the land of the future, but for Alves London was still the source of imperial might and financial weight. Finally, to see the streets he knew in his head—Poultry, Old Jewry, Cornhill, Threadneedle, Cheapside—to watch the black-suited, bowler-topped men whose lives revolved around the endless resources, to recognize from his reading the silk tophats of the stockjobbers, to simply be there sent his heart pounding. When he surveyed his team, he was not displeased. They all wore dark suits, shined shoes; only the mustaches and the gray Borsalinos might have given them a signal of foreigners . . . and, in any case, foreigners were common in London.

The Bank of England . . . the Stock Exchange . . . the ceaseless, relentless motion, the swinging of furled umbrellas, the absence of women in the streets. He'd read in Plum Wodehouse about the dependency of the typical Londoner on his club—he wondered if he might ask where, in fact, the Drones Club was—but he didn't want to appear overly inquisitive, being an Oxford man and all. . . .

He would have drawn it to the attention of the others, this quite indescribable sensation he was feeling, but they most surely would not have understood. It was something in himself, a pilgrim at the shrine. This was the home ground of Money and Power. He felt more at home here than he did in Lisbon.

Great Winchester Street was a great disappointment. He could have thrown a stone its entire length. Waterlow's was a grayish yellow four-story structure that curved around the sharp corner that formed the middle of the street. It was not an impressive sight. He cast a quizzical look at Marang, who nodded yes, this was it. Above the plain heavy street door was affixed the coat of arms of a Royal Purveyor. Now, he smiled to himself, that was more like it. Several Rolls-Royces and Daimlers were arrayed outside in the narrow street; that, too, reassured him.

The huge first-floor room was spartan, crowded with dozens of clerks bent scribbling over their ledgers. He could actually smell the ink from the bookkeepers' area, heard the hard-nibbed pens on the paper. And it was all devoted to money. . . . Marang stopped at a large wooden inquiry desk to the right of the door, announced himself to the uniformed commissionaires, who relayed the message to a runner, a youth who bolted up the narrow stairs. A minute later he was back, gulping his breath; he led the way back up the stairs.

"Dickens," Hennies muttered. "Nothing ever changes in England. That'll be their undoing, mark my words."

The runner tapped on the door, waited ten seconds, then carefully opened it and motioned them all inside. It was a large, comfortable but simple office, globes and books and framed maps, leather club chairs, a heavy ornate couch, framed photographs of stern, solemn Waterlows, a palm in a large pot—a dry, stuffy room with sunlight streaming in the windows, motes of dust dancing slowly in the air. At the far end of the space, flanked by aspidistra, was a huge rolltop desk. Standing beside the desk, red-faced and very tall, immaculately turned out in striped trousers and a black coat, smiling thinly, was a man who spoke loudly, like a cannon. He came forward as he spoke, extending a huge pink hand to Alves, who realized that he was in the lead.

"Good morning," boomed the man. "You must be the chap from Lisbon! I am Waterlow!"

*   *   *

Indeed he was Waterlow, Sir William. And that morning he had the feeling that he was at the top of his game. He was ruddy well fit as he'd ever been, and he proved it once today by mauling a broker neighbor of his on the tennis court he'd had installed at Whyte Ways. Fellow had a good bit of Italian blood in him, or so Waterlow suspected, and

calling himself Reggie Laughton wasn't going to fool anyone. Wops, Spics, Yids, Micks, it was all a matter of
establishing the proper relationship at the beginning. They
weren't all bad fellows, and no one could convince him
they were. Brave, many of them, die for their country—or
rather *his* country, since they surely couldn't claim to be
Englishmen, regardless of the uniforms they wore in the
trenches. Brave, yes; loyal, often. No morals, but then a
damned fine pointer or jumper didn't have much moral
sense either. Straight from the start, one simple rule: you
tell them what to do, they do it. Foundations of every
great civilization. A class who gave the orders, a class who
followed them. Made perfect sense, anyone could see that.

Once he'd left the tennis court, after leaping the net in
a show of sportsmanship that left the broker paralyzed with
fear and hope—both relating to the possibility that Sir
William might trip and kill himself—once he'd left the
broker with the order to buy him some additional railway
stock, he had been reflecting on this perfect social contract
that existed between the tellers and the told. On his way
to the handsome mansion he'd stopped for a word with
the mick gardener who was pruning the hedges.

"Good morning, Boylan," he barked. "Lovely weather
for early December, eh?"

"Aye, sir, very nice it is." He took off his cap, ground
out his fag so he might speak properly to Sir William.

He slapped Boylan on his narrow, bent back. "Well,
then. Bushes are all right, are they? Hedges? Borders?"

"Oh, yes, sir."

"Well, then, carry on, carry on. You're a good man,
Boylan. Reaffirms my faith in the Irish, eh?"

The problem was, as Sir William saw it, there was never
anything to say, actually, to these people. They were all
around you, of course, serving their small, wretched purposes, but once you'd told them to hop to it, well, what
was there to say? Not great when it came to conversation.
Give them a hoe or a shears, though, and they were quite
as happy as clams.

The chauffeured black Daimler eased him gently toward
the city. Consulting his schedule, pigskin with a fine gold
pencil from Harrod's, he relaxed against the cushions and
saw that the morning, damn and blast, was given over to
some sweaty little Portuguese . . . or were they? Marang?
He was Dutch, of course . . . poor devil, Marang van

Ysselveere! Did he think that fooled anyone? But the matter had something to do with the Portuguese, his clerk had told him that. Ah, what a lovely morning. His eyes roamed the green expanses of a park, huge trees, emerald carpets. . . . Ah, yes, what a perfect day for Cousin Edgar to be visited by a plague of boils. Rain of toads.

The morning ride was perfect for his happiest daydreams. Beyond Cousin Edgar's immediate dismemberment by howling gypsies, the continuing increase of Waterlow's new business made him most expansive. No one before him had ever done quite so well. Not only had he shepherded the firm through the scandals of the recent past, but he had pushed it to new heights. And enough new business —that might be the key to unseating Edgar. It would have to be a naked, unadorned power play, but it might just be possible. If his successes made him the one truly indispensable man, it was just possible that he could deliver an ultimatum—that is, Edgar or me.

And the Portuguese deal, whatever it was, might mean new business. There was, he admitted, something slightly out of the ordinary about this Marang thing. In the past, any communication regarding Waterlow's work for Portugal had come directly from the Portuguese Embassy in London. Now there was a Dutchman with a bogus name bringing word . . . Still, the Portuguese were different, and they doubtless had their own colorful, childlike intrigues.

The only intrigues that held any fascination for him involved his determination to become Lord Mayor of London. And that was proceeding nicely. Orderly. This was England.

* * *

"Good morning," he said heartily, the soul of welcoming aristocracy. "You must be the chaps about Portugal. I am Waterlow."

"Sir William," the first one said. He struck Sir William as being rather woplike, actually, which was no doubt simply Portuguese. "I am Artur Virgilio Alves Reis, representing the Bank of Portugal. These are my associates." At which point he rattled off a confusing series of names and hands were shaken. "May I begin by saying that we are on a mission requiring the utmost secrecy and discretion. . . ."

Waterlow sat in a club chair and the others arranged

themselves about the room. Marang, the Dutchman, headed the financial syndicate lending money *sotto voce* to Portugal —why, he reasoned, was none of his business, thank God— and Reis was the liaison between the bank and the syndicate. Slowly and with fiendish detail, all to the good, of course, they told him of the arrangement aimed at once again propping up Angola. Money down a rat's hole, of course, but Portugal was an ally after all. Government was crooked, yes, but you expected that. Somebody getting rich on the deal—but that was nothing to him. Waterlow printed banknotes, not morality leaflets.

"Well, of course," he said, "I am familiar with Portugal's misfortunes with Angola. Never mind, the story has been told in detail in the financial pages of the *Times*. As you know, during the past two years we have been of some service to Lisbon, printing several low-denomination notes for Angola—a tribute to the continuing efforts of our man in Lisbon, late of Angola—our man Smythe-Hancock." He heard a curious sound and turned to Reis. "I beg your pardon, sir? Did you speak?"

The Portuguese shook his head, covered his mouth with a bit of handkerchief, manfully struggled with the coughing impulse.

"You're quite all right? Yes? Good. Well, as I was saying, we've done that work, but these orders came from the Portuguese Embassy and were verified by Smythe-Hancock, as well as by personal letter from Rodrigues himself. Governor Innocencio Camacho Rodrigues—nice ring to it, eh? This matter you bring me is very different, isn't it?" He stroked his slablike pinkish chin, searched their faces with watery blue eyes.

"You grasp our point, then." Reis had apparently recovered from his fit. "This is totally unlike any previous issue of notes. Of all the elements Camacho stressed in our conversations, utter secrecy was foremost. There must be no communications beyond ours with you . . . and the document we have in our possession at this moment. Smythe-Hancock, for instance, must play no part in this."

"He is the soul of discretion, you know."

"He's human. His office could be burgled, his mail intercepted, under torture the man could break—"

"Oh, I say, old man," Waterlow chuckled. Excitable Portuguese. Quite like children.

"This is most serious, most serious, Sir William. Believe

me, the fate of Angola hangs in the balance. There is no question of overstatement, not when you listen to me. Through me, the Bank of Portugal speaks to you."

Fiery Latins, no point in setting them off. "Well, then, let us see this document of yours." Marang seemed to be leaving it all to this Reis fellow, deferring to him, you might say. He must amount to something. The contract was surely in order: not the normal thing but then this was, as they said—the man was an absolute bug about secrecy! —not the usual kind of matter. The notes appended to the contract were, however, not the work of Waterlow's, which created a problem. They had been printed, he realized at once, by his great London competitor, Bradbury, Wilkinson. Staring at them, looking back through the document again, he camouflaged what was spinning urgently through his mind. The accepted thing to do was face up to it and send them packing off down the street to Bradbury, Wilkinson. But damn and blast! Why? This was new business and highly confidential business at that, brought to him on a silver salver. Why turn it away? New business, another step toward ridding himself of the unspeakable Edgar . . . Might this not force Bradbury, Wilkinson out of the Portuguese market altogether?

"These notes," he said, waving them before him, "were printed by an American firm." It was a technicality, rather than an outright lie. Bradbury, Wilkinson was a subsidiary of the American Bank Note Company.

"Could you duplicate the notes?" Marang asked. The one with the long drooping mustache lit a cheroot. He looked as though he belonged behind a blackjack table in a casino.

"Probably. But it would take months of engraving alone."

"We must have the notes by February."

"Impossible. *But* . . . had you brought us the note we have already printed for the bank, then there would be no difficulty meeting your schedule, the Vasco da Gama five-hundred-escudo note." He took a large leather volume from the desk and dramatically threw it on the table, flipped it open to the Vasco da Gama note. "Our work, as you can see. Is it possible to substitute this note, gentlemen?"

Reis bolted from his chair and moved to the bank of windows giving onto a view of Great Winchester Street.

He lit a cigarette; smoke billowed around him. "I don't know if this is possible—"

"But, Senhor Reis, it is a simple enough change. It represents no problem at all to us at this end. And, as you say, time is of the essence. The less time required, the less risk of the truth leaking out . . . that new currency is being printed for Angola, eh? This is your best hope."

Clearly it was this Reis fellow who was the decision maker. Sir William did not want to push too hard, but the instincts swelling in his breast were those of the hunter moving in for the kill.

"Really, my dear fellow, it's simple as simple can be. Why, it doesn't even require a change in the denomination of the notes—you have both the thousand and the five-hundred-escudo note attached here. We will merely do the entire issue in the smaller denomination, using the Vasco da Gama note."

"As you say," Reis said slowly, nervously polishing his spectacles for the second time since he'd arrived, "it is a simple change. Still, there are reasons for my hesitancy which I cannot explain."

"But it is the only way."

"Yes, well, if it is, it is." Reis sighed melodramatically. "Use the Da Gama notes, then. But let me stress again the confidentiality of the entire matter. And let me make another point here."

Good heavens, who did he think he was dealing with? A garrulous drunk?

"As you know," Reis continued, "the Banco Ultramarino is normally the only agency that is allowed to issue bank-notes for our colonies. Complicating matters is the fact that two brothers, the Ulrichs, serve as directors of both the Bank of Portugal and the Banco Ultramarino. For this very reason only a few directors of the Bank of Portugal have been informed of this secret arrangement to pump new capital into Angola. The fact is, only the governor of the bank and the deputy governor know the details. Consequently, there must be no risk of revelation . . . your past connection with the bank is another area where an information leak could develop. The contracts which you already have could be a problem . . . a seam in the fabric of this arrangement which might burst. That is why we would have preferred a new printing of notes with which you had had no previous involvement." He sighed mightily,

shoulders heaving. "But if it is impossible . . ." He
shrugged. "We shall have to rely on your total discretion."

Outside the Rolls-Royces came and went. Alves heard a
boy hawking newspapers, recognized the banalities of great
moments.

"Believe me, Senhor, we are businessmen well versed in
the most delicate arrangements. Money is something we
never—let me put it this way, our instructions are nothing
less than Holy Writ. However, you understand that we will
need the personal authorization of the governor of the
Bank of Portugal to use the Da Gama plates for this new
printing."

"But why? Each time there is a communication, the risk
of losing secrecy is increased." Reis was sweating, pacing
again, lighting another cigarette. "No, I really cannot understand why there must be further authorization. . . . You
have in your hand the document containing all the authorization you need. I cannot go back to the bank and tell
them, no, there is a further delay. They expect results."

"But we cannot deviate from the notes attached to the
document without instructions to do so," Waterlow said.

"I am giving you the instructions."

"I am sorry, Senhor, but you are not the governor of
the bank. You are not an officer of the bank. I must have
a written authorization. But, if you wish, I can undertake
to acquire that myself, either through the embassy here or
directly from the bank by wire. As you know, I am well
acquainted with the governor—"

Reis interrupted: "No, you must not do that. It would
undoubtedly result in both Waterlow and our syndicate
losing the contract. That is precisely the kind of communication that I have been instructed to avoid at all costs."
He finally came to rest in a chair. "I will have to get the
proper authorization myself. I will return to Lisbon at
once."

"Well then, gentlemen, we have a deal. Waterlow is
completely at your service. If any help is needed in Lisbon,
rest assured that our man Smythe-Hancock will be ready
at a moment's notice."

"Very kind of you, Sir William," Marang said.

"But I hardly think that will be necessary," Reis added.

The arrangements concluded, Waterlow allowed a strict
five minutes for conversation with the other members of
the party and then determinedly saw them to the door.

What a bunch, he reflected as they trooped down the stairway, and how could a fellow like the Dutchman get involved with a bunch of Portuguese? But business was business, he supposed, and someone might as easily have asked
the same question about Waterlow himself. New business . . . He returned to his office and summoned his director of the foreign banknote division, Frederick Goodman, who had been with the firm since 1881 and a staunch
supporter in the unending battle with Edgar. He outlined
the arrangement to Goodman, who took it quickly, nodding
agreement but making one suggestion. Secrecy, he pointed
out, was all well and good, but we can hardly allow these
Portuguese lads to run our business for us. Whatever they
said, Smythe-Hancock, as our man in Lisbon, should be
informed of what was going on. Sir William agreed.

The meat of the wire they sent to Smythe-Hancock,
whose cable address was ENERGETIC LISBON and fitted him
to a T, pointed out the details of the deal and the fact that
further authorization was needed from the bank.

THE PRICE IS ALREADY ARRANGED: DO NOT REPEAT DO
NOT DISCUSS PRICE. DO NOT INSTIGATE CONTACT EITHER
WITH THE BANK OR WITH THE SYNDICATE. THIS IS BACK-
GROUND INFORMATION. DO NOTHING.

Sir William made it clear that Smythe-Hancock would
realize that the wire had originated with him personally.
Then he went to lunch at his club, satisfied that an excellent morning's work had been done and he hadn't had to
treat his clients to so much as a cup of tea.

*   *   *

Marang herded them to the darkened corner of an ancient
restaurant to celebrate. As their congratulations and high
spirits swirled around him, Alves fought off a feeling of
faintness. Hennies slapped him on the shoulder blade and
he managed a weak smile. José insisted on shaking his
hand, telling him how masterfully he had handled "that
overgrown side of English mutton!" Arnaldo drank his
warm stout, his bookish features lightened by what seemed,
no doubt, a hurdle crossed.

"A simple authorization and the deal is final," Marang
said, licking foam from his tight little mouth. His eyes glit-

tered behind his spectacles, almost threatening in a quiet, unobtrusive manner.

"My people at the bank aren't going to like it," Alves said, "not a bit, but with a little lubricant they'll provide the authorization."

Hennies' face lost its glow.

"Lubricant be damned! This isn't our fault. Why the hell should we have to grease any more of their greedy damned palms? They've gone this far. So who would they turn it over to now? By God, we've got them by the balls, I'd say." He laughed roughly.

"We haven't got anybody by anything," Alves said. "In the eyes of the bank, we're having the wrong people print the wrong notes. Now, while they may be too deeply into this deal to cancel it completely, if we try to throw our weight around we are damned well going to cut ourselves out of doing any further business with them. Do you see my point, Hennies? Use your thick German head, man . . . Five hundred pounds properly placed will take the sting out of the bad news I'm bringing them. And it could mean more, and larger, commissions in the future. Understand?"

"He's quite right," Marang said.

"Listen to him," José said. "He may need a better tailor, but he's a smart little bastard. . . ." He winked at Alves, apparently pushing Greta out of his mind now that money was being discussed.

"Five hundred pounds?" Hennies said. "That means our commission is down to seventeen thousand five hundred pounds."

José laughed. "Mind like an adding machine." He cackled happily, looking from face to face.

Hennies nodded, frowning. "*Ja, ja,*" he said.

Alves' mind wandered during the remainder of lunch. The stout and some hearty food—beef sliced from a rolling cart, hot Yorkshire pudding, a gooseberry tart—was reviving his equilibrium. God, what a morning! Smythe-Hancock . . . he'd nearly fainted when Waterlow had dropped that into the conversation. The abominable man he'd feared most in Luanda—possibly the only man in Angola who could have demolished his celebrated Oxford diploma! Fate had been with him, however. The two of them had met only at functions of an official nature. Alves had seen in the man's eyes the supercilious Englishman at his worst. In Luanda he'd had the impression that Smythe-

Hancock was a banker, or perhaps a broker. Now he turns up a trusted agent of the world's largest printer of banknotes . . . who must surely know of Alves Reis's business ventures in Lisbon, the Oporto jail. . . . Who might legitimately wonder at such a man representing the august Bank of Portugal in a convoluted issuance of banknotes. . . . Who might with great ease make inquiries at the bank. The more he thought about it the worse it became. He pushed his gooseberry tart away. The heat and noise in the small, low-ceiling dining room was oppressive. Secrecy. The man simply must be kept in the dark. But could Waterlow be trusted? One word from Smythe-Hancock to the bank and the entire scheme would be ignited like nitro, blowing Alves and his dreams right back into a jail cell. . . . Could Waterlow be trusted to maintain absolute secrecy?

He didn't know which was worse, Smythe-Hancock or the fact that Waterlow was insisting on printing notes they had printed before. The one thing he had sought to avoid was having men at Waterlow printing notes for men they knew at the bank. It was, at the moment, very much like finding himself locked into the locomotive halfway across the High Bridge and hearing the bridge supports starting to give way. . . .

There was nothing left but to forge another document. Yet surely each new forgery increased the odds of detection, either in Lisbon or London, at least tenfold. He had purchased a packet of digestive mints at breakfast; by the time he left the luncheon table the supply was exhausted.

With Hennies' bank draft tucked in his briefcase he and Arnaldo checked out of the Great Eastern and entrained for Harwich. There was no way to manage the forgery anywhere but Lisbon. In any case, it was expected by the others. The single bright spot was the five hundred pounds for his own bank account.

Hennies and Marang decided to remain in London until Reis' return. José chose to accompany Alves and Arnaldo as far as Paris.

"I'll try to make it up with Greta," José said by way of explanation, as they waited on the train platform. "Who knows what goes on in the woman's mind? She baffles me. What do you really think of her, Alves? Forget my behavior in The Hague."

"She would be more than a match for any man. I wish you luck with her."

Arnaldo returned with the tickets. They were standing by a soot-blackened pillar. The train was building up steam, firing it in jets along the grim platform. "She'll never give you any peace of mind," he said, parceling out the tickets for the train and the boat.

"Peace of mind," José cried scornfully. "We are too young to speak of that."

Alves stared at him, his face a map of impatience and doleful resignation.

"Of course, José," he said. "I am just tired. This traveling, it's bad for my stomach. . . ."

"Listen to your Uncle José and relax. There's nothing to worry about. . . ." He tilted his Borsalino jauntily and strolled toward the railway coach, Arnaldo and Alves in tow. "Nothing can go wrong now. . . ."

* * *

Anthony Smythe-Hancock's secret passion, confined to the dim cubbyhole of an office he maintained not far from the quarters Arnaldo found for Alves, was perhaps a throwback to all the soldiers his family had provided for England in centuries past. Decoding. Smythe-Hancock loved decoding: it was, he felt, about as close to military activity as he was likely to get in the banknote business. He enjoyed the secrecy, felt like a spy keeping clandestine meetings by moonlight. A coded wire from Sir William was an event. With quiet care and an increased heartbeat, he hunched over his neat, polished desk and slowly printed the message in black capitals with a worn stub of a pencil.

Years before Sir William had chosen the energetic Smythe-Hancock for his attack on Bradbury, Wilkinson. First he had sent him to Latin America to learn the strategies of the banknote business; then posted him to Luanda to begin the war on Bradbury, Wilkinson's Portuguese contracts by attacking from the least expected direction—Angola. The strategy, circuitous and patient, had produced Waterlow's first work for Portugal. Now, with the arrival in London of Marang's syndicate and Senhor Reis, the big breakthrough was at hand. Smythe-Hancock saw it in military terms. He was a loyal field officer, a by-the-book man. Which was why, as he read through Sir William's cable for the third time, he found himself in a quandary.

The message was clearly in error. Yet, how to handle it without disobeying orders?

Sir William had quite specifically instructed him in the utterly secret arrangement with the Bank of Portugal . . . and that was the crucial point: the Bank of Portugal had never had the slightest involvement with the issuing of banknotes for Angola. Drumming his fingers on the table, sucking the stub of pencil, he debated what to do. Finally he encoded a brief reply:

REFERRING TO YOUR WIRE OF YESTERDAY. BANK OF PORTUGAL HAS NOTHING TO DO WITH THE MATTER. BANCO ULTRAMARINO IS THE BANK DEALING WITH PORTUGUESE COLONIES. TELEGRAPH WHAT AM I TO DO.

But the wire was not enough. He composed a longer message in the form of a personal letter to Sir William.

You suggested that I might be called upon by a representative of the syndicate. They should have made the journey by now, yet I have heard nothing! What kind of behavior is this?

I cannot help thinking there must be some confusion in your mind with regard to the connection of the Bank of Portugal with Angola. The Bank of Portugal has never issued any Colonial notes to the best of my belief at anytime!!! So far as I know the Banco Ultramarino is the only Bank that has anything to do with Portuguese Colonial notes. I think it well to let you know as soon as possible that to the best of my belief you are confusing these two banks!!!

On December 9 Sir William, at a definite boil, fired off his reply to Smythe-Hancock.

YOUR TELEGRAM SHOWS YOU DO NOT APPRECIATE POSITION. DO NOTHING! SAY NOTHING! DO NOT PRESUME TO TELL ME I AM CONFUSED. IT IS YOU WHO ARE CONFUSED!

Smythe-Hancock was shaken by this peremptory disregard of his suggestions. Another man might have gone out for a stiff one. But Smythe-Hancock was made of sterner stuff, a company man with a deep belief that he could save the firm considerable humiliation. With his career quite possibly dangling by the most frayed of threads he sent off a long, encoded wire.

I QUITE APPRECIATE YOUR CABLE AND I CERTAINLY KNOW NOTHING OF THE POSITION BUT WHAT I DO KNOW IS THAT THE ISSUE OF PORTUGUESE COLONIAL NOTES HAS ALWAYS BEEN IN THE HANDS OF BANCO ULTRA-MARINO AND SO FAR AS MY KNOWLEDGE GOES THE BANK OF PORTUGAL HAVE NOT ONLY NOTHING TO DO WITH THE FINANCES OF THE PORTUGUESE COLONIES BUT IT WOULD BE NECESSARY TO HAVE A NEW ARRANGEMENT WITH THE PORTUGUESE GOVERNMENT AND A NEW DE-CREE SIGNED TO ENABLE THE BANK OF PORTUGAL TO ISSUE NOTES FOR THE FINANCING OF ANY SCHEME IN CONNECTION WITH ANGOLA. NOT ONLY THAT BUT THE PAPERS AT THE PRESENT MOMENT HERE IN LISBON BEING FULL OF ANGOLA FINANCE AND THE DISASTROUS STATE OF THE COLONY GENERALLY I CANNOT HELP THINKING THAT THE BANK OF PORTUGAL WOULD NEVER CONSENT TO THEIR PLATES BEING UTILIZED FOR A PORTUGUESE COLONY WHOSE FINANCES ARE APPARENT-LY IN A STATE OF ABSOLUTE CHAOS.

OF COURSE, PER YOUR INSTRUCTIONS, I AM DOING NOTHING BUT I TAKE THE LIBERTY OF CAUTIONING YOU IN THIS PROPOSED TRANSACTION.

The train ride following his second Channel crossing was an exhausting, debilitating affair for Alves, who wobbled off the swaying monster in Rossio Station, pale and indifferently shaven. Arnaldo saw to the bags and found a taxi. Alves slumped wordlessly into an upholstered corner.

What had Waterlow done once they'd left his office? The fear had gnawed at him across the hundreds of miles as the train had pounded southward from Paris. If Waterlow had taken any kind of a second look at the situation and notified Smythe-Hancock . . . well, there was no point in considering the horrendous possibilities. If Smythe-Hancock learned of his involvement the cat would be among the pigeons. Whatever happened, they would certainly not contact Smythe-Hancock at this end. But Waterlow had spoken highly of him. . . .

"Alves, please stop grinding your teeth." Arnaldo was tired too, nervous because Alves was nervous.

Alves groaned and lit a cigarette. God, if only he could tell someone the truth, somehow share the agony.

They were so close, not merely to the commission of one hundred thousand dollars, as the members of the "syndicate" thought, but close to the entire printing of two hundred thousand banknotes . . . *five million dollars.*

Smythe-Hancock. He could destroy the entire scheme.

And how was he going to forge a personal authorization from Governor Camacho?

"I am ill," he moaned.

"You are train sick. It will pass."

Alves groaned. It was very nearly too much to bear. If only he could discuss it with someone. *Greta* . . . Her name and her face and the low, hoarse voice floated toward him out of the night. *Greta.* She would understand; she was worldly and sophisticated. She . . . was in Paris. Listening to José. In bed with José.

* * *

At noon the next day Alves met Arnaldo for lunch at the Avenida Palace. He had arisen early, soaked in the tub before the children and Maria had begun their day's noise-making, shaved, doused himself with cologne and walked to the dingy office. For several hours he had sat at his desk, doodling on a note pad, jotting down several lists and reminders. Though pale and tired, he looked and felt rather more presentable as he strolled through the crowded streets to the hotel. He had decided on a new document.

He tried to eat, but food seemed superfluous at the moment. "Well, I have spent the morning—a most harrowing morning, let me assure you—with the High Commissioner of Angola and Governor Camacho of the bank. Both of them are almost ready to call the entire deal off. They don't like using these Waterlow notes, as I expected. But I finally was able to soothe them."

Arnaldo's face darkened with concern. "The authorization is in doubt?"

"No, Camacho said that it was not unusual, though he hadn't really thought it was necessary."

"Thank God!" Arnaldo sighed.

"But he doesn't want to exchange any correspondence

with Waterlow—because there's nothing easier than for a letter to go astray. Such a letter in the wrong hands . . . The deal would be off. Finished."

"Yes, yes, but Waterlow said he wanted *a personal letter*—"

"Don't try me, Arnaldo, I'm warning you. I am fully aware of what I'm doing."

"I realize that," he persisted stubbornly, making his point by rapping his forefinger on the table. "But the Englishman said he wanted . . . a personal letter! And we've already given him the wrong thing once—"

"Enough," Alves cried harshly, "enough, enough, enough! You are an imbecile!"

"I am not an imbecile," Arnaldo said with withdrawn severity. "Retract the imbecile, please."

Alves stared at him, this unfamiliar monster. There was a change in Arnaldo recently: he couldn't put a name to it, but it was there, nonetheless.

"Of course, you're not an imbecile. But you do not grasp the essence of the present situation as firmly as I. . . . And I'm telling you that what Camacho is providing me with is more than enough." He watched Arnaldo make a face and settle back in his chair.

"And what is this wonderful document?"

Briefly Alves described it. Arnaldo nodded silently. The lunch was not a success. When it was over Alves went off to commit his latest bit of larceny to paper. *Papel selado*.

During the hours spent forging the new contract Alves' mind drifted away from the task at hand. What had gotten into the faithful Arnaldo? Never before had he evidenced such a cool attitude in their personal relationship. Obviously the problem deserved more attention, just as Maria and the boys deserved more attention, but where was he supposed to find the time? Sighing, cramming more cigarette ends into his ashtray, he bent back over the typewriter.

CONFIDENTIAL CONTRACT
The undersigned,

　　Banco de Portugal, duly represented by its Governor Innocencio Camacho Rodrigues and its Director Joao da Mota Gomes Junior, as First Contracting Party, of the one part, and the Government of Angola, duly represented by its High Commissioner Francisco

*da Cunha Rego Chaves, as Second Contracting Party,
of the other part, declare:*

*First: That the First Contracting Party authorizes
the Second Contracting Party to cause to be manufactured up to two hundred thousand Bank Notes of five
hundred Escudos and one hundred thousand of one
thousand Escudos of the issue of the First Contracting
Party and of the types attached to this contract.*

*Second: Each Bank Note will bear the special des-
ignations of the Second Contracting Party, numbers
series and signatures, which shall be printed by the
First Contracting Party.*

*Third: That the Second Contracting Party guar-
antees to the First Contracting Party the privilege of
the issue of Notes in Angola and that it will endorse
to Artur Virgilio Alves Reis, Engineer, a married man,
all the powers granted by this Contract in the part
relating to the manufacture of the Notes, which powers
and conditions are set forth in their entirety in the
Contract to be drawn up on this date between Second
Contracting Party and the said Artur Virgilio Alves
Reis.*

*Done in Lisbon in the Agency General of the Col-
onies in the year 1924 on November 6 by me, Delfin
Costa, as I certify. Done and signed in duplicate there
being no other copies.*

His hands were shaking when he finished. Rereading the
new document, he was struck again by the immensity of
what he was doing. But it read well.

He copied the signatures onto the *papel selado*. With a
long shoemaker's needle and stout thread he sewed the
two documents together, added the separate page of
notarial signatures from the original contract. He attached
a five-hundred-escudo Vasco da Gama note on yet another
sheet. He sealed the packet with wax and applied the
Portuguese crest with the little ring.

For an hour he sat at the desk, glasses on the table, eyes
squeezed shut against the world, hands folded monkishly
in his lap, almost too tired to think. There was just enough
strength left to worry.

*   *   *

A few minutes' walk away, Smythe-Hancock sat equally disconsolately at his own desk, wondering at this late date if the banknote business had been a stupid choice all those years ago. Apparently he was squandering his store of good will in London; yet, he was simply acting responsibly and prudently, trying to alert Sir William to the extreme oddities in this Alves Reis situation. He paced to his office window, lit his small bowled black pipe and crossed his arms, a telegram dangling from the fingers of his left hand. "Alves Reis!" he said aloud. It was incredible that this ridiculous little confidence man should bob up to imperil his future with Waterlow. He brushed his lank blond hair back from his forehead. He remembered the High Bridge; he'd been there and lost a packet. He knew of the Oporto jail fraud, and he had always thought there was something fishy about his Oxford background. And now he presented himself as an agent of the Bank of Portugal. There was something wrong, and if Waterlow would only turn him loose on it he knew he could bloody well ferret it out. Frowning, he reread Sir William's latest wire.

WE MUST EXPRESS OUR SURPRISE THAT YOU DO NOT GIVE US CREDIT FOR KNOWING THAT THE BANCO NACIONAL ULTRAMARINO DEALS WITH THE PORTUGUESE COLONIES. OUR WIRES IF YOU HAD STUDIED THEM WOULD HAVE SHOWN THAT SPECIAL CIRCUMSTANCES HAD ARISEN. ABOVE ALL NOT A WHISPER OF THIS SHOULD REACH THE BANCO ULTRAMARINO. ALL WE WANT YOU TO DO IN THIS CONNECTION IS TO DO NOTHING. NOTHING.

Smythe-Hancock impulsively wadded the wire into a tight ball and banged it angrily off the wall into his wastebasket. Here I am, on the scene, experienced with proven judgment, and I am instructed, even *warned,* to do nothing.

Later he fetched the crumpled wire from the wastebasket, pressed it flat and put it carefully in the proper folder in his correspondence file.

*   *   *

Friday night they were once more on board the Sud Express heading back for The Hague. Alves had barely spoken with the children, and Maria had been getting her Christmas preparations underway. The holiday was less than two weeks away. Never had he felt less like Christmas. Arnaldo remained civil but distant. When Alves tried to engage him in conversation the responses were monosyllables. Eventually Alves gave up, returned to his compartment and struggled with another Wodehouse, picturing Sir William in a variety of roles. Somehow he didn't quite fit. He thought about Greta, too, and that was a mistake, because Greta made him think about José, whose behavior was becoming as unpredictable as Arnaldo's—jealous and ready to fight one moment, chagrin and camaraderie the next. Perhaps it was the pressure of bringing the deal to fruition.

But that didn't make any sense to him either, since only he, Alves Reis, the mastermind, knew that it was all a swindle. . . .

As if to give weight to these solitary reflections, José joined them in Paris for the final leg to The Hague. The wolfish grin, the bandit's careless demeanor, the quick chuckle and the friendly slope of the eyebrows—all that was gone, whatever the reason.

"Well, did you patch it up with Greta?" he asked, man to man.

José spoke flatly without looking up from his newspaper. "I have nothing to say about Greta."

Later Alves prevailed on him to have a look at the new document. Uncharacteristically José read it with considerable care. "I don't know if it will satisfy Sir William. He said he wanted a personal letter. This isn't one."

"Believe me, it could not be more official. It's better than any personal letter."

"I hope so, Alves. It seems to me a letter would have been easily arranged. . . ." He shrugged.

"The personal letter was out of the question. Impersonal, that's the way the bank wants it."

"All right," José said. "You know best. They are your friends."

*   *   *

Monday morning and the Portuguese were back. My God, to read Smythe-Hancock's idiotic wires you'd think they

were a pack of criminals, riffraff. Something had obviously
snapped in Smythe-Hancock's alleged brain—pique, perhaps, at not being included in a deal emanating from Lisbon. Well, hurt pride was not the concern of Sir William
Waterlow. New business was his concern, striking a blow
at Bradbury, Wilkinson. He patted the great beaming pink
slab of face with cologne, emerged from his private bathroom and set out across his office toward the door, hand
extended. Optimism was his boon companion this morning,
a quality that would have suited Smythe-Hancock in very
large doses.

Smiling broadly, he hardly noticed the reserve exhibited
by his foreign visitors.

"Of course, this is most acceptable," he announced
upon completing his perusal of the new document.

Alves Reis smiled for the first time since he'd entered
the room.

Since conversation seemed a trifle stiff, Sir William made
a show of shaking hands all around. Perhaps they would
care to join him later in the day here in Great Winchester
Street for sherry. By that time he would have had his
solicitor check over the contracts—purely routine, he assured them—and there would be copies available in an
English translation. Gravely, the deputation assented and
filed quietly out and back down the stairs. He watched
them go, more nails in the coffin of Edgar's hopes. His
face clouded as it always did when he thought of Edgar.

An elderly clerk was waiting in the hallway behind him.

"Another wire from Mr. Smythe-Hancock, Sir William."

Sir William's eyes narrowed in the great dry Yardley-
bathed face. The round pink cheeks with their tracing of
broken veins beneath the watery blue eyes twitched.

"Throw it away, Cubbage. I will have no more wires
from Lisbon. But do encode one more to him."

Cubbage produced a pad and pencil, poised himself.

" 'We will accept no more carping. Further wires will be
at your own expense. Stop, cease, desist.' And make sure
he knows it is from my office. Personally."

Having recovered his good humor over lunch with two
fellow titans of the City, Sir William consulted his solicitor
in the early afternoon. A steady December rain dripped
outside his windows.

"A couple of peculiarities here, Sir William," the solicitor said, much in the manner of a good personal physician, "but nothing of great importance. The contracts are bound in the wrong order—probably the work of an inexperienced clerk or a high officer of the bank unused to such menial tasks."

"That would be consistent with the high degree of secrecy involved." Sir William nodded sagely, staring at the rain-spattered toes of his otherwise spotless black boots.

"And the contract is not particularly clearly written. Again, not a crucial matter. Undoubtedly the contracts contain sufficient authority for Reis to manufacture these notes, and if they were manufactured by anyone authorized by Reis, the bank could not possibly question their manufacture."

"Just as I expected," Sir William said. "The business, then, is ours."

The solicitor bundled himself into his raincoat and retrieved his bumbershoot from the brass boot inside Sir William's office door, then turned back.

"One more thing, Sir William."

"Yes, what is it, for heaven's sake?"

"I think it would be a very good thing if you wrote a confidential letter to the chairman of the Bank of Portugal requesting his personal, specific authorization. . . ."

"All right, all right," Sir William cried impatiently. "Get your coat off, sit back down and dictate the letter." He pushed a button on his desk. "I'll get Cubbage in here right now; these little wogs are due back in an hour."

The solicitor replaced the bumbershoot, hung his raincoat back up and patiently sat down to await Cubbage. The rain drummed against the glass, blown by the wind trapped outside in Great Winchester Street. Cubbage brought steaming tea as well as his pad.

*   *   *

Something over an hour later, the sherry poured and the group arrayed before him, Sir William proposed a toast to the future of their mutual arrangement. Copies of the contract were dispensed. Alves Reis drained his glass and Sir William quickly refilled it.

"There is one more very small requirement," Sir William said, withdrawing an envelope from his inner breast pocket. He felt five pairs of eyes shift toward him.

"One more requirement?" That was Reis.

"It's nothing. But my solicitor is adamant and he is well paid to give me such advice. He does insist that I send a personal letter to Camacho Rodrigues requesting his personal authorization—surely a small matter."

"Of course," Marang said quickly.

"But . . ." Reis again, but Sir William went on, unfolding the letter Cubbage had typed.

"Here, now let me give you the sense of it." Sir William adjusted the pince-nez at the end of his nose. "You will realize," he read, "it is impossible for a banknote manufacturer to print banknotes except with the direct authorization of the bank, and I shall therefore be much obliged if you will kindly let me know that in accepting the order to print the notes in question, and using the existing plates for that purpose, we shall be acting with your approval." Sir William plucked the glasses from his nose. "You see, merest formality."

"I do not like it," Reis said.

"I beg your pardon, sir?" Sir William took a close look. Was the man trembling? High-strung, he supposed.

"Or rather Camacho will not like it. One more communication, one more opportunity for a slip-up—"

"Nonsense, Senhor Reis! You worry too much. This is normal business procedure. We can bend the rules of the firm no further. Surely, you can understand such a simple request. I, for one, cannot imagine your letting this stand in the way of our arrangement."

Reis visibly sagged, turned away and lit a cigarette. Yes, by god, the man's hands were trembling!

"Certainly not," Hennies interjected. "Nothing will be allowed to stand in the way—certainly not a simple letter."

Reis turned back, engulfed in smoke, calmer.

"All right. But you must realize that it is I who bear the full weight of the bank's displeasure. In any case, we must under no circumstances use the mails. I personally will deliver your letter to Camacho Rodrigues. It will not be a pleasant meeting!"

"But you're the man who can handle it, Senhor Reis!" Sir William's booming voice filled the room, one of his favorite sounds. "Gentlemen, we're in business together."

He clapped Reis on the back. The little Portuguese grinned weakly.

*   *   *

The Sud Express had become a portable hell for Alves. Exhausted, confounded by the endless requirements dragged out by Waterlow, he spent half-sleepless nights on the rocking, swaying train and helpless days watching the increasingly familiar landscape quiver past. Christmas decorations festooned the dining car. Many of the passengers traveled laden down with parcels. Alves stared at his dog-eared Wodehouse.

In Lisbon, rumpled and freshly nicked from shaving on the train, which seemed to have developed a malevolent, leering nature of its own, he went directly to his office. Dismayed but not altogether surprised, he discovered that at least three more creditors were sending angry letters threatening suits. Immediately he composed a tersely worded wire and dispatched it to Hennies.

RECEPTION AT BANK AS EXPECTED. NO GOVERNOR SIGNATURE UNTIL 1000 RECEIVED. IF NOT FORTHCOMING AT ONCE I DECLINE ALL RESPONSIBILITY. REIS.

Hennies wouldn't like it, but Alves felt certain that beneath it all Adolf knew perfectly well how the world worked. With the thousand pounds Alves could more than settle with the creditors; the rest he would give to Maria as a Christmas surprise. Just perhaps it would make her stop complaining about the size of the apartment.

The matter of the personal letter from Camacho Rodrigues gave him reason for concern. How to acquire the personal letterhead stationery of the governor of the Bank of Portugal? After considering a variety of pitiful subterfuges he left the office convinced there was nothing to do but make it.

The printer he called on was a distant cousin, easily impressed by Alves' claim that his dear friend the governor of the Bank of Portugal had asked Alves to bring him back some engraved writing paper from Paris. Alas, he had forgotten, but rather than disappoint his friend he would have the job done in Lisbon. If, of course, the printer thought he was equal to the task.

Having decided on the paper, Alves designed the stationery itself.

In the upper left-hand corner:

BANCO DE PORTUGAL
Cabinete do Governador
Particular

"Now, cousin," he said, "I need hardly caution you not to leave any sheets lying about or even in your dustbin. There is always the chance of an unscrupulous individual using them improperly. Burn the trial sheets."

While the type was being set he crossed the street to see an engraver.

"I am secretary of the Portuguese Sporting Club. You've doubtless heard of it." He smiled engagingly, affecting his idea of a sportsman's stance. "We have chosen a design for our new club seal—namely, the Portuguese crest with the club's designation."

"Aha," the printer said, nodding approval. "Very handsome, indeed. Now what type face have you chosen? If you please, may I suggest—"

"Excuse me, sir, but that matter is still the subject of some debate among the stationery committee. You understand"—he chuckled—"how committees work. As our American friends say, all chiefs and no Indians, eh? Just make an engraving of the seal and the printer can handle the typography. And this is an emergency—we must have the engraving by tomorrow morning. The committee has, of course, left everything to the last moment, and now I, the innocent secretary, must do the dirty work."

"But tomorrow morning, it is impossible, Senhor."

"Money, may I add, is no object. . . . This is a crisis! The honor of the Sporting Club may hang in the balance!"

"All right. Tomorrow morning it is, but it will be dear—"

"And the club members, many of whom govern great companies with engraving needs, will not forget the service you have rendered." Alves worked up a small smile. "Naturally, the lower the price, the more frequently we are apt to remember your great assistance!"

By midafternoon of the next day Hennies' thousand pounds had arrived, the creditors had been settled with and Alves was back at his desk with one hundred sheets and envelopes of bogus letterhead and a typewriter. He composed Camacho Rodrigues' letter to Sir William, taking pains to congratulate Waterlow on his great discretion.

Although it is to be recognized that the contracts held by Messrs. Marang and Reis, et alii, are documents sufficiently valid to free from all responsibility any printer, I cannot but thank your firm for your attention and special care in consulting me before employing the plates of the Bank which are in your hands and have great pleasure in informing you that you may accept the order from Marang and use the Bank's plates.

You would highly oblige me by dealing directly with Marang and Reis on all points connected with the printing of this Bank's Notes. Should any further data be required from me, I should beg you to apply for it in a Confidential letter directed to Marang and Reis or sent me, through their interposition, and in likewise confidential form.

The delivery of the Bank Notes may be made to Marang and Reis in London.

As to the numerating, dating, signing, etc. of the Bank Notes, the same gentlemen are empowered to make the Bank Notes as they wish—that is, to have them numbered, signed etc. and printed by your firm or any other, as they choose.

After concluding with the assurance that the notes would subsequently bear the ANGOLA overprint, Alves traced Camacho Rodrigues' signature from the five-hundred-escudo banknote and enlarged it. On another sheet he quickly forged a receipt for one hundred thousand escudos —the equivalent of the thousand pounds Hennies had just wired—and signed it with the name of Mota Gomes, the Bank's vice-governor, acknowledgment of the latest bribe. He mailed it at once to Hennies, hoping to forestall any more of Hennies' complaints; it proved beyond doubt the money had been well spent. Which, God knew, it had.

Arnaldo and José arrived on the Sud Express a few days before Christmas, and at a family dinner it seemed to Alves like a return to the happiness of the past, the days before he had hatched his great scheme and set it rolling. Maria led the singing of the traditional Christmas songs, and the boys portrayed the Three Wise Men and the baby had no

trouble with the role of the Infant Jesus. In the evening
they walked the brightly lit streets, swept along by the
crowds and the Christmas processions. Alves turned and
saw over the heads of the throng the impassive gray walls
of the Bank of Portugal. He could not escape the shadow
of the scheme, and at such moments he felt as if he'd
fallen into the embrace of the Iron Maiden. Like his
father's poverty, Alves found his grand plan equally per-
vasive.

"Now this is more like it," José said once Alves had
given him the personal letter from Camacho Rodrigues.
"Waterlow should find this exactly to his liking."

Arnaldo read, frowning. "But why couldn't we have just
gotten this in the first place and saved all this time?"

"As I have said," Alves said, "it was the question of
personal involvement—Camacho wanted to avoid that if at
all possible. There was no other reason." He caught Arnaldo's cool eye. "What else could it have been?"

Arnaldo shrugged. "How should I know . . . we could
have saved time." He handed the letter back. "This is fine,
Alves, just fine." But there was a muted quality to what
he said and did. No excitement, no joy, and his glance
flickered like eyes watching from the jungle.

José set off to see his father, who was relieved to have
spent a holiday season with José free of any incarceration.
Arnaldo spent most of his playing with the Reis children
and escorting Maria to concerts, on shopping trips, on
strolls through the parks, evidencing his quiet concern for
her well-being. His brotherly attention was necessary because of Alves' continuing preoccupations with the scheme.
No sooner had one obstacle been overcome than another
presented itself. As Christmas passed unnoticed, one problem remained—the ordering of numbers, letters and signatures on the banknotes Waterlow was waiting to print.

Since the numbering system was not described in any
of the Bank of Portugal materials Alves had researched,
there was only one way to learn it. He had to have enough
banknotes to find a pattern for himself, essentially an exercise in cryptanalysis. The pledge to overprint the notes
with ANGOLA would quiet any fears that Waterlow might
have about duplicate bills being put into circulation, but
still the designations on the banknotes would have to conform more or less with established practice. There was

also only one way to get his hands on a large enough sample of notes.

He wired Hennies, requesting another thousand pounds.

The answer, an immediate return wire, was NO.

In a soaking, cold sweat, Alves responded with a dramatic plea: YOUR PETTINESS ENDANGERS ENTIRE OPERATION.

Hennies was obdurate: THESE OUTRAGEOUS DEMANDS ARE WHAT IS ENDANGERING ENTIRE OPERATION. NO MORE.

Reis, after a totally sleepless night and the loss of everything he tried to eat, was at the telegraph office when it opened the next morning.

NO TIME FOR ULTIMATUMS. SUGGEST YOU CONSULT MARANG. REMEMBER YOU WILL BE REPAID FROM PROCEEDS.

Reis waited. Everything bad he'd ever heard about the Germans crossed his weary mind. With obviously inaccurate designations the notes must be recognized at any time, then all would be lost. He touched the tiny thunderbolt pendant at his neck.

On the second day he re-sent the same wire, adding:

PLEASE REPLY AT ONCE. ONE THOUSAND POUNDS URGENTLY REQUIRED. SILENCE INCOMPREHENSIBLE.

The next day word finally came.

FULL MEETING IN PARIS NECESSARY. CLARIDGE'S HOTEL. DECEMBER 31. HENNIES.

Alves had no more cards to play. Numbly he told José and Arnaldo that a final bribe was necessary and that Hennies was cutting off funds. José swore and angrily broke his new walking stick, a Christmas gift from his mother, over a restaurant railing. Arnaldo looked bleak, as if he had half expected it.

"Do those crooked bastards at the bank think we're made of money?" José picked up the two halves of his stick and vainly tried to push the broken ends together. "I should have broken it on the head of a bank director, by God!"

"You don't understand finance," Alves said.

"There's no end to it," Arnaldo remarked glumly. "It's hard to believe that such men are so totally unscrupulous. . . . I've never heard of such a situation."

"The fact remains," Alves said, "it is so and we must play by their rules. We either get the money from Hennies or the deal is off. What can I say? It's all part of life's rich pageant. . . ."

That evening Maria had an idea.

"Take me to Paris with you, Alves. You've been so busy —now we can go to Paris together and greet the New Year!"

"My darling, this is business, I'll be busy there."

"Not on New Year's Eve, Alves." She flung herself at him, arms around him, her cheek to his chest. "Please, Alves . . . Please."

Arnaldo spoke from a deep chair where he'd been napping after dinner. "It's a good idea, Alves. Your wife deserves a treat." He stood up and smiled grayly, yawned. "We could use some of the fun we used to have in the old days." He looked from one face to the other. "Then, it's settled. We all go to Paris in the morning!"

Alves forced a grin, nodded. "Of course, of course, we could all use some fun. . . ."

*   *   *

They arrived in Paris beneath gray, threatening skies that carried a hint of snow. Leaving Arnaldo to handle tickets and luggage, Alves waited with Maria beneath the soot-stained superstructure of the rail station, feeling her fingers squeezing his excitedly. Miraculously, the trip had worked a calming spell on him: he and Maria had retired early for their first lovemaking in what seemed an eternity. Her passion, followed by the placidity that had always hallmarked her behavior, had brought him a sudden return of his old confidence. It was as if one of his grandmother's thunderbolts had touched him again, this time for the better. Maria had presented him with a pearl-gray Borsalino with a soft, crunchy crown for Christmas. He had bought a grand camel's-hair polo coat, which gave him a swagger. For the first time since he had gone to the Oporto jail he felt at one with himself. Settling back into the taxi, Arnaldo and the children following in a second vehicle, he glanced at José, who was looking apprehensively out at Paris whisking by. Very soon he would see to it that all these worried faces were a thing of the past. Wordlessly, he leaned forward and clapped José's knee and winked.

The Claridge suited his mood perfectly. At the top of the Champs-Elysées the Arc de Triomphe loomed through the faint mist. Elegant black automobiles swept by on the boulevard and the colonnaded shopping vista off the lobby pleased his new frame of mind. Anything less than the pinnacle of style would have been out of character. He wished that the rolling carts of Vuitton luggage dotting the carpeted expanse were his own. A bit more patience . . .

Marang was waiting in the lobby, pacing, wearing a long fitted black overcoat that matched his funereal air. He shook hands glumly and began to speak.

"In a moment, old man," Alves said, turning to the desk clerk. "There is a mistake in our reservations. My wife and I require a large suite, as well as single rooms for Senhor Carvalho and Senhor Bandeira." He favored the clerk with a knowing look.

"But Herr Hennies made the reservations most specifically—"

"Herr Hennies made a mistake. Rectify his error at once and I promise you Herr Hennies will be remarkably grateful."

Marang blinked and turned to Reis, mouth agape.

"Over here, Karel," Alves said, leading him away from the bustle surrounding Maria, the children, the bags. José followed him while Arnaldo instructed the bellboys. "Now, what is of such great concern?" Alves lit a cigarette nonchalantly. "Speak up."

"It's Hennies," Marang muttered. "He says there'll be no more money. If you can't handle them at the bank he's ready to take over the entire business, go to Lisbon, meet with Camacho. It's his money and he says he has the power—"

"Ah, poor Hennies," Alves said. "I will take care of him, Karel, don't worry."

"He's waiting for you to call him. He told me he wants to see you at once, as soon as you're here."

José said, "It sounds like he means it, Alves."

"He may mean whatever he wishes. But it will all be done exactly as I say. You may count on that."

The clerk appeared at his elbow. "Your accommodations

are ready now, Senhor Reis. And may I extend our apologies for the misunderstanding?"

"Of course you may, my good man," Alves said, pressing bills into the man's palm. "Simply remember in the future that I am Senhor Reis of Lisbon."

Installed in the suite that spread lavishly in all directions, with windows overlooking the Champs-Elysées, two telephones, three baths and a dressing room in addition to a master bedroom, an exquisitely appointed sitting room in mauve and green and gold thread and a bedroom for the boys, Alves looked at his watch. It was ten o'clock in the morning. He rubbed his hands together, sniffed the bowl of fresh yellow flowers on the Directoire table.

"Now, may I suggest that you call Adolf?" It was Marang, still shifting from one foot to the other. Maria was unpacking the bags and busily putting things in drawers and closets, humming gaily.

Alves rang the German's room, his face becalmed and darkly handsome. He caught sight of himself in a gilt-framed mirror. The recent loss of weight suited him.

"Adolf? Reis here. You had the wrong rooms booked. A suite was necessary, but . . . tut, tut, never mind. I repaired the situation myself, no great harm done."

"I want you down here at once," Hennies barked at the other end of the line.

"I'm having a swim and a steam bath in a few minutes, work the stiffness out and relax. You should do the same—you sound a nervous wreck." Alves leaned back and gestured to Marang for his cigarette case.

"Cancel your swim, Reis. I got you here to talk business, not to pretend it's a spa. I want to talk now, do you understand? I'm making some changes in the scheme!"

Alves laughed aloud. "Adolf, I must say that bluster becomes you! I'll be happy to hear your story, of course. Let's say in an hour. And I'm sure we'll be more comfortable in my suite. One hour." He hung up.

"He's not going to take that," Marang muttered.

"Then he can come down and talk to me in the pool." Alves slipped out of his coat and headed for the dressing room.

The swim, in one of Paris' few indoor pools, soothed him, and the steam bath followed by a cold shower left him eager and alert, anxious to get it over with. He knew his luck had changed. Somehow he was willing the change.

Back in the suite, he saw Maria off on a walk with the children. He hadn't seen her so happy and animated since the dinner party in Lisbon. Now he spied the glitter in her eyes, the anticipation as she set off.

Hennies arrived on the hour, his face red, a thick cigar clamped tightly between his teeth. The monocle flashed. He stood for a moment in the center of the room, getting his bearings. Alves nodded. "Sit down, Adolf. Arnaldo, bring him an ashtray. Please extinguish your cigar, Adolf. The smoke will linger most offensively, and there is Maria to consider." He watched while Hennies scowled, ground out the expensive cigar. "Now, Karel tells me that you're full of interesting ideas—"

"You're damned right I am. I've been bled dry by these crooked friends of yours, and I've decided to take matters into my own hands and go directly to Lisbon. I'll talk some sense to your Camacho Rodrigues. What do you think of that, Senhor?"

"Before you interrupted me I was about to say that I have no interest whatsoever in your interesting ideas and no inclination to hear them." Alves shrugged. "Unfortunately I have now heard them and they are even more imbecilic than I'd expected. If you have finished you are free to go." He extracted a cigarette from the case and slowly fondled his old gold lighter. "I have nothing more to say to you. The deal is off. I will inform Waterlow to that effect." He lit the cigarette.

"What do you mean?" Hennies cried, leaping to his feet. "Your bluffing doesn't fool me, damn it! Reis, you've been playing me for a fool."

"Goodbye, Adolf." He blew a series of smoke rings, smiled as they floated toward Hennies. He could feel the three sets of eyes following the conversation like the ball in a tennis match.

Hennies sank back in his chair. "What are you pulling, Reis?"

"Nothing, don't be absurd. Many business arrangements collapse. I have other interests. I have put myself out to consummate this one. Apparently I have fallen short. It's time for me to pursue my other interests. You are at liberty to do whatever you wish."

"Just like that?"

"Just like that, Adolf. After all, a few weeks lost, what is that? I am exceedingly well connected in Lisbon. There's no shortage of enterprises seeking my attention. It's fate. . . ." He smiled amiably. *"Au revoir,* Adolf."

"What do you intend to do about my losses?"

"I? I intend to do nothing about your losses. I'd have thought they were exclusively yours. . . . Perhaps Camacho Rodrigues and Mota Gomes will give you your money back." He chuckled, glancing at Marang, whose mouth had dropped open. "And perhaps they won't. A business risk, nothing more."

"But, Reis—"

"I am sorry," Alves said. "I wish you luck with Camacho. He hates Germans. His brother-in-law was killed during the war, so make quite sure he believes you are Swiss. Just a word of advice." Alves straightened the crease in his trousers, aimed the pointed toe of his shiny black shoe at the base of a brass floor lamp.

"I *am* Swiss," Hennies mumbled. "And he owes me thousands. . . ."

"Godspeed, Adolf."

"If I should reconsider . . ."

"There is only one reconsideration possible, Adolf," Alves said gently, insistently. "Pay up another thousand pounds, old fellow, or count your losses. As for myself, I am perfectly capable of repairing my relationship with Camacho—you forget who I am, the Hero of Angola, a man of substance. Camacho will understand that I have been betrayed by a German. . . . But you, my fine friend, will have lost through impetuous shortsightedness every advantage you have acquired here and will have caused your associates a good deal of inconvenience. That is nothing but a passing irritation. But what are you planning, Adolf? A return to the Singer Sewing Machine Company on the upper reaches of the Amazon?"

Hennies flinched at the attack, his face paling. He hunched forward, hands on knees, collar cutting into his throat.

Alves pressed his advantage. "Besides money, be good enough to tell me what you brought to our arrangement? A past so checkered that it has become a maze of false documents and faked identities, a questionable reputation as a German spy, membership in the most despised race in Europe. . . . Did you look upon these as your contribution? No, you brought *money.* . . . Now you back out on me,

on all of us." Alves shook his head in mock sorrow. "Are
you so misled as to think I will forget your behavior?"

Hennies roused himself. "Are you threatening me, sir?"

"Are you backing out on our agreement?" Alves lifted
his eyebrows and frowned. "The fact is, you owe us another thousand pounds."

There was a pause during which Alves stood up and
went to the window, folded his arms and watched the traffic below. Finally, against the sound of the ornate ormolu
clock ticking on the desk, he spoke with his back to Hennies: "I am sorry, Adolf. Goodbye."

"All right, you win," Hennies whispered, unfolding his
checkbook.

"There is no time for checks now. I want the money in
escudos, small denominations, no later than one o'clock
this afternoon. I am very much afraid that you'll miss
your lunch, Adolf. You had better be on your way."

Hennies limped out of the room.

The room was silent again, the clock ticking.

"You've made an enemy," Arnaldo said at last.

"Nonsense," Alves said. "I know my man and I know I
have been much too timid from the beginning. Hennies is
the one deriving benefit from this arrangement. He owes
his inclusion entirely to me . . . lazily, I had let him forget
it. Now he will remember. Now we go forward." He
looked from face to face. "Well, then," he said heartily,
clapping his hands, "it is time for lunch."

There was something different in their faces and, on the
whole, he liked it. He had his feet on solid ground again.
No more desperate hours in the tiny office bent over the
typewriter.

*   *   *

At one o'clock Hennies appeared meekly with an aged
satchel full of escudos. Smiling broadly, Alves took it and
placed it in the middle of the large table beneath a set of
windows.

"Reis," Hennies began, standing stiffly at one side, jowls
quivering. "About this morning. I wish to make it clear
that I have been under much strain. . . . There is not an
endless supply of money to draw on." He polished his
monocle with the white handkerchief from his breast
pocket.

Alves slapped him on the shoulder. "We have all been under a good deal of strain. Confidentially, let me tell you that even I have been near to it at times during these past few weeks." He smiled benignly. "I foresee no more demands of this kind—from here on, we should be making money, not spending it."

"Then all is well?" Hennies asked softly. "Between us?"

"Of course, Adolf. We understand each other perfectly. Have an extravagant lunch, have a swim and some steam! You've earned it."

Hennies retired, awash in relief.

For the next two hours, in his shirtsleeves and with the door securely locked, Alves covered six pages with notations of banknote designations, trying to discern the pattern. It was just beginning to take shape when Maria returned with the children. Her excitement filled the room. After she arranged the children with books and games, she returned to Alves and perched on the edge of the desk, barely noticing what he was working on.

"You've had a pleasant afternoon, my darling?" Alves inquired, slipping his spectacles off and rubbing his eyes.

"More than pleasant! We walked all the way to the Arc de Triomphe and it was so exciting that we forgot about the cold. And you will never, *never* guess whom we saw. . . ." She waited expectantly.

"No, I'm afraid I haven't any idea, dearest."

"Well, just as we were turning back and thinking about a bite of lunch, who should come striding up in a very grand fur coat but the famous . . . Greta Nordlund! A chance meeting and what a wonderful time we had! Isn't that amazing in such a large city?"

"Perhaps it is amazing. In any case, you are surely amazed."

"As was she." Maria began to stroll about the room, arranging ashtrays, turning on lamps, fluffing pillows. She found the remains of Hennies' cigar and dumped it into a wastebasket. Watching her move, her shapely figure and heavy breasts shaking as she walked, he recalled the previous night and felt himself quickening. He wished, however, that Greta had not turned up. His new frame of mind had not provided him as yet with a means of handling her.

"And we lunched together at a charming little café and she took me to some shops. Beautiful bags and shoes and scarves. Such taste the woman has! And, of course, she asked about you and I said you were meeting with your associates at Claridge's." Maria's voice dropped to a whisper and she came closer. "Alves, is there some trouble between her and José? She said she hasn't seen him since you were all together in The Hague."

"And what else? Surely she must have had new amours in the days since then."

"Alves, don't be unkind. She is a lovely, friendly woman with great style, and José has probably treated her badly."

"I had no intention of being unkind, my dear. I'm sure she is all you say. But who understands such matters? Not I, not with the sweetness of our marriage. I know nothing of their personal problems."

"But couldn't that cause conflicts in your group?" She had grown unusually interested in this new gossip, and Alves wondered how he might head her off. He turned back to his calculations, stacks of banknotes, none of which Maria seemed to have noticed.

"Perhaps we won't be seeing much of her if José is no longer involved with her—"

"Ah, but that's what I'm leading up to," she cried. "The most exciting thing of all—a New Year's Eve party, here in Paris!" She put her hand over his, stopping his shuffling of papers. "We're all to meet at her apartment at nine o'clock—including José. . . . She says there's no point in having a party unless we're all there."

"Oh, Maria," Alves said at length, "I really don't believe we should have quite so much to do with this woman. After all, we hardly know her. . . . I don't really approve of mixing business with our private life. So, please, my darling, let's celebrate New Year's Eve alone, together."

"Alves," she began, her voice troubled, "Alves, I am always, unfailingly a good wife, but tonight I was hoping we could go out, see Paris, do something exciting—*live,* Alves, *live.* . . . Greta wants to have a party—dreams are answered! And you, sitting here surrounded by money and scribbling and your business deal, you say we cannot spend a few hours doing something I want to do!" Her face crumpled up in sobs. "I just don't understand why you would be so cruel when I was so happy." She broke off in mid-wail and ran into the bedroom, slamming the door. Alves stared after her, bewildered. She would never have behaved in such a way before meeting Greta. Now she had seen another kind of woman and the trouble was beginning. What to do? Obviously, he could not allow her to run his life. She would just have to cry; she could then apologize and he would arrange a private candlelit dinner in the hotel and everything would be back to normal.

The telephone rang shortly after he returned to his compilations and frightened him into knocking his ashtray onto the floor. Smoke rose from the carpet. He leaped up, grinding his heel into the smoldering mess, and grabbed the infernal ringing machine.

"What is it?" he said sharply.

"Alves, is it you?" The low husky voice with the peculiar intimations he could never quite identify: he wasn't surprised.

"Of course, Greta. How are you?"

"Hoping to see you this evening. I thought it would be such great fun for us all to celebrate together."

"Well, Greta, I'm afraid we're both very tired from the train trip. And we have the children here, you see."

"You drive me to an indiscretion, Senhor . . ."

"I don't understand—"

"I will be frank with you and, please, don't think me mad. Do you promise?"

"Of course." The carpet was still smoking. With his free hand he reached one of the slender vases of flowers, withdrew the flowers, which wetted his hand and sleeve, and poured the water on the small but persistent fire.

"You sound peculiar, Alves."

"The carpet here is on fire."

"What did you say?"

"Nothing. The carpet is burning."

"My indiscretion, then, is that I very much want to see you—you personally, Alves Reis."

"Greta, what are you saying?"

"Only that I want you to come to my party. With your wife and all our other friends. Simply that. Whatever happens will happen."

Maria poked her head through the doorway. She held a damp face cloth and looked from Alves to the wet, black debris on the carpet and back to Alves. "Is that Greta?"

He nodded.

"Are you coming now, Alves? As a personal favor to me? Now that I've delivered my little indiscretion?"

"Yes, of course, Greta, we will be very happy to attend

your soirée. . . . Forgive my devotion to my work; sometimes I am very selfish."

Maria flew to Alves, flung her arms around him, kissing
his cheek.

"I shall look forward to it," Greta said softly, a smile
in her voice. "Maria has the address. Goodbye, Alves."

Her voice lingered in his ear as he put his arms around
Maria, heard her warmly whispering tiny privacies as she
moved her body against his. Quietly, she took his hand and
led him to the bedroom. Behind him on the table his
researches went uncompleted.

*   *   *

With the exception of José, who had agreed to meet a
friend for a quick drink and would be along later, the
entire group arrived at Greta Nordlund's Left Bank flat
precisely at nine o'clock. She inhabited the top floor of a
squat old building with a view of Notre Dame and the Ile
de la Cité. There were skylights in a cavernous studio room
heated by two large fireplaces, the logs crackling and spit-
ting in the flames. A light rain dripped cozily on the skylights, and through the wall of windows all Paris seemed
to glow with New Year's Eve light, blurred and softened
and enlarged by fog banks slipping up off the Seine. Oriental pieces were scattered about the room, statues of in-
scrutable gods, vases that seemed alive with curling
dragons, incense burners that gently gave the space a hint
of exotic practices carried out by the famous actress and
her Bohemian friends. Soft, deep cushions outnumbered
the low bamboo chairs. There was a peacock-backed chair
set on a platform with an oddly Scandinavian wallhanging
behind it, creating a throne effect; on the walls there were
several large framed theatrical posters celebrating the
owner's career. A huge canopied bed of Oriental design
could be glimpsed past an archway hung with beaded curtains. A Javanese maid greeted them, led them into the
studio, where a low table was spread with curries and
champagne. Greta was standing near one of the fireplaces,
seeming immensely tall in loose-fitting beige trousers and
blouse with a lavender belt cinching her waist, lighting a
long, thin black cigar. The whole thing struck Alves as
rather stagily produced, but, on the other hand, he'd never
seen such an extraordinarily dramatic setting or such a

remarkably beautiful woman. As he'd grown older and seen to his own education, he'd come to realize that vaguely similar places and people actually existed. But to be in their presence was an awe-inspiring experience. Maria leaned against him for a moment when the full impact of the room struck her. A smile crossed Greta's face as she exhaled thick aromatic cigar smoke; then she broke the pose and came toward them.

There was a quick tour in response to Maria's cries of delight at the furnishings and the views of the cathedral, the bridges, the lights across the water. Champagne flowed, curries were sampled with toasted almonds and apple slices and cocoanut and chutney and raisins. There was a spinach and mushroom salad and several more guests arrived: a sculptor whose partially completed bust of Greta was ceremoniously unveiled to applause and toasts; a Belgian drama critic dressed in puce velvet; José's diplomat brother Antonio Bandeira, who came from The Hague and wore a chestful of intensely colorful medals; several painters and poets; the newspaperman Jake Barnes, who apologized for his pal Hemingway, who was at The Select and unlikely to leave. There was Covarrubias, who had done the pink drops with watermelons and hams in cornucopias for Josephine Baker's *La Revue Nègre* at the Theatre des Champs-Elysées; and there was the tiny Rumanian poet—though everybody thought him French, Greta said with a wink of her lavender eyes—Tristan Tzara, founder of what Greta informed him was the Dada movement, and his Swedish wife, the daughter of a fabulously rich industrialist and an old friend of Greta's.

Alves was leaning against the wall near an open window, sipping champagne and feeling its liberating effect, when Greta touched his arm. Fog blew past the windows and someone was singing in the streets below.

"Being a hostess is such a bore," she said, "particularly when I want to be spending my time talking with you."

"I am very flattered," he said. Her face was close to his. He smelled her perfume, longed to touch her cheek, run his fingertips over her face. "But why should you want to spend time with me?" She shrugged.

"Because I am terribly attracted to you. Surely I have made that clear."

"I am a married man."

"I didn't ask you to commit bigamy, Senhor."

"You know what I mean." His throat was dry. He tilted the champagne to his mouth.

"You are a very strong man. So few men can truly dominate. Hennies and José, they both are in thrall to you. . . . You should hear them speak of you—you hypnotize them. Maybe that's what I feel. I like to listen to you, the sound of your voice. . . . Do you remember The Hague? I felt it then, your power over me." The wind at the window moved her hair, the soft material of her blouse.

"But you are always laughing at me."

"I am laughing at myself, the way my mind is behaving like an adolescent schoolgirl's. I want to kiss you, do more than kiss you. . . ." She took a deep breath, standing so near him that he felt it. A gramophone was playing something familiar and emotionally potent behind them, and he forgot to worry that Maria might see them.

"You must forgive me," he said, stroking his mustache, feeling the power she attributed to him, "but why tell me such things?"

"What good is there in denying your feelings? Or keeping them to yourself? This is New Year's Eve in the twentieth century, and if a woman wants to tell a man that she . . ."

"Tell him what?"

"No, really, I've said more than enough. I am an emotional actress and sometimes say things I shouldn't." Abruptly she stiffened, her face darkened. "José is here," she said.

He felt José's heavy hand on his shoulder and smelled the liquor on his breath. The hooded eyes squinted past cigarette smoke and the slick black hair was mussed.

"Alves," he said, "Happy New Year . . . and where is the faithful little wife? With Arnaldo running along behind her, keeping her occupied while you tag along after this . . ." He jerked his head toward Greta.

"I'm tired of this, José," he said. "You're an old and dear friend, but my patience is wearing thin."

"Too fucking bad about your patience," José said, biting off each word as best he could, considering his condition. He tilted slightly, as if preparing either to launch or receive an attack.

"José, I'll have you thrown out," she said.

"I don't see Hemingway here. I thought he did all your throwing out for you . . . stupid ox."

"José, please, you'll ruin my party, darling. Now behave."

"I saw the party you and my dear friend Alves Reis, Hero of Angola, Oxford graduate, were having over here by yourselves, standing nice and close together. I've seen your work, Greta darling, I watched you work on me—how's that for a joke?" Sweat was beaded up across his forehead and an eyelid twitched nervously. He shook his head like a fighter getting up and holding on. "You're after him now and you'll damn well have him, whatever it costs him . . . but you think he'll just buckle like all the rest of your men, eh?" He held onto the window frame, swayed for a moment before steadying himself.

"You're making a fool of yourself," she said, moving away.

He grabbed her arm, yanked her back. Out of the corner of his eye, Alves saw Maria and Arnaldo turn to watch.

"It's you that's the fool, Greta," José said, voice louder and more insistent. "Because no matter how much you talk and let him look at your tits and tell him you want him in your bed . . ." His voice cracked. The room at large could not hear them, but Maria and Arnaldo had drawn closer, heard every word. Alves looked quickly at Maria as if to say there was nothing he could do about this drunken madman.

"No matter what whore's tricks you play on him, Alves Reis is not like me! He is a man of proven character, a respectable married man with children, and Alves Reis will tell you to go straight to hell!"

Immediately he swept away toward a tray of champagne. Maria ran to Greta's side and put her arm around the actress' shoulder, comforting. Arnaldo watched the two women in amazement. Alves sank back against the wall, releasing the tension.

"Maria," Greta said laughing, "you are so good! José is such a poor fool. And so madly jealous. He sees me chatting innocently with your husband and the drink goes to his head, he becomes a crazy man. . . ."

"Have you ever seen José behave in such an offensive manner, Alves?" Maria's horror was palpable.

"Please," Greta said. "Let's not let this spoil our evening. I have an idea—shall we go dancing? Isn't that a good idea?"

"Wonderful!" Maria exclaimed. "Alves, please . . ."

Relieved at the way it had all turned out, Alves nodded.

Arnaldo stared at him once the women had moved away. "What was Greta saying to you? Before José arrived. . . ."

"What's the matter with you? She was going on about some play about Cleopatra. . . . She's always talking about things I don't understand. Come on, old fellow, cheer up. I'm ready to watch you dance, you sly fox."

The procession of taxis moved through the chilly mist up Rue Vaugirard to turn down Montparnasse, past the dim, dreary buildings toward the warm glow emanating from the corner at Raspail where the cafés bloomed like flowers in the night. The crowds were thick. Less than an hour until 1925.

Riding with Greta and Maria on either side of him, Alves saw for the first time the Dome, which was seething, people spilling out from the interior onto the terrace. Next door, with an even longer terrace, the Coupole's crowd was a trifle more controlled, maintaining a certain order in the chairs at the long rows of tables. There was a good deal of singing going on as they left the taxis and the sound of the bands intermingled in the boulevard. American jazz, of course, but unidentifiable as it mixed with the horns of dozens of taxis bringing merrymakers to the Left Bank. The gendarmerie was out in full force.

Greta squeezed his arm as she led the way, spoke to both of them: "Here, across from the Dome, is the Rotonde, our destination. I always feel more at home there; it's where most of the Scandinavians go. The Americans go to the Dome as a rule and the Coupole is international. We all mingle, of course, everyone seems to know everyone else." Friends, or admirers, who recognized her cleared a path and welcomed the actress to several tables where room was made at once. There were cries of "Bravo!" as she nodded, inclined her head, and Maria's face glowed in Greta's reflected fame. Alves smiled as if some of the attention was for him, wishing in a way that it were but also enjoying being the man of mystery with the women on his arm. It was like the champagne, a fizz of excitement beneath the pink and white and blue lamps. Braziers of coal glowed behind their table, and the chill was lessened considerably.

"Don't order any champagne," Greta whispered. "It will come." She glanced, smiling, at the crowd banked around their tables. "I'm sorry to subject you to all this attention, but it's one of the prices I pay . . . and they do supply me with champagne on occasion." She leaned closer; he felt her breath on his ear. "I'm so glad we're here, together on New Year's Eve. It is right that we are, don't you see? And what José said? Well, he was not altogether mistaken." He felt her lips move in a smile against his ear. "I am in pursuit of you." A laugh caught deep in her throat. "But don't worry. What happens happens." She turned quickly away, and when he looked she was pointing out someone to Maria. Champagne arrived and was poured into goblets. The band grew louder and dancers threw off their coats and began stamping rhythmically. A bald man whose beret was slipping appeared with an accordion strapped across his chest, followed by a trumpeter and a clarinetist, all of whom gathered near one of the braziers and began to play, heightening the excitement on the terrace. It all reminded Alves of the party of the past summer, celebrating his release from Oporto. It had been different then, of course, but there was a feeling that night that he had never known before—the feeling of beginning anew, full of confidence in himself and his plans. Somehow in the complexity of the months that followed he had lost that sense of his own destiny and let himself grow weary and mired in the mechanics of what had to be done. He could do anything, anything at all. It was quite fitting that there be a party. As for a new woman . . . Whatever would happen would happen.

"Le java!" a voice cried, and a handsome young Frenchman took Maria by the hand and with only a quick, tentative backward glance at Alves she followed. With her quick instincts she began the dance, caught up in it at once, coat open, eyes flashing.

Greta nodded approvingly. "Very good, your Maria! Lively. Would you care to try?"

"No, thank you." He put his arm around her shoulder.

"I thought not." She smiled, her thin mouth barely moving. It was her eyes that communicated: a code they both understood. Hennies and Marang chatted with her other guests; Arnaldo's eyes followed Maria, would then flicker back to Greta and Alves, then move restlessly on across the crowd. A large blond woman closed in on him shortly before midnight and resistance was hopeless: she pulled him into the dancing and Alves applauded, shouted, "Hooray, Arnaldo! The dancing man!"

"Le fox!" another shouted, and the band segued into a popular American foxtrot.

"And now, Senhor Reis," Greta said, standing, "this is our dance. Le fox . . ."

Her mink coat draped open, and he was conscious of her nipples stiffening beneath the thin fabric of her blouse. She smiled, watching him watching. Playfully, she shook her finger at him. She was pliable in his arms, moved where he wished, bent gracefully, didn't speak but looked frequently into his eyes. She conveyed the frankest suggestions possible, without a hint of self-consciousness.

At midnight the terrace had become a dance floor and the mass of people was impenetrable. He could not see Maria anywhere. The band was counting off the seconds, and as the moment came the cafés exploded with sound, music and cheers and the riotously loud horns of the taxis. The mist was caught in the lamplight, balloons floated away like the travail of the old year. Greta took his hand and placed it against her breast beneath her coat, drawing herself close against him. The lights were extinguished, and a sparkling device was lit on the sidewalk, casting a faint red glow across the terrace. Someone began singing "Auld Lang Syne" across the street at the Dome, and it was taken up from one café to another.

"Happy New Year," she said. There were tears on her pale cheeks and she wiped them away, her lips parted.

"Yes, Happy New Year."

She closed her eyes and leaned forward. He felt a catch in his chest, a lightheadedness. He kissed her, at first a mere touching of their mouths, then harder, pulse quickening, his ears closing out the sounds around them. It was as if he heard her heartbeat, felt the throbbing of blood in her veins. It was almost like the first kiss of his life, a first step into mystery. He tasted the tip of her tongue, the pulse beneath it. . . .

When he finally drew back she clung for a moment, eyes closed, her fine head tilted to one side as if listening for some distant applause. He knew even then that he would never quite be certain of the difference between the truth of the matter and her performance.

Later as the crowd returned to their tables and the dancing grew less frenetic, he found Maria pushing her way through the chairs and coats to throw herself into his arms. She was tipsy, slurring her words and laughing at herself. She kissed him, missing his mouth. He knew Greta was watching as she spoke with Marang a few feet away.

"I danced le java, my love," Maria cried. "Did you see me? Were you proud?"

"Of course I saw you and of course I was proud!"

"And your wife is the mother of four! Think of it! Oh, Alves," she cascaded onward, "I am so glad we came—to Paris, to Greta's party, to this place, whatever its name is. . . . Aren't you?"

"Very glad. And Happy New Year, my darling."

"It will be our best year ever! Do you promise, Alves? An unforgettable year?" Her grip tightened on his hands. She was staring up at him, but the dark eyes were glazed.

"The best year of our lives, Maria. I promise you. Unforgettable. . . ."

Later as he stood smoking, his collar turned up against the cold wind, he noticed snowflakes in the glow, drifting down over the scene like smoke.

Arnaldo came up, a worried look on his face.

"José is back drunker than ever and looking for you. I tried to get him to give it up, but he wasn't making much sense." He cast searching glances behind him at the crowd.

"Damn him," Alves said tiredly.

"He's jealous," Arnaldo said. "How can he know your relationship with Greta is innocent if it doesn't appear innocent even to me? You are not being wise, Alves."

"And what do you think I should do?"

"Take Maria and get out of here. She's about ready to pass out, anyway. Call it a night. . . ."

They found Maria sitting next to Greta, a faint smile fixed on her mouth, snowflakes lacing her hair.

"Come, my darling," he said. "It's time to say good night."

Maria giggled. "Good night, my dear Greta. I'm afraid Alves knows me too well. . . . I should be in bed."

"It has been a long night," Greta replied. "You see her safely home, Alves. I'm so happy you could join us. . . . We did launch the New Year handsomely, didn't we?" She kissed Maria's cheek, smiled at Alves and clasped his hand.

Arnaldo, Maria and Alves were halfway across the street, gesturing to a taxi, slipping on the suddenly slick paving, when José saw them. His coat bore the marks of a recent

fall in the snow, and he was carrying a bottle of red wine
in his left hand. He waved with it, slopping wine on his
hand. "Hey there, Reis!"

"Yes, José, here I am."

"Well, I've had enough of you," José shouted. People
began to stare. "You rotten bastard . . ." He seemed to forget what he was about to say, stood confused in the street.
He took a drink from the bottle. "I'm telling you to leave
my whore alone! My whore is . . ." He lurched forward,
flailing again with the bottle, wine floating through the air
to spatter Alves' coat. Arnaldo pulled Maria toward the
waiting taxi. "My whore is my whore!" He belched and
glared drunkenly at Alves.

Alves straightened him up, gently, balancing him on the
snowy street, and struck him on the side of the face, the
blow carrying on past his cheek to glance off the bridge
of the nose. José waved both arms like a windmill in an
attempt to keep his footing. His hat fell off. The wine bottle
described an upward trajectory and stopped abruptly when
it contacted Alves' nose. José, staggering backward, cried
out, clutched his own nose, slipped desperately in the snow
and sat down heavily on his hat. Alves' nose was dripping
blood. He left a trail in the snow as he went toward José,
who was using the bumper of a taxi to get back on his feet.
He had just drawn erect and was shouting "Whore!" when
Alves arrived and slammed a right into his midsection. José
collapsed forward over the fist and forearm and, when
Alves stepped back, fell face downward. The skin on his
nose had been broken and was beginning to bleed. A stain
spread in the snow, pink.

Glancing up from his efforts, Alves saw a taxi growling
past with Arnaldo's face, expressionless, in the window and
the shape of Maria's head slumped forward on his shoulder.
At the first sight of the fight the taxi drivers had edged their
vehicles closer, lights on, motors running, the drivers egg-
ing the combatants to keep at it. The crowds at the cafés,
aware that something interesting was happening, had
pushed in behind the taxis and were now seeping through
to the site itself. "Come on, get up and give us a fight."
"Two bloody noses, that's not bad." "*Ach*, two drunks,
let's go back and have another drink. . . ." Hennies pushed
his way to Alves' side, while Marang went to bend over
the inert figure of José. "You're bleeding," Hennies said.
"I saw him, he threw the bottle at you. . . ."

"He didn't mean to," Alves said. He took the handkerchief Hennies offered. "I'm all right."

Hennies clapped him on the back, laughing. "Well, I'm
glad you didn't deal with me like that!"

"Don't be ridiculous, Adolf. I don't do this habitually."

"Damned lucky for José you don't. . . . Hey, Karel, will
he live?"

"I expect he will," Marang replied. The horns were still
honking and the gendarmes were having considerable difficulty getting to the scene of the fisticuffs. Marang tugged
at José, who was suffering the effects of being drunk rather
than of any blows received. He ineffectually slapped José's
face. José grunted, wiped snow on his face.

Greta had reached Alves' side and was dabbing at his
nose with a white handkerchief. "You knocked him out!
A veritable Georges Carpentier you are. . . ."

"I suppose you know *him*, too," Alves muttered.

"But of course," Greta said, licking the handkerchief
and continuing her repair work. "Dear Georges never did
a quicker job in his life! How do you feel?"

"All right. . . ."

"Oh, look at your hand! The skin is all broken. . . .
Fighting for my honor, too. What can I say to you?"

"You heard what he said?"

"Yes, of course I did. When he gets an idea he certainly
does cling to it, doesn't he?"

Hennies returned from his inspection of José, who was
by now propped against the wheel of a taxi with several
drivers gathered around toasting him from their own supplies of wine.

"Adolf," Alves said, "I am counting on you to take care
of this as quietly as possible. José may not even remember
it by tomorrow."

"Of course, exactly. Discretion, eh? Leave it to me."

"Good. You may begin by dealing with the gendarmerie."

Hennies went to explain the situation to the uniformed
officers, who had finally arrived in force and were looking
around for culprits. Leaning over José, one of them slipped
and fell down. The drivers laughed. The police decided to
get the taxis moving and unclog the corner.

Greta led him back past the Rotonde, where the scene
was growing much quieter. It was something past one-
thirty and the snow was still drifting lazily down in the

lamplight. "Please, come back to the flat with me." She spoke without urgency, as if she already knew his reply.

*   *   *

By five o'clock, the night still dark outside the bedroom windows, they were finally quiet. The sheets had all come loose and were now drawn tightly around their bodies as they lay cradled by pillows. He had retrieved the heavy comforter from the floor and piled that on top of the sheets. Now he smoked, eyes open, body limp, feeling her naked legs clasped around his thigh, her pubic hair soft on his flesh.

"Are you awake?" he asked, whispering.

"Yes," she sighed. "I am utterly exhausted, but I cannot possibly sleep." She kissed his chest, fondling the amulet on the cord around his neck.

She burrowed against him. He smelled her hair, the sweat that glued their bodies together and made a sibilant sucking sound when they shifted, pulled apart. A lamp glowed in the large studio room beyond the beaded curtains. It seemed to him in the haze of spent passion that he was somehow playing a part in a stage production or a film. The whole thing—the taxi moving through the falling snow, the elderly driver who had chuckled indulgently at the kissing in the back seat, the quiet street with the smell of the cold Seine, the climb up the squeaking stairway, the way she had dropped her coat on the floor inside the door, the quiet complicity with fate as she led him to the bedroom and slipped out of her clothing while he watched, the sound of her washing in the bathroom and the cold sheets against him as he waited—there had been a dreamlike quality, a heightened reality unlike anything he had ever known before. . . . Never had there been such an opportunity, never such a woman, not even in his fantasies.

Cool and smooth and white, she had before his eyes grown warm and moist, an urgent and demanding woman, responsive yet concerned for her own sexual satisfaction. Nothing at all like the cuddlesome, childlike Maria, who had always looked upon lovemaking as something playful and amusing, not something that led deliberately to moans and sweat and pushing, driving thrusts, cries of passion and bodies wracked with the violent spasms of need and irrepressible climax. . . . No, she had been wholly unlike Maria, and he couldn't shake the thought from his mind. He wanted to think only of these hours with Greta, but Maria, with her innocent pleasures, would not fade away. Yet Maria had never drained him so thoroughly, so insistently. Closing his eyes, he could taste again her thighs, feel the texture of Greta's warm flesh beneath his tongue, straining against his mouth, holding his face against the thick darkness. . . . Now he knew more about her than he had ever known of Maria, more, he feared, than there was to know. . . .

"What is this you wear around your neck?"

He looked down, leaned across and circled her nipple with his tongue, felt it harden until she pushed him away.

"Behave, Senhor, I beg you. . . ."

"My grandmother gave it to me on her deathbed. It is a thunderbolt, very old—it protects me, though it has not always done a very good job."

"A thunderbolt," she mused, laughing. "It is you, I am quite sure, who are the thunderbolt." She leaned up, pushed herself back on the pillows. "Alves, did my behavior shock you? I cannot help myself sometimes. I do those things which, I am told, proper people don't do. . . ."

"You are most womanly—more desirable than I thought possible." He kissed her hair.

"I am not what José calls me, but I am not innocent. I don't believe I was ever innocent, not completely. Does that bother you?"

A draft shook the glass in the window frames. Far off an automobile engine coughed into life.

He took her hand and placed it on himself. "Does this bother you?"

He pulled her over on top of him, looked up into her eyes, felt the long blond hair falling like a drapery around his face.

"Yet again?" she whispered.

"Yet again. . . ."

Dawn came gray and wet, and still they had not slept. Together they dressed and found a tiny patisserie in a narrow crumbling street nearby. The morning was cold and cutting. He felt cleansed. The croissants were freshly baked, the coffee strong and mixed with hot milk and sugar. New lovers, they held hands across the small table, the sounds of the bakery a few feet away. He felt drunk with the smell of the ovens, the touch of Greta, yet his head was clear.

"Come," she said. "I have a surprise for you."

He followed her down another side street, stopped behind her as she unlocked a garage door. Inside there was a Bentley roadster, green with gleaming spoked tires and the steering wheel on the right.

"My car. Get in. Ask no questions."

There was only one other car in the street as she passed her flat, the driver hunched like a shadow behind the wheel. As they went past he came to life, turned on his headlamps. "We've awakened him," she said. She drove intently, enjoying the act. New Year's Day. They seemed to have Paris to themselves, gray and wet and foggy. The snow clung to the streets in patches.

She drove to the stables in the Bois de Boulogne. She parked the little car and with another key opened the door into the horse barns. He followed her across the hard-packed earth. A stableboy greeted her. Lights glowed in the huge barn. Horses snorted, clomped their feet. The smell of hay permeated everything, hay and oiled leather. Birds darted noisily among the rafters.

"You said you used to ride in Africa. We will ride my horses. They can use the exercise and it will be good for us." She threw him a heavy jacket to replace his coat. She saddled one large gray, the stableboy attended to an even larger chestnut stallion. He watched her work with the economy and strength of a man. He felt his heart pounding again. He had not ridden since Africa, had not realized how much he missed it. She mounted easily, the stableboy holding the stirrup; he swung up quickly, and she slowly led the way out onto the paths crossing the green grass, the wet trees muffling any sound from the world beyond. Fog shrouded the landmarks of the city. The horse moved easily, smoothly beneath him, snorting, shaking the cobwebs out of its head. He moved up to ride beside her. She smiled across at him. "A good idea, don't you think? Does it feel good?"

"Perfect."

"I knew you'd like it."

"These are your horses?"

"Yes, I keep four and ride whenever I can. José used to fall off . . . but he was always superbly dressed." Her laugh floated and she rode off ahead. He marveled at her:

that there could be such a woman. He had never considered riding as a form of pleasure; suddenly he saw it very clearly.

She waited for him a couple of hundred yards ahead. Together they sauntered on in silence. She wore a serious, intent face, patting the horse, whispering to it as she leaned forward.

"Have you thought about us?" she asked. "Why we did this, spent the night together?"

"I believe in fate. Just as I believe in myself. . . . Some things are fated to happen—"

"But in the beginning you didn't like me much. Be honest."

"I was frightened of you, of your world, you were too sophisticated. I had just come from Africa."

"More accurately, you had just come from jail."

"Ah, yes, jail. . . . I owe a great deal to my stay in the Oporto jail. But you frightened me yourself, you are so frank, if you see what I mean. And you are quite incredibly beautiful, of course. . . ."

She rode on in silence. The fog had completely swallowed them. Even a few feet away the outline of her was blurred.

"But you have so much to lose. . . ."

"Not at all," he said. "I have gained a night with you." He took a deep breath. "I have fallen in love."

"Oh, no," she said, reigning up and turning in the saddle. "Love comes much later. This is excitement, this is romance, my dear Senhor."

He watched her wheel the gray and set him off down the path at a gallop. Slowly he walked the chestnut back along the path. "Don't be anxious, horse," he said. "We'll just walk back. We can think about what the day will bring us. We have all the time in the world." He lit a cigarette and settled back in the saddle, the way he'd done so often in Africa when he was never quite sure what lay ahead.

* * *

Arnaldo, muffled thoroughly inside a heavy overcoat, was pacing nervously outside the Claridge when the Bentley pulled up to the curb. With a wave and a smile, Greta was gone.

"We must talk," Arnaldo said, his mouth hidden behind the scarf.

"All right," Alves said. "But I hope you are not about to cause me more problems. . . . I have had quite enough unpleasantness within the past twenty-four hours with Hennies and José. I'm tired of having to bully everyone—"

"You seem to have a natural gift for it."

"It is foreign to my nature, you know that. I have been driven to it, and you can be sure you'll all be thanking me when it's over and our business is producing. Come on, let's walk."

Their footsteps clicked on the sidewalk. New Year's Day and the Champs-Elysées was almost empty. The Arc de Triomphe loomed ahead, oddly devoid of traffic at its vast base.

"I cannot contain myself any longer," Arnaldo began with a rush. "What you are doing to Maria is unforgivable, Alves. What has happened to you? Why have you lost your senses over this creature who is nothing but an adventuress and quite possibly much worse than that? You heard what José called her . . . and he is in a position to know."

"You find her a whore, then?"

"I see no evidence to the contrary. She has blinded you, that much is apparent."

"I suggest you retract your insult. I suggest as well that you refrain from discussing matters about which you know nothing."

"But I do know about Maria—"

"Take back your implications about Greta Nordlund!"

"Alves, for God's sake! What are you talking about?"

"You heard me. Apologize at once or we can settle it another way. . . ."

"All right, all right," Arnaldo cried impatiently. "I am withdrawing my implications about her moral character."

"Thank you, Arnaldo."

"But the fact remains that you are doing your wife a terrible wrong!"

"Nonsense. I have done her no harm at all."

"You deny you spent the night with Greta Nordlund?"

"No. You have just witnessed my return."

"You deny you went riding with her in the Bois de Boulogne at dawn? Don't look so shocked. You were seen . . . followed there actually."

Alves remembered the car near her flat, starting up as her Bentley passed by.

"José," he said. "José waited outside her place all night. Incredible." There was wonder in his voice. "Then he followed us. . . . I don't believe it."

"You deny you committed infidelity this past night?"

"Arnaldo, stop harping! You sound like a particularly dimwitted prosecutor. . . . It is none of your business."

"This, to me?" Arnaldo grabbed Alves' arm, his face white, shocked. "To Arnaldo Carvalho? Your old friend, your companion at the High Bridge—you tell me it is none of my business?"

"A man's life is his own. . . . I'm going to make you rich—"

"You have impaired our friendship!"

"Ridiculous!"

"You will make me rich," Arnaldo repeated scornfully. "You are giving me charity, is that what you are saying?"

"You're crazy, you're my right hand, you know that! Come to your senses—we will grow rich together!"

"All you think of is money! Money, money, money! You're obsessed. . . ."

"What are you saying? When was I ever any different? Why did we go to Luanda in the first place? Because we knew we weren't run-of-the-mill men, doomed to struggle to survive. We went off, we proved ourselves, we made money—a man must have a singleness of purpose, and that has been my strength. I have always known what I was about. . . . Don't you see that?"

A lonely car honked angrily as they crossed a sidestreet without paying heed.

"You never used to hurt people . . . and now you are bullying Hennies, knocking José down in the street, telling me to mind my own business, and you are—God help you—betraying your sweet innocent bride! And you, you . . ." He nearly choked over his emotions. "You tell me it was never any different!"

They pushed on in silence, approaching the Arc de Triomphe, vast like something found in Egypt. Alves crossed his arms, puffing a cigarette, squinting.

"It's very large, isn't it?"

Arnaldo scowled. "Yes, very."

"A symbol, Arnaldo, of the great world, the great deeds men can do. . . . Don't you see what is happening to us,

Arnaldo, friend of my boyhood, don't you see that we have gone beyond the small world where we learned our capabilities? How can I make you see?" He regarded his glum, sour-faced comrade. "Life is opening for us its store of treasure . . . we must not waste the opportunities the great world offers us. Remember all the reading I did in the Oporto jail? You brought me the books. . . . And as I read them, as I scoured the newspapers and books of history, I began to grasp the fact that there was a great world far beyond the boundaries of Portugal . . . opportunities, and I made the decision to face the opportunities and accept their challenges. . . . The framework of our lives is changing, we are being offered new things—we must grasp them forcefully, whether it is a woman or the chance to make some money. Now listen, I cannot give you the details yet, but the bank has led me to believe that we can expect more, *much* more, to come. . . . And I want you with me, I want to say, aha, there is my Arnaldo, I can count on his loyalty! To the end. . . ."

"Don't talk to me of loyalty."

"Don't be a fool, Arnaldo. Take what life has to offer."

"Life has already offered you the love of a sweet wife, four children, the opportunity to recover your reputation and start again. . . . Those are the things that count."

Arnaldo began to move off around the Place de l'Etoile, trudging slowly. Alves followed him, suddenly quite desperate to make him understand.

"There is more, my friend," he cried after the stooped figure. "Arnaldo, I cannot turn my back on it all. . . . I may die tomorrow, no more chances."

Arnaldo stopped, said sadly, "She is worth all this, then?"

"You don't understand it—yes, of course I slept with her, but don't you see that it was more than that, the act of sex? I had real power over this unattainable creature, Arnaldo. Don't say it. Hennies attained her, José attained her, I know, I know, but they are not me, and I never imagined such a thing . . . why, my God, Arnaldo," and Alves' voice fell to a whisper as they turned around the monument, the cold wind whipping at their legs, "I could make her do what I wanted, things I never imagined with Maria, *anything I wanted.* . . . It's a matter of new powers and Greta is only one part of it but, I admit, she's a symbol of it all. We are making the world do things our way rather than our having to conform to the world's way of doing things. And you, Arnaldo, must be part of our success. I, Alves Reis, demand it!"

Arnaldo, confused and frightened, shook his head.

"You're not the same man to whom I gave every last shred of my loyalty. . . ."

"Ah, that is the point—"

"But there is something . . . I don't know quite what's going on here. I can't understand it, but it's not right. . . ."

"You must merely grow accustomed to it, my friend. Can I count on you? To stay at my side?"

"I cannot condone your behavior with the woman."

"Maria will never be hurt, you must believe me. Just continue to be our dearest friend. . . . And you will be amply rewarded."

*   *   *

Maria had spent New Year's Day asleep, while the children were minded by a day nurse provided by the ever capable Claridge. Arnaldo had seen to that. Now, when Alves returned, the children were quietly doing puzzles with the nurse, and Maria was propped up in bed with a tray, a plate of toasted rolls and a soft-boiled egg. A pot of tea perfumed the room. She smiled happily when Alves entered the bedroom and kissed her cheek. He had bathed, napped briefly and returned to his calculations of banknote numbering and lettering. It was five o'clock in the afternoon when Maria received her breakfast. The bedroom was brightly lit and cheery. Outside the light was nearly gone.

"Did I misbehave terribly at the party? I cannot remember much, I'm afraid, my love. I have no head for champagne. . . ." She looked up shyly. "Don't look at me, I must be a terrible hag. . . ."

"Maria, your behavior was exemplary and your appearance as beautiful as ever." He kicked off his shoes and sat beside her on the bed.

Buoyant with happiness, she went on to tell Alves how much he reminded her these past few days of the man who made the trains run in Angola—the man who became the hero of the colony. But now he struck her as even bigger, stronger. "Oh, my darling," she sobbed at last, delighted at the turn life had taken. "I will love you forever."

Eyes closed, Alves listened, his heart torn between her familiar voice, excited and childish, and his intense memories of Greta. When would he speak with her again? They had left the future indefinite.

"Oh, Alves, we must move to a new apartment . . . or, better yet, a house! When can we? I will furnish it in the style of Greta's. Did you ever see anything so perfectly beautiful? Our home will be the envy of Lisbon!" She cocked her head, birdlike. "And what happened after Arnaldo brought me home?"

"Ah, you remember my little problem with José. Well, he'd had too much to drink, of course, and apparently he's insanely jealous over Greta, the poor woman. What a burden, a drunken José following her about! In any case, since Arnaldo had whisked you away before I could join you, Greta invited me back to her place and attended to cleaning up my nose and scraped knuckles. I'm afraid your Alves is not such a great fighter."

"You won, didn't you?" She spooned egg onto a triangle of toast and popped it into her mouth.

"And then we chatted for a while. I'm afraid I was a terrible boor, keeping her up all night. But I was too excited myself by all that's been happening. Anyway, soon it was morning and we went out for breakfast and she showed me her horses—yes, she keeps horses right here in the city—and I went riding with her . . . very nice it was, too, and then she drove me back here and I bumped into Arnaldo. We went for a walk. Thus, New Year's Eve." He opened his eyes wide and yawned.

"She must be so rich and famous, too. . . . The champagne just kept coming to the table. . . ."

After dinner, which they had brought to the suite, after the children were in bed, Maria situated herself in Alves' lap and pecked his cheek.

"I forgot to call Greta to thank her for the party," she said pensively. "Will you be seeing her again before you go to London?"

"I doubt it, my sweet. I will be very busy, I'm afraid. You can write a nice note from Lisbon."

She traced a fingertip along his mouth. "Take me to bed, please. . . ."

"Of course, my darling, but please forgive me if I am tired. . . ." He smiled weakly, standing up with her in his arms.

"Don't talk to me of how tired you are," she chided.

"You have your husband's responsibilities and I have never known you to fail."

"I know, but tonight . . . really . . ."

"Alves, remember that I am leaving for Lisbon in the morning. I won't see you for days and days."

"Of course, my darling," he said, carrying her to the bedroom.

It had been an immensely long day.

* * *

The gray crushed stone paths of the Luxembourg Gardens spread away in clockwork precision, matching the color of the low, cloudy morning. Women bundled in tight-fitting coats pushed babies in prams determinedly along the paths, faces down to shelter against the cold wind. The mighty chestnut trees creaked and rustled overhead. José, with a small white bandage across the bridge of his nose and a discoloration at the point of his left cheekbone, stared across the dead gardens at the cold, bleak palace itself. Alves puffed on a cigarette, flexed his fingers in new black calfskin gloves.

"Am I fired?" José spoke with uncharacteristic temerity. Presumably he grasped the enormity of his transgressions. He had been left to stew throughout New Year's Day, without so much as a word from Alves. During those hours remorse and, so it appeared to Alves, even fear had set in. José weighed his own life; he must have known he could not lightly discard his relationship with Alves Reis, who was quite possibly the only man on earth who would turn a blind eye to his relentlessly irresponsible past. There were circles under his eyes and his mouth was pinched.

Alves turned his back to the palace and leaned against the balustrade, watching a group of old men pitching chestnuts at birds. "I'm at a loss, José," Alves said casually. "What can I do with you? I am bereft of patience. . . ."

"I don't know." José would not look at him, stared off toward the faint rumblings of the city beyond the trees and shrubs and gates. "I have made my peace with Greta, for whatever that's worth. Everything is over between us. Do with her whatever you wish." He sighed, made a helpless gesture with his hands. He still wore a flower in his buttonhole, smelled of fine cologne, wore gray gloves with pearl buttons and spats beneath razor-creased trousers. "It's up to you, Alves—my life, my future, all in your hands. You know best. I'll abide by whatever you say. . . ."

"We are old friends, José. But you must realize that we are no longer reckless children selling fake relics to foreigners. You are part of me, José, but you must understand who is the leader now. As children, things were different, but those years are long gone. Now we are men and the balance has turned. You must accept that."

"I know," José said, suddenly contrite, struck by the reality.

"And as far as Greta goes . . . It is entirely my own business and I will tolerate no interference from anyone. None."

He began walking the length of path away from the palace, toward the gate far ahead. The wind blew dead leaves across the playgrounds and the tennis courts.

"I wish you luck, of course," José said, falling into step beside him. "Have you spoken with her since—"

"No. I am trying to think this through." The claim was only partially true: he had not spoken with her but not for lack of trying. Repeatedly during the morning her telephone had gone unanswered.

They walked several hundred yards in silence.

"Well, Alves. I humble myself . . . no more trouble." José kicked at a patch of snowy moss, impatience showing through for the first time. Alves saw, ignored it.

"Then there is no problem between us. Next step, Waterlow. . . ."

*   *   *

The weather in London was foul and Sir William was fed up with it. It had been raining and sleeting ever since Christmas, and now the Thames was bloody flooding! He couldn't believe it. The roads entering Whyte Ways resembled nothing less than the Grimpen Mire. . . . And he'd had a nasty head cold for two weeks that had required constant ingestion of hot rum toddies, the one bright spot of his holiday season. On top of it all, his doctor had spent the morning telling him that the excessively empurpled coloration of his normally pink face was an indication of a dangerous rise in his blood pressure. And why not? he had thundered. Floods, illness, the vile Edgar! He should have died of apoplexy, given the burdens he bore. . . .

Fortunately, the little men from the Bank of Portugal were on the day's schedule, and that brought a smile to his face. Another nail in the coffin of Edgar's miserable career! New business! He went to his private water closet and swallowed two high-blood-pressure pills and drained off a glass of water. Lots of fluids, his old Harley Street quack had said. And for this sort of advice he was required to pay coin of the realm! One day, while being attended by the doddering old butcher, Sir William knew he would be summoned to join the Choir Invisible—and his widow would be left to pay old Moggenthorpe's final due bill! The man was obviously no better than a murderer on the loose, but he was reputed to be the most expensive and therefore the best in London. Which only went to show you the state of the healing arts as 1925 dawned. . . . Ah, well, thank God he was in his prime and soon to be the Lord Mayor of London! The largest printing firm in the world at his command. . . . Yes, the best was very definitely yet to be, as one of those simpering damn scribblers had written.

The Portuguese envoys—my God, the whole lot of them, including the German, the Dutchman and the two lackeys who never seemed to say anything, as well as Senhor Reis—arrived after lunch. Reis seemed quite a different man this time, much calmer, less transparent, which was good. Sir William loathed seeing the messy interiors of the minds of business associates. Keep up a damn good front, mind your p's and q's, keep an eye out for the main chance and business was a piece of cake . . . if, of course, you were a Waterlow. Breeding had a good deal to do with it, but you couldn't expect a wog to understand that.

"The letter from Camacho," Reis said, withdrawing two envelopes from a leather case, "and the designations to be printed on the banknotes. I believe that should satisfy your needs in every way." He smiled. "I am certainly not empowered to draw this out any longer. You will understand the view of my principals."

"Of course, most understandable." Sir William glanced at the letter from Camacho and rang for Cubbage. The faithful aide appeared on the instant. "Have this translated at once." With a nod Cubbage departed. Sir William then inspected the envelope of numbering data, nodding his approval. "Fine, fine," he rumbled. "All is in order."

"Of course," Reis agreed. "Now, if it is not too much trouble, we require a delivery date, Sir William."

"Ah, yes, let us inspect the printing schedules." He leafed through a heavy, clothbound ring binder. "Today is the sixth of January," he muttered, running his finger down various columns, "and we can deliver ten thousand five-hundred-escudo notes on the first of February . . . and the remaining one hundred and ninety thousand notes on the tenth. Is that—"

"Perfectly," Reis said, "perfectly acceptable. We will, however, pick up the notes, all of them, on the tenth."

"Pick up, Senhor?"

"Take delivery. Here at Waterlow. We will then see to transshipment ourselves." Reis pursed his lips. "And the cost, Sir William?"

"Fifteen hundred pounds."

"On our acceptance of the notes."

"If you wish, of course."

"And we also need the measurements—"

"I beg your pardon?"

"A stack of one thousand notes, we need to know the dimensions of such a stack." Reis smiled distantly. "Today."

"I see." What the hell were they about, anyway? Sir William rang for Cubbage, who appeared with the translation of the director's letter. "Cubbage, get me the dimensions of a stack of one thousand five-hundred-escudo notes." Nodding, Cubbage retired. Sir William read the translation of Camacho's letter.

"The letter is, I trust, in order?" Reis inquired.

"Oh, yes, I say, certainly."

"The director asked me to personally thank you for your aid, Sir William. And to caution you not to conduct any correspondence about this arrangement with him—except through us."

"Yes, yes, secrecy and all. I have quite grasped that point." He chuckled indulgently, but it made no impression on Senhor Reis's cool stare.

"I should very much hope so, Sir William. There is, I assure you, far more to this arrangement than you have thus far glimpsed."

"Is that so? Did the director himself say so?"

"Would I be telling you if he had not?"

Sir William could barely control his smile.

Cubbage reappeared. "The measurements, Sir William."

"Read them, read them, man."

Cubbage consulted the sheet of paper he was carrying.

"The one-thousand-note packets measure four and three-quarters inches. The packet weighs about five pounds, gentlemen." Cubbage permitted himself a small smile. "I couldn't resist calculating the value per ounce of such a packet."

"And?" Sir William prompted indulgently.

"The packet is worth about sixty pounds an ounce, or three hundred dollars an ounce American. When you think that gold itself is selling for four pounds an ounce . . . Such a packet is worth fifteen times its weight in gold," he said, chuckling. "Puts it in a new perspective, you might say."

"Thank you, Cubbage. We see your point."

"Thank you, Sir William." Cubbage was gone in an instant.

"Good man, Cubbage. Head for figures, you see. Point well made, though. Take good care of your money, gentlemen."

"Portugal's money," Reis corrected him.

"Of course."

"And you need not trouble yourself as to our precautions." Reis stood and shook hands. The appropriate good-byes were observed, and they all trooped off down the worn staircase.

Musing later in the afternoon, Sir William enjoyed a tot of rum from a hammered silver flask in his desk and picked up the file that he had relabeled, changing "Banco de Portugal" to "Senhor Alves Reis." Thank God he'd been able to shut up the absurd Smythe-Hancock! Obviously, Smythe-Hancock wasn't half the man this Reis chap was, albeit he had to be counted a wog. . . . With the rum there came a confident warmth at the day's work, the unexpected promise of more business conveyed from Camacho Rodrigues himself through Reis. . . . By God, it had been a good day after all.

This Camacho must be quite a fellow, carrying out such a little snatch of intrigue as this. He read the translation of the letter again, then went through the most important plate notations. Well, surely there should be some acknowledgment from the head of Waterlow to the head of the Bank of Portugal . . . nothing detailed, nothing to break the secrecy that was obviously an obsession of these people, but just a personal acknowledgment of the letter. Why, it would be a true breach of etiquette simply to ignore the man's letter. . . .

The rain rattled steadily at the window, and Great Winchester Street lay bathed in yellow light. With a self-satisfied sigh, Sir William drew a sheet of his personal stationery from its shelf and dipped his pen in the pewter inkstand:

> *My dear Senhor Director,*
>   *I have the pleasure of acknowledging receipt of your confidential letter of 23rd December, the contents of which I have noted, and for which I am obliged.*
> *Yours faithfully, William A. Waterlow,*
> *Chairman of Waterlow and Sons Limited.*

There, that should aid good will and what not. He rang for Cubbage.

"I say, Cubbage," he said to the elderly man whose appearance never underwent a change during the long day required of him. "I'd like you to personally post this for me. See that it goes in the slot yourself. That's a good fellow. Do it tonight in the City, when you leave, eh?"

"Yes, sir," Cubbage replied. "Without fail."

*   *   *

At the conclusion of their business with Waterlow, the group dispersed. Marang returned to The Hague, where his other interests required his attention. José accompanied him with plans to see his brother Antonio and the intention of visiting the shadier districts in nearby Amsterdam in a carnal attempt to put the memory of Greta Nordlund to rest. Hennies set off for Berlin without offering any particular explanation: he had his deals to attend to and he was a close-mouthed man. Arnaldo accompanied Alves to Paris, where Alves intended to remain for a time.

"I must have the House of Vuitton build our cases for us. We'll need them often. They should be made to last."

"Alves, you don't have to explain to me." Arnaldo was drinking beer and nibbling on cheese and crackers. They sat in a depot restaurant. In a few minutes Arnaldo would board the Sud Express for Lisbon. "I understand why you must remain here, but, while you are enjoying yourself with her, please remember you have Maria at home. . . ."

"How can I forget? In any case, I may not even see Greta. Now, serious matters. Do you need some money?"

"No, I can get by on what I have. I'm rather worried about the way money is being spent. . . . Do you really have so much? Paris, all this traveling, it must be costing a fortune. . . ."

The train hissed and snorted like an anxious beast. Alves flinched at the sound. He glared at it, munched cheese.

"If you must know, after our discussion the first day in Paris, Adolf Hennies has become most cooperative about taking care of our various bills."

Walking toward the black, throbbing train, Alves threw his arm around Arnaldo's shoulders, stooped with the cares of his imagination.

"Now take good care of Maria," he said huskily. "You know how she is . . . if she wants to look for a new apartment, humor her, go with her, let her rattle on, make her feel good. I know what she's been through . . . and I know what lies ahead. Don't worry. And before you know it I'll be there."

The two men embraced.

"I count on you," Alves said.

"Yes." Then Arnaldo swung aboard and was gone.

Returning by taxi to Claridge's, Alves could think only of Greta. Where was she? Had she already forgotten their night together? Had it been a matter of curiosity satisfied? He had no experience of such a woman, whose life was so busy and full and, God knew, financially remunerative.

Once again there was no answer when he called her. Where was she? Fears of another man fled, faceless, before him. . . . He couldn't bear the thought, yet he was frightened by his passion. It grew each day; she was always with him. . . .

After a quick lunch he strolled across the Champs-Elysées, turned at the corner pointed out by Claridge's doorman and entered the House of Vuitton. He found himself a few minutes early and took the time to browse: the merchandise was irresistible. He chose a note case and a manicure set for himself, fondling the tiny gold mustache scissors, the miniature comb, file, cuticle tool. For Maria he found a case for stationery, designed for use while traveling. A wallet for Arnaldo. And for Greta a small purse:

why not? he asked himself. He left them with one of the salespeople to be wrapped individually and picked up following his meeting with the manager.

The manager himself, pale, perfumed, minced forward, extending a small boned hand from a mauve cuff. He executed a mandarin inclination of his pointed foxlike face and put himself at Alves' disposal. Yes, of course Vuitton would have no difficulty in supplying such an order by the appointed date. And how many cases would be required?

"Five identical cases," Alves told him, feeling the power of command, giving the dimensions he had calculated to accommodate the stacks of banknotes. "Sturdy brass fittings and corners, triple-sewn handles . . . as indestructible as Vuitton can make them. By the twenty-seventh of January."

"Certainly, without fail."

"Fine," Alves said, crossing his legs, enjoying the procedure. "Bill me personally at Claridge's. If there is any doubt as to the extension of credit you may contact my bank in Lisbon, the management at Claridge's, Antonio Bandeira at the Portuguese consulate in The Hague, Karel Marang at the firm bearing his name in The Hague—"

"Please, Monsieur, there will be no problem. It is an honor to build such cases."

Alves rose and shook the Frenchman's delicate hand. "By the way, there are a few small gifts I had wrapped downstairs . . ."

"Thank you, Monsieur. We feel that nothing conveys one's appreciation and respect quite like a gift from Vuitton. They will be included on your final statement. There is certainly no need to pay for them now." He bowed, tilting his narrow head above a floppy mauve tie.

"For accounting purposes," Alves said softly.

"But of course, Monsieur. It has been a great pleasure serving you."

Upon leaving Vuitton with his packages he returned to Claridge's, left them in his suite and had the doorman hail a cab. There was nothing left but to visit Greta's apartment. A drizzle clung like moss from the clouds. The wipers clacked erratically on the Citroën's windscreen. Water ran in rivulets down the inside of the rear windows. The light was fading outside, and headlamps gleamed on the streets. He felt as if he were hunting for a wonderful party that kept eluding him, just out of reach.

"This is it," he said, tapping the driver's shoulder. Standing in the rain, he pressed bills into the driver's hand. Patches of wetness stained the flat front of the building. The windows were shuttered, paint chipped and peeling, old and blistered by the centuries. The only door opened into a darkened courtyard, which he vaguely remembered. Up two steps to the right was an interior hallway where two electric lights shone dimly from what had once been gas brackets. He went in. An old woman in a heavy black sweater sat behind a counter. A radio muttered softly in the dark. The concierge stirred, eyes peering up like gleaming marbles.

"Monsieur?" she croaked. A cigar glowed in her ashtray. He smelled cooking odors, so old that he couldn't identify them.

"Mademoiselle Nordlund," he said. "Is she in?"

She cupped a hand to her ear, stuck the cigar into the corner of her mouth. He repeated his inquiry.

"No, she is not in, Monsieur."

"When will she return?"

"I don't know." She shrugged elaborately, dribbling ash into the folds of the shapeless sweater. "She is in the country. She did not say, a few days, perhaps . . . a week? Who can say?"

"I see. May I leave a message for her, then?"

"Certainly." She slid a scrap of paper across the counter, extended a stub of pencil.

He dated the sheet. *I am at Claridge's,* he wrote. *Call me if it is convenient. Alves.* There was nothing else to say, though it seemed a pitiful attempt at communication. But how could he put on paper the agonies he felt?

He laid two folded banknotes on the counter and went back outside. The street was still empty, rain dripping from the gutters, running in the sewers. He set off walking, the rain in his face, wandering from one cramped, ancient street to another. He saw the patisserie where he and Greta had breakfasted, ducked in and settled behind the same small table and drank two mugs of hot coffee, two fresh brioches. Greta filled his mind as much as if she'd been there beside him. He got up abruptly and went back into the street. Eventually he reached the Sorbonne with its cafés strung like beads on the Boulevard St.-Michel fading away in the rain toward Notre Dame. Vaguely reassured by the crowds in the street and the steamed windows of the cafés, he entered another and drank two cognacs, engulfed in the constant babble of French on all sides of him. The cognac burned in his stomach, warmed him against the chill. Outside he found another taxi and nearly fell asleep during the ride back to Claridge's.

For three days he was alone, prowling the streets, walking for hours down the endless corridors of the Louvre. He lit a candle for his grandmother in the foggy darkness of Notre Dame, then crossed the bridges and stared at the black wintry Seine. Each day he checked back with the concierge. Nothing.

*   *   *

On Alves' fourth day of waiting in Paris the drama of Sir William's letter to Camacho Rodrigues was being played to its climax within that faceless, gray building in Lisbon, the Banco de Portugal. Camacho himself had been under substantial pressure from both his stockholders and the government, the problem being, as it always was, the general state of the economy and the hopelessness of the Angolan situation in particular. A disagreeable early-morning meeting had concluded with one of the government ministers scowling at him—as if the problems were somehow of his making!—and whining loudly, "Show me a man who can get this nation out of the trough and moving forward again, economically speaking, of course, and I'll show you a man who will have my support . . . to head the bank! No, by heaven, to head the government itself!" Clearly, in the minister's eyes, Camacho Rodrigues was not the man.

Leaving the meeting fairly well shaken, his mind engaged with the idea of public hangings for disloyal officials among whom he numbered the minister, he drove his black sedan directly into the side of a vegetable vendor's cart, whose presence between the Praca do Comercio and the Banco de Portugal was never explained to his satisfaction. The cart was not going to be good for much in the future, and there were two noticeable dents in the sedan; the vendor was a raving lunatic, and settling the matter required two policemen and an hour of the director's valuable time. He was in a rotten mood when he arrived at his office and began barking nastily at Antonia de Fonseca, his secretary, who had not herself put in a particularly pleasant morning.

The problem was no longer that she was in love with a man some years her junior of whom her parents did not

232 THE MAN FROM LISBON

at all approve. After all, at thirty-two, Antonia de Fonseca
was in no position to be overly demanding of any suitor
and certainly not of a young and virile one. She had overcome her parents' objections. Now the problem was substantially more desperate: she was pregnant. Although the
father's identity was reasonably certain, Antonia was unable to foresee a marriage being accomplished in time to
hide the fact that she had been no virgin on her wedding
day. She had managed to staunch the flow of tears by the
time Camacho appeared, face like an ax murderer and
shouting at her. His suit jacket, it seemed, had somehow
become spattered with fruit stains and required immediate
steaming and sponging. And, equally urgently, she would
have to take several long letters to such mighty individuals
as a pair of highly critical newspaper editors, several ministers who were insisting on specific answers to specific
questions and a lengthy reply to the damnable economics
professor who had written a lengthy article taking bank
policy nastily to task ... whatever his name was, academic
sniper!

"Professor Salazar," Antonia de Fonseca replied, her
memory unimpaired by present difficulties.

"Damned nobody!" Rodrigues cried, handing her his
coat. "I am beset by enemies, absolutely beset! Now see to
this coat at once!"

Closing the door behind her, she returned to her desk
with its single flower in a bud vase, its typewriter, its engagement book, its stack of newly delivered mail. The
flower had been given her by her young and too virile lover
while they were on their way to work that very morning,
before she had kept her secret doctor's appointment. Now,
the sight of it brought tears to her eyes once again. She
dropped the director's coat on her desk, sat down and withdrew her lace handkerchief from the sleeve of her severe
black dress. Face down on the desk top was a sheet of
bank notepaper on which she had begun a letter to her lover
explaining the morning's unhappy turn of events. Her fountain pen lay across the paper, the ink bottle, uncapped, sat
nearby. What to do first? Dabbing at her eyes, she picked
up the stack of letters, began flipping through them. It was
the customary day's worth, with two interesting exceptions
she would deliver unopened to the director: one from Professor Salazar and one from Waterlow in London, a firm
with which she knew the bank had conducted some small

business through its Lisbon agent. Both letters were marked *Personal,* and she set them aside near her own.

Sighing disconsolately, she swept up the director's coat, and in so doing she knocked over the uncapped bottle of black ink. Frozen in horror, she watched the black stain spread like an explosion across her desk top, flooding her own letter, Professor Salazar's letter and the Waterlow letter. . . . It happened too quickly. Then there was nothing to be done. The letters were ruined. Ink dripped from the edge of her desk. She sank into her chair, still holding the director's coat.

The door to his office exploded open, like a gunshot, and like a wild animal his squat figure stormed through the anteroom and out into the hallway. The close escape brought Antonia de Fonseca to action. She dropped the blackened, wet items into her wastebasket, covered them with several crumpled sheets of scratch paper and summoned the janitor by telephone. He could clean up the mess. . . . Anyone could have an accident. Somehow things would all work out. The director's stained coat over her arm, Antonia de Fonseca went in search of a cleaning establishment.

*   *   *

Alves was in the bath when the telephone rang. Leaving wet tracks across the Claridge's fine carpet, he reached the telephone on the fifth ring, stood shivering and naked in the cold.

"Alves," she said.

"Greta, my love," he whispered, his relief obvious. "Where have you been? I was about to leave for Lisbon—"

"Please forgive me, Alves," she said with audible feeling. "I thought you were returning straight to Lisbon. . . . And I have been in the country, what a shame! When can I see you, my sweet?"

"At once," Alves said. "Sooner!"

"Tonight, then. I'll be busy all day—rehearsing. The play, do you recall? We open at the Comédie Française in three more days."

"Have you been rehearsing in the country?" Suspicion gnawed at his relief, happiness.

"Precisely. The director, Jean-Claude de Valoix, took us to his country home, a lovely chateau on the Loire, to

work while the set was made ready. . . . Oh, we've had
such trouble with the set! It requires a sphinx for one thing,
and as of today we are on our third sphinx! And do you
realize what this means, my little thunderbolt? You must
stay for our opening night! It will be excessively grand,
and my performance is really remarkably bad. I believe I
told you that I am too old, too tall and a complete bust
at looking like an Egyptian—but you must stay, you will
enjoy it, the parties, excitement—and we will make such
love. I cannot describe to you how much I have dreamt
of closing myself around you again, feeling you within
me!" Her voice dropped to a whisper, festooned with implications he was already envisioning.

"Come to me at eight. There will be a small supper. Does
that suit you?"

The evening was all he had hoped. Greta met him in a
robe, accepted the Vuitton bag with quiet pleasure, told
him that she needed him immediately. Emerging from the
bedroom two hours later, they shared the supper of bread
and sausage and wine, with cheese and fruit from a cutting
board, with coffee and Napoleon brandy. Shortly before
midnight she took him outside for a walk, along the Boulevard St. Germain. They sat on a bench outside St. Germain
des Pres: she told him it was the oldest church in Paris.
"Can you imagine this. . . . It was built in 542 by King
Childebert, the son of Clovis, and he is buried here, beside
us, Alves!" There was wonder in her voice, a sense of the
drama that had been almost fifteen centuries before, with
the mists of darkness and destruction rising from the plains
where now great cities stood. "He brought back a piece of
the True Cross and some of St. Vincent's tunic. . . . He'd
come from Spain, and he built this church to house the
relics. . . ."

"Some day I will take you to the Castle of San Jorge.
You will like that, too, my love. It is very different from
this. Older, even."

Still later he stood in the beaded doorway of her bedroom. She lay naked on her belly, asleep, the sheet halfway up her thighs, her blond hair plastered wetly to the
nape of her neck. He pulled the sheet and comforter up
over her broad shoulders, went downstairs, past the dozing
concierge. Outside his taxi waited.

The days between her return and the opening of Shaw's
Caesar and Cleopatra at the Comédie Française left him

more time to poke about the city, thinking of her in ornate fantasies while she went through final rehearsals. It had all come right again: walking in the Luxembourg Gardens, watching the old men playing at bowls, he found himself skipping on the path, like the child in Lisbon that Easter Sunday so long ago. He couldn't stop smiling, even when people noticed and hurried past or stopped to return his smile. . . . He felt younger and altogether happier than he had in years. . . . The days were spent in wide-eyed enjoyment of the city, eagerness to spend the evening with her. And the evenings, though they began very late following dress rehearsals, were lush with her finely honed sense of the erotic, the flair for abandon and the slight intimation of violence she brought to her lovemaking. Her energy drove him to excesses he'd not have believed possible had he heard them as part of a braggart's line. She never seemed to tire, though he would collapse, aching, half asleep in the taxi on the way back.

Opening night was enormously festive. He wore a hired suit of formal wear, white tie, top hat, a cape and arrived shortly before curtain time. He had dined alone at Fouquet's across from Claridge's: Beluga caviar and Mumm's champagne, sweet tender veal and peas, a crème brûlée. He enjoyed the lonely dinner, the waiter hovering, pouring champagne, lighting his cigarettes. A man of mystery, he thought, a man of means and style. He made a mental note to order his own formal wear, to get the name of the best tailor in Paris and have his entire wardrobe made to measure. Such a difference, he reflected, how unlike the mere boy who had set out for Luanda, or the nerve-wracked entrepreneur who made use of the slow boats to the New York bank.

The foyer of the Comédie Française was shoulder to shoulder with the first-nighters, the men in black and white like dominoes, the women with bare shoulders, diamonds and gold and shingled hair and opera glasses. Houdon's bust of Voltaire: Greta had told him to pay it his respects, as well as the very chair Molière had been seated in when mortally stricken while performing in Le Malade Imaginaire in 1673. His head was swirling by the time he took his own seat, sixth row center.

His French was rudimentary at best, but the words being recited on stage were irrelevant: he barely heard them. His attention was fixed on Greta as Cleopatra, somehow seeming smaller, a worldly child full of her own immense power, made up to an appropriately Egyptian duskiness with the black ropes of hair seeming not in the least ridiculous. Poor Caesar, how could he resist this delicious creature? The audience, the play, the applause and laughter faded as he lost himself in thoughts of her, the passion and lust, but even more the love, the glow of her attention and the comfort of her touch. . . . He closed his eyes, saw her naked and vulnerable, heard the sound of her crying out as he filled her, tasted her tears as he overflowed within her and left her clinging, weeping—only he had known her this way, as only she had seen the man he became in her presence. It was the truth of what existed between them. It gave them life, transformed them.

He waited for the crush of well-wishers to subside, stood waiting at the end of the corridor. The flowers he had sent were in a vase on her dressing table, reflected in the mirror. The other countless vases were together on a table against the wall behind her. She sat with a wrap around her shoulders, applying cream to her face. She saw him in the mirror, turned smiling, reaching for his hand.

"I was horrid," she said, mocking herself. "You needn't tell me I was wonderful. . . ." She squeezed his hand, then wiped it off with a towel. "Was I all right? Really?"

"You were superb . . . such a transformation. I hardly recognized you, then I heard your voice. . . ." He made a gesture of futility, words proving inadequate.

"My critic!" she cried, laughing, turning back to her table, catching his eye in the mirror. He kissed her hair.

The next few hours were passed at a party, given by someone in a tuxedo whose name he missed. He met the gentleman who portrayed Caesar, a rather scholarly type, civil but remote; he met the director, several of the actors, patrons of the arts who came and went with metronome regularity, embracing Greta, kissing her cheek, paying court to the star. There were several Scandinavian dignitaries who wore medals and proclaimed her a national treasure.

He was watching the process, smoking, leaning against a doorway, when she came to him, held onto his arm.

"Let's go," she said. "I've been toasted and fondled and gushed over until I feel quite faint. . . . Come quickly before they catch us!"

He drove the Bentley through the deserted streets. She

curled up beneath the mink coat, eyes closed. He knew the route.

"Stay the night, please. Please, I want you with me when I fall asleep and I want you beside me when I wake."

In bed she kissed him briefly.

"Hold me while I go to sleep," she whispered.

"Of course." He brushed his lips against her hair. "You were wonderful."

"I know," she said. "I know that." She was almost asleep. "I am always quite wonderful."

The next day he told her he must return to Lisbon on the evening train. She nodded. They breakfasted quietly with a fire roaring. He hated the thought of leaving her.

In the afternoon they went for a walk that curled around St. Germain des Pres, up the Rue de Rennes, back along the Rue de Vaugirard to the Place de l'Odéon, where she impulsively held his face in her hands and kissed him. They were standing beneath the columned porch of the theater, across the Rue de Médicis from the Luxembourg Palace, in whose grounds he had had it out with José.

She took his hand and led him into the garden. By the side of a long flat pool she sat down and made room for him. The pool was littered with dead leaves like fairies' rafts and reflected the plane trees all around; a huge cyclops glowered threateningly over an unhappy pair of lovers. She saw him looking at the fountain statuary.

"This is the Médici Fountain," she said, her voice a monotone as if she were a tour guide whose mind was somewhere else. "The scary fellow about to leap on Acis and Galatea is Polyphemus . . . I think it is the most beautiful fountain in Paris." She turned back to watch the people walking intently on the path. "You must go tonight, then?"

"Yes, I am afraid that I must. It is not that I want to. . . ."

"I know, I understand. . . . I shall miss you, you know that."

"I must see Maria. . . ."

"Will she know about us? Will you tell her?" The broad brim of her slouch hat hid her eyes.

"No. She trusts me implicitly, of course. . . . And why would I want her to know? What would be served? Besides, she thinks you are the most wonderful creature she has ever met. . . . She thinks I am much too hard on you, not sympathetic. She thinks you are beautiful, brave, a little sad. No. I won't tell her. I wouldn't know how to explain it, all that's happened. . . ."

"I'm sure you're right." She paused, then rushed on: "I couldn't explain what's happened either. I don't know what has happened between us."

He put his arm around her, hugged her to him.

"And when will I see you again?" She wiped her eyes with a gloved hand.

"I'll be back in Paris in February, just a few weeks."

"Alone?"

"I hope so."

"I will long for you, Alves," she said, reaching toward him, brushing his cheek with the tips of her fingers.

"I love you," he said, his voice small, shadowed by the scale of what he felt under the softness of her touch.

Finally they rose and went back to Rue Vaugirard, where he found a taxi, kissed her goodbye and left her standing on the curb. She was waving to him when he looked back a block away. He turned around and settled back, tired, missing her already. What was he going to do? What?

*   *   *

By the morning of a gray and blustery tenth of February, Sir William Waterlow had almost forgotten the fact that Camacho Rodrigues had never responded to his personal note of a month before. For that matter, it had not required a reply and he had not really expected one, though an increasingly personal relationship with the director could not but be helpful in the line of business. He was, however, somewhat disconcerted by a mix-up at the Scrutton Street plant, where the Portuguese banknotes were being printed. They had fallen behind schedule and had informed him of it only a few days before. And now here they were, all five of them snorting and pawing the turf and ready to collect their money. . . . There was, he observed with considerable wonderment, a most remarkable matched set of Vuitton cases that threatened to stretch, a river of brown, from Great Winchester Street to the outer reaches of Golders Green. They must have cost, he reflected, a treble fortune . . . and Smythe-Hancock had thought there was something not quite right about the deal! Fool!

"Gentlemen," he said heartily, tearing his eyes away from

the brass-fitted cases, "how excellent to see you on this momentous day! The fruition of the first in what we hope will be many such associations, what?"

"Undoubtedly, Sir William," Marang said. "As you can see, our cases bear the orange diplomatic seals. We are ready to move. . . . And I have a check made out to Waterlow for payment in full."

"Excuse me, gentlemen," Sir William said, circling behind his chair, turning to use it as a lectern or a first line of defense, depending. "But I must beg your forbearance in one matter. . . . Due to absolutely unavoidable mechanical delays with our presses in Scrutton Street, we are slightly behind the agreed upon schedule. . . ." For some reason Sir William was not quite able to grasp, Senhor Reis, who had previously orchestrated these meetings, was waiting leisurely in the background, leaning on the credenza, watching the traffic in the street.

"Not at all far, certainly nothing to worry about. . . ."

"How far, precisely?" Herr Hennies was not smiling.

"Today I am delivering fifty thousand notes—"

"One hundred and fifty thousand notes short," Hennies said grimly. "What kind of business procedure is this, may I ask?"

"Unavoidable, I can only repeat it." Sir William shook his great red face mournfully. Leave it to the bloody Hun to get prickly. "Believe me, this is not customary Waterlow procedure. . . . Any of our clients will be more than happy to vouch for our customary promptness. In any case, we can deliver the remainder of your order by the first of March. . . ." He spoke with a dying fall. Somewhere within the firm, namely at Scrutton Street, heads would roll.

"A month's delay," Marang mused. "And how are we to be recompensed for this inconvenience?"

"I propose you accept these notes now but withhold all payment until the remainder are delivered. You may continue to draw interest on your own money, you see. What could be fairer?"

"A reduction of, say, three percent could be fairer," Hennies barked.

"You have me at a great disadvantage, I admit. But still . . ." Sir William had begun to perspire under this frontal barrage. He was playing for time when Reis stepped forward, smiling, gesturing for calm.

"Sir William," he said, "we are all men of affairs, are

we not? We have all faced situations where problems not of our own causing have been inevitable. . . ." He surveyed his colleagues. "I have stories from my days in Africa that would—well, that is neither here nor there. Naturally we are disappointed—it would be less than honest to deny that—but we are also men of principle and good will. In that spirit, there will be no delay in paying for the job. Marang, give him the check."

"I say, Reis," Sir William sputtered, "dashed decent of you!"

"Personal honesty and trust, the foundation of every successful business arrangement . . . my watchwords, Sir William."

"Well, I like it, I like your style!"

"Now," Reis said with an ease and command Sir William had to admire, "shall we fill these handsome cases?"

Cubbage supervised the wheeling in of the two reinforced, metal-banded wooden crates. Carefully the packets were divided into five equal stacks, and Reis himself fitted them into the cases. Meticulous, Sir William thought, watching the procedure. This little fellow will go damned far before he's done. . . .

There should have been a chorus rattling the windows in old Great Winchester Street, something majestic and godlike, with piping cherubim and thundering organ tones. Alves could almost hear it, anyway, as he stepped out of the portal into the plain street, newly born, a rich man! He stopped at the top of the steps, having bade Cubbage a good day as the old man held the door personally for their exit. Rich! He was rich at last. . . . And he had managed it on his own, against great odds, by means of a master plan that defied detection. . . . His heart battered the walls of his chest. Here, at the heart of the City, he stood at last, no longer on the margin of great things but within the cloister of wealth and power. . . . The Rolls-Royce limousines by the curb swam before his eyes.

He looked from one face to the other, each caught in a timeless moment of happiness. Their eyes locked for an instant, roved on. Arnaldo. José. Marang. Hennies. Watching them, proud of the way they had seen it through, Alves almost felt as if they knew the whole story, the truth of his ingenuity and daring and courage. . . . To tell them, to hold them spellbound with the drama of it all! But that, he knew even in the glorious instant, was out of the ques-

tion. He could never tell them. Absolute secrecy was the
keystone of the plan. . . . The documents he had forged
now existed, palpably, in the files; they were real by the
very fact of their existence.

Their own hired Rolls-Royce limousine waited, shining
and black, at the curb. The uniformed chauffeur opened the
door, stacked the cases on the floor carpet, ushered them
into the dark vastness.

"Fifty pounds of notes in each case," Hennies mused,
quiet for a change. "Two hundred and fifty pounds of
money. . . . I've never thought of currency in terms of
poundage before." He suddenly laughed, his eyes squinting.

"One million one hundred and sixty thousand dollars!"
Arnaldo whistled softly.

"Why did you go so easily on Waterlow?" José asked.
He sniffed at the red flower in his buttonhole. "We could
have put some pressure on him, pushed him a bit . . ."

"There was no point in it. It wouldn't have hurried the
delivery and would have put him off. Now, he is quite
plainly in our debt for a very small favor, one which cost
us nothing, but will grow in size in his mind. . . . A matter of psychology." Alves smiled, shrugged indifferently,
full of his triumph.

"I've never heard you mention the subject before,"
Arnaldo remarked.

The boat train and the Channel crossing proved un-
eventful. Alves walked the deck heedless of the spray from
the choppy seas. His excitement, the fingers of power moving along his nervous system, had not diminished with the
passage of hours. He needed the solitude, the opportunity
to contemplate what was happening. His life was being
shaken to its foundation.

The success of the day in London helped him to forget
for the moment the tedium of the weeks spent in Lisbon
between leaving Greta and returning to Paris to take
delivery of the Vuitton cases. There had been no indication of suspicion or concern on Maria's part. On the contrary, she had exhibited good spirits as they visited one
apartment after another, Maria listing the features of decor
and architecture and location. Arnaldo frequently accompanied them on their rounds, and Maria's matchmaking instincts had finally produced a young woman who had
caught Arnaldo's eye. Consequently he was not as available
for house hunting as he might once have been. Silvia seemed

a nice girl, plumpish and of a solid, middle-class family,
her father a bureaucrat. It was good for him, Alves and
Maria agreed. But there was little else, however slight, to
attract Alves' attention in Lisbon. The days passed slowly;
there was none of the desperation he'd almost grown accustomed to as he'd worked out his forgeries. There was
nothing to be done but play with the children and trot along
after Maria in her search for the proper abode, a new
necklace, a new dress, a new pair of shoes. She seemed to
be readying herself for the large amounts of money Alves
had promised her were coming, practicing, waiting. Alves
was undismayed: Maria had seen most of their possessions
go up for sale at the time of his imprisonment, had seen
the accouterments of her everyday existence dismantled and
dispersed. He was sure that he had never been able to
sympathize fully with what she'd undergone, since he had
not surprisingly been preoccupied with his own misfortunes.
But now there was the opportunity to indulge her. He took
it and promised her even more to come. . . . It was a
pleasurably powerful sensation. But it grew tedious, there
was no getting around that.

The point was that his mind was in Paris with Greta.
The quiet of Lisbon, instead of calming him, had thrown
into sharper relief the sense of life, burgeoning, cascading
life, that he had discovered with Greta.

*   *   *

Yellow lampshades, liberally fringed and affixed to heavy
metal bases, gave the front parlor of Marang's home the
mellow glow of a library. It was just past midafternoon,
but the day was dark, windy and cold. Clouds rode low,
like watery ink blots resting on the treetops by the canals.
Marang's wife and children were away visiting in Amsterdam. The men sat around the heavy mahogany table with
feet like the claws of a monstrous bird. The Vuitton cases
stood against the wall. Raphael reproductions covered the
wall, attesting to Madame Marang's taste in art, and Em-
pire-style bronze pieces cluttered every surface. A radiator
hissed. Marang himself brought a tray of tea things and
passed around the cups, the china rattling.

"Now, gentlemen, your attention, if I may? There is a
change in our plans that I am bound to tell you." Alves
sensed the quickening of interest, the tinge of anxiety.

"The High Commissioner of Angola has resigned in a dispute over Lisbon's attempts at financing the colony. Without ever becoming a matter of public concern, Camacho Rodrigues' scheme, which we are executing, was supported by the High Commissioner. What he objected to was a Parliament bill with a great many conditions attached. But Camacho and the bank have been forced to adjust the plan. The money will not be overprinted with the word *Angola* as originally intended. Instead it will be left as is . . . and circulated in Portugal and the *Azores.*" He paused and looked at the faces. Their rapt attention pleased him: they had never had the slightest inkling of his actual intentions from the beginning.

"But, Alves," Arnaldo said slowly, "that means that this batch of money will be indistinguishable from all other money. There could be duplications, couldn't there? A new one and an old one, with the same serial numbers?"

"Quite possibly," Alves allowed. "It is not our problem, is it? You must not forget our role in this. We carry out our instructions. . . ."

"So the money will stay in Portugal?" Hennies thumbed his lower lip, quizzical. "I don't understand. How will it benefit Angola? Which was the purpose, if memory serves, of the entire operation. . . ."

"The adjustment in the plan is this," Alves resumed. "The major part of the money will be invested in Angolan companies, thereby accomplishing the original end—getting the money into the Angolan economy."

"Who will invest this money?" Marang sipped his tea, stared at Alves over the cup's rim.

"We will invest the money, Karel."

"At the bank's discretion?"

"I'm sure that Camacho will not leave me uninstructed. But there will be nothing put in writing. . . . There must be no evidence that the bank or the government is involved. That has been the case from the beginning, of course."

José brightened. "You mean it is ours to invest? Alves, you are brilliant. . . ."

"At the bank's discretion, my friend," Alves smiled.

"But I don't understand," Arnaldo pressed on, tortoise-like. "Does this change our remuneration? Where does our commission fit into this?"

"May I remind you that we are agents, following whatever instructions the bank gives us? We certainly have no right to dispute or question those instructions. We benefit as ever."

"Ah, yes, you're quite right." Arnaldo sighed, running his fingers through his hair. "It's just that I sometimes find it difficult to follow the machinations of those in power at the bank . . . but what you're saying is that it's none of our business. Which is true, I realize."

"Exactly." Alves looked around for questions. Everyone seemed satisfied. "For your information, gentlemen, the first large investment we have been authorized to make is Angola Mining. . . ."

Arnaldo looked up, startled. "Angola Mining, you say?"

Alves nodded, aware of what was going through Arnaldo's mind, almost hearing the sparks in his brain. There was no way around it, however. Get it out on the table. Only Arnaldo was aware of how heavily and disastrously involved in Angola Mining Alves actually was. . . . There was a flash of doubt: Arnaldo had never been able to mask his thoughts. There was no time to deal with his doubts at the moment.

"Angola Mining," Alves said. "Now we might as well move on to the main purpose of this meeting. The distribution of our commission. There will be three equal shares—one for Hennies and Marang, one for José and Arnaldo, one for me. Are there any questions about the disbursement?"

Marang bristled. "You have forgotten about the expenses. They were to be paid first, that was our agreement. And Hennies and I, between us, have invested nearly fifty thousand dollars American."

"So much, Karel?" Alves smiled, shaking his head. "Fifty thousand dollars American?"

"If not more!" Marang exclaimed. Hennies stared at the table; he had been bloodied in a head-to-head with Reis and the fight had gone out of him. "We can substantiate the figures. . . . Bribes, travel expenses, the high living, your expenses in Paris—"

"Relax, Karel, drink your tea."

Hennies said, "For the love of God, what are you quibbling about, Karel? We're still far ahead, don't you see?"

"Our commission remains a hundred thousand dollars *over and above our expenses.*" Alves nodded toward the

Vuitton cases. "I suggest we attend to that matter right now."

It concluded the meeting on a properly exuberant note.

*　　*　　*

Late that night Arnaldo spoke with Alves in the bar at the Hotel des Indes. They were almost alone; the room was dim.

"Alves, I am worried. This is fraud."

Alves lit a cigarette, leaned back in his chair, folded his arms across his chest.

"And who is being defrauded, Arnaldo? The bank has authorized the printing of a certain quantity of bank-notes—"

"But that money was intended for Angola."

"It is the bank's money. By law. They can do with it whatever they wish. It is none of our affair. How many times need I say it? We are agents of the bank."

"But Angola Mining—that's your firm. Nothing but coincidence?"

"Hardly a coincidence. It is a very prominent Angolan firm that happens to need some propping up. A logical place to put some of this money to work, wouldn't you agree? Any objective investor might choose it . . . my involvement is irrelevant. . . ."

"But what if it should come out? It would look awfully peculiar, your investing the bank's money in a firm with which you have had so many dealings. . . ."

"How it looks is of no concern. In the first place, it won't come out, and in the second, if it did it would quick-ly become apparent that I was acting under special instruc-tions. . . . Arnaldo, you look exhausted. Go to bed, old friend. You deserve a rest."

*　　*　　*

The morning brought another meeting, this time in Ma-rang's office.

"Karel," Alves said, "you will retain the banknotes here until you meet me in Paris three days from today. By then I will have concluded my business there—among other things, I must order cases, large ones, for the shipping of the money to Lisbon in March. I will be at Claridge's as

usual. Adolf, you will join us there and together we will
all go to Lisbon. Arnaldo, you and José should go straight
to Lisbon. Immediately arrange to have new office space
for A. V. Alves Reis, Limitado . . . absolutely respectable,
elegant, understated as befits a firm such as ours. Money
is no object. Just have the office ready for me to look at
when I arrive, understood?"

Everyone understood.

"All right." Alves returned to the next point. "We will
begin circulating the new banknotes at once, making use
of both black-market sources and selected legitimate outlets. Naturally, Camacho prefers to have the notes changed
into one of the very hard currencies—dollars or pounds—
but he realizes that there are realistic limits." He took an
envelope from his coat pocket, handed it to Arnaldo. "This
is a list of the names and addresses of several men I have
worked with before, men we can trust to do the circulation
work. Most of it can be accomplished in Oporto. Tell them
we will pay a two percent commission on every exchange.
I need hardly tell you that any suggestion of the bank's
involvement would be disastrous!"

"Why Oporto?" Hennies asked.

"The wine merchants there have made it the center of
black-market money changing. They deal all over the world
and keep their money outside of Portugal."

"What am I to do with these black-marketeers of yours?"
There was an unmistakable sarcasm in Arnaldo's voice.

"Have them at the ready. I will meet with them within
twenty-four hours of my arrival in Lisbon. And don't for
a moment think they should be treated with anything but
respect. They are small businessmen, and they know what
they are doing."

Arnaldo nodded.

*   *   *

Alves checked into the Claridge that same evening. Having
wired Greta before leaving The Hague, he was waiting in
the dressing-room corridor, rain glittering like confetti in
the single bright bulb over the alleyway door. She leaped
from her dressing-table chair to hug him. The sight of her
as Cleopatra still gave him pause before he kissed her.

"You are radiant, darling!" She stood back and gave him
a thorough looking over. "The cat who has eaten a cageful

of canaries!" She hugged him. "Things went well for you in London?"

"Very well, yes. I thought of you constantly."

"And I you, every day, every night . . . Always."

Her performance as Cleopatra had charmed Parisian theatergoers and critics alike. She showed him the reviews: "The Scandinavian Bernhardt, Greta Nordlund, once again has brought Paris to its knees—and to her feet—this time with a piquant comic grace and charm seldom equaled on any stage, anywhere. . . ." The tone of all the notices was much the same. "You prefer your critics to me," he whispered sternly, and she replied, "Only sometimes . . . but not always," and they laughed, her breath warm on his neck. He was filled with pride in her, regretted a lifetime's ignorance of her obviously noble profession. But that provincialism was in the past: his life was beginning again. He told her, spoke of her effect on him, and she kissed his nose. "You have been learning different things," she said. "We have so much to teach each other, haven't we?"

They went in the green Bentley to Fouquet's, where her table was ready, champagne in a sterling ice bucket, hothouse roses on her table, admirers watching as she passed through the room toward the secluded corner.

Now, leaning across her plate of Beluga and lemon, she told him that two more articles, in serious theatrical journals, had appeared since he had left. She would read them to him. "Also I have received a letter from Maria."

"Indeed?" He felt the breath being squeezed from him.

"No, darling, there was nothing worrisome, just a chatty, friendly note. She's looking forward to shopping with me in Paris, visiting the couturiers, the jewelers, the galleries. She described some of the apartments she has been looking at. . . . She invited me to Lisbon when my play closes."

"I put you in a difficult position with her. What can I do?"

"Do nothing, of course. There is no reason why I cannot be her friend, at least at long distance. Obviously it would be more difficult if she were here . . . but that is in the future. . . ."

"And we are not to think of the future," Alves said slowly. "I know."

"It is the best way. For now." She stroked caviar onto

a wafer, squeezed lemon, tasted and grinned with pleasure. "Now, tell me about London."

"Our syndicate concluded its first major deal."

"And you were the mastermind, of course."

"Yes, that is an exact description of the event." He chuckled.

"Are you very rich?" she whispered, a happy conspirator.

"Actually, yes, I'm fairly rich right now. . . . I shall be very rich quite soon."

"I am very pleased for you." She clasped his hand across the table, candlelight reflected in the lavender eyes. "It is terribly important to you, isn't it?"

"Six weeks ago I would have said it was more important to me than anything else in the world. It is a shocking thing to say—I have never said it before—but it was more important to me than my wife and children . . . an obsession."

"And now," she said, "you are free of the obsession. . . ."

"No, I am afraid that is not quite the case, Cleopatra. I have exchanged one obsession for another. . . ."

He lit a cigarette, pushed the plate away, poured more champagne. When he looked up, she was smiling brightly, eyes glistening. "Tell me more about London," she whispered, her voice shaking.

Never before had he been tempted to discuss his business affairs with a woman. And now the temptation was almost overwhelming. Nothing had ever made him so proud of himself, not the ride across the High Bridge, not his triumphant return to Lisbon from Angola . . . yet he knew he must say nothing. He skirted the issue. "Complicated finance," he said. "Nothing really to tell." She gave him a knowing look: she understood.

Later, in the dark hours of the early morning, they lay in bed and talked tiredly, happily. . . . "The money is power," he said. "The power to put so many of my plans into action, the power to make Portugal great again. . . ."

"The power to be a great man," she said. "It is . . ." She paused for the right word. "Your destiny. . . . How lucky we are, each of us at one with our destinies."

"It is you," he whispered, his voice catching in his throat. "You have brought me to life."

"I feel the same way every night when I am on the stage, when I hear the applause. . . . It is all new, knowing you have seen me . . . it's as if I'm always on stage for you, wherever you are." She shifted her body against him; he felt her lips against his chest. "You become my life. . . . And you benefit—we both benefit. . . ."

* * *

In the morning he left her sleeping and went to the Claridge. He knew everyone there now, they knew him. They remembered the way he wanted things. He tipped very well. It was a perfect relationship. Once settled, with the single locked Vuitton case in the hotel safe, he bathed, put on fresh clothing, had his shoes shined and his nails and mustache done. He walked across the Champs-Elysées, passed Fouquet's. The day bore the hint of spring. The sun dipped among the clouds. The city smelled clean, young. Workmen sprayed water in the streets, women walked their dogs.

The manager at Vuitton greeted him warmly. He wore a pale-green tie as if he were celebrating the first thought of spring.

"Yes, monsieur, the cases gave us great satisfaction."

The manager inclined his head. "Thank you. I was quite sure they would do nothing less. And what may I do for you today?"

"I need three more cases, much larger this time, each capable of carrying two hundred and fifty pounds. Zinc-lined. Absolutely waterproof, fireproof. . . . In short, indestructible. What does Vuitton say to that?"

"An interesting challenge. The delivery date, Senhor Reis?"

"The twenty-eighth of February."

"Aha. . . . Perhaps you can give me the specifications as to the size?"

He certainly could. He even drew a sketch, locks, brass fittings, belting and all. He also ordered three bags for his personal use, the initials to be stamped in gold, for delivery to Claridge's the next day.

"It will be a very great pleasure to be of further service to you, Senhor Reis." He bowed slightly, having seen Alves through the street-floor showroom to the door. He shook hands. "Until the twenty-eighth, then. . . ."

Before leaving The Hague, Alves had prevailed on José for the name of his Paris tailor. From Vuitton he went to the tailor. The remainder of the day was spent in the company of Monsieur Henri, who carefully conducted him through the bolts of cloth, the shirtings, the silk for cravats; they went through books of sketches—sketches of lapels, cuffs, belt loops, pocket flaps, shoulders and knee widths, waists suppressed and straight, buttonholes, collars . . . He was measured from head to toe, up, down and around, for business suits, country suits, formal cutaways, dinner jackets and sporting jackets, jodhpurs, pajamas, everything he might imagine wearing. It was exhausting. The first suits would be available on the twenty-eighth of February.

In the evening he went to the theater to see the play again. The weather had held and the evening was balmy. Afterward Greta suggested a walk. She led him through the Place du Palais-Royal to the Rue de Rivoli, with the cafés glowing on one side and the Louvre looming on the other. Hand in hand, they turned and crossed the Pont Neuf. Lovers leaned on the railing, kissing, inspired by the weather. An hour's stroll and they had reached her apartment.

"Stay again," she said.

"We'll open the windows and light just a small fire."

"I do believe that I am in love with you." She laughed lightly.

"And why not? I am a great man. You said so yourself, if I may remind you." He was only partly in jest.

"I know." She laughed in the darkened hallway. "I am attracted to greatness."

"Then how," he chided her, "do you explain José?"

"He was a great dresser." She fitted the key into the old lock. "After all, greatness is greatness. Years ago my husband was a painter. We both thought he would achieve greatness, but, alas, he did not. I was the one . . . we parted." She turned to kiss him. "Don't ask me about Hennies. Every woman owes herself at least one German . . . afterward, everything else seems so wonderful!"

They did not speak seriously during the remainder of the night. Alves successfully ignored the question mark in the corner of their new life together.

In the morning, before he left, she said, "Everyone lives by something, a law. I think that we should remember this . . . our future is now, we must live as if we will never see each other again. We have our own lives to lead when we are apart—and when we are together we will share what matters to us. What else can we do? How can we plan for the future?"

He wished desperately that he could convince himself, but in his heart, in his mind, they were never apart.

"I don't know. I wish there was a way . . ."

"I know. So do I."

* * *

At the train station preparing to board the Sud Express, Hennies pointed to Alves' new matched Vuitton suitcases.

"New," he said, "and very handsome. But . . ." He shook his head.

"But what?"

"The initials. Most unwise, I'm afraid."

"What are you talking about? The initials identify them if some fool of a porter loses them. What's unwise about that?"

"Listen, my friend, I speak from experience. There may well come a time when you will wish to conceal your identity . . . and the luggage will give you away."

"Give me away? Don't be ridiculous, Adolf. I've waited a long time for luggage like this."

Hennies clearly didn't understand him. Alves had had enough of being anonymous. Very soon his name would be on everyone's lips: it was inevitable. He intended to enjoy it.

The fresh diplomatic seals sufficed to pass the banknotes through customs at the tiny Spanish border village of Vilar Fomoso. In Lisbon Alves promptly chose a large suite of offices in the Baixa, the financial district, not far from the cramped, unpleasant quarters where he'd worked during the autumn. It positively glowed with a quiet, satiny polish, less obvious than the baronial splendor of the rooms where Chaves had come with his desperate hopes but far more impressive to anyone who understood such things. Since it was immediately available and decently furnished, Alves moved in, ordered the antique furniture he'd had an eye on, left the choosing of paintings and statuary and occasional pieces to Maria. He engaged a secretary, ordered stationery and arranged for José and Arnaldo to bring in the gentlemen whose names had appeared on his list.

They were a faceless bunch, known to Alves for discretion and a total lack of curiosity. Drones, they were called, men professionally engaged in handling black-market currency. Alves offered a standard 2 percent commission; each drone was allotted five hundred thousand escudos to start. José, whose familiarity with such goings-on was considerably greater than Arnaldo's, accompanied the crew on the eight o'clock overnight train to Oporto. He would act as foreman.

The first day on the job saw one hundred and fifty thousand dollars purchased. José arranged to pay commissions on a daily schedule. Once the escudos were changed and the dollars in hand, José immediately deposited them in new accounts opened in Oporto banks under the name of Alves Reis, Lda.

In Lisbon Alves was opening several more accounts in a variety of banks. All the money not being passed in Oporto was deposited in these Lisbon banks. After a week's wait, he began making withdrawals, naturally receiving old, unremarkable banknotes rather than the new ones he had deposited. The deposits were made in many small branches of the major banks; withdrawals were made from the large, parent banks in the heart of Lisbon.

José returned with an interesting anecdote, the significance of which he had no way of knowing. One of the drones had gone to an Oporto bank the first morning to change one of the five-hundred-escudo notes into smaller bills. Among the less trusting drones it was common practice: if you had been given counterfeit notes to change it was best to find out immediately. The teller, confronted with an absolutely new note, examined it minutely, then retreated to the manager's office for further consultation. He returned without a word and exchanged it for the smaller bills. The note was clearly genuine.

Quietly the drones went about their work.

Alves told Arnaldo that Camacho would be very pleased.

* * *

Lying half asleep in the small apartment, the taste of Maria still on his lips, his thoughts would turn to Greta. She might be returning from the theater, or reading herself to sleep in the deep chair before her fire, or walking the

Pont Neuf. . . . Of course, there might be other men in her life, surely there were in one way or another. Parties, dancing in the cafés, casual kisses, trips to the country, riding in the Bois de Boulogne . . . But in Lisbon a feeling of guilt about his infidelity surpassed the itching of jealousy that he could still tell himself was human nature.

He could not seriously consider telling Maria the truth. And he could not dream of a life devoid of Greta, the style and excitement she had brought. The romance . . . With her he felt like a hero, a man of the world. Maria had never seen him as Greta did. She had known him as little more than a boy, half drowning himself at Cascais, seasick on the voyage out to Luanda, anxiety-ridden as he tried to build a life in Africa . . . and desperate, a nearly hysterical ruin in the Oporto jail. There was no erasing the past; and Maria knew the past, the good and the bad, which revealed him as just a man. Greta—now, she knew him only as Reis, the entrepreneur, the financial wizard, *a great man.* . . .

To ease the anguish he felt when Maria caught his eye and smiled her wifely smile, he made a point of accompanying her on more rounds of apartment hunting. After one long day that had turned up nothing quite right, he took her to dinner at the Avenida Palace, promising a surprise.

"Maria, darling," he interrupted, halting the torrent of her chatter, "forget all about a new apartment."

"Alves . . ." The disappointment showed, her eyes lowered. "What do you mean? I thought . . . I mean, you said we could afford—"

"A house! Something great, grand, a house you can decorate as you wish, furnish as you wish—it's yours! Nothing is too good for Senhora Reis. Maria, what is the matter? You are crying." The sight of her tears still stung him. He could not bear the thought of hurting her: that would never change, and who could say that it was not the deepest love, the most enduring love of all?

"You frightened me and then you make me so happy! You are a devil! I want a hug. . . ."

"Sit down, dearest, and drink your wine. I have a toast . . . To a new home, the pride of Lisbon!" He lifted his glass and touched hers. She drank with tears on her cheeks like diamonds.

"To us," she replied eagerly. "To a life forever in our new home, the happiest family in Lisbon!"

They drank to their happiness.

*   *   *

The house Alves had in mind was one of the best known in Lisbon, in all of Portugal for that matter. He knew it was available for purchase and had arranged with an estate agent for a private showing. He kept it a secret from Maria, bundling her into the old Daimler he was using while he decided on which car manufacturer he would bestow his business. Up the narrow streets they drove until finally they saw it—a massive structure set pink and high on the crown of a hill giving a distant view of the Tagus harbor, the Castle of San Jorge off to the left, with the sprawl of the city far below. Around the entire building was a six-foot-high wall decorated with azulejus, the blue-painted tiles found everywhere in Lisbon, these depicting peasant life on one façade, a variety of cherubim and seraphim on another. Atop the wall was an ornate, equally high wrought-iron fence, affording protection against all but the most determined intruder.

"Alves!" she gasped, confronting the establishment as he maneuvered the sedan through the iron gates, conveniently held by the estate agent, into the tiled, minutely designed courtyard. The tires slid momentarily on the polished tiles. "Alves, you cannot be serious. . . . Not this, the grandest house in Lisbon. . . ."

He put his arm around her, squeezed her. "If you approve, the house is ours. . . ."

"I am certain," the agent said unctuously, bowing as if in respect to the building itself, "the Senhora will approve."

"The Menino d'Ouro . . ." Maria was uncharacteristically speechless. Her voice trailed away as she took Alves' arm and followed the agent across the courtyard toward the front door with its overhang of clouded glass and wrought iron. High, arched windows set in multiple mouldings flanked the doorway. Above the doorway were three even taller French windows which led onto a narrow matching wrought-iron balcony with three angled flagpoles, flagless at the moment. Here the owner might incite his servants and staff to greater efforts. Or thank his guests for joining him as they danced the night away in the tiled

smoothness of the courtyard below. The breeze rustled
the treetops. The walls of the exterior were a pale dusty
pink; the columns and carved mouldings that appointed
every imaginable seam were beige and rich cream in color.
They went inside, saw the broad staircase sweeping toward them as they stood in the foyer. Huge vases towered
on either side of them, the sunlight lay in vast patches on
the acreage of gleaming floor, the handles on the door
were burnished gold. Maria very nearly fainted at the
splendor of it all, the extraordinary sense of its perma-
nence.

The Menino d'Ouro was by no means an ancient mansion, despite the extent of its fame. Its curious name—the
Palace of the Golden Boy—was given it by a childless
Portuguese couple, spectacularly rich. Deeply religious,
they vowed that if blessed with a child, on the boy's first
birthday, gold, equal to the boy's weight, would be given
to the Church for God's greater glory. And so it happened.

The house was also said to bear a curse, this stemming
from the days of the Inquisition when the grounds were
rumored to have been made a graveyard for the anonymous
bones of torture victims.

"The cornices and mouldings are entirely gilded," the
agent was saying. "The fixtures in the bathrooms are gold,
much of the furnishings of the house are antique pieces
imported from France, England, Spain and Italy. There
are also examples of the finest Portuguese workmanship.
And please note the walls. . . . Many of the less formal
rooms, you will discover, are paneled with the rarest
Brazilian woods." The tour wound on, room after room,
one story after another. The wine cellar; the billiard
room with the enormous table; the music room with the
bay window and the chairs in neat, precise rows waiting
for the concert to begin; the bedrooms and the master
suite with the canopied four-poster and two adjoining,
gold-appointed baths; the ballroom; the parlors; the library
with the shelves lining the walls top to bottom.

"An interesting feature here, Senhor Reis," the agent
said, peeling back the carpet in the library. "Really, no one
knows about this—but in the case of so serious a prospect
as yourself I see no reason to hide it." He had gotten the
carpet two-thirds of the way back and knelt in the middle
of the room, removed a small round disk of wood from

the floor, revealing a metal ring handle. He lifted the handle and a two-foot square section of flooring came up easily: beneath it the black metal and gold printing, the somewhat ornamental door of a custom-designed safe!

"For important documents, the Senhora's jewelry, whatever you cannot bear to have out of reach." The agent, now sweating with exertion, laboriously pulled the safe open. "Lead-lined, steel shell—impregnable to fire, impossible to detect, and as you can see, very large in volume. . . ." He lowered the door.

"Most interesting, isn't it, my dear? What a place for safekeeping."

"Maybe they put the Golden Boy in there when he didn't behave!" Maria giggled happily. "Alves," she whispered while the rug was being replaced, "I have never seen such splendor. . . ."

"You deserve far more, putting up with me as you do." He felt a surge of warmth. This is real, not what happens in Paris. . . . This is my life, this is what matters. Watching her happiness, he sighed, knowing that his mind would change half a dozen times during the day on the subject of what was real, what truly mattered. If only he had two lifetimes.

"Will you buy it? Please?" They were driving to her parents' home for dinner.

"I said I would buy it if you approved."

"Oh, I approve! I approve!"

"The house, then, is yours."

It was, he reflected, a kind of supreme happiness, giving another human being such intense satisfaction.

At dinner Maria told her parents while Alves calmly spooned his soup.

"The Menino d'Ouro!" her mother exclaimed. She put her hands to her mouth in shock. "Alves, is she teasing me?"

"Ah, she is as truthful as ever."

"But, Alves," her father said, "it must cost a fortune. . . ."

"Yes, a modest fortune, that seems to me an accurate description—"

"I'd put the price somewhere near a million escudos." That from Manuelo, Maria's brother, for whom there had been the graduation party so long ago. Alves had never satisfactorily thanked Manuelo for the party, nor had he ever told him about what effect it had had on him—the sight of all those babbling fools paying such homage to a man with a leather-bound piece of parchment. But the party had given him that first insight into how it might all be managed and come right in the end.

Alves smiled gently at Manuelo, who had been named for King Manuelo I, known as Manuelo the Fortunate, who in 1496 had given the Jews of Portugal the choice of expulsion or conversion to Christianity. Manuelo in 1925 was making a career of a less historical nature: Manuelo the Accountant. He had wound up working for his father in the English firm, regardless of his fine diploma.

"A million," Alves repeated, shrugging. "Not far off."

"My God, you are on to something." Maria's father peered into his soup as if it were a heap of tea leaves wherein he might read the reasons for his in-and-out son-in-law's success.

"Just sound investments, sir," Alves said. "It's all a matter of knowing what you are doing. I have spent my life learning my lessons."

"And now the Menino d'Ouro," Maria cried proudly. "Mother, you must see it, the gold bathroom fixtures . . . gilt everywhere and the bedstead, you won't believe it if I tell you—and, Father, the wine cellar is a dream, a room for billiards . . ."

Manuelo was clearly torn between astonishment and envy. Maria's mother listened in varying degrees of pleasure at her daughter's good fortune and shock at the extravagance of it. Her father kept stealing covert glances at Alves, his face a vision of puzzled re-evaluation. For Alves, it was considerably more enjoyable than most evenings *chez* D'Azevedo.

Before the week was out Alves paid exactly one million escudos for the house and set up an account of half a million for Maria to draw on while adding whatever furnishings she fancied.

* * *

"Your great romance goes well, Arnaldo?"

"We are most compatible, yes, Alves. We are not grand. We stay in a great deal with Silvia's mother and father . . . we walked on the beach at Cascais last Sunday. It took

me back. I remembered other Sundays on that beach, years
ago, eh?"

"The day you met José," Alves said, seeing it all again,
watching the dawn beside the Tagus, listening the night
away as José talked of women and their various uses. "The
day I first saw Maria . . . such a long time ago. Yet, not
even a decade . . . several months short of a decade."

"So much has happened."

"More than in most people's lives, I expect."

"Great moments, Alves. The memories will already last
a lifetime."

"And I need hardly remind you that we are beginning
our finest period. . . ."

"No," Arnaldo mused, his face markedly older than it
had once been. It struck Alves as odd that he'd never
noticed it before. "But it will never be the way it was,
never excitement like that again. . . ."

"That's because it was our first taste . . . of anything,"
Alves said. "We were virginal, presumptuous young men,
Arnaldo, and we couldn't be quite sure how it would all
turn out. That's why it was different. Now we know what
we're doing."

"You may know," Arnaldo said. "I'm not at all sure I
understand it. . . ."

"Don't worry."

"It's my nature."

*   *   *

Evening. For most Portuguese businessmen the workday
was over. The streets of the Baixa were deserted. Alves sat
behind his new desk, which had required a delivery crew
of four. Arnaldo in his shirtsleeves stood at the bar cart
pouring two glasses of port. Alves looked up from a pile
of papers, removed his spectacles, commenced cleaning
them on his breast pocket handkerchief.

"In two days we leave for London. Would you prefer to
remain here? You could attend to the office and not have
to be away from your little friend. . . ."

"Yes, I would rather stay here."

"All right, then, that's settled."

"How long will you be gone?"

"I don't know." He replaced his spectacles, stacked his
papers and replaced them in a heavy folder. He lit a ciga-

rette with a heavy gold table lighter. "There is something important I am going to do. You should know about it. It is a matter of honor and dignity. . . ."

Arnaldo handed him his port and eased himself into a deep leather couch facing the desk. He waited attentively. *Honra e dignidade,* they inevitably went together in the Portuguese lexicon. It was almost as if they were a single word.

"As you are aware," Alves began slowly, "I have done nothing to vindicate myself in the matter of my difficulties with the treacherous directors of the Royal Trans-African Railway Company of Angola. I brought all my ingenuity to bear on old Chaves' problems, I brought stability to the railway, enabled their stock to rise and restored confidence in the firm . . . and for my troubles I was betrayed by three of the directors, accused of embezzling! From their positions as directors of Oporto banks, my accusers had me thrown into a dungeon in a city where I was friendless." He spoke more deliberately than Arnaldo had ever heard him. "Yet I was found innocent of embezzling Ambaca money. Innocent in a court of law! But still, they had me *jailed.* . . . The stain remains on the record of Alves Reis. I close my eyes and I can still see it, smell it, hear the incessant dripping when it rained. . . . My Maria was forced to sell everything, to beg our creditors for more time, forced to undergo the vilest humiliations . . . all because of the Ambaca directors in Oporto.

"Now, Arnaldo, we have come to a time of reckoning. Honor and dignity will be restored. . . . Do you understand? It is not a matter of simple revenge—that is for Italians. This is a Portuguese matter, honor and dignity.

"While I am in London I want you to begin the process of buying Ambaca stock." He tapped the folder that lay before him. "The directions are here. They are self-explanatory. There is a blank check. Spend to a limit of one million escudos while I am away. My calculations tell me that a total investment of two million escudos will give me control. We will conclude the purchase upon my return. Then we will have a surprise for the directors from Oporto." He stared through a bridge of fingers at Arnaldo. "Is this entirely understood?"

"I am to buy the shares for A. V. Alves Reis, Limitado?"

"Yes."

"But, Alves," he said hesitantly, "this money is the Bank of Portugal's, is it not?"

"I am following my instructions, Arnaldo. I ask only that you follow yours. Obviously I must not buy them in the name of the bank. . . . May I depend on you, old friend?"

"Yes." Arnaldo sighed, smiled feebly. "You know that."

Alves lifted his port. "To the conquest of Ambaca!"

Arnaldo replied, "To honor and dignity!"

Smiling confidently, Alves drank. Two million escudos had cost him one hundred and forty-four dollars in printing costs.

*　*　*

He stopped over in Paris late in the evening and went directly to the Claridge. He immediately rang Greta. There was no answer. It was nearly midnight: where could she be? He contemplated taking a taxi to her apartment. How childish! She was a grown woman, she had friends, admirers. Undoubtedly she was having a late supper. He hadn't told her when he was arriving. It was his own fault, after all. But he could not ignore the feeling of disappointment, the uneasiness in his stomach. Finally he slept—badly, waking frequently, standing at the window, drinking from the tooth glass, returning to the rumpled bed only to toss about and come awake yet again in the darkness. His train for The Hague left early. There was no time to call her. He would only have gotten her up for a confused conversation without time to see her. He settled for scribbling a note telling her that he would be passing through again in a few days and would call her. He also instructed the assistant manager to send flowers in his name. To the theater. He collected the new cases at Vuitton and checked them through to The Hague. The new clothing would have to wait until his return.

Hennies and Marang, who had remained in Lisbon only a few days to see the money-changing process begun, were waiting for him at the station. They went directly to the Hook of Holland in Marang's Winton, the Vuitton cases packed on the rear seat. It made for a crowded ride. They caught the night ferry with less than half an hour to spare.

In London all went smoothly. The Scrutton Street printing works had held to the schedule. Sir William wished them well. He told them of his present involvement in the preparation of the Waterlow Pavilion for the Second British Empire Exhibition at Wembley.

"The King, as you may know," he confided over the customary sherry, "is a noted philatelist, a particular admirer of several of the stamps we print. A fine man, The King. . . ." The implication of personal friendship was clear. Sir William produced a copy of the souvenir book that would be available at the exhibit. It was handsomely bound in tooled English leather. He asked the three financiers to listen as he read.

" 'There has been no attempt on Sir William's part,' " he read, "'to exalt the House of Waterlow at the expense of other businesses. The statements made are statements of fact. Nothing has been exaggerated. The House of Waterlow was founded more than a century ago—it has gone from strength to strength, under Waterlow guidance. There is no certainty in earthly affairs, but it is not too much to hope that in A.D. 2015 there will be occasion to chronicle another century of uninterrupted success on the part of Waterlow and Sons, Limited.' " He looked up, beaming. "That, gentlemen, is the sort of house you're doing business with. I sincerely hope we have given satisfaction."

"We are very pleased," Alves said.

"You would do me a great honor, Senhor Reis, if you would accept this especially bound copy with my compliments."

"Indeed, it is I who am honored, Sir William."

"Tell me, Senhor, do you expect further orders in the foreseeable future?"

"I am bound to maintain official silence, as you will understand. But let me say this, when I leave your office today I say *au revoir,* not goodbye."

Chuckles all around.

Waterlow porters loaded the three two-hundred-and-fifty-pound cases into two taxis. Following in a cab of their own, Hennies, Marang and Alves saw them to the Liverpool Street Station Main Line Departure Cloakroom. Marang checked them, receiving three two-piece cloakroom tickets. The three trunks were worth more than three and one half million dollars.

They proceeded to a leisurely lunch at Pimm's in Cheapside. The day was warm, surprisingly sunny. They looked through the Waterlow souvenir book.

"There is a certain magnificence about it, eh?" Hennies puffed on a cigar. He ran his fingertips over the tooled leather. The Waterlow coat of arms stood out in relief: a great snake swallowing its own tail. Within the circle was a sheaf of wheat and the motto *Vis unita fortior*. Union is strength.

The conversation turned to automobiles since all three men were contemplating the choices open to them. Hennies staunchly championed the Rolls-Royce, "English or not." Marang thoughtfully demurred. "I have already two cars to replace the faithful Winton—a Lincoln and a Kissel. You, Alves, you know the world of automobiles, you've sold the steady Nash. What's your choice?"

"The Hispano-Suiza. I have decided to have a pair made to my own design."

"Very expensive," Marang noted slyly. "Don't spend all your money on cars," he cautioned.

"Don't worry yourself, Karel," Alves said. "I've told you from the beginning I am very diversified."

"And the bank's investments in Angola will do no harm, I trust." Marang pursed his lips, almost coyly, playing the innocent.

"You may be right."

"Ach, I dare say he is," Hennies guffawed, draining his Pimm's cup.

The cases of banknotes were checked through to The Hague, where Hennies would pick them up and see that they arrived safely in Paris, where he and Alves would shepherd them to Lisbon. Marang's other companies required his attention in The Hague. He would receive his share of the commission before Hennies left for Paris, as well as a "bonus" Alves told them Camacho had very generously authorized. The last thing he wanted was malcontented partners in larceny. He couldn't help but wonder if they had developed any doubts as to the legitimacy of the operation. But, then, why would they? They had seen the contracts, they had seen Waterlow accept everything Reis gave him, and they had seen Reis come up with one document after another to meet Waterlow's demands. Why would they doubt at this late date, as the money poured in?

* * *

His first stop in Paris was at Boucheron, in Place Vendome, where he purchased two sapphire rings in gold, one for each of his women. From there he went to his tailor. The suits and riding gear were ready, as well as several of the shirts. Using a changing room, he put on a pearl-gray suit and waistcoat over a cream-colored shirt, a navy-blue silk tie with a pearl tack. Surveying himself in a three-way mirror, he drew a startled breath: he had never seen himself looking so elegant. Less self-conscious, too, he noted. He'd discarded that absurd cape, the pretentious silk shirts that had appealed to him in the first flush of wealth. Now it was fine broadcloth, the best collars, wool worsteds, silk only in the ties. Now they would remember the man, Reis, not what he wore. He smiled at himself, seeing a man truly to be reckoned with.

It was early afternoon when he called Greta. She seemed enthusiastic, happy to hear from him. He did not ask her where she had been a few days before.

"It's such a lovely day," she said. "Shall we have a picnic? Let's, please. I'll pick you up at Claridge's. One hour. . . ."

Picnic or not, he would wear his pearl gray!

He was waiting when the green Bentley pulled over to the curb. The top was down. Her hair was windblown, a flush in her cheeks. She kissed him in the sunshine as he settled into the passenger seat. The white wicker hamper was nestled in the space behind them.

"Your new suit . . . You are so handsome, I am driven mad!"

He felt his face flush. "You notice everything. Do you like it?"

"It is exquisite, darling. Understated."

"You know just what to say, don't you? Just what I wanted to hear."

"I know, but it is true, nonetheless."

He leaned back, feeling the sun on his face, slipping easily into his new world. Here he was free, his own man, without family or responsibilities. And so much money.

She drove to the Ile de la Cité and parked behind Notre Dame, beside a small triangular park, tree-shaded and quiet, insulated by the Seine on either side. Pigeons watched them intently as they left the car, bringing the hamper, then strolled on about their business.

"Is this nice? Do you like it? Lovers come here in the

summer, and when the *bateaux mouche* drift by they kiss and wave, most amusing. So why can't lovers come in the early spring?" She was carefully unpacking the hamper, arranging the chicken with truffles, the tomatoes and cucumbers in oil, the fresh moist bread with the hard crust, the wine and the Brie. "Now kiss me again before we gorge ourselves. . . ."

The afternoon drifted slowly past, like the boats on the river. She would kiss him whenever she noticed a boat and they would wave. She told him theater tales and he laughed, shook his head at the craziness. She asked him what was happening, how his business was going. He told her of the matter of honor and dignity, the history of his relationship with the railway: how he had made the trains run, how he had worn his monkey suit and damned near died in the heat of the boiler, and how he had ridden the High Bridge. . . . He lived it all again as the sun faded and the sky over Paris grew cloudy. He told her how Chaves had applied to him for help in Lisbon and how he had given it and saved Ambaca while at the same time propping up Angola Mining and how the Oporto directors had paid him back for his help. He told her what he had in store for the directors. She listened intently, questioning intelligently.

"I have never discussed such things with a woman before. I hope I didn't bore you." It was time to leave; she had to go to the theater.

"Alves, we are now part of each other's lives. We must share our experiences, know what the other is living through. . . . I would have it no other way. If you cannot confide in me, then it is not love between us. With José it was not a great love and there were no deep confidences. . . . With us, my thunderbolt, it is very different. You could never bore me."

She drove back to her apartment, where he relaxed, napping, reading while she worked.

He had the chilled champagne ready when she returned, flushed with the evening's success. No matter how tired she might be, the excitement of the stage always left her sexually hungry, eager to open herself to him. She kissed him and slid out of her blouse, leaning over him so that he could see her chemise fall loose, revealing her taut nipples. She took his hand and placed it against her flesh, laughing low in her throat, her breath steaming on his spectacles. "I can't wait," she whispered. "Do it here, in the chair. . . ." She was pulling her skirt off, stripping desperately. "Let me ride you," she said, leaning over his face, kissing his forehead, taking his spectacles off. She straddled him and lowered herself. His head swam with emotion and his own need. She made him lose control, made him the helpless victim of desire, as no one else ever had. Moments like this frightened him, but there was no going back: when she wanted him it was a force greater than his. He sunk his fingers into the flesh of her hips, guiding her, rocking her rhythmically, tasting her sweat as she pulled his head against her breasts, hearing the moans as she thrust herself down on him, again and again, going on long after he had emptied himself inside her. . . .

Drained, dizzy, they flung themselves on the bed's cool pillows, covered their damp bodies with the sheet. When their breathing had quieted he reached the night stand, felt for the small box from Boucheron, held it aloft like a prize. She smiled exhaustedly, reached for it.

"A trinket," he said.

She opened it and held it, turning it to watch the reflection of the candlelight.

"A trinket," she repeated, teasing him. "A sapphire trinket. . . ."

"You don't already have one, I hope."

She leaned forward, the sheet falling away, slipping the ring onto her finger. "I have several sapphires . . . but only one is a gift from Alves Reis." She lay back, admiring the ring. "And that makes all the difference. Thank you. You are much too generous."

"Don't be ridiculous and don't play that game with me." He was irritated out of proportion, but there was nothing to do about it. "I am not one of your admirers to whom you can say that . . . that I am too generous. . . ."

She leaned sideways, pulling the sheet back up, staring at the ring. After a while she said, "I'm sorry, darling. Of course, you are right. I love the ring . . . and tomorrow I will buy scarves to match it and I will wear it every day. Because it is a gift from you." She looked up, blinked.

He hugged her, nodding his face against her pale hair. He felt an unaccountable sadness and tried to ignore it. His beautiful new suit hung on a rack across the room; he noticed it like an old friend. He thought about his tailor and the lovely cut of the suits. He was very tired. He leaned across her body and pinched out the flame. She was already asleep.

*   *   *

Alves met Hennies on schedule. The trunks of money were loaded aboard the Sud Express. They bore the diplomatic seals, but to ensure smooth passage Hennies was carrying a passport naming him Commercial Attaché of the Liberian Legation, a far more recent document than Marang's.

"Better safe than sorry, eh?" the German barked with his customary energetic good humor. "Nobody will dare fiddle with these trunks now. In my travels I've learned that you can never take too many precautions. Someone, some busybody is always out there, waiting to catch you up when you least expect it."

Night was falling beyond the windows of the dining car. They sipped their coffee quietly, contemplated the dimming French countryside.

"It's all gone the way you planned, eh? The money is in circulation, the investments being made. We're all making more money through Camacho's generosity in the matter of bonuses. . . . You've done very well out of this, I must say." Hennies smiled broadly.

"I was fortunate in my connections," Alves said.

"I've know men who would have killed for such an opportunity. Many such men . . ."

"Are you including yourself, Adolf?"

"Quite possibly." The German chuckled. "At least when I was younger and less cautious . . ." He puffed his cigar, watching Alves. "I'm very curious about you, you know. I don't really know what kind of man you are . . . an enigma, so you remain to me. Oh, yes, you're a thinker, a planner, a clever fellow. But I knew that in Luanda, the night I met you. Your reputation had preceded you. An entrepreneur . . . then I learned of your stay in Oporto and I put what I knew of your African career together with that and I said to myself, the man is an adventurer . . . possibly a bit on the far side of the law, but, please, I am not judging you. Many of us have spent much of our lives in that no man's land where right and wrong grow confused. It is very easy to collide with the law. It can happen to anyone."

"I was found innocent in court, you may recall."

"I know, I know, but it has been my experience that anyone who has resided for a time in a jail cell has usually earned it, one way or another. So, I said to myself, the man may be something of a swindler—again, without passing judgment, I assure you."

"Of course not. You are in no particular position to pass any judgments." Hennies was making a blind probe. Surely he knew nothing.

"How right you are! But then you came to me with this remarkable offer—and once again I was set to doubting my opinion of you. Your connections with the bank—the highest levels of Portuguese finance! Surely not the province of a swindler, however clever, eh? Nor even of an adventurer. No, here is a man with extraordinary dimensions, I said to myself. But—" he sighed heavily—"what are those dimensions? You have hidden yourself away. . . . And now I think again. This bank, what kind of men are they? Here we are suddenly in the position of investing the bank's money through your company, as if it is ours. And we are given bonuses and the size of the bribery grows like . . . like nothing I have ever seen! Well, can such things not be part of a swindle? But who is being swindled, I ask myself, and I see in my mind all those contracts and letters . . . and I cannot see anyone being swindled. But I still have my riddle: what sort of fellow is this Alves Reis?" He shrugged his shoulders elaborately. "Perhaps he is some sort of financial genius, eh? You'd agree with that, I dare say. You don't mind my little speculations, I hope. . . ."

"I don't blame you," Alves said. "But there is no great mystery. I am just a man with a restless mind, determined not to be poor. . . . There is always a way to succeed, if you can only see it. You must be ready when the chance arises, when you come up with the idea that will work. But I am not a difficult man to understand, Adolf. . . . I do what I can to make my own luck, and once I have set out I don't look back. The future is only marginally interesting. . . . The future is now, Adolf. Remember that. What counts is now. . . . Confidence in what you do, always have confidence!"

Before retiring to their compartments for the evening Hennies winked at Alves.

"Perhaps you're a salesman. How about that, eh?"

"It's as good as anything. Whatever you decide, remember that it makes no difference. I am as I am."

"Well, that's good enough for me. Good night, Reis. Sleep well."

The next day Alves went to buy newspapers at Rossio Station while Hennies went to pick up the trunks. The papers folded under his arm, he was approaching the customs counter when he realized that something was very wrong. He stopped, stepped back into the crowd, propped himself against one of the pillars and surveyed the counter from behind the paper. He'd been through too many tight spots to miss it: his instincts set off the alarm, along the back of his neck, in his stomach. Danger . . . Hennies was arguing with the Chief of Customs, who watched him impassively, shaking his head in an unmistakably negative manner. Hennies threw his Liberian diplomatic passport down on the counter between them, pointed at it vigorously. The Chief of Customs curled a lip, regarded the document with disdain and folded his arms across the brass buttons on his chest. Hennies threw up his hands, wiped his forehead with a handkerchief.

If the Chief of Customs insisted on opening the trunks the world would blow up in their faces. Alves shrank against the pillar, trying to make sense out of the scene before him. He could see that seven hundred and fifty pounds of freshly printed banknotes spilling on the floor would set off a round of questions that would lead to Camacho Rodrigues—the *real* Camacho—and the earth would crack apart, swallow them all. Hennies looked ashen, trapped, eyes flickering. He was at a standstill with the Chief of Customs and had realized the consequences of a search through the trunks. The Chief of Customs pointed to the trunks that reposed in full view on a cart behind him. What was he contemplating? Alves watched for any sign, analyzing the situation like a man watching the fin of a shark circling in the water and weighing his chances of survival. Then, as the Chief of Customs moved back from the counter and reached for the three Vuitton trunks, Alves decided, slipped on an old mask of confidence and strode briskly up to the counter, smiling pleasantly.

"Trouble?" he inquired. The customs official turned abruptly. "Some difficulty here?"

"I cannot seem to convince this lunatic that the trunks are diplomatic property, sealed and protected by law. . . ." Hennies was holding onto the counter, jowls trembling.

Alves swallowed dryly, froze his smile in place, offered his assistance.

"I am quite within my powers to open whatever I choose. I am unfamiliar with you and I have never been offered a Liberian passport in my life." The Chief of Customs was not about to be intimidated. His eyes were very close together and glowed like coals. "I see no reason not to check these trunks."

"Excuse me, my good man," Alves said soothingly. "You are certainly within your rights. It is men like you who have made the Portuguese Customs Office one of the nation's prides! But this is a special case, if I may explain." He nodded to the man to come close, lowered his voice, as if to impart a weighty confidence. Hennies' eyes glazed over, staring past the counter at the trunks. "I am Senhor Alves Reis of Lisbon. These trunks were given to my care in Paris to hand-deliver to certain individuals in our government. As for myself the contents are entirely unknown to me or to my associate here. I fully understand your concern . . . but to avoid any difficulty for myself— you know how government ministers can be, I dare say— might we leave these trunks in your care overnight? Surely they will be safe with you and we'll send someone round tomorrow. Someone with more authority, if you understand. Then I will be out of any difficulty with my associates in power and you may deal with them as you wish." His shirt was soaked with sweat; his collar seemed to be choking him. It had to work.

The Chief of Customs sized him up, then nodded judiciously. He acknowledged with stern dignity that the trunks could be no safer anywhere else in Lisbon. Alves nodded. "They are in your trust, then."

Alves guided Hennies quickly away to a taxi. The German was still a sickly gray. They barely spoke until Alves saw him installed at the Avenida Palace.

"Don't worry, Adolf. Confidence is the watchword. Tomorrow I will have Camacho himself go down and show that officious dimwit what for. There will be no problem. Relax."

He left Hennies fussing. He took the checks for the trunks with him. He also took the Liberian diplomatic passport. God, what next?

The next morning he went to Rossio Station and positioned himself to watch the customs counter. For nearly

an hour he watched without seeing the culprit from yesterday. There would not be a shift change until after noon.
With a commanding air he approached the counter, heading straight for an elderly fellow with a round, happy face
who had been seen to smile several times during the hour of
surveillance. He too wore the badge of a Customs Chief.
Quickly, with an engaging humble smile on his own face,
Alves explained the problems the diplomat Hennies had
experienced the previous day. The elderly fellow nodded
sympathetically.

"It's not important, you understand," Alves said, "but
you know how zealous these diplomats are of their
privileges. Now Hennies plans to make a formal protest to
the Foreign Office this afternoon, and of course he needs
a morning coat and striped trousers . . . and, as luck
would have it, they happen to be in the trunks he's pro-
testing about!" Rolling his eyes over the childish behavior
of impetuous diplomats, Alves extracted an elegant croco-
dile-and-gold key case preparatory to opening the trunks
then and there.

"That must have been my young colleague," the Customs Chief said, "who shall remain nameless to save him
any further humiliation. I wonder sometimes what gets
into him—maybe he has stomach gas, who knows? Such a
blunder!"

"Ah, how true. I was hopeful that your maturity might
prevail."

They chuckled together, men of the world.

"Well, I will be delighted to release the trunks, Senhor,
upon the presentation of a diplomatic passport."

"No sooner said than done." Alves presented the document in question.

In a matter of seconds the trunks were being carted
toward the waiting taxi. Alves followed behind, his clammy,
trembling hands jammed in his coat pockets. He didn't
trust himself to light a cigarette. Much too close. *Much.*

*   *   *

José was sitting on the couch smoking a black cigarette in
an ivory holder, a veritable bouquet in his buttonhole.
Maria was trying to learn to smoke, coughing over an
identical cigarette and holder. Alves, returned from taking
the trunks to the office and leaving them with Arnaldo,

stood in the doorway of the old apartment, mouth agape. For a moment he thought there was a fire in the room.

"What do you think you're doing, Maria? What is going on here, anyway?"

"Now, Alves, don't be angry." José grinned.

"Your flower will die, it will suffocate!"

"José is teaching me to smoke, dear. It's nothing to get upset about."

"She's doing very well, too." José's grin seemed a permanent fixture. "I've stopped her swallowing the smoke and that's the battle, of course."

Maria belched softly. She held the cigarette holder as if it might go off at any moment.

"And we've done some shopping as well," she said, moving briskly on. "José has been helping me. I never see Arnaldo anymore, he's always off with his ladylove. You're always in London. . . ."

"Or The Hague or Paris," José said. "A very busy fellow."

"So I wanted to go out and needed someone to take me."

"All right, all right," Alves said, lighting a cigarette of his own. "Where are the boys?"

"In the park with Nurse. Let me show you what I bought."

"With what, may I ask?"

"Well, José said I could use credit. . . ."

"I merely pointed out that the owner of the Menino d'Ouro should certainly be a good credit risk. Once I told the shopkeepers precisely who Senhora Reis was, well, there was no question about an extension of credit—"

"I see," Alves interrupted. "Wasn't that a trifle presumptuous, José?"

"Please, Alves, I told him you would be pleased. After all, this way you won't have to take time away from your business to go shopping with a silly wife. . . ."

"I don't quite understand," Alves said. "I am more than happy to accompany you anywhere you—"

"I know that, but José explained to me how terribly busy you are, how much depends on what you're doing—"

"He did, did he? Very kind of you, José."

"It's nothing, Alves, nothing at all."

"Come, dear, look at what I bought." Maria led him to the dining table. It had taken on the look of a jeweler's display case. With what he saw as a delicate kind of greed,

Maria presented her purchases. There was a pearl necklace with three hundred and ninety-nine perfect pearls. Diamond earrings that glittered on the table like a scattering of stars in the night sky. Eight diamond rings. Gold and diamonds in a bracelet. A platinum lorgnette—and, for the evening, a diamond-encrusted platinum lorgnette. Fifty thousand dollars' worth of pearls, gold, platinum and diamonds.

"Good God," Alves sighed.

"Do you like them?" Maria prodded them with her forefinger as if they might come to life. "Oh, I know this awful apartment is a grim setting, but our new house, that will be perfect. . . . We must live up to our house!"

"This is incredible," Alves said.

"It's not too much, is it? We can afford it, can't we?"

"I don't know what to say, really I—"

"José said you—"

"Don't tell me what José said. Yes, of course I can afford it, I suppose. But it is a great deal all at once. . . ."

"Now, Alves, I knew you'd want Maria to have the best. From now on the sky's the limit. Everything is going so well for you—hell, for all of us! Maria is growing up after all these years of bearing your children, staying at home all locked away and protected. . . . It's time she got out into the world and became a sophisticated lady of means."

"That's true, isn't it, dear?" She stood before him, her fingers wrapped in the lapels of his coat. The corners of her mouth twitched, unsure of themselves. "You want me to be sophisticated, fit for such a rich and powerful man?"

"Rich and powerful—"

"That's what José called you."

"Stop, stop, yes, rich and powerful. Go home, José!"

"He's joking, José."

"I know."

"I am not. Go home, José."

"Stay, José," Maria said, confidence growing.

"Fifty thousand dollars," Alves murmured.

"Are you angry, dear? Tell me truthfully."

He put his hand in his pocket and touched the second of the two small packages from Boucheron. There was no point in that now.

"Of course I'm not angry," he said, forcing a smile. What could he expect, after all? He was in Paris with Greta every chance he could get. If the price he had to pay

for his infidelity was some jewelry and an extravagant
house, well, that was little enough. But when would the
price come down to something other than money?

"Alves?" she asked. "Are you all right?"

"Yes, I'm fine, just thinking how dazzling you will look
in our new home, draped in diamonds and beautiful
gowns. . . . Quite awe-inspiring I must say."

"You see," José cried, leaping up, sweeping his arms
in an expansive gesture, "I knew he'd approve!" He
squeezed Maria's shoulders while she smiled happily from
one to the other.

Maria went off to bathe away the exertions of the
shopping trip. José smiled at Alves, waiting.

"You may go too far," Alves said quietly. "She's a very
simple woman, not sophisticated, not a clothes horse."

"She's never had the chance. . . . It's not fair to her.
You've developed a sudden taste for worldly women, well,
then the least you can do is let Maria enter the competition and battle for your affection on even ground."

"You understand nothing, José," Alves said, forcing
himself to control his exasperation. "Maria has my love,
my undying devotion, but not because I want her to become
a sophisticate, a worldly woman. I love her for what she
is. I don't want her to become a second-rate copy of
Greta—that would be ridiculous."

"You underestimate your Maria." He picked up his
walking stick and slipped his fingers into a fawn-colored
glove. His suit was a shade darker than the gloves, and he
wore a chocolate-brown necktie. His hair was oiled slick
against his small skull. He smelled of French cologne.
"She intends to enjoy your new wealth. She is pursuing her
instincts. That house has transformed her, my friend,
but when she speaks you are either in Paris with Greta or
you don't listen because you think it is only empty-headed
little Maria who has nothing of interest to say." He waggled a forefinger in Alves' face. "Well, you are in for a
surprise."

"What are you talking about, my new wealth? You
know how much I made on the bank deal. . . . You know
I can't afford these jewels." He had to probe, find out what
José was thinking.

"Don't kid me, not old José. It won't work. I've been
there and back, time and again. All those bribes for the

bank? You're skimming some of that for yourself. You've
got some private arrangements with them, I know that.
All legal, don't get me wrong. . . . But you're making a
hell of a lot more than a commission!" He laughed,
punched Alves' arm. "And the investments in Ambaca and
the mining company? You'll gain a fortune as the stock
rises even if the investment money isn't yours. . . . Hell,
man, you can afford the jewels and, believe me, I love
being along for the ride. Anything I can do, you name it."
He paused at the door. "What I'm saying about Maria,
I'm not joking. She may not have thought it through, but
she knows there's something wrong, that she's seeing less
and less of you, losing you—to your business if not to another woman. And she has to replace you in her life. Either
with another man—yes, another man—or by embellishing
her own life. As it happens, she is doing the latter . . . for
now. You should be delighted she's not cuckolding you, my
lad."

"Perhaps you are right, perhaps she is losing me . . .
but I cannot bear the thought of losing her. . . ."

"Then you, my old chum, are in one hell of a quandary.
You'll figure a way out of it, you always have. And look
at the bright side—while you worry about it, you'll be
rich!" He left with a broad grin spreading beneath the
sloping wings of his mustache.

Alves went to the bedroom and lay down. Maria was
singing a nursery rhyme in the tub. Perhaps José was right,
but if he was, what then? She would have to be indulged.
Another man! My God, what a thought . . . Maria! Incredible, utterly out of character. But the jewels and the
house and the inevitable parties: yes, she would have to be
indulged. And in the meantime he would try to make some
sense of the two halves of his life.

At least José hadn't stumbled across anything like the
truth behind Alves' scheme. José saw things as he would
have arranged them, the skimming of bribes. Which was,
of course, why he'd spent so much time in jail and Alves
had devised the perfect plan. These problems would all
work out, he was sure of it. The silk-cased pillows felt soft,
pleasantly expensive, against his face as he drifted off,
one hand in his pocket, clutching the Boucheron box.

*　　*　　*

A representative of the Hispano-Suiza motorcar works came to Lisbon to consult with Senhor Reis on the coach-work of the two vehicles that were being built. That same week they moved into the Menino d'Ouro, and for three days the vans rolled into the courtyard with the furnishings—carpets and tables and couches and chairs and tapestries and silver and crates of leather-bound books for Alves' library. The tiled courtyard was jammed with deliverymen and gardeners attending to the plantings and painters repainting with the original colors, of course.

Carpenters and masons began work on the double garage designed to accommodate with ease the two automobiles that were in preparation. Architects supervised the construction, perfectly matching garage to house, attending to details, screaming instructions, demonstrating with hammers and chisels. Iron gates were mounted matching those guarding the courtyard. Azulejos were commissioned, duplicating those on the walls surrounding the estate. During the excavation the workmen called to Alves; he must come look at what they had unearthed. The bleached, splintered bones of the victims of the Inquisition. Alves shuddered, went back inside.

One day he was passing a small art gallery in a side street, saw a Morocco bound, gilt-stamped atlas of considerable antiquity and went inside. While paying for the volume his eye was caught by a dim old portrait of an admiral of the Portuguese fleet. The small oval plate screwed into the intricately carved frame struck him like a cannon ball.

The great Admiral Reis . . .

"Oh, that," the shopkeeper said. "It's been around here for years. My father had it when I was a boy. Nobody's ever shown the slightest interest in it, I'm afraid."

"But he was a famous admiral," Alves said. "There is a street in Lisbon named for him. . . . A great man."

"Maybe so. Not much of a painting, though."

"I want it. Clean it up for me. I'll wait for it, if you don't mind."

That set his mind to working. Of course he'd always been one for having photographs taken every chance he got. He recalled the wedding portrait of Maria and himself the photographer had kept so long in his shop window. They proved that you'd been here, that you had existed. Your children and their children would some day look slowly through the albums and see just who you had been. Photographs had always struck him as quite wonderfully sufficient. But now . . . The next day he arranged to have the best portraitist in Lisbon undertake two works: one of himself on horseback with a background representing the High Bridge, one of himself and Maria as they were today, him in his dark-blue suit from Paris and Maria in a lovely crimson gown with bare shoulders, a demure shawl and a great many diamonds. Maria was enchanted.

One evening he called Maria into his new library, where he had spread out on a long table the hundreds of photographs they had accumulated over the years. Carefully, without noticing the passage of time, they worked until dawn, choosing which ones would be framed. The next day the framer came to the house, with a crate full of samples, and went away with the largest single order of his life.

Yes, Alves thought, I have been here, no doubt of that.

* * *

Arnaldo entered Alves' private office with the air of a man who was being led to the scaffold. He was growing increasingly tired-looking as the weeks went past, and there seemed to be nothing Alves could do to cheer him up. What his problem was Alves could not quite figure out. The work load was not all that heavy. He had plenty of money. Silvia was as true as any man could wish. Yet, Arnaldo's face grew wan and pinched. He sighed too often and ate like a bird when they were together.

Alves sat with his back to the windows. Venetian blinds sliced the spring sunshine into blocks that lay across his desk like toy stones for building castles. On the wall before him above the couch hung the gleaming portrait of Admiral Reis.

"What's the matter now?" Alves leaned back in his leather padded swivel chair, folded his hands across his vest. "You look even worse than usual."

"This," he sighed, "this is no joke." His sleeves were rolled up and his tie loosened. His shirt was crumpled like tissue paper under his suspenders. There was apparently nothing to be done about his inability to dress befitting his new station. He wiped his head with a red bandana. "We've got trouble, Alves. . . ."

"Sit down, relax, tell me about it."

Arnaldo dropped like a stone onto the couch, moved his head when he found himself squinting into the sun.

"There are rumors in the street, among the bankers and the moneylenders and even some cabinet ministers. . . . I heard them for the first time yesterday at lunch. Now my friends tell me there will be something in the papers tomorrow." He chewed hungrily at a fingernail.

"Rumors? Not about us, surely?"

"Not us personally, no. But about what we're doing."

"No, about what is happening, not what we're doing."

"Look, have it any way you want it, Alves. I didn't come in here to quibble over words. Whatever you call it, there are several million dollars' worth of new five-hundred-escudo notes in circulation somewhere—here, France, England, in the Portuguese economy. Things are getting thrown off balance." He stood and jammed his hands into the pockets of his rumpled trousers, began pacing. "I'd have thought that your friends at the bank would have instructed us to go more slowly."

Alves shrugged. "Well, the fact is, they didn't. Continue, please."

"Well, the rumors say that there is a flood of counterfeit five-hundred-escudo notes. A flood. I'm told that merchants are very reluctant to accept them, that business in some of the smaller towns has come to a standstill."

Alves made a face. "We know the notes are good, the bank knows . . . We have got to get the word out that the notes are good. Leave it to me. I'll call Camacho and see what he wants done." He watched Arnaldo until he stopped pacing. "It's going to be all right. Have faith in me, Arnaldo."

Arnaldo nodded. Sweat stains spread from under his arms. At least, Alves thought, it wasn't an expensive silk shirt.

He decided to call José Armando Pedroso, the Bank of Portugal's expert on forgery.

"Senhor Pedroso, this is Alves Reis of Reis, Limitada. May I take a moment of your time? As you may know there are rumors circulating about possible counterfeit notes—five-hundred-escudo notes, to be precise. Now they look fine to me. I am accepting them. But some of my clients are reluctant. . . . Could you possibly take a look at some of the notes if I sent a few to your office? I want to remain completely anonymous, of course."

"Of course, Senhor. In any case, we are looking at some notes now. I'll be glad to have yours included . . . and I doubt very much if you are involved with any counterfeit notes. We haven't found any thus far. This little scare should die out in a few days. But, by all means, send them over."

Alves dispatched an office boy with a bundle of new notes and instructed José to inform the drones that a rest was in order. There would be no more money changing until Alves sent the word.

Senhor Pedroso was on the telephone first thing the next morning.

"Senhor Reis, your notes are on the way back to you by special messenger. I have checked them personally and rechecked them. I have calibrated them, the finest measurements I can make—anyone can make. I have magnified the tiniest details, I have chemically removed ink for analysis . . . and, by God, I have smelled them with a nose that is the envy of the industry! Senhor Reis, these notes are absolutely perfect. No possibility of counterfeit whatsoever."

Alves summoned Arnaldo to his office, told him the story.

"The bank is sending very discreet letters to all of its correspondents across Portugal, personal letters from Pedroso, whose authority in these matters is absolute. The rumors will be put to rest. . . ."

"Well, thank God for that." Arnaldo managed a smile. There was a soup stain on Arnaldo's tie that somehow struck just the proper note in his ensemble.

"Yes, it's just what I asked for. But we must understand that it will take time for confidence to be restored in the marketplace."

José threw the door open and strode jauntily into the office, the perfect boulevardier. No stains on his tie.

"You're supposed to knock," Arnaldo said tonelessly.

"It's important, my lad. When can the drones go back to work?" He sat on the edge of Alves' desk and popped open the cigarette case on the desk. His nails were manicured, buffed to a high sheen. José Bandeira, Alves thought, ravisher of manicurists. No wonder Greta had not found him a great love. . . .

"It will be a while," Alves said. "I'll let you know. Call them in a week, tell them we're giving them a vacation."

"Without pay," José said. "They'll balk—"

"They've done very well off us," Alves exploded, "now they'll do what they're told."

"As the Americans say, keep your shirt on, Alves." He lit a cigarette in the ivory holder and slowly expelled a brownish cloud. "Did you hear the elephant story, by the way?" He was already chuckling, his slender body quaking lightly.

"What elephant?" Arnaldo asked.

"The famous elephant in the Lisbon Zoo, the elephant that can tell the difference between silver and copper coins. It seems he takes the copper ones and flings them into the ditch. The silver ones he takes to a little box, deposits them and then lumbers off happily to tug on a bell rope that alerts his keeper, who then delivers a fresh bundle of grass in exchange for the silver coin! Quite a brilliant pachyderm!"

Arnaldo peered up wearily. "What's so brilliant about turning silver into grass?"

"He misses the point," José said blandly. "In any case, they're taking a bunch of notes—our notes—to the elephant in the hope that he can tell if they're counterfeit!"

"What if he pees on them?" Arnaldo muttered. "It's a boring story, José. . . . There's nothing amusing about the public at large snickering over money. I don't like it."

Alves listened to them babble on. It was the perfect time for the next step in the plan. Undoubtedly the biggest step of all.

"Arnaldo," he interrupted. "Send wires to Hennies in Berlin and Marang in The Hague. The message is simple. 'Most important meet Claridge Paris April twenty-nine.' Get them off at once."

"What's so important?" José was pouring a glass of port at the rolling cart.

"You will discover on April twenty-ninth," Alves said.

José shrugged. "Whatever you say. Boss. Chief."

"Arnaldo, get the files on the wheat and match deals ready. We can take care of those in Paris, as well as more important things." The thought of doing business with the Swedish Match Company gave him a pleasant pause, reminded him of the new breadth of his horizons.

"Wheat and matches." José nodded appreciatively. "You *are* diversified. . . . Ooo, la, la."

"Money has to be put to work as well as spent," Alves said briskly.

"Ah, but it's the spending that makes it all worthwhile."

"So you say."

"Incidentally, I hope you recall that I am invited for dinner this evening."

"Yes, yes, yes, I recall."

José had increasingly filled the void left by Arnaldo's devotion to his Silvia. His appearance at the Menino d'Ouro for meals and evenings in the music room or at the billiard table was most common. Alves didn't really mind. José was good company and helped overcome Alves' own not particularly playful nature. And he amused Maria, who occasionally modeled new gowns for the two of them after dinner. There had always been someone to occupy Maria's mind, he reflected, always someone to keep her busy while he attended to serious matters. Why, he wondered, had there always been such a need? Perhaps it was one of life's imponderables. Just a fact of life. . . .

The morning of the twenty-seventh the entire caravan arrived at Rossio Station for yet another trip on the Sud Express. There were the four boys and their nurse and their governess. There was Maria's newly acquired personal maid. There were José, Arnaldo and Silvia. There was Maria herself and her various trunks, several of which were empty in anticipation of purchases in the City of Light. And there was Alves himself. An even dozen. An entourage. When he thought of it, Alves was oddly pleased.

*   *   *

After everyone else had retired, Alves relaxed with Arnaldo over a brandy. The train rocked gently, steadily through the night.

"Are you going to marry Silvia? I wouldn't want to think you hadn't told me . . . oldest friends and so on." The very question brought a rush of memory, made him feel youthful again.

"It's not as easy to talk to you as it used to be."

"Nonsense! What do you mean?"

Arnaldo shrugged, looked out the window. "It's not simple. . . . You've gone so far. You know I've always admired you, followed you around, done what I was told."

"You make yourself sound like an errand boy," Alves

snorted. "You have always been my right hand, supported me in every crisis. . . . Friend, partner. Those are the words that apply."

"I don't know. We have so little in common. I've never wanted power or great wealth or women, the things that come with money. I'll always be pretty much the same. . . . These past six months you've worked a miracle on yourself, on all of us but mainly on yourself. Do you see? Now we're all running along behind you trying to catch up, trying to be what you want us to be. Well, I'm having a hard time, Alves, and I'm not sure I can handle it. I don't understand what we're doing with the bank, how it can be that we have all this money at our disposal—I don't understand why the bank deals on the black market with the drones. It makes no sense to me. I don't understand all the rumors about bad money . . . and the things I don't understand are the things that frighten me. It makes me want to pull up and get out, Alves." He caught Alves' eye in the window's reflection.

"You're just tired," Alves said. "You'll come around and be like new. Particularly when you hear what I have in store for you in Paris . . . the next step! That'll perk you up, I guarantee it."

Arnaldo smiled wanly. "Alves, you just don't listen to me anymore. The next step—I don't know if I care about the next step."

"Don't be so sure, old friend. You've never dreamed of anything like it." He smiled reassuringly, sipped his brandy. "And you've ignored my question. Are you going to marry Silvia?"

"Yes, when the time is right. I want her to be my wife, have our children . . . yes. We haven't set a date, but she's accepted my suit."

"Arnaldo," Alves said, clasping his hand impulsively, feeling a tightness in his chest. "Arnaldo, my dear fellow, I am so very pleased for you. So very happy! Does anyone know?"

"Only you—only the three of us."

"Not even Maria?"

"I don't see her so often anymore, you know. . . ." He shrugged.

"Well, I leave it entirely to you. I won't let on to anyone, not even Maria or Silvia. She's a lovely young woman, she'll make you a grand, loving wife. . . ."

"If she is another Maria," Arnaldo said, "I couldn't have asked for more."

"Arnaldo, do me a great favor, no questions, just do me a favor."

"Of course, name it."

"This," Alves said, fumbling for a moment in his pocket. "Take this and give it to Silvia. From you, a small present—no need to mention me. I'd appreciate it if you didn't. Just call it a gift in celebration of your future together."

Arnaldo opened the tiny hinged box.

It was a small sapphire-and-gold ring.

*   *   *

"Oh, Greta, you must come to Lisbon and see our house! It even has a name! The Menino d'Ouro. And a wine cellar and a music room and Alves' library full of leather-bound books! Promise me you'll come for a visit." Maria's face was flushed, and her champagne glass was nearly empty. The evening was warm. Greta's apartment seemed crowded, even though it was the same old group. But Alves could not shake his own memories of what had happened again and again in the same rooms. Greta's cries echoed faintly in his mind, and he could smell her body as he watched her with his wife.

"I'd love it, Maria, I really would love it. You and Alves could show me all the places he's mentioned, the Castle of San Jorge and the Alfama and the harbor and the beach— now where was the beach, yes, at Cascais. . . . And I would love seeing your house." She held her glass out, and José filled hers and Maria's. "Though I'm positive I would be hideously envious. Alves has described it to me too. . . . Heavenly! And what a story, the baby's weight in gold!"

"Alves can't resist a good story," Maria said. "He didn't tell me he'd seen you—"

"He called me one night, passing through on his way to The Hague. I asked him to come see me in my play— thank God, it's over at last—and we went to dinner at Fouquet's. He was so excited at the thought of the house, I couldn't get him to stop."

"I'll bet on that," José interjected. "He's a hard man to stop."

"I'm so glad he has at least one friend in Paris," Maria

said. "I'm always afraid he'll be lonely on his trips." She sipped the Mumm's and flicked a point of tongue across her lips. "He's always gone, always in London or The Hague—or Paris. It seems I don't see him at all. . . ." Her happiness was fading. "I think I've had my limit of champagne."

"I'm afraid I have also reached my limit," José said. "I grow voluble beyond this point, as we all have reason to know."

"And regret," Greta added with sarcastic good humor.

"Too much to drink and, as the Americans say, I spill the beans!" José said, frowned, shook his head. "What could they have had in mind? What does spilling the beans have to do with talking too much?"

"As much as letting the cat out of the bag, I suppose." Greta smiled. "I'm very up on my Americanisms too, you see."

"Well, I hope it does you some good." José wandered off.

Alves moved away from the cold fireplace and joined the two women. The Javanese maid glided past, more champagne.

"Greta has promised to visit us in Lisbon," Maria said, taking his arm. "Isn't that wonderful?"

"I'm overwhelmed by our good fortune," he said.

"You are too kind," Greta said.

"Alves and I met on the beach at Cascais, let's see, a little over one hundred years ago." Maria giggled. "As mere children, of course. Do you remember, dear? It was so funny, the rope broke and Alves nearly drowned. . . ."

"I had no idea you were such a funny fellow," Greta said. "I've never seen that side of you, have I?"

"Oh, there are worlds of Alves Reis you haven't seen," Maria said. Her voice was trembling a bit. Alves knew it was the champagne that might be the very best way out of this grueling evening.

"Well, let's not go into that," he said jocularly. "Much too boring."

Plumpish, shy Silvia, with her Madonna's face, heavy browed with full lips, joined the group with Arnaldo behind her looking customarily rumpled and vaguely ill at ease.

"You have a lovely home," Silvia said. "Exotic . . . is that the word I want?"

"I'm sure it is precisely the word you want, my dear," Greta said, inclining her long white neck. "Are you having a nice trip thus far? Have you been to Paris before?"

"I never have," Silvia said, "but I am having a wonderful trip." She looked adoringly at Arnaldo, who blushed. "I've already had a lovely present—look. . . ." She held up her hand and the sapphire caught the light.

"Why, that is very beautiful," Alves said. "Arnaldo's taste is unsurpassed."

"It is very beautiful, I agree," Greta said, "and I say that quite objectively even though I happen to be wearing the same ring." She held her hand out to view. "Isn't that an absolutely remarkable coincidence?"

"From an admirer?" Maria asked.

"Who else would give one such a ring?" Arnaldo said. He put his arm around Silvia lightly. "An ardent admirer, I'd say. Wouldn't you agree, Alves?"

"So it would seem."

Maria waved her own hand, fanning her fingers across her face, peeking tipsily between. "Platinum and diamonds for me. And gold." She pouted. "But I had to buy them for myself. My ardent admirer was away or busy. . . ."

Greta said: "But the diamonds are a very nice consolation, aren't they? I've always found diamonds wonderfully comforting at difficult, lonely moments. Take away money and Boucheron and Cartier, and loneliness would be far worse than it is." Everyone laughed appreciatively.

"Sweet Georgia Brown" on the phonograph gave way to "Why Do I Love You?" and Greta uncovered the silver chafing dishes. Maria remarked that she was hungry, and José went to the steaming, aromatic curry.

"I had the food sent in," Greta said to Alves, winking. "So don't compliment me on it. You bought two rings, I see. You are a complex man."

"One was for Maria, but when I saw her acquisitions I decided the gesture would be wasted. I gave it to Arnaldo."

"That was very sweet. Silvia seems just his type, chubby and faithful and boring. She won't give him any trouble. Or he her, for that matter. How long will you be in Paris? Will I see you alone?"

"I don't know. A few days. . . . I'll try to get away."

"Don't make trouble for yourself. . . . What are you

here for, actually? More big business deals!" She mocked him softly.

"Yes, very big this time."

"You must be growing very rich. Those diamonds she's wearing tonight are quite breathtaking."

"José's influence. . . . I couldn't have her take them back. They make up for . . ." He left the thought dangling.

"Me?" Her lavender eyes took on a bluish cast in the dim candlelight. Bracelets rattled on her long wrists.

"Yes, you. I have betrayed her. . . ."

"If that's the way you feel, stop."

"Don't say that. You know what I mean."

"I have never looked at it as betrayal, even when there was someone. I see it as enjoying myself, a far healthier attitude, I think."

"I'm seeing the great man himself," he told her, seeking firmer ground. Hennies put another record on the machine. "Sleepy Time Gal."

"And who may that be?"

"Kreuger, the match king."

"You're doing business with Ivar Kreuger?"

"Yes. It's a matter of factories in Portugal. He's all around us, heavily in Spain, but Portugal has eluded him. I will help him rectify that. . . ."

"My darling, you should have mentioned this before. Ivar is a very dear friend of mine, Scandinavians together. He has a fatal weakness for actresses. . . . They say he's homosexual because he's never married, but it's not so. He's very fond of ladies . . . but Swedish Match and Kreuger and Toll, that is his life, his businesses. It's a game for him, and he plays it better than anyone ever has."

"How dear a friend, Greta?"

"A very dear friend," she repeated. "Do I hear jealousy?" She took his hand. "You have no need, darling. We are not that kind of friends. But he is a lovely, sweet man— he is like you, incredibly generous because he can never give people the personal attention they deserve. He actually carries diamond rings with him. I saw him give one to a serving girl in a small restaurant once, simply because she had been courteous and attentive without knowing he was Ivar Kreuger. He gave me the Bentley."

"Are you serious?" His hand tightened on hers.

"He saw me give a performance and invited me to dinner every night for a week without ever committing the slightest impropriety . . . beyond inquiring if he might see my breasts."

"And you showed him?"

She laughed. "Of course. I'd never heard of a man asking such a favor so solemnly. It was harmless. He didn't touch me. We were dining at his apartment, an entire table between us, so I slipped the straps of my dress down. His expression never changed. He just kept on chewing his pheasant and said, 'You are quite beautiful, my dear Greta, but you have the breasts of a twelve-year-old.' "

Alves shook his head. "I don't understand you sometimes."

"Would you like to see him socially? At home? I'm quite sure it could be arranged."

"I don't think I'd like him. . . ."

"Silly. Of course you would. He is a quiet, retiring man, carries his own bags when he takes a trip. . . . I'm afraid I shouldn't have told you my little story. Now you have the wrong impression. Let me call him. . . . Maria would enjoy seeing his apartment. She could tell her friends she has met the greatest man in Europe, the most powerful financier in the world."

"All right. If it is convenient."

She brushed her mouth against his ear. "My breasts are for you, Senhor Reis. Would you care to accompany me to my bedchamber? I would gladly prove it."

"Stop, for heaven's sake. Anyone can see you." He drew away, saw her laughing at him. "And don't laugh like that. . . ."

She sighed. "But I want you desperately. I'm not working every evening now. Think of all that excess energy I could devote to you."

"I would rather not," he said. Hennies was moving their way. "Ah, Adolf, old man, join us. I was just telling Greta what a big surprise I have for all of you tomorrow."

Hennies set his plate on the wide windowsill. He dabbed perspiration from his forehead.

"He's lying, Adolf. We were having an intensely private discussion and you've interrupted us."

"Ach, too bloody bad, my dear. Alves has to keep his mind on increasing our wealth! Ignore her, that's my advice—she's a lovely, troublesome wench. . . ." He kissed her cheek. "And she says terrible things about me, calls me a Hun!"

"Indeed, I do and you deserve it. Did you see the gift Adolf brought me?"

"Not a sapphire ring, I hope?"

"A book. What was it called, Adolf?"

"*Mein Kampf,* the newest thing in Berlin. Jailbird politician wrote it, Hitler, Adolf Hitler. You need to know things German, my dear Greta. You have a great following in Berlin. The man has all sorts of interesting ideas."

"Have you read it?" she asked him. "Truthfully."

He made a face. "Not exactly; I don't have time for books and such. But I've heard it discussed. He hates the Jews, I'm told, which meets with considerable approval. . . . I don't really give a damn, Greta. I'm just pandering to your intellectual pretensions." He began to eat noisily.

"Perhaps I should read it," Alves said.

"Is your German up to it?" Greta said.

"I could manage."

"Fine, take it. Give me jewels next time, Adolf. Or a new car. I'm tired of my poor Bentley. It's too green. Or flowers . . . just send flowers." She handed the book to Alves.

"Bah. You're such a materialist!" Hennies sniffed, turned to Alves. "Life is a joke to her. Take out of it what you can and when it is finally empty, it is time to go!"

As they were leaving, Greta kissed Maria's cheek. Alves bowed and she kissed him as well, chiding him for his formality. In the hallway he could still hear the music. "Rings on your fingers," someone was singing. Rings on your fingers—that was amusing, he reflected sourly.

* * *

No one ever seemed to have a very clear memory of the evenings in Paris come morning, and Alves never knew quite why, because he invariably recalled them with considerable lucidity. Perhaps the tension he'd felt at Greta's apartment had existed only in his mind. But, still, there had been something in the air, a kind of overpowering implication never quite stated. The story of Greta revealing her breasts to Kreuger had bothered him more than he liked; he woke up picturing her calmly exhibiting herself. . . . But he seemed to be the only one who had sensed anything out of the ordinary. Maria had awakened, gulped a pair of headache powders, and called Greta. They were going to her couturier in the afternoon, then on to other shopping. Maria seemed a bit less talkative than usual, probably the effect of the champagne. The governess had herded the children off to the park.

"All right," Hennies prodded him, "we're here in solemn conclave yet again, eh? Give us our surprise, Alves. . . ."

The familiar suite fairly glowed with the spring sunshine. The management had made sure there were flowers everywhere. The windows were thrown open to the warm breezes.

"We have come a great distance since we began," Alves said. "A long way in a very short time. And I am here today to extend the deepest thanks for our friends at the bank. Circumstances make it impossible for them to thank you personally, as you will understand, but nevertheless their appreciation is sincere. We are no longer merely in their employ. . . . We are crucial to the future of the bank, necessary elements in their battle with those directors of the bank unsympathetic to their final aims: . . ."

"And what does all this gratitude mean?" Marang asked. "How does it translate?"

"Let me be methodical," Alves said, glancing at his notes. He sat with his back to the windows. "First, we have ordered a temporary cessation to the distribution of the remaining banknotes. We are agreed that there is nothing to be gained by drawing attention to the new issuance.

"Second, I take great pleasure in telling you that we are going to create for ourselves nothing less than *a new bank!* Our bank—the Bank of Angola and Metropole!"

Hennies looked up, startled. "What?"

Marang's eyebrows arched dramatically. Arnaldo sighed and removed his spectacles, pinched his eyes shut.

José looked skeptical. "What do we need a bank for? To pay more salaries? More rent?"

Alves felt an immense serenity. This was the moment he had dreamed of in the Oporto jail. My God, it seemed so long ago, an age ago. But less than a year. . . . The power would be his now.

"Our friends at the bank support and encourage us in this step. We have reached the limit of how far we can go just by using our free-lance money changers, our drones. Inevitably their turning up day after day, week after week, with only new five-hundred-escudo notes will direct certain unwelcome attention to them . . . and to us. A bank, on the other hand, can do these things with ease, through private, unobserved channels. . . . Obviously, we can also save the two-percent commission we've been paying. This is not to say there won't be any problems. We must have the permission of the Banking Council and the Inspectorate of the Banking Trade. I have already begun some preliminary discussions and there are difficulties to be overcome. They have requested that one of my proposed directors be dropped." He paused and drummed the table with his fingertips. "José, I'm afraid your past has caught up with you. . . . The arrest for embezzlement, even though you were finally acquitted, has made you a liability. There's no point in having them digging too deeply into your past. You do understand, I hope?"

José nodded glumly. "The mistakes of a man's green years never leave him. . . . What can I say? Things are as they are."

"Hennies and Marang are perfectly acceptable, men of substance. The three of us will be required to pledge substantial capital—but that is no problem with the bank authorizing our use of the notes we've had printed and more notes to come, as well. Arnaldo will remain my personal aide, with a wide responsibility across the entire scope of Reis Limitado interests—including my arrangements with Swedish Match."

"And me? What of me? Am I of no use anymore?" José struck a plaintive note.

"I have an immensely important task for you, José— more important, I might say, than anything you have ever dreamed of doing. I will explain in due course, José."

The sun was warm on the back of Alves' neck. An image flitted across his mind, other trips to Paris when he'd been less sure of himself: remembrance of the first meeting in Biarritz with the storm outside, trying his idea out on these men. . . . He had been someone else then, Arnaldo was right. "Our Bank of Angola and Metropole will have several goals. All of Reis Limitado will pass through it, for example. Through it we will be able to dispose of the rest of the banknotes we have from the first printing— and all the subsequent banknotes as well, and of which you may be sure there will be a great many—"

"That's a bit of damned good news!" Hennies cried. "More bonuses, too, I'll wager!"

"Quite possibly," Alves said, raising a hand to retain order. "The new bank, too, will be our instrument for investing in land and real estate in Portugal. And ideal for acquiring control of certain Angola corporations. The profits should be considerable. Very considerable, gentlemen. And much of that will be set aside for our ultimate goal. . . ."

"I'm confused," Arnaldo said, pouring himself coffee from the silver service. His coat hung on the back of the chair, and his bow tie was undone, dangling loosely from his collar. "Who is this 'our' anyway? Is it us, here in this room? Or does it include your friends at the bank? I mean, they're still in this, they have to be, obviously, but—"

"Please, Arnaldo," Alves said, gesturing for him to resume his chair, "you make this needlessly complex, old fellow. Certainly we are using the word 'our' in its most inclusive sense. Now, let me continue as to the ultimate goal. . . ."

"I'm sorry," Arnaldo mumbled, stirring his coffee, the spoon rattling.

Alves waited until there was absolute silence, then spoke very softly.

"That goal, my friends, is nothing less than . . . *mastery of Portugal itself*. And the way we will achieve that aim without resorting to revolution or a *coup d'état* is by . . . *buying control of the Bank of Portugal*. . . ."

They were astounded. A small smile forming, Alves surveyed them slowly. It was a warming sight.

"Buy the Bank of Portugal," Marang repeated slowly, his eyes widening. "Buy the Bank of Portugal?" He turned to the others as if to say, What is this? What does he mean?

Hennies fished his monocle out and jabbed it into place, furrowed his brow, stared at Reis. "Yes, and then we should buy the Eiffel Tower, eh? And Mont Blanc, I suppose!"

"You heard me correctly, gentlemen," Alves said, rising and leaning forward on the table. "The time has come for us to show our appreciation for our friends and colleagues at the bank—Governor Camacho and Vice-Governor Gomes—by giving our substantial assistance in their secret battle against the backward directors of the bank. When we have a majority of the bank stock we will be able to override these captious critics, the reactionary dead hands of the past. . . . Which brings me back to José. Who will with utmost discretion set about buying up as much available Bank of Portugal stock as we require for a take-over. . . ." He leaned back, waiting, the faint noise of traffic drifting up from the Champs-Elysées. The curtains moved. Sunlight glinted on the coffee service and the polished surfaces of the tables. The scene was imprinted forever in his mind. Everything else—Maria, Greta—paled in comparison to this moment.

"It's true, all this?" José asked tentatively.

"Quite true. The fact is, to gain our support, Camacho and Gomes are giving us more power than anyone in the history of Portugal has ever had—that's what it comes down to. We will become truly rich men."

"Like Kreuger," José said.

"Perhaps, in time . . . but we will stand alone in Portugal. We will remake Portugal, gentlemen, as it should be . . . as it once was and will be again."

"Alves," Hennies cautioned, "don't overreach yourself."

"Ah, Adolf, my faithful counselor!" Alves said expansively. "Who knows this situation best, I ask you? I, Alves Reis, and I have never gone too far. . . ."

"Well, then," Hennies said, standing, hooking his fingers into his vest pockets, "I think it should be said now once and for all that we—all of us in this room—owe what we are today and more importantly what we will become in the days ahead . . . to you, Alves Reis—one of the great financial geniuses of our time, of all time . . . the uncrowned King of Portugal!"

"Alves, you have done it!" José shouted, clasping his hand, and Marang embraced him. Hennies draped his arm around the royal shoulders. Arnaldo was the last: "I am very proud of you," he said quietly. "Very proud, my friend."

*   *   *

Ivar Kreuger was en route from Stockholm and would not arrive until evening. Consequently Alves met with Kreuger's chief representative in Paris, Gunnar Cederschiold, a man about his own age. Their meeting went well. The Match King was prepared to go ahead with his purchases of two match factories in Portugal, streamline them and build an entirely new plant as well. Alves pledged a large capital investment, although, as was his custom, Kreuger would retain complete control. The idea was to force the Portuguese match business to become another Kreuger monopoly. Alves left a check with Cederschiold. In return he was presented with a formal pledge of stock certificates in the new operation. Kreuger moved quickly. As his agent in Lisbon, Alves was empowered to buy the existing factories at a good price. "Kreuger never cheats anyone," Cederschiold remarked gravely. "It is his watchword. The golden rule."

*　　*　　*

As promised, upon Kreuger's arrival in Paris the next day, Greta arranged for him to host a small dinner at his apartment, No. 5 Avenue Victor Emmanuel III near the Seine.

"He eats very lightly," Greta had warned them when she called in the morning, "so you might have a late-afternoon tea. There will be only a main dish, a dessert and some very fine Bordeaux—it never varies. He says eating makes him lazy, and he can't afford to be lazy. Eight o'clock sharp. Ivar is never late."

From the street No. 5 Avenue Victor Emmanuel was indistinguishable from its equally dignified, somber neighbors. A pointed black, gold-tipped iron fence fronted on the wide sidewalk bordered by tall trees newly leafed out. A wobbling cage lifted them to the third floor, where the great man lived while stopping in Paris.

Maria wore white, Alves a dark business suit. Hennies, Marang and José had arranged to arrive together. Arnaldo and Silvia accompanied Alves and Maria. The door was opened by a tall, pallid man with a large face and short, thinning hair that offered a great dome of forehead. His deep-set eyes focused above a long, straight nose. He wore a black suit, white shirt, black tie with a tiny, plain gold stickpin.

"How do you do," he said without vocal or facial expression. "You're the man from Lisbon?"

"Yes," Alves said. "We are joining Herr Kreuger for dinner."

"Of course," he said, reaching for Maria's diamond-braceleted hand. "I am Ivar Kreuger. I am delighted to make your acquaintance." He bent over Maria's hand and brushed his lips across her wrist. He nodded to Alves, who introduced Arnaldo and Silvia, over whose wrist he slowly, like a large and dignified elephant, performed the same ritual. "Please, come in. I have only just arrived in Paris, and you must forgive my lack of adequate preparations. I find it superfluous to maintain a staff to care for these five rooms. Your wrap, Senhora." He helped Maria with her brocade cape. He acted, Alves thought, more like a butler than the most powerful financier in the world. He led the way across the small parquet foyer and into a large parlor filled with great heavy furniture, deep masculine chairs and couches in dark wood and fabrics. The light was dim and an indifferent fire struggled in the grate, lighting the oppressive darkness. Greta was sitting near the fire sipping a goblet of red wine. "You, of course, know my dear Greta." His smile came and went, a phantom. "Please, if you would excuse, I hear the lift again. . . ." He went back the way they had come.

"Not exactly what you'd expected," Greta said perceptively.

"I thought he was a servant." Maria smiled.

"People can't believe he lives so simply. But, of course, he maintains an absolutely magnificent place in Stockholm and a lavish penthouse in New York, apartments in Berlin and Warsaw—he's always coming and going. His work is everything to him. He's never married and I can't imagine he will. . . ." Greta poured wine and passed it around as they all sat stiffly. "Don't be nervous, Alves, he's a very dear man but shy with strangers."

"You shouldn't have forced us on him like this," Alves said. "We're intruding on his privacy."

"He told me he felt badly about being unable to see you personally yesterday. He's delighted to have you here. You're business associates, and think of that . . . an associate of Ivar Kreuger. I thought you'd be so pleased to meet him, Alves."

Voices could be heard from the foyer, and immediately Hennies, Marang, José and two other gentlemen entered the parlor. Kreuger began to move among them, calmly, speaking in quiet tones, nodding agreement, bestowing time, remote smiles. Alves recognized Cederschiold, and they spoke for a while. Alves could not keep his eyes from tracking his host as he glided about, paying proper heed to the women. Eventually several more men and women arrived, including two eye-catching blondes with the overt, dramatic style of Folies-Bergère chorines. Alves was watching the girls when he heard a connoisseur's gentle whisper at his shoulder.

"Decorative women take the attention away from one who gives the party, don't you agree, Senhor Reis? You seem to have an eye for them." Kreuger spoke slowly, as if measuring the words. There was no hint of carnality in the remark but a realistic appraisal.

"By all means," Alves said tentatively. He didn't want to say anything stupid. Greta was speaking with the girls as if she knew them, drawing them toward Maria, who was talking energetically to Cederschiold and Marang.

"Parties are not for men, in any case. I seem always to be invited to parties where I am overcome by the idiocy of the guests and the host. I always long for the sight of a beautiful woman, but more often than not I am doomed to disappointment with the result . . . so tonight I protected you on that count and drew some attention away from myself." He did not look at Alves as he spoke but seemed to be staring off into a general area in the center of the room.

"I hope we aren't inconveniencing you," Alves said. He watched Kreuger roll the twenty-year-old Bordeaux on his tongue, the small deep-set eyes closing for a moment.

"Not at all. I am very sorry that I wasn't able to meet with you yesterday. Sometimes I could swear I spend half my life on shipboard going or coming from New York. But there's no need to tell you."

"For the last six months I've spent most of my time on the Sud Express. Yes, it's tiresome, but when business requires one's presence, what is there to do but be there?" Talking with Kreuger, man to man, about the common difficulties of international tycoondom. Incredible. There was so much to learn from such a man. "I want to tell you how grateful I am for this business opportunity, Herr Kreuger. We shall do very well together, I'm sure."

Kreuger's gray-green eyes caught a shaft of light; they seemed to be mocking, but his resonant voice lost none of its conviction. "Perhaps you envision further dealings between us. . . . And who knows, perhaps they will come. Time will tell, time always tells." His eyes moved slowly about the room. Alves had yet to look into them.

Kreuger took a Turkish cigarette from a black leather-and-gold case.

"People always find it terribly amusing when I have to

ask for a match . . . but I never seem to have any on me."
He lit the cigarette from Alves' Dunhill lighter, then rolled
the piece of gold between his fingers. "Poor Ivar," he said,
"having to compete with such elegant trinkets. Fortunately
the world is very poor and only the rich can light their
cigarettes with such devices. Do you know, Reis, that a
hundred million matches are struck every hour? There
will come a day when every match will be a Swedish Match.
We must have goals, don't you agree? It's all so incredibly
simple. Reduce the number of matches in a box by three
or four, raise the price a penny . . . profits increase quite
literally by millions of dollars."

Hennies, Marang and José had joined the group, and
Kreuger personally, humbly topped off their goblets.

"The great mystery," Hennies said, "the making of
money. Everyone tries and almost no one succeeds. The
human comedy. . . ."

"I've never found anything comic about money," Marang
remarked. "But, then, I'm often told I have no sense of
humor."

"It's not easy to laugh," Kreuger said, staring off, "at
money or the human comedy. At least not when all human
beings are so reprehensible. . . . Especially those who can
get everything they want." He drew his mouth tight. "You
must tell me to be quiet. With wine I grow ever more
voluble. Soon I'll begin telling you about Charles the Second. . . ."

José was inspecting a painting beneath a dim yellow
light.

"You are an art collector, I see."

"Me?" Kreuger affected surprise. "Goodness, no. I have
no interest in art. No, I have just two interests, the match
and Kreuger and Toll . . . a third would split me. I can't
ever succeed in turning off my mind, and I always think
business. No, I have no interest in art."

"But this is a Rembrandt," José said, "and this a
Rubens. . . ."

Kreuger almost looked at José but let his eyes slide away
toward the women, then went to attend to his other guests.
José raised his eyebrows. "He wants me to believe he
doesn't know he has a Rembrandt and a Rubens six inches
from my face? Is it a game?"

"Possibly it is a fact," Marang said. "He is not an ordinary man."

Greta had been quite correct about the menu. There were several racks of lamb on the table, a tureen of vichyssoise. Another Bordeaux. Kreuger sat at the head of the table with Maria on his left, Greta on his right. Alves was seated next to Greta with one of the blond girls on his right. She spoke with a thick Swedish accent and looked to be straight from a convent school, dewy and pale and well muscled, the perfect picture of a Scandinavian beauty. Marang was across from him, next to Maria.

Kreuger mentioned his recently concluded arrangement with the Spanish dictator, de Rivera: a twenty-five-year match monopoly for Swedish Match.

"We've taken a large step ourselves," Alves said. "We are forming our own bank in Lisbon. . . ."

"Indeed," Kreuger said, daintily chewing a tiny morsel of lamb. "You must be doing very well, Senhor. It will reflect well on Kreuger to be associated with you. A bank is a very convenient possession. . . ."

"It is the bank that will benefit from its association with Kreuger—that goes without saying."

"Not at all," Kreuger said, sipping the Bordeaux. "I once wanted a bank, years ago, and then a friend gave me a toy abacus . . . and I discovered I was more amused by it than by the bank. I could count up all the millions I wanted on my little toy." He sighed, put his elbows on the table before him and rubbed his fine, small hands busily before him. He seemed to be staring at the remains of one of the racks of lamb.

"And let me add," Alves said, feeling the effect of the wine, "that I can only barely believe that I am at table with Ivar Kreuger. This is most rare . . . One of life's great rewards. . . ." Feeling a trifle foolish, he stopped and emptied his goblet.

"To our host!" Hennies' ebullience rang like cannon fire in the quiet dining room. He lifted his goblet. "I give you the greatest financier of our age, a model for us all!"

A murmur of approval trickled along the table; wine was sipped by way of salute. A slight flush crossed the great man's face, like a shadow. The Swedish girl cooed gently. Alves felt the unmistakable pressure of Greta's hand on his thigh.

"You embarrass me," Kreuger said with quiet sincerity. "I am always given far too much credit. Making money, a child could do it. . . . The fortunes of nations can be made to turn on apparently trivial things. I am called an earth shaker." He shrugged. "And I am, but it is a trick. I have made countries swing upon a match. It could just as easily have been hairpins. Or buttons. . . ."

"But you are a man of your times, a titan," Marang said.

"Our times," Kreuger repeated distastefully. "When I compare our contemporaries with the people whose biographies I have read, I am struck with the desperate pettiness of the world today. Most people are tedious and boring. They are only barely aware they are alive at all. This one speaks of nothing but his dentist, that one about his family's bad luck and a third about the job he didn't get. . . . What are we to think of times that produce such ciphers?"

Alves nodded sagely. He reached for Greta's hand, held it still. The Swedish girl was watching from the corner of her eye.

"To succeed," Kreuger went on in his weighty, deliberate manner, "one must understand our times and the people populating them. This is the key. In the end, you depend on little men, your accountants. . . . Every period of history has its own gods, its own high priests, its own holy days. It's been true of politics, religion and war. Now it's true of economics. We've created something new, Reis, men like you and me. Instead of being fighting men, as in days of old, we're all in business; our high priests are called accountants. They too have a holy day—the thirty-first of December—on which we're supposed to confess. In olden times, the princes would go to Confession because it was the thing to do, whether they believed or not. Today the world demands balance sheets, profit-and-loss statements once a year. But if you're really working on great ideas . . ."

Alves looked up from his plate, searching out Kreuger's eyes. *Great ideas . . .*

"If you are," Kreuger went on, "you can't supply them on schedule and expose yourself to view. Yet you've got to tell the public something, and so long as it is satisfied and continues to have faith in you, then it is really not important what you confess. Someday people will realize that every balance sheet is wrong because it doesn't contain anything but figures. The real strengths and weaknesses of an enterprise lie in the *plans*. . . ."

Alves sighed to himself: how true. Kreuger leaned back,

hands curled around the arms of the chair. His face looked suddenly tired, the skin tight, shadows spreading beneath his small eyes.

"I hope you have all eaten enough. I'm told I set a rather meager table. I apologize. . . ."

"I must tell a story on Ivar," Greta said. Her hand was gone from Alves' thigh. He missed her touch. "One night he was very hungry for a cheese sandwich. So off he went to one of our establishments here in Paris. A cheese sandwich, he suggested to the waiter. The waiter sniffed, said nothing, but the chill was ominous. Well, the great financier reconsidered. Yes, he told the waiter, some caviar, a lobster, champagne and some bread and cheese!" The table rocked with laughter. "Fifty dollars American," Greta said, "to get a cheese sandwich! Only dear Ivar . . ." She put her hand on his, gently. Kreuger smiled.

"But that is not the end of the story," she went on. "Carefully he conceived his solution—he bought Palliard's! With a restaurant and wine cellar of his own he now can go out for a cheese sandwich whenever he wishes. . . ." Tears of mirth appeared on cheeks, hands clapped on the tabletop, candlesticks shook.

"The grand gesture!" Hennies bawled, red-faced. "Bravo, Kreuger!"

Over coffee in the parlor Maria sat next to Kreuger. Alves leaned against a lovely little Renaissance table in the shadows near a window. Greta made her way inconspicuously to his side. "What do you think of him?"

"Certainly an unusual man. Brilliant thing he said about the importance of plans. . . . I'm a believer in plans, you know. A surprisingly accessible man, the common touch. Or is it an act?"

"No, this is the way he is. Polite, distant, full of thoughts you would appreciate. . . . I sense an affinity between you." She brushed his hand with hers. "You handle yourself very well in his presence. I'm proud of you, darling, but . . ." She shuddered involuntarily. "I can't claim you, turn to you, be yours on evenings like this. Maria takes you for granted, she knows the diamonds will keep coming, she doesn't see in you what I do. . . ." She shook her head, looked away, biting her lip. "It isn't jealousy . . . it's envy, and there's a difference. I've fought it, I've tried not to be too solemn about you, about *us,* but I need you. I feel myself coming undone sexually without you." She brushed at her eyes, hand shaking. The sapphire crossed her face and in the dim light left an afterimage in his mind.

"You've never talked to me this way before. . . ."

"Have you assumed I'm faithful to you?"

"I've hoped. I've tried not to think about it."

"Well, I have been, ever since our first time in bed. But how long can I go on, never knowing when I'll see you? I'm not made for celibacy, Alves. I need a man." She sniffled, her face still lovely in repose. "Tell me, what do you want me to do?"

"What are you asking of me? Are you asking me to leave Maria?" The bottom of his stomach was slipping away. He felt faint.

"You deserve more than she can give you. You deserve the grand life. . . . You are on the world stage now, a financier, one of Kreuger's kind."

"You would marry me? Is that what you're suggesting?"

"I don't know. I've said I'd never marry again. . . . But we could be together, here in Paris."

"I must be in Lisbon. Everything is there, everything I am. . . ."

"You are now a citizen of Europe, darling. You will have interests everywhere. You will move through the great cities like the wind. You must not limit yourself."

"Greta . . ." He made a gesture of confusion. "I must think. It is not simple. You must see that I am between my love for you and the responsibilities of a lifetime."

"Something will have to happen, that's all I'm saying. I cannot go on like this indefinitely. I have never tried to be faithful before. I have always been free to do as I please. I've always made that a condition. . . . I don't know what's gotten into me."

"I thought the future was now," Alves said.

"Don't tease me, darling."

"Don't push me, then. I can't simply make a decision that is bound to smash lives to bits. . . . It's not fair."

"Fair," she said, jaws clenched. "Fair? To whom? I have willingly closed my life to everyone but you. . . ."

He was sweating and felt ill. "Do as you please. I cannot command your fidelity . . . you must give it but only if you choose."

She turned away angrily, stared out the window into the shadows of trees.

"Leave me alone, then," she said. "Just leave me alone."

Weak with anger and frustration, he went away, pretended to inspect the Rembrandt.

"Alves, come sit by me." It was Maria, making room on the couch. "Are you all right, my dear? You look so pale."

"No, I'm fine." He sank down on the couch. He saw Greta with the Swedish girl who had sat beside him at dinner. They went off together.

"I was just asking Ivar why he'd never married," Maria said. Alves flinched. How could she be so familiar with such a man?

"I cannot marry," Kreuger said solemnly. "It would take at least eight days. I can't spare the time. . . ."

"Be serious," the other blond Swede said. Her mouth was wide, her lips thin like Greta's. "You must not joke about such important matters."

"I'm sorry, my child. Could I tie myself permanently to a woman? Well, I believe I could, externally—because I should see her only occasionally anyhow. But spiritually, I must honestly say no. And I don't care about children. I'm sure you have lovely, beautiful children, Senhora Reis. But they always seem to do things differently from what one would like, which must be so annoying. Nor do I wish to be burdened with love. . . . Love requires time and attention. Swedish Match is my son, my only child."

Maria was watching him, appraising him as he spoke. She seemed more mature to Alves. It was the same thing he'd noticed in Arnaldo, a process that must have been going on without his noticing it. Everyone was growing older and time seemed to be going faster.

Maria was pulling his sleeve, speaking to him.

"Alves, you're somewhere else. Come back and join the party." There was an edge to her voice. "Ivar has an entertainment planned."

He stood up, gave her his hand. She led the way, and he watched her move ahead; yes, she had changed with the years. The girlishness was going, and a woman, less yielding, more substantial, was appearing. The past year had been difficult, taking its toll on the girl she had once been.

They entered a smaller sitting room with soft low chairs facing a raised platform where a plush chaise longue stood, bathed in a warm, dim red glow from spotlights hung from the ceiling. Greta and José sat nearest the platform. Alves and Maria moved in behind them. He saw Arnaldo wiping his brow, Silvia clinging to his arm. Hennies had attached himself to a gaunt woman. Marang sat stiffly, curious. There was a sweet aroma of incense. He thought he saw Kreuger in the doorway. A jazz record began very softly and the voices died.

The two Swedish girls appeared at the edge of the platform, mounted it and sat on the divan. Their eyes met, and slowly one reached out, stroked the other's pale cheek. They kissed, their mouths open. The aggressor carefully pushed the other backward until she was at rest, then began undoing the front of her dress, exposing large white breasts. She leaned down, sucked the small, hard nipples while the girl moaned softly. Alves shook his head. He heard the distant breathing of the audience. A small gasp escaped Maria, who leaned forward. Greta smoked a cigarette, her attention riveted. One girl was naked, her legs spread to rest on either side of the chaise longue. The hair between her legs made a blond halo in the light. The other girl, his dinner partner, slipped out of her gown and knelt between the spread thighs, slowly burying her sweet face in the hair. The legs bent upward, the knees holding her partner in place, fingers working in the blond hair, holding her face while the lips and belly began to push rhythmically.

Maria's face was wet, her lips parted.

"My God," Alves said under his breath. The girl being acted upon let out a soft cry, said something in Swedish. With one hand she squeezed her breast, pulling the nipple tight. She grunted deep in her throat, bucked against the burrowing face. "This is too much," Alves said aloud. "Maria!" He grabbed Maria's wrist and pulled her to her feet. There were tears on her face. She was biting her lip. Arnaldo and Silvia bolted for the door. "Greta," Alves said. "Please leave with us. . . ."

José turned, caught Alves' eye, winked. "Sit down, Alves," he said. "It's a harmless diversion."

No one seemed to hear them. The girl had moved from between her partner's thighs and had slid lengthwise the other way, settling her own parted hips across the eager waiting mouth, crying out thinly as she received the tongue's probe. Her fingers clutched the air. The music was louder, more insistent. The spotlights had gone blue.

"Greta . . ."

But Greta was straining forward, watching the darting

tongue. José bent toward her, said something, laughed soundlessly. Alves turned, holding Maria's elbow, propelling her out of the room. The light in the outer chamber struck like a blow, burning his eyes. Arnaldo was talking to Silvia, who listened solemnly. Maria was sobbing. Alves looked around in a fury, spotted a wineglass and hurled it against the wall.

"What does he think he's doing? We need dirty shows to enjoy our evening? Dinner and whores?" He trod on the broken glass. "Maria, calm yourself. Arnaldo, let's get out of here. Maria, my sweet little wife," he cooed, holding her against him. "Forget it, forget it. . . ." He mumbled on until Arnaldo returned to help Maria into her cape.

Alves glowered. "What a nightmare. How can they sit there and watch, I ask you? How?"

"Human nature." Arnaldo opened the door to the first parlor. "Take your own advice, forget it. We're above this, that's what it amounts to."

A movement on the small balcony overlooking a courtyard caught his eye. A huge figure loomed, a red eye glowed.

"Senhor Reis." Kreuger moved into the opening of the French windows. He was smoking one of the Turkish cigarettes. Smoke hung in the cool night behind him.

"Please," Kreuger said, "accept my apologies. Some of these people expect such a show. I'm told it is very much the rage in Paris these days. However, among my countless faults, I do not number voyeurism. Senhora . . ." He turned to Maria. "Can you forgive me? How can I make it up to you?"

"Don't try," Alves said harshly. "When you come to Lisbon, I can assure you, you will be spared such an exhibition!"

"You are truly offended," Kreuger said quite calmly, "and rightly so. Well, I must make it up to you. Maria and Silvia," he said with perfect recall of their names, "a small token, an apology." He handed them each a small leather pouch. "Now, ladies, don't peek until you are home for the night. Promise. . . ."

The women nodded. Alves felt as if they were all children Kreuger was placating. It was like passing out candy to remove the pain of a scraped knee. Kreuger turned to escort them to the foyer, across the parquet floor, heels clicking.

"The two girls came to me, you know," he said, "asked if they could perform. They needed the money and they know of my generosity. . . . What could I do? Odd thing," he mused, pursing his lips, looking down at them, "the Spaniards always love this sort of show, emerge telling me what a grand fellow I am."

"Apparently a difference between Spaniards and Portuguese," Alves said stiffly.

"Please accept my explanation, Senhor. We must be friends. We are two of a kind."

They shook hands.

* * *

Maria went to bed without speaking further of the evening's events. Thunder in the early-morning hours woke Alves. He lay still, waiting for his head to clear.

It wasn't the two girls that had upset him. It was the fact of Greta's reaction, the way she had pressed forward to see the girls, had refused to leave. He could not explain it, at least not to his satisfaction.

In any case, given their disturbing conversation, he would have to see her again. They would have to straighten things out. He went to the window and watched the rain falling on the Champs-Elysées, making it shine.

* * *

They were sitting on opposite sides of the breakfast table, Alves dressed for the day, Maria in a filmy peignoir over her nightgown. He poured hot coffee and milk, buttered a flaky croissant and vowed to take a swim and a steam bath. "Kreüger was certainly most generous to you." He nodded to the bedside table where a tiny leather bag lay, a gold, diamond-encrusted pin beside it. The diamonds formed a matchstick with rubies at the tip.

Maria set her cup down with a clatter, splashing coffee onto the heavy linen. "I can't eat. Oh, Alves . . ." She broke off, threw herself on the bed, hiding her face. Her body shook. "I am losing you." The words were muffled.

"Have you been talking with José?"

"Why? Does he know the truth about you?"

"No, my dearest . . . but he is a mischief-maker—and I am your Alves, your husband." He kissed her hair.

"Something has gone wrong with our lives," she said, half choking. "I don't know what you want of me. . . . What do you want me to be, Alves? Do you want me to be like her?"

"Like whom?"

"Alves!" she screamed, turning, fists flashing at his face. He felt the nose piece of his spectacles cut his face. He reached to stop her too late. She hit him again and the spectacles fell to the floor. "Don't treat me like a fool. . . ." He had her by the wrists, holding her away. "Like her, like her," she croaked, face screwed into an ugly mask. "Greta, Greta . . . Greta . . ."

"For God's sake be quiet," he shouted. He had no experience with madwomen. "The children. . . ."

"I watched you with her last night at Ivar Kreuger's," she gasped, trying to whisper. "I saw the way she looked at you." She pulled loose and threw herself back on the pillows. "Don't think I'm blind just because I'm your little wife. Don't underestimate me, Alves Reis." She thrust out her jaw, wiped her eyes. "I'm more than you think."

"I love you."

"Don't say that to me, Alves."

"What do you want me to say, then?"

"Nothing, I want to go home." She swallowed with difficulty. "Come back with me. . . ." She softened. "I don't know what's happening, Alves. I'm afraid. . . ."

"You go," he said. "I have business for another few days. See your parents, relax . . . and I'll be home by the end of the week." He kissed her nose, hoping that the worst was over. "And stop being so silly."

She lay back and closed her eyes, spent. Alves watched her until her breathing steadied and she fell asleep. He wiped blood off his face, retrieved his spectacles from the floor.

He couldn't see that he had any choice. He'd give José and Arnaldo their instructions. But he had to stay in Paris. He had to see Greta. . . .

*   *   *

He had never had such a scene with Maria, nothing remotely comparable. Seldom had there been so much as a cross word. Now he had somehow driven her to striking him. Had he given himself away? But the fact was that

she'd seen nothing between him and Greta. She was guess-
ing it, speculating on a possibility. Damned complexity,
way too much on his mind. To succeed in business you
had to have some peaceful retreat, a haven, somewhere to
rest. That was what he had had with Maria, and, being
human, he had never realized it, had assumed it would
always be there. Now it was slipping away from him. It
had begun slipping when he had committed his energies to
the scheme. He had grown impatient with her silliness,
bored by the pettiness of her world. He had sought a new
kind of peace—brought about by the distraction and excitement of a romance—and Greta had eased his mind of
the cares of the scheme. Rather, to his surprise she had
returned his passion and desire with a fervent gift of her
own. He had come to depend on her. Undeniably, he
knew, he had been influenced by her worldliness. He had
ignored the subtle implications of his infidelity. He felt as if
an earthquake were rumbling, sending fissures shooting
across the foundations of his life.

Now Maria was gone, her eyes so lifeless and dull, remote, hurt, not understanding what was happening but
afraid and angry, as if a phantom tiger had been loosed on
her soul. . . .

And he had let her go. Because of Greta. Her hold on
him was too great, and the time was at hand to face up to
it. He was a man alone, if he only had the courage.

He walked the streets of Paris, ignoring the people
around him, moving like a man in a dream, his lips silently forming the words in his mind. Kreuger had the
answer. Somehow there was no time for anything other
than Swedish Match; it was his *life*. Kreuger knew. And
fate had placed Kreuger in the path of Alves Reis, had
put him there for Alves to learn a lesson. . . .

Greta was wearing a lime-green sleeveless dress that
had no waist and hung straight from the shoulders to cling
briefly at her hips, pleats swinging from her thighs. She
smiled to him when he opened the door, went on humming, watering her plants. The Javanese maid followed her,
wiping up any overflow with a white cloth. Sunshine
streamed in the windows, and the plants seemed to be
exploding with green health. The phonograph was playing,
and he recognized Josephine Baker's voice. Greta was cool,
civil, told him her manager had just called to tell her she
was being offered a wonderful role in a play for the fall.

Outward Bound. She asked him to sit, dismissing the Javanese girl with a nod of the head.

"You are angry with me." She sighed, crossing her legs, staring at him. "There's no point in asking why, I suppose." She was smiling faintly, tolerantly. "I, who have every right to be angry. I was forced to watch you with your wife all last evening. I was very frustrated, do you understand that? Sexually frustrated. . . ."

Alves' head had begun to throb. A thought crossed his mind: none of this would have bothered José in the least. José was no romantic when it came to women.

Greta lit a cigarette and went to the window, touched the leaves of an immense fern. "I have said all I intend to say. I take what life offers me. If you want me, take me as I am."

"Last night we talked of my giving up Maria. . . . Now you calmly give me the gate."

"Listen to me, Alves." She knelt beside his chair. He thought, she should be on the stage; there should be an audience waiting to applaud. "I would not have given up my other small amours, my sweet careless afternoons, if I didn't love you. I want you and I need you. You must realize, however, that I am not an ordinary little housewife, subordinating myself, my desires, my needs to yours . . . and you must see, my darling, that you are a great man, that the rules for us are different. . . ."

"Maybe I am ordinary, after all. . . ." He took her face in his hands, gently searched the lavender eyes.

"No, not you, not Kreuger, not me. . . . It's part of us, inevitable. Either love me and accept me, or go back to Lisbon and stay there, making your money, shrouding Maria in jewels. . . ." She kissed his fingertips. "And be careful of her, my love. I have never spoken of her this way, but now—well, we're past good manners, aren't we? She is boring, tedious, and she can be a dangerous woman, too, believe me, a woman knows. She doesn't know how to behave, she lets you walk on her and she will wait, wondering what to do, and then, I warn you, she will go crazy and you will wish you'd never set eyes on her that day at the beach. If you understand what I am saying, stay. I love you, but understand that I am as I am. . . ."

"I do, I understand." He took her hand, squeezed.

"Do you love me, then? Are you prepared to love me?"

"Yes."

"Then we will go on, Alves, but you must solve your problems in Lisbon. You are making the choice."

"I know."

"Well, there is hope for you." She smiled again, at last.

They went to bed rather solemnly, as if sealing their new agreement. The shadows outside were turning the day a velvety purple. He heard the wind in the trees; the softness teased him, like a dream. His guard was down, he was tired. He felt as if he had passed through hazard and emerged intact.

"You say I am a great man," he said absently, stroking her hair. She used his chest as a pillow, toyed with the thunderbolt around his neck.

"You are," she said softly.

"I've done more than you know," he said. "You have no idea. . . ."

And leaning back, looking up at the shadows slanting across the ceiling, he let the flood of his secret accomplishment wash across them. It all came out: from the days in the Oporto jail where he dared to conceive the scheme, on through the assembling of his syndicate and the first sets of stationery and forgeries. He told her of how he had given all that was in him in Angola, how he had returned to Lisbon and been treacherously brought down, how he had decided that a great success required great daring. She listened silently as he told her of the agonies of the past winter, when everything hung in the balance, dangling by the frayed threads of his nerve.

"You mean to tell me," she said at last, propping herself on one elbow, a puzzled smile crossing her wide mouth, "that there are no connections between your syndicate and the Bank of Portugal? It is all the product of your own mind?" She brushed the hair from her eyes.

"Yes." He nodded proudly, his voice hushed. He couldn't quite believe he was doing it. "The only connections are the forged documents, which, on the face of it, are decisive. . . . But they are forgeries. Yes. I dreamed it up in the Oporto jail. . . ." He let a smile creep into his voice.

"My God," she said, straightening pillows behind her, sitting up straighter. "And I thought you were a business-man."

"No, this kind of power, this kind of economic leverage, is simply not attainable in the normal course of business.

You must bend the system to your own needs, you must risk it all. . . . I'll wager Kreuger knows what I mean."

"Can they catch you?" There was a kind of excitement, a quiver in her voice.

"No, my darling. The money is perfectly legitimate, printed from the Bank of Portugal's plates. . . . There are no counterfeits. The only way anything can possibly go amiss is within the structure of the bank itself. Waterlow and the bank must be kept apart; there must be no communication from the printer to the bank . . . and Waterlow has been told of the secrecy required. No, nothing is likely to go wrong . . . and, should the worst happen, the documents *prove* that I was acting as an agent of the bank!"

"It is perfect, isn't it?" She hugged him. He felt gooseflesh rise on her arm. "I can't believe it. . . ." Her voice trailed off.

It was dark outside now, and all he could think about was that he wasn't alone anymore; someone else knew. . . .

"There's more," he said, sliding his arm around her shoulder, cradling her. "My aim . . . from the beginning has been for something bigger, something more than mere wealth. I have plans for Portugal . . . for my country. I will control the economy, you see, everything, when I have gained control of the bank." He fumbled on the bedside tabletop, got hold of a cigarette and his lighter. The smoke calmed him. He hadn't realized how excited he was, what a speech he was making. But the words tumbled onward; he couldn't stop. "Once we have control of the Bank of Portugal, we not only control the nation's economy . . . we also have erased any possible detection. You see, in studying the bank's bylaws in the Oporto jail I discovered an amazing thing: only the Bank of Portugal can initiate action against counterfeiters of its notes. *Only the bank!* Whether we counterfeited the notes or not, we are in possession of them illegally, which could be interpreted as counterfeiting. . . . It sure as hell would be if they ever caught us!"

They looked at each other, grinning. She tasted his cigarette, inhaled deeply. He had never spoken aloud of his scheme before, never told the whole story, never heard the words. The plan had its own life: now it had been given a voice. He squeezed Greta's hand. She was with him now— he was no longer alone inside the plan. . . .

"So the bank itself is the only possible source of danger. When I control a working majority of the bank's stock, well, then I would never tolerate the presence of any bank official who would want to initiate such action against us. . . . Control of the bank is the final step. . . ."

"Does anyone else know? How could they *not* know?"

"No, no one else knows. Everything is completely acceptable once you know that I am an agent of the bank. We're buying up the shares because there is an internal power struggle going on. . . . My friends at the bank are using us to help them gain control." He laughed aloud. "It is so perfect . . . like an egg, smooth and seamless and perfect. No one knows, no one will ever know until it is much too late. Once we are in control we secretly regularize all the unauthorized issues of banknotes. We sweep the bank as clean and fresh as the egg. No evidence, nothing but Portugal in our hands. . . ."

*   *   *

In the morning he left her with a kiss. Had he been wise, telling her? How could one ever know? He pushed the doubt aside. He felt better, knowing that someone else knew. Whom else could he have told? Greta was the only person on earth he felt sure of. . . .

The morning was bright, the streets alive with strollers enjoying the spring sunshine.

"I . . . am . . . Alves . . . Reis," he hummed as he walked. He bought a flower for his buttonhole. It was all going to be all right, one way or another.

Before he left for Lisbon he spent ten minutes in an automobile showroom on the Champs-Elysées buying a replacement for Greta's Bentley. An Isotta-Fraschini would be delivered to Greta Nordlund with his compliments. Already in the taxi that took him to the railway station he missed her, felt the vague emptiness. He tried to concentrate on Paris passing by, but the charm was gone. He was leaving her behind, and the uncertainty tore at his happiness. He lit a cigarette. Life without her was a pale travesty, colorless, only a half life. When would he see her again? When?

*   *   *

Soot-caked Rossio Station had never looked better. He had rested surprisingly well on the long ride from Paris, losing himself in one of Wodehouse's novels. He did not expect wonders at the Menino d'Ouro, and there were none. Time would see it all resolved. His plan for the Bank of Portugal, the creation of his own bank must come first. His personal life . . . well, sacrifices would have to be made in the short run. Kreuger would have understood. Greta, too. Maria would simply have to adjust.

Upon his arrival in the grand foyer she met him with a cool embrace, a kiss on the cheek, polite inquiry as to the trip home. She was civil and avoided his eyes. His memory served him badly: where had things gone wrong? Precisely. At what moment? At Kreuger's, yes, and when she struck him and made him bleed. . . . Yet, he'd insisted he loved her: there was no doubt about that. He would always love her. But was that enough? He sat alone in his library late into the night, watching the flickering lights of Lisbon. Greta had called her dangerous. . . .

There was little more than cursory communication between them, nothing overt. It was best to leave her to herself. She busied herself supervising the staff of servants, having her friends in to visit, building a series of activities that excluded Alves. "You're always off somewhere, anyway," she said. "Yes, don't say it, I know how busy you are. José explains it to me. He is very thoughtful."

She was making all the discoveries Greta had mentioned. The change worked in Alves' life was so fundamental that he found it difficult to think about. Maria no longer offered comfort. Well, perhaps it would make his decision an easier one. . . . But that was nonsense and he knew it. The only thing to do was to put it all off as long as possible.

*   *   *

Away from the house his energy and confidence had never been greater. It was as if the onrushing heat of summer set him aflame. Each day brought new triumphs and opportunities. While he busied himself with the official paperwork and interviews attendant on the creation of the Bank of Angola and Metropole, he deputized Arnaldo to expend the monies required to achieve control of Ambaca. Within ten days the railway was his, owned by A. V. Alves Reis,

Limitado. He was at the portrait painter's studio, sitting astride an angled wooden horse, posing with a wide-brimmed white hat on his head, a white silk shirt with an open collar and belled sleeves, when Arnaldo burst in, stopped short.

"Where did you get that hat?"

"Never mind, I got it. Dashing, don't you think?"

"You never wore a hat like that in Africa. . . . Nor a shirt like that. You'd have sooner been boiled alive!"

"Arnaldo, this is called artistic license. Tell him," he said to the painter.

"It will be a portrait in the heroic style," the painter began. "It is accepted heroic dress. A blend of truth and fiction . . . a heightening of the essential realities of Senhor Reis' experience—"

"That's enough," Alves interrupted. "He understands. Now, why are you here, Arnaldo? It's like walking in on a man sitting on a toilet . . . worse, there is nothing more intimate than having your portrait painted!"

Arnaldo had sidled around to have a look at the canvas. He pinched his lower lip dubiously. The painter stepped back appraisingly. "There is much to be done yet." Arnaldo nodded.

Alves slid awkwardly down from the horse. "What is it, Arnaldo?"

"A man from the Public Prosecutor's office," he said, still regarding the painting. "He came by to see you this morning. He's coming in again this afternoon."

"The Public Prosecutor's office . . ." For a moment it was like the old days: icy dread in his chest.

"I think you should see him," Arnaldo said. "He was nervous. Ah, I have it," he cried. "There's something wrong with this painting—you aren't wearing your spectacles!"

"Not heroic, idiot," Alves snapped. He was already unbuttoning the silk shirt, heading for the dressing room.

*   *   *

Breathing a sigh of relief, Alves saw that the man from the Public Prosecutor's office was an old friend, a small fellow who always looked nervous. His eyes flickered restlessly, his fingers drummed and fluttered. Not a dangerous man. Pleasantries quickly exchanged, he seated himself on the first six inches of the chair, dangling his straw hat on his knees.

"It has come to my attention," he said carefully, "that you have acquired majority holdings in the Royal Trans-African Railway Company of Angola." How like him not to say simply *Ambaca,* how characteristic not to reveal his source. Alves could not resist a smile.

"Quite so."

"Which automatically makes you a director of the Oporto Commercial Bank."

"Right again, old fellow."

"Alves, as an old friend and a new director, you should know something that has not as yet been made public. I asked myself, what are friends for, and I decided to come around and put this in your ear. We at the Prosecutor's office have discovered certain serious irregularities at the Oporto Commercial Bank, involving two of the directors." He placed a finger to his lips. "Two directors known to you personally," he whispered. "We are investigating and I can tell you there's something very crooked going on up there. I am here to suggest that you clean house before we complete our inquiries. Beyond that my lips must remain sealed." He drew a thick folder from his briefcase. "There is nothing, however, to keep you from reading this material. Remember, I have *told* you nothing. . . ."

"I see," Alves said. "I am in your debt. Tell me, are you and your lovely wife free for dinner on Saturday? Maria and I would love to have you come and visit us in our new home. . . . There will be some people you might enjoy." He rattled off a list of several names drawn from Lisbon's social and financial circles. The little man's face beamed like a child's.

"We would be delighted, my dear Alves. You know, my wife could hardly believe it when I told her what friends we'd been in school. . . . The Menino d'Ouro!" He pulled a long face. "She will make me buy her a new gown!"

"Believe me, if this information is useful to me, you will not be forgotten by Alves Reis!" He saw him to the door. "Splurge, buy her the gown!"

Alone for an hour, Alves read the file. It was, on the whole, too good to be true. Fate had once again smiled on him.

* * *

The board room of the Oporto Commercial Bank was as somber as his memories of his last visit to the city. The twelve directors sat in their heavy chairs, staring up at him, not knowing what to expect. Black severe suits, high detachable collars, narrow black ties on white shirts, frowning faces revealing nothing but their ill-ease. Alves looked at them, tight-lipped, impassive, his bearing and expression full of unbending rectitude. The chairman tapped a gold pen on the table, scowled. "All right, we're here, Senhor Reis, but let me say at no little inconvenience to ourselves. We are all busy men, so let me suggest that you get to it. And, speaking for all of us, let me say that you had better have a serious reason for convening this board."

"If you will stop being officious I will tell you just how serious I am." He looked at the directors. Two of them he knew: they had personally made certain he went to jail. "You are now dealing with Alves Reis, gentlemen, an honest man . . . a powerful man, as you are about to find out. I have in my possession incontrovertible documentary evidence that extreme—'shocking' is perhaps the better word—irregularities have occurred here among you and involving certain bank directors. . . . The irregularities and the men who perpetrated them are known to the Public Prosecutor's office. An investigation is very nearly complete."

The chairman glared around the table. "I know nothing of any investigation. Do any of you? Has any of you been approached?" He had bitten through his cigar, ashes spilling on the polished tabletop.

The directors uniformly shook their heads. One of his two accusers leaned back, laughed. "I don't believe you, Reis. You're trying to scare us, make trouble. . . . We know you, we know your tricks!"

"We are being given the opportunity," Alves went on, "to clean our own nest . . . solely because of the respect with which I am held in the Public Prosecutor's office. Anyone else but me and they would be on you like wolves in the night." He picked up the folder, weighed it in his hand, looked pointedly at the two directors. "These two must go—their names dot every document here, like punctuation marks."

"You are a known swindler," the second one cried. "A

jailbird! Your word means nothing, Reis! You're out for revenge, plain and simple." He leaped out of his chair. "I'm leaving. This is ridiculous!"

"Would you care to see the evidence?" Alves offered the folder to the chairman, who brushed the mound of ashes aside and placed it before him. "The two documents on top should satisfy any doubts you have had." The man stopped short of the double door, came back to the table and sat down.

The large ormolu clock on the credenza ticked loudly in the silence. Alves sat down and lit a cigarette, inspected his manicured nails, the perfect crescents. Ten, fifteen minutes passed. Directors were sweating, pacing; the room grew thick with cigar smoke. Finally the chairman wiped his forehead with a white handkerchief and looked up at Alves, running his tongue shakily along his dry lips.

"This," Manuel, slouched disconsolately back in his chair, having failed in his final attempt at defiance, began, "is a time for harmony. I . . . I . . . What do these charges amount to? We have a right to know!"

"By all means, tell him," Alves said, nodding to the chairman.

"It is very bad, Manuel," the chairman whispered. "But, Reis, we can clear this up, you know. . . . There's no need to drop these directors." He fought to compose himself, placed his wrinkled old hands flat on the table. "Why, dropping them from our board would be nothing less than an admission of guilt, Reis!"

"And why not?" Alves said, shrugging. "They are guilty."

"Let us think about it, give us two weeks. . . ."

"Two weeks? Chairman, I admit that you shock me. Two weeks and the funds could be replaced, the tracks covered over. . . . These two criminals would go free. That, Chairman, is not the way we do things in Portugal. No, I must have your decision when I leave this room."

"Impossible!" Manuel studied the tabletop. The other, red in the face, shouted, "You are forcing us!"

"We must have time," the chairman said.

"All right." Alves sighed. "Until tomorrow morning. My train leaves at eleven o'clock. I want these two dismissed. Promptly."

*   *   *

Alves was just finishing his after-dinner coffee at the hotel when the two directors presented themselves at his table. They were pale, smelled of drink.

"We are at your mercy, Senhor Reis."

"Unnerving, isn't it?" Alves dabbed his mouth. "Your resignations should be tendered to the chairman, I believe. I certainly don't want to breach protocol in this matter."

"Now, now, Reis, what do you get out of this vendetta? Can revenge be so sweet?"

"This is not a matter of revenge," Alves said, chuckling. "I simply don't want to be associated with criminals. A man in my position, it is simply unthinkable."

"Give us a chance to clear this up. Let's handle this man to man, what do you say? We are in a position to make it worth your while. . . ."

Alves laughed. "Ah, you make it worse and worse. Now you have compounded your offense by attempting to bribe me. Do you seriously believe that Alves Reis is for sale? I have already given you far more opportunity to extricate yourselves than you gave me a year ago."

"Reis, for God's sake, we're begging you—"

"The answer is no. Resign from the board and hope the Prosecutor goes easy on you. Or stay. Perhaps you feel the evidence is inconclusive. You are certainly free to fight it out. Now, good evening, gentlemen. Do as you wish."

There was no word from the chairman in the morning.

He returned to Lisbon and gave the material back to his friend in the Prosecutor's office. He then wrote a detailed letter of "concern" to the Banking Trade Inspector, outlining "rumors" he had heard regarding the activities of two directors of an institution of which he had just become a director. Naturally he felt an obligation to bring his fears to the attention of the Inspector.

When he saw his friend at dinner Saturday night he was pleased to learn that the Public Prosecutor had wasted no time.

"The Oporto Commercial Bank will not be allowed to reopen on Monday. And the indictments against your two friends went down yesterday morning. They're through. . . . Sorry about closing the bank, you being a director."

"Think nothing of it," Alves said magnanimously. He clapped the man's shoulder. "There are some things more important than one's own interests, eh? The good of Por-

tugal comes first . . . and those two bastards belong in
jail!"

*   *   *

At breakfast one morning Maria told him that she had
received a letter from Greta.

"She wants me to visit her in Paris."

"And what was your reply?"

"I thought I should ask you first. Would you object to
my going?"

Several objections leaped to mind, notably his fear that
Greta might be taking it on herself to tell Maria the truth
about their affair. Greta had seemed satisfied when he had
left Paris, but that was a few weeks ago. Women, God
knew, can change as a matter of principle. Perhaps she had
decided simply to take matters into her own hands. . . .
But she was not a stupid woman, and running the risk of
telling Maria and possibly losing Alves was stupid. Wasn't
it? His mind was overburdened, too many details, too
much to control. This trip to Paris was too involved to
worry about.

"Go, by all means, my dear. You haven't seemed yourself lately. . . ." He reached for her hand. She chewed
tentatively on her brioche, a drop of marmalade caught in
the corner of her mouth. For a moment she seemed about
to speak. He wanted her to say something about the distance
between them, anything. But the moment passed; she licked
at the marmalade. "Enjoy yourself, meet her friends, lunch
on the Champs-Elysées, shop to your heart's content. It
will be lovely in Paris now."

In the office he called Arnaldo for a conference.

"Maria is going to Paris. Greta invited her."

"That's a very tasteless joke, Alves."

"It's not a joke. Hopefully it'll do her some good. She's
not been herself."

"Please, Alves, I don't want to hear about your problems
with Maria. It has nothing to do with our business enterprises. You know what I think, there is nothing more to
say. It's your life."

"Yes, I forgot," Alves said. "We're all business now.
Alves the monster, no longer worthy of your friendship!"
He'd intended to tease Arnaldo, but there was a bitterness.
He heard it himself and he couldn't remove it. "I do have

some business for you to transact in Paris. I want you to accompany Maria, see her safely to Claridge's, and then bring back the contents of our safety-deposit box in the safe at the hotel. I'll give you a letter of permission. Just give it to the manager and bring the contents back. I believe everything is packaged. There's some jewelry and some money. I want it here in Lisbon."

"Why don't you go?"

"I don't want Maria to feel that I'm tagging along, and there's a great deal to do this week with the chartering of our bank. Stop by at the end of the day and pick up the letter. My secretary will have it ready for you. . . . And have a pleasant trip. Stop by my tailor, have him measure you for some suits. On my account."

* * *

Establishing a new bank was not an easy task. Full of confidence and determination, however, Alves persuaded a retired navy commander, Joao Manuel de Carvalho, to accept the presidency of the Fiscal Council of the Bank of Angola and Metropole. The old commander was impeccably connected through his family and the contacts of an illustrious career. The position was offered as an honor of some note, a means of joining together the great Portuguese naval tradition with a new era in financial prosperity. Carvalho had a great advantage over a few other men Alves had considered, and it weighed heavily in his favor: his daughter was married to the son of Luis Viegas, the Inspector of the Banking Council.

Alves needed all the heavyweights he could bring aboard because, unknown to his associates, he had one significant antagonist who was fighting against the birth of the new bank.

Dr. Mota Gomes, vice-governor of the Bank of Portugal and known to Marang, Hennies, José and Arnaldo as one of Alves' best friends at the bank, was unhappy about the application for a charter. He finally summoned Alves to his office for a private discussion. It was the first time the two men had set eyes on each other. Alves dressed for the occasion: spats and morning coat, striped trousers, a homburg, gray gloves, mustache and hair pomaded to a fine gleaming shine.

Mota Gomes was a fat man whose double chins overflowed his shirt collar. His voice rumbled deep inside his vastness. Sweat beaded his dark face and spread from his armpits across his shirt. He did not rise upon Alves' arrival. He looked like a giant toad squatting half hidden behind his desk.

"Sit down, Senhor Reis," he wheezed resonantly. A huge cigar looked like a sixth finger in his left hand. Papers were strewn across the desk. "Forget the preliminaries. I am Gomes, you are Reis, it's a very hot day, my fan is broken, and I don't like the looks of this bank of yours."

"Have you discussed it with Senhor Rodrigues?"

"Yes, yes, he is not a skeptic, I am, and I am the man you have to satisfy. I've done some research on you. . . . You're the man who bought the fancy house, the railway shares—there's word out that you do business with Kreuger. I ask myself, what does all this mean? What have you done in the past year to make yourself such a big man? A year ago you were going to jail. Now you're up to your ears in high finance. Rodrigues may call it a success story. I call it damned strange! Talk to me. What have you got to say for yourself?"

"I was charged in Oporto and acquitted. Portuguese justice still counts for something, I assume? Even to such a skeptic as yourself, one hopes. Is an association with Kreuger, the greatest financier the world has ever known, a crime now? What is it that turns you against my bank?" He felt none of the old fear; he trusted himself.

Gomes snorted, puffed the cigar wetly, shuffled some of the papers on his desk.

"That doesn't explain your sudden wealth. Am I missing something?"

"I am an able businessman. I made my first fortune in Angola. You may know that I have been called by men of judgment the 'Hero of Angola.' I returned to Lisbon, still a young man, and made another fortune only to be stripped of it by my enemies, who had me accused unjustly and thrown in jail. What is so surprising about my making a third fortune? Money, the making of it, is child's play. . . . Kreuger himself told me that. I agree with him."

"Then you are either a genius or a criminal, Reis."

"I am a financial genius. I was born at a time when I could prove it. My humble origins did not hold me back."

"Yes, yes, we've all heard that these past few years. What do you want a bank for, anyway?"

"To finance the development of Portugal and Angola, to help raise the value of Portuguese currency, to bring our country back to its previous might. . . . I want a bank for the sake of Portugal, not for the sake of Alves Reis. . . ."

"Such a saint!" Gomes rumbled, coughing wetly. He pulled a towel from a desk drawer and laboriously wiped his face. "But some of your associates are not so saintly. . . ."

"Commander Carvalho, you question him? This is indeed a surprise!"

"Not Commander Carvalho, but there are others. This Bandeira fellow—"

"But Bandeira has nothing to do with my bank, as you perfectly well know, Vice-Governor. Let's stick to the point."

"He is a close associate of yours. You cannot deny that, and the man is unquestionably a rogue!"

"Bandeira is a trusted employee who made youthful mistakes. His name does not arise here."

"Then there's this German, Hennies. . . . A *German*, Senhor, as a director of a Portuguese bank? Come, come. Everyone knows that Germany, having lost her colonies to the Allies, covets our colonies in Angola and Mozambique. . . . Your choice of a German is unwise."

Alves watched Gomes sweat. "I have twenty-three shareholders listed on my application. Bandeira is not among them, and you pick out one German for your objections. There is a government deputy on my list, a former Minister of Agriculture, two prominent professors of economics, influential businessmen—do you have questions about them? I thought not. Karel Marang has been decorated twice by the Republic of Portugal for services in its behalf in the business arena. . . . Herr Hennies is immensely respected not only in Berlin but in half the capitals of Europe. Please, don't interrupt me, Gomes."

Gomes frowned, then motioned Alves on. It was too hot to fight.

"As you may know, I have personally had a hand in bringing two directors of the Oporto Commercial Bank to task for their recent embezzlements . . . and I have seen the bank closed, even though I myself was a director of the bank! What greater proof can you have of my honest concern for the good of the nation? I have placed the integrity of the system above my own profits. . . . How many bankers can you name who would have gone out of their way to do the same?

"And, finally, Luis Viegas, the Inspector of the Banking Council, is a friend of our enterprise who has already intervened with Camacho Rodrigues on our behalf to get this application approved. Now, unless you have some substantive complaints about my bank, I will leave you to your skepticism." He rose and bowed slightly. "Good day, Vice-Governor. I await your report to Governor Rodrigues."

Gomes' eyes were narrowed to slits and the great puffy jowls sagged moistly.

"You had better keep your operations very clean, Senhor Reis. I personally will be keeping an eye on them."

"Then you withdraw your objections?"

"I will put them in storage, Senhor. Good day to you."

Buoyed by his rout of the vice-governor, Alves spent the remainder of the week acquiring certain real assets.

For one hundred and twenty-five thousand dollars he bought a building in the Rua do Crucifixo, in the heart of the *Baixa*, to house the Bank of Angola and Metropole. Carpenters and painters were set to work at once.

He paid fifty thousand dollars for a building in Oporto to house the first large branch of the Bank of Angola and Metropole. There had been no question of turning his back on Oporto. He had, however, succeeded in seeing what would have been a major competitor close its doors.

For eighty-eight thousand dollars he bought the building in Lisbon that housed the ever-expanding offices of Alves Reis, Limitado.

The charter for the new bank was officially approved two days after his meeting with Vice-Governor Gomes. Immediately he invested heavily in several large Portuguese and Angolan enterprises. But a problem had arisen. He was running out of money. Waterlow was going to have to run off some more because, incredibly, Alves had ninety thousand banknotes he couldn't use.

Originally these particular notes had somehow been overinked at the Scrutton Street printing plant. Upon unpacking them in Lisbon, he had been upset by the overpowering smell of ink clinging to them. They not only looked brand new, they smelled it, and he decided that together the look and the smell would serve to draw too much attention to them. Better to be on the conservative side and take no unnecessary risks. But ninety thousand notes . . . worth two and a quarter million dollars!

At night he had removed the packages of notes from the safe at Alves Reis, Limitado and transferred them to the library's floor safe in the Menino d'Ouro. To the notes he added a liberal application of camphor, hoping it would absorb or at least cover over the smell of ink. It struck him as an altogether practicable idea, possibly even a small stroke of genius.

With Maria safely out of the way in Paris and the six servants asleep in their quarters, he retired late one night to recover the newly defumed money. He carefully rolled back the rug, removed the oak disc and swung the trap door up, then the heavy door to the elaborately gilded safe.

The blast of camphor rocked him back. He sat down heavily, wiping his eyes, gagging. Christ, I'm poisoned! Like mustard gas! It wasn't *that* much camphor. . . . He leaned forward tentatively. The fumes still rose, almost visibly. Sighing wearily, he staggered to his feet, threw open the windows, made windmill gestures with his arms, trying to push the camphor odor out of the room. He pointed the heavy black fan at the hole in the floor and switched it on.

In a few minutes he could get close enough, handkerchief over his nose and eyes, to remove the bundles from the safe. Ninety bundles carefully wrapped, each with a thousand tightly packed banknotes. Gingerly he sniffed, frowning. He took several bundles to his desk, spread them out, brought the fan from its stand and directed it to blow across the money. He sat down, lit an Upmann cigar and waited. He drank some port.

Finally he took a bundle and sniffed it.

The notes reeked of ink and camphor.

He recognized the fact that not every idea could be a good one. He stacked the notes across the desktop and left the fan blowing across them. Then he locked the door to the library, having closed the safe and replaced the carpet, and tramped groggily off to bed.

In the morning he called José, asking him to stop by the house. "There's a slight problem," he said, staring at the desert of odoriferous banknotes. "I need your opinion."

Breakfast was waiting in the library when José arrived in his Pierce Arrow, which was yellow and black like a mammoth bumblebee. Alves watched from above, waved.

Alves told him how things stood. José began to shake with laughter.

"We're talking about more than two million dollars," Alves said soberly. "I've run across funnier things, to be frank with you."

"What did your chums at the bank have to say about this? You could gas half the bank tellers in Lisbon with these notes!" José dissolved in laughter.

"I haven't told them yet," Alves admitted. "There'll be no problem with them. They can just cancel the notes and we can have Waterlow reprint them. . . . Or print new notes, for that matter. It's only a question of bookkeeping." He stared malevolently at the notes. "I'd rather not have to inform them of my blunder. . . . I admit it, my blunder. I asked you here, if you can restrain your mirth, to see if you had a suggestion. . . . Is there anything you can think of to, ah, fumigate these things?"

"Oh, God, I've never heard of such a thing!" He slapped his thigh.

"Your thoughts, please," Alves said.

"Sure, I'll think of something. But I've got a busy day ahead of me—a big chunk of bank shares are coming our way." He stood and brushed the crumbs of pastry onto the floor, grinning. "I'll come back tonight, ten o'clock. I'll think of something." He shook his head, holding his nose, beginning to chuckle again. "Don't worry, Alves, I suggest you leave the fan on, ha, ha. . . ."

The night was warm and Alves was waiting in his undershirt. José, suit as wrinklefree as it had been twelve hours before and flower fresh as the dawn, arrived with a large brown paper bag.

"Lemons!" he cried, emptying the contents on top of the banknotes.

"My fan broke," Alves said disconsolately. "What do you bring lemons for?" The lemons were rolling off the desk, bouncing on the floor.

"Forty-eight lemons," José announced. "Get two knives and a bowl. We squeeze. . . ."

An hour later the bowl was full and both men were sweating. Lemon rinds filled the wastebasket. "Jesus," Alves said. "I hope this works, whatever it is."

"Just follow my directions. You are in the hands of José Bandeira, world's greatest money fumigator!"

José led the way to the bathroom, Alves carrying the

bowl of lemon juice. José turned the golden water faucets and they watched the tub fill. "Now, pour the lemon juice into the water." Alves poured. Steam clouded the huge gilt-framed mirror.

They carried the bundles in three trips from the library.

"Trust me," José said. Carefully, one bundle at a time, José placed the bundles at the bottom of the tub. Through the water the money seemed to squirm, come alive. "Let's go to work on your billiard table, two gentlemen of leisure."

"Stop laughing," Alves said. "You're driving me crazy."

It was two o'clock in the morning when José straightened up from the table. "They should be ready by now," he announced.

They stood looking down into the tub.

"They don't look right," Alves said.

"It's the water makes them look funny. Don't worry. They're going to smell just fine, you can take my word for that."

They removed the bundles, placed them on thick towels on the bathroom floor. José blotted them, held one bundle to his nose, sniffed.

"See, no camphor, no ink . . . clean and pretty as a baby's bottom!" He waved the packet of notes beneath Alves' nose.

"José, don't you notice something wrong?"

"Wrong? I suppose you're referring to the color, is that it?"

"Yes, José, I am referring to the color." Alves was gritting his teeth, speaking with some effort from behind tight lips. "The money is pink!" Alves screamed. "Vasco da Gama notes are not supposed to be pink! Have you ever seen a pink Vasco da Gama note?"

"Well, I suppose you're right about that . . . but all I promised was to take care of the smell."

"You could have set fire to them and gotten rid of the smell. . . ." Alves threw the notes to the bathroom floor, where they landed with a wet smack. "Christ," he groaned, "you have turned two million dollars into big pink shrimps!"

"Dry them," Alves muttered derisively. "It can't get worse."

Through the night they ironed the notes, one at a time. By dawn's light there were a thousand ironed notes. The pinkness had darkened somewhat as the notes grew crisp. But the smell of ink had returned.

"Alves, you look terrible," José said, yawning. "Bags under your eyes, you need a shave."

Alves set the iron down, lit a cigarette and perched on the windowsill. "Listen to the birds. We've been up all night playing with this money. . . ." He shook his head, ruffled his hair. He began to laugh quietly. "Well, genius," he said, "what next?"

"I do have a final idea," José said.

Later the same day, after they had napped briefly and attended to their business engagements, they met again in Alves' library. José brought glycerine.

"Back to the bathroom," José said.

Alves carried several bundles of crisp, newly dried and ironed notes back down the hallway to the bathroom.

"A very strong solution of glycerine and water," José explained. "That should take care of the smell of ink and who knows, maybe it'll restore the color. . . ."

Several bundles were submerged. They waited. José finally reached in and brought them out. They returned to the library and began ironing.

"You see, this time the smell of ink is gone. This smells very much like money, Alves."

"But I ask you, José, does it look like money?"

"It's still a little pink, I must admit."

Alves took a note from his trouser pocket and placed it on the table. He covered it with one of the new pinkish notes.

"Our notes have shrunk, José. Your glycerine has shrunk our little pink notes by—oh, what would you say, José?"

"A quarter of an inch?"

"Yes, I think that's fair. We now have tiny, pink Vasco da Gama banknotes, José. . . ."

"They don't smell bad, though. What should we do?"

"A big fire," Alves said. "Then I'll go see Waterlow."

"Just one of those things, eh, Alves?"

Now that he was accustomed to it, the new forgeries proved no problem for Alves. The first letter was from Camacho Rodrigues to Waterlow and Sons, Ltd., authorizing the printing of three hundred and eighty thousand Vasco da Gama notes. He stressed the continuing secrecy and the need to adhere to all the previous requirements. The second letter listed the serial numbers and directors' signatures. The few errors he had made in Paris were not repeated, since in the meantime he'd had plenty of bank-notes to use for research. Waterlow hadn't noticed the original errors, in any case, but it was better to get it exactly right. When they were finished he ordered José to London to get the wheels moving.

Since her arrival in Paris Maria had wired every few days for more money. Alves always sent it, a total of forty thousand dollars in the course of a week. If it made her happy, then it was a reasonable price. That was the only way he could see it. Then Arnaldo returned to Lisbon. Alves was glad to see him. Marang was investigating some opportunities in Norway, and Hennies was bargaining intensely with the Albanian government for the rights to create a new central bank under the Alves Reis umbrella. Thus far fifty thousand dollars had gone into the Albanian enterprise and the news was not what one hoped for: Hennies had sent a coded wire fearful that Albania was flirting with the idea of granting the banking rights to the Italian government. Marang had sent a carping wire from Oslo, questioning the wisdom of Alves' quarter-million-dollar investment in the South Angola Mining Company that had yet to produce an escudo's worth of ore. So, Alves was glad at the prospect of seeing Arnaldo. He was also pleased at another idea, a suggestion from José: Alves was going to take the family to the spa at Carlsbad. He'd been working terribly hard, José had argued, and a week of taking the waters would do a world of good.

Perhaps, Alves wondered, Arnaldo and Silvia might care to join them, all expenses taken care of, naturally. Maybe it would alleviate some of Arnaldo's sourness.

Arnaldo never looked worse. His eyes were bloodshot and he was indifferently barbered. His suit was rumpled, the cuffs of his white shirt were smudged. He had come to the office direct from the Rossio Station. Alves tried to ignore his appearance.

"And how was Paris?" he asked heartily. Carlsbad was certainly just what Arnaldo needed. "Were the girls having fun?"

"Fun?" Arnaldo croaked wearily. "Alves, we must talk seriously about this. I tell you, I was disgusted by what I saw, nauseated . . . the extravagance! It's as if Maria has gone mad, been taken by a fever. Alves, I wish I could make you understand . . . Nothing I said to her made the slightest impression. She's possessed. . . ."

"My God, Arnaldo, the woman is enjoying herself! Her husband is a rich man—"

"No, no." Arnaldo shook his head vigorously. "You don't understand. It's a sickness, I tell you. She buys everything she sees. And Greta urges her on, presents new possibilities. Gowns, diamond necklaces, shoes, underclothes . . . the boxes, I've seen them delivered, ripped open, glanced at, stacked on the floor. An army of deliverymen march through the lobby of Claridge's each day. One day there were nineteen gowns delivered and a Russian mink coat from Jenny de Paris. . . . Watching her was obscene, and Greta just laughed, told her she deserved to treat herself . . . and Maria kept telling me that José had told her that money is for spending. I asked her what you had told her, but she'd make a face, said you didn't care, you were busy buying cars. . . ."

"Well, she has a point there," Alves admitted. "Come on, old friend, don't worry—she's having a fling!"

"Why can't you face it?" Arnaldo whispered. "You've killed the Maria we all loved. She no longer exists. . . . Why must you make a joke of it?"

"We're going through a phase of our lives. We must live it as best we can. Our lives are in process, not completed stories—"

"You're fooling yourself, Alves." Arnaldo was literally wringing his hands, realized it and clamped them hard on his knees. The office clock ticked. Sunlight lay across the portrait of the old admiral. "You've driven Maria to this, you've taken yourself out of her life and left her empty and terrified. So now she's in Paris trying to buy back happiness. . . ."

"How do the two of them get along?"

"It's pupil and teacher. Maria is a good student."

Alves diverted the conversation in an attempt to brighten the gloom. He told Arnaldo of the ink smell and the pink, shrinking money. Arnaldo would not be cheered.

"It's no problem. The bank has already authorized the printing of more money. José has already left to see Waterlow. For God's sake, cheer up."

Without comment Arnaldo placed a briefcase on Alves' desk.

"The contents of the strongbox," he said. "Perhaps you should check it."

Nonchalantly Alves opened the case and emptied the contents before him. His heart very nearly stopped beating.

The last item fluttering to the desk was the stationery marked with the name of I. Camacho Rodrigues. There were several sheets and a handful of envelopes. He had forgotten he'd left the stationery there since he had plenty in a locked drawer of his library desk.

"Ah," Alves said.

"I brought the strongbox to Maria's suite and she dumped it on the bed. She couldn't wait to get her hands on some of the jewelry she'd left in it. She saw the envelope—it was sealed. She just grabbed it without thinking and ripped it open. . . . And in it was Camacho's private stationery, with a receipt from the printer in Lisbon, not the government printing office." Arnaldo's eyes had not left the sheets of stationery. His voice had grown almost inaudible.

"It's easily explained," Alves said.

"I'm sure you have an explanation. . . ."

"Camacho personally authorized me to use it. With my own signature, of course. He thought it would lend weight to my communications with Waterlow. . . . I don't know why he chose the printer he did. He just told me to pick it up. That's all there is to it."

Arnaldo was shaking his head. His face shone with the evidence of his nerves.

"No, I can't accept it, Alves. Something is very wrong here, something I can't understand. You are either being used by the men at the bank or you are using them. I don't want to know which it is. But I must leave Alves Reis, Limitado at once. José can take my place. You rely on him more now anyway. This sort of thing doesn't bother him, never has. I am used to the ways we used to do things, you and I. . . ."

Alves straightened the stationery into a neat pile, slid it into a large envelope. He did not want to look at Arnaldo.

"Are you accusing me of something?"

"I am accusing you of bad judgment. Money cannot just become ours, not honestly . . . you cannot just have money printed when you need some. Those men at the bank, Alves, they must be acting irresponsibly at best, illegally at worst. And there will be a reckoning. . . . I only hope that you can survive it, my old friend. But I cannot remain part of it. . . ."

Alves already felt the cold sense of loss. A joint trip to Carlsbad was unthinkable now.

"I have been offered a partnership in a small import-export firm. I'm going to take it."

"But I won't see you anymore," Alves objected, feeling like a helpless child.

"I've got to do what I think is best for me."

"I shall miss you."

The two men embraced, held each other tight without speaking. Alves finally turned his back, stood by the window, pretending to survey the street below through eyes veiled with tears, waited until he heard the door close behind his dear old Arnaldo.

*   *   *

The telephone roused him from his memories. He had no idea how long he'd been sitting at his desk, eyes closed, dejected. The earpiece crackled. Paris calling. The new long-distance lines were rotten, and no one in Lisbon depended on them. While he waited for the caller to be rung back he wondered who it was, Greta or Maria.

But it was a man. He didn't catch the name, but it was unnecessary.

The two Hispano-Suizas were ready. Would Senhor Reis care to take delivery in Paris or would he prefer to have them shipped to Lisbon?

"Paris," he said. "I will be there within the week. I will take delivery at the Claridge. Did you make the color change I requested?"

"By all means, Senhor Reis. I have the list of requirements right here. Perhaps I should go through them in case changes are needed."

He listened to the voice droning on: all wood and steel trim, hand-finished wood interior, slanted windscreen, handle-operated separation screen between front and back seats, convertible top, four doors, upholstery in black Morocco leather of first grade, hood in black cowhide, small wooden cabinet in rear. Floor to be covered with carpeting, cushions filled with horsehair, speaking tube between rear and front, exterior painted red with silver trim, fenders black, extra accessories: three Vuitton valises, Barker headlight dippers . . .

Yes, it was all to his specifications. He wondered if anyone else in the world had such automobiles. . . .

He wired Marang in Oslo and Hennies in Albania to meet with him in Paris in one week. He no longer had to tell them Claridge's. It was all old hat by now. There was only one great difference. There would be no Arnaldo. He wired José at the Carlton in London: once he'd seen Waterlow he might as well come to Paris, too.

*　　*　　*

Maria and Greta were drinking champagne in his suite when he arrived. Seeing them as Arnaldo had described them, surrounded by boxes and tissue packing with the bottle of Mumm's in an ice bucket, he felt numb.

"Alves!" Maria ran to him with a flash of her old affection. It faded as she drew near. He kissed her cheek. "My darling . . ." She stood back. Greta nodded, smiling.

"And take a look at your wife," Greta said. "A transformation, don't you think?"

Maria stepped back, spun slowly. Her long hair was gone, cropped down to a black helmet, revealing her tiny ears, the nape of her smooth neck. Her hair seemed even darker, a raven's shade with glints of steel blue. Her full breasts had been flattened by the tight tubular dress. Her eyes seemed even larger.

"Whoever you are, Senhora," he said, "you are exceedingly beautiful. But, may I inquire as to my wife's whereabouts?" He pantomimed looking behind a chair. "Come out, Maria, wherever you are. . . ."

"You don't like it,". Maria said. "I knew you wouldn't like it."

"Of course he does," Greta said, leaning back languidly, crossing her legs. "Have some champagne, Alves, you look like Dracula!" She poured another glass.

Maria clutched his arm. "It's the latest look. . . . I was going to come home a new woman."

"My love, new or old, you are lovelier than a summer morning in Paris." He never felt comfortable saying such things, but the pain in Maria's eyes as she had looked for his reaction struck through his shell of concern. He wanted to soothe her. For himself there was a flood of relief: obviously the two women were still at ease with each other. Maria chattered on, a feverish cheerfulness in her voice.

Anxiously she showed him her new acquisitions, flinging gowns and dresses and sweaters across the couches, tables and chairs. Shoes were deposited carelessly in the middle of the floor.

"Don't forget the lingerie," Greta teased.

And out it came, box after box of intimate underthings, dripping like foam wherever she tossed them. It all struck him as forced, unnatural, sad. At the conclusion Maria swept by him to a closet and emerged with the Russian coat that almost flowed, a waterfall, a cascade of mink. . . .

"Bravo!" he cried, trying to take part and feeling foolish.

They sipped champagne, out of breath, and then Greta made a telephone call and he followed Maria into the bedroom. He watched her mood shift, he reached for her, she moved away, shaking her head. He kissed her. She did not break free but was dead in his arms, unresponsive. She lifted his glasses, looked at the scar on his nose. "I'm sorry," she said from a great distance, "I didn't mean to hurt you. . . ."

"That was a long time ago," he said. "It was nothing."

He didn't want to poke at the embers of their life together. He couldn't see the gain in it.

"I'm going to have a bath," she said. "Take Greta down to the bar. I'll meet you there."

When he closed the bedroom door behind him, Greta took his hand, kissed him.

Downstairs she ordered French 75s, made sure his Turkish cigarette was lit. "Your initials on every hand-rolled cigarette . . . ooo-la-la." She pulled his suit coat open. "Initials on your shirts."

"Yes," he said, "and on my dressing gowns, pajamas and my velvet carpet slippers. In case I forget who I am. Don't laugh, it could happen. . . . It might be a blessing."

"Poor dear, I could see that you need babying. Maria and I have been having quite a time. Your wealth agrees with her."

"Arnaldo says you've been goading her into this mad spending."

"Oh, I should think that's a bit strong, but she needed some advice. She's never shopped in Paris before. You might say I've been encouraging her, teaching her what is the *crème de la crème*."

The champagne cocktails arrived. She lifted hers. "To the enjoyment of money!"

Alves nodded. "Why are you taking this sudden interest in Maria's education? You've told me she's tedious and dull. . . ."

"And dangerous, don't forget that. I'm trying to cap the fangs. I'm trying to give her something else to think about."

"I don't understand."

"Something other than you. Alves, my sweet, she knows that her role in your life is growing smaller, and she's seeking a way to get you back. It's a very common female experience. . . . I'm trying to show her that there's more to life than you, that she may have to face life without you."

"I see," Alves said. The bar was slowly filling with shoppers from the Champs-Elysées, hotel guests, salesmen, beautiful women. "And her reaction?"

"Beneath the surface I'd say she understands it." Greta tilted her graceful head to exhale a jet of smoke. "Who can be absolutely sure of another person's mind? She senses the turning point in her life. And she's learning that there is enjoyment to be had without you. Alves, you must accept the fact that you are becoming expendable." She touched his arm, comforting. "It's not easy for her."

"You've been through it before, I suppose."

"Yes, and I've watched it happen to others—men and women. There's always a pattern. Soon she will have an affair. And you will have to accept that. It's the price of your own freedom. First she will fill her life with things, then with a man . . . or men. There's no trouble on that front, particularly if a woman is wealthy."

"Not Maria," Alves said emphatically. "I know her better than anyone." He finished his drink and nodded to the waiter for two more.

"Try to believe me," Greta said. "When she talks about you she tells me that she's already lost you. And don't ask me if she knows about us because I simply don't know. She says she's lost you to your new life, that it consumes you. . . ."

He looked into Greta's eyes until she looked away. "I'm taking her away, to Carlsbad. . . . I could use the waters myself, I could use something." He sighed, rubbed the back of his neck. "Greta, I don't know what to do with her. I still love her, of course."

"Well, you must talk it out with her in Carlsbad. . . . Then come back to Paris and you and I can talk. We'll have our own life." She took his hand and pressed his fingertips to her mouth. "Rainbows every day. . . ."

Maria joined them as their third set of French 75s arrived. Alves ordered one for her. She sat, fitting one of her own cigarettes into a holder. He leaned across the table to light it. He felt as if she were someone he'd never met before. Someone who wasn't terribly interested in him.

"Well," she said, flashing brilliant crimson nails around the drink, "did Arnaldo tell tales on us? I couldn't imagine why else you'd drop in like this."

"Arnaldo came to me in Lisbon to tell me he was resigning from Reis Limitado. . . . I called a meeting of our group here in Paris."

Maria flashed an accusing glance. "Why did he resign after all these years? What will he do?"

"He was offered a partnership in an import-export firm. He was never comfortable with high finance. . . . He hasn't been really happy since we left Africa. Some men are just meant for smaller things. . . . He'll be fine."

"I thought him a nice man," Greta said.

Maria struck an obvious pout. "Yes, but he was becoming an old sourpuss, no fun anymore. Take José, he is always so gay, so much fun. . . . He knows how to live, not like poor Arnaldo. . . ."

"Poor Arnaldo," Alves repeated. Her eyes were blank, yet Arnaldo had been closer to her than any man but Alves.

Later when they lay in bed Maria whispered to him, "Why did Arnaldo really leave? Don't lie to me, Alves, or pretend I'm a child and can't understand. . . . What was it? He was terribly upset when he saw the stationery from the governor's office. . . ."

"No, nothing like that. He just didn't understand what we were doing. He wanted out. Now go to sleep. . . ."

"He wanted out," she repeated.

"Maria, when I'm done here in Paris, I thought we might go to Carlsbad. . . . For a rest. You could wear your new clothing, display your jewelry. Would you like that?"

"I suppose," she said. "How are the children?"

"They're fine. They send you their love."

As he was falling asleep he thought he felt his wife crying. But what could he do? He was very tired.

*　　*　　*

Alves had told Marang and Hennies that he wanted someone with stronger diplomatic connections to see the next shipment of banknotes to Lisbon. The mess with Hennies' documents at Rossio Station was not to be repeated. At the meeting the next day they presented their solution. His name, they said, was Count Simon Planas-Suarez, the Venezuelan minister to Portugal. Marang knew him from The Hague, and José's brother Antonio vouched for him, had in fact heard him deliver a series of lectures at the Academy of International Law in The Hague. He had written a dozen books, was wealthy and at forty-six was a Commander of the French Legion of Honor, holder of the Order of Christ of Portugal and a Count of the Holy See.

"He knows nothing of the banknotes, of course," Hennies said.

Marang smiled smugly. "I told him only that we had a great number of confidential documents we needed brought to Lisbon from The Hague as diplomatic baggage. I told him we'd be happy to cover his expenses, which will of course be fairly heavy. . . ." He laughed abruptly. "I doubt if he realizes fully just how many official documents we have! In any case, he's not the kind of man who asks questions—been a diplomat too long for that."

"You've done well, gentlemen," Alves said.

Marang shrugged as if to say, What else would you expect?

The Albanian matter was not so happily resolved. There was little to be done now, Hennies admitted. Mussolini was establishing a firmer hegemony in Albania than any of them had thought likely. The plain fact was that they'd been beaten out by the new dictator of Italy.

"In other words," Alves said, "we kiss our hundred thousand dollars goodbye. Cut our losses and get out."

José, fresh from London, acknowledged that he was buying Bank of Portugal shares as quickly as he could but that, in fact, it was a slow process. There were a great many shares, the price was rising almost daily since there was known to be a new buyer in the marketplace, and it was important not to arouse too much outside attention.

Marang brought the group up to date on the real-estate purchases made by the group's newly organized Holland and Portugal Trading Company, headquartered in The Hague. The intention was to sink as much of the bank's resources as possible into countries other than Portugal. Thus far nearly a million dollars was in use in England, France, Switzerland and Holland. The future, Marang reported, looked very promising in Norway and Sweden as well.

Alves concluded the meeting with the word—which he tried to soften with a smile—of Arnaldo's resignation but moved quickly on to news from Lisbon's banking community. While their own new bank was prospering splendidly and the Bank of Portugal was healthy enough, several banks in Lisbon and smaller cities were on the verge of closing their doors, primarily because the government had withdrawn its money from African branches. Things were desperate in Angola and Mozambique, and the banks were already going under—five already.

"The closings," Alves said, "work to our advantage. The Bank of Angola and Metropole will have much less competition in buying up hard foreign currencies. We should be thankful for each and every blessing."

At dinner he sat and watched them, prosperous, worldly businessmen who had been at best marginal cases when he'd brought them together. Did they ever question how he had done it? How bright were they all, really? In their position, having seen what they had seen, would he have known? He considered the question during the course of the long dinner, through the brandies and the Upmann cigars. Would he have known that the man on the top was a swindler? Yes, he suspected that he would have known. But he also knew that he wouldn't have admitted it to himself. It was just too good a thing to squander. . . .

*   *   *

He had the two Hispano-Suizas delivered to Claridge's the next morning. The sun was bright and hot, and the trees stood motionless as the startlingly beautiful automobiles were wheeled up the Champs-Elysées. Alves stood at the back, watching. He had waited with considerable anticipation for the cars, and now they seemed a trifle meaningless —lovely, yes, but nothing really more than an accumulation of bits and pieces of metal and leather. He frowned at himself. Perhaps he was growing jaded. He'd heard it could happen.

"You must be very happy with those cars, Senhor Reis." It was the doorman, by now an old friend.

"Yes, Claude, of course I am very happy with them." He clapped the doorman on the back.

"A matched pair," Claude said with a wink. "Very stylish. You know how to live, Senhor. *Magnifique!*"

"Well, Claude," Alves said, stroking his mustache with a knuckle, "that's why we're here. . . . It's a question of style."

Alves drove the lead car and José took the wheel of the second. In a caravan the two enormous red-and-silver coaches wheeled gaily through the streets of Paris, along the Seine, circling the Eiffel Tower, moving swiftly across countless ancient bridges, through the shadow of Notre Dame with the pigeons scattering, past the Invalides and St. Germain and countless other places he had visited with Greta.

But it wasn't as much fun as he'd hoped it would be. The fun—God, the fun was supposed to have been so important—was draining off like the water the street cleaners ran in the gutters.

Night came and there was another dinner with too much to eat and drink and too many cigars and brandies. Maria got tipsy, and Greta let José take her home, blowing a kiss to Alves, and then everybody was sleepy and the day of the Hispano-Suizas was over.

In the morning Alves and Maria loaded the car to drive to Carlsbad. At the last minute José decided he would come too, and Maria said quickly that that was a wonderful idea; the party wouldn't be over after all.

Alves left the second car with Claude to break in. He gave him a hundred dollars in francs, and Claude's smile of surprise and gratitude was the nicest thing that had happened to him in Paris. Then they drove to Carlsbad, which turned out to be a longer trip than they'd expected. Alves didn't mind. He had plenty to think about, and as he drove time seemed to be moving too quickly. It was almost as if he heard a clock ticking.

*   *   *

Carlsbad was not a great success, at least not from his point of view. On the first day, while strolling along the picturesque streets, José saw a photographer's studio and insisted on having several pictures taken. He knew of Alves' fondness for photographs; and the afternoon was spent posing under the lights, waiting for the explosive flash. Alves, intent on looking his best, wore a gray homburg, a double-breasted suit in banker's gray, a three-pointed white handkerchief in his breast pocket and carried a Malacca cane. The summer heat notwithstanding, he had José go back to the hotel and fetch Maria's mink coat. Then the three of them posed. Staring into the camera's lens, it occurred to him that there was something wrong. José didn't really belong there. The problem was that Arnaldo wasn't there, the way he'd been in all the other pictures taken in all the other photographers' studios.

The photographs turned out very well. Alves ordered two dozen copies to be made for mounting in the new stand-up, cut-out fashion. It was always nice to send copies to associates, a homey touch, a testament to your stability. It spread confidence. A personal inscription was always nice. He would send one to Ivar Kreuger.

You could never have too many photographs.

But that was the high point. Over tea, Maria was quiet, watching him. Her face had lost its rounded softness, the oval grace it had once presented so happily to a world full of promise. Now her cheekbones projected ever more angularly and she wore varieties of makeup that gave her a French look, somewhat haunted and mysterious. Had he been meeting her for the first time he'd have taken her for a woman with a past. He felt her eyes on him until he could stand it no more, looked at the stranger's face inquiringly.

"I was just thinking," she said evenly, "what a farce that picture-taking was. The happy couple—rich and well dressed and smiling—having their picture taken. Remember that when you add it to your collection and flood the mails with copies for your friends."

He watched her, trying to recognize her. There was nothing to say. She'd been unable to stop the bitterness at the end.

* * *

Alves sat in a white lawn chair on green grass and dozed and went to the terrace for lunch. He read a new Wodehouse novel, vowing for once to keep the plot clear in his mind. But it was hopeless. He drank mineral water. He took the baths with José. The three of them dined each evening, and it was rather like being aboard ship. Occasionally they met a German baron or an English duchess and a party would be made up. Maria's clothing and jewels were striking, acting as a magnet on the curious, drawing them into her orbit, where she was at times talkative and at other times withdrawn, shy and, he had to admit it, seductive. It was as if she were acting, trying out a series of masks. He'd forgotten what the reality of their lives had been. . . .

He derived little benefit from the waters. There was no comfort to be had with Maria. One night with too much champagne in him he took her very messily in her bed and she seemed hardly to notice. After that the thought of sex with her was unimaginable.

As their stay progressed he took the baths by himself more often than not as Maria was completely taken up by the princesses, countesses and dowagers and those who were simply very rich. He saw less and less of her, glimpsed her at card tables with her new friends, saw her at cocktails with a group of haughty Germans, and later she sped by him in an open Mercedes, her face oddly serious, absorbed in what someone was saying.

José introduced him to an Italian with only one eye and an Englishman with a Guards mustache and only one arm, the sleeve of his dinner jacket pinned up to his shoulder. They smiled benevolently, and it turned out that they were wartime heroes who had decided to become gamblers. They moved from spa to spa but did not work as a team. The four men became chums. Within two weeks Carlo and Hugh had won thirty thousand dollars from José and fifty thousand dollars from Alves. They were terribly embarrassed about it, but as Hugh said with his nasal public-school voice, "You two can afford it a damn sight better than we can!"

José and Alves saw them off at the railroad depot. Alves hated to see them go. Losing money to them was considerably more enjoyable than taking the waters.

One evening he called Greta.

"Are you a new man?"

"No, but I've lost fifty thousand dollars at cards."

"Well, that should make you feel like a rich man, darling."

"It's raining."

"That's too bad. . . ." He could barely hear her. The lines crackled.

"I wish you were here. We could stay in bed all day."

"Have you had your talk with Maria?"

"Not yet. I hardly ever see her. She has new friends."

"Darling, I can't make out what you're saying. I'll ring off now. Call me again in a few days. I'm anxious to be with you."

It was true: he seldom saw Maria. And he was afraid to have a serious talk with her. What was there really to talk about, anyway? This difficult time between them would either pass or it wouldn't. What could he say? Divorce me? I'm abandoning you? Would she care, one way or the other? He had seen her twice walking in the garden with a handsome young German, very courtly and polite and polished. Someone said he was a medical student. She had drinks one evening with a fiftyish Englishman, a lord, he thought, and he had watched them dance and had gone home early by himself.

One day, beneath an iron-gray sky that seemed to be resting on the conical treetops like an Indian on a bed of nails, she told him she wanted to talk to him. She had lost weight and wore a dusky green dress that hung loose, elegant with all the tiny gold appointments. She led him to the terrace, where they sat at a little round table and drank Cinzano. The breeze was almost cool. She told him that she wanted him to go away.

"You don't fool me, you know," she said. "I know all about you and my wonderful friend Greta . . . and I don't blame her. I blame you, I trusted you, I never gave you a moment's cause to betray me. Our marriage was the one exception to all the others—you weren't a man who had a mistress. Your wife was enough. Well, we turned out no better than all the others. . . . Surprise."

"I don't understand what it is you know about Greta and me," he said. "I've not hidden the fact that I've seen her on occasion in Paris, that we're friends—"

"For one thing, foolish man, I saw the sapphire ring!

Arnaldo told me that you'd given him one to give to Silvia, a duplicate. . . . Obviously the rings came from the same man."

"And what does that prove? The one I gave Arnaldo was intended for you, but it looked so silly the day I brought it home, like nothing among all your diamonds, I was embarrassed to give it to you."

"My God, you bought the same ring for me you bought for your mistress . . . She and I, we're equals in your eyes, is that what you're telling me?"

"I have no mistress, no kept woman—I forbid you to say that to me!"

"How pathetic you are, how earnest. In Greta's apartment, just a few days before you arrived, I saw one of your initialed handkerchiefs on a table beside her bed, neatly laundered and folded, for you to place your spectacles on the next night you spend with her. . . ." She gazed at him appraisingly and he felt his stomach sliding away. "Greta must have left it out for me to see. Intentionally. I'm not sure what I think of her—it may be that she's trying to protect me and have you for herself. You're very rich, you know. You're like Ivar Kreuger, soon you'll need bodyguards and private railway cars—"

"I still love you. I will always love you. . . ."

"Did I say you didn't? I said that Greta is your mistress and that I want you to leave me alone, go away. She is more than welcome to you."

"I must go anyway. I've been away from business too long as it is. I'm not going because you told me to. . . . You are distraught, you don't know what you're saying."

"Ah, I see. Well, just so you go, the reason is immaterial to me."

"What are you going to do here alone? Are you planning an affair? To make me jealous?"

Her laughter pealed across the terrace.

"And they say you have no sense of humor. . . . No. I am not planning an affair, my dear husband. I simply want to be alone. . . . Before you go, please put ten thousand in a bank here for me. You wouldn't want Senhora Alves Reis destitute in Carlsbad, pawning her diamonds for her next meal. And leave the car, if you don't mind. I may learn to drive it. Or I may just buy a chauffeur. . . ." She stood up and leaned down to kiss the top of his head. "I have an engagement. I must go. Have a pleasant stay in Paris. Give Greta my love."

He had another Cinzano and watched the clouds darken overhead. He was relieved that she'd told him to go. He'd been concerned. . . . Could he have taken the thing by the horns himself? He didn't think he could have done it.

Arnaldo had seen the stationery.

Maria had seen the sapphire.

He had been careless.

The party had lasted for years and now everyone was leaving.

One morning José and Alves took the train for Paris.

*   *   *

In Paris they escorted Greta to the races and passed some cool hours in the Louvre, retreating from the summer sun. The Parisians were leaving on holiday. They checked in as usual at Claridge's, where Claude had the car waiting for them; but Alves spent his nights at Greta's flat. Alves and Greta had never been so quiet together before. They sat on the couch and read with the gramophone playing behind them. They walked along the Seine. They sat in the cafés and sipped cold beer. Greta didn't bring up the subject of Maria after Alves told her they had had words. To Alves the marriage was in limbo, which, at least when he was with Greta, seemed a good place for it. Sometimes he wondered about the comments the women had made about each other. The Maria whom Greta called tedious and dull hardly existed anymore. But Greta had also called her dangerous, and for the first time he saw how that might be appropriate. He wasn't sure exactly how Maria might endanger him, but it was no longer a ridiculous idea. . . . And she had implied that Greta was being attracted to Alves' wealth. He searched for clues, but there were none. She had not asked for the car he'd given her, nor for the sapphire. She took care of herself. He was not keeping her. The idea had never arisen. This was a matter of love. As such he supposed it might be more capricious than an economic bargain. But in other ways it was stronger. He would watch her over the top of his book as she read. She seemed at peace.

*   *   *

The time had come to pick up the new money.

In The Hague, Marang introduced him to Don Simon Planas-Suarez, who was tall and so dignified that Alves very nearly winced. Don Simon was not too dignified, however, to ask for more money to see the "official documents" through to Lisbon. He had, he said, misunderstood Marang's original suggestion.

José smiled at Alves. "Let me handle him. I understand his type." José's confidence was growing like a patch of weeds. As managing director of the Bank of Angola and Metropole he was anxious to prove himself. He made a new arrangement with Don Simon, who agreed to store the trunks in his apartment in Lisbon, which doubled as the Venezuelan Ministry. Yes, José had grown, and Alves felt confident at the way this onetime reprobate and jailbird had matured.

The total of the new printing was ten million dollars in the same five-hundred-escudo notes. Two hundred thousand notes, accounting for the first delivery of the second printing and worth five million dollars, were packed into eight Vuitton cases and deposited at the Liverpool Street Station cloakroom. Hennies and Marang had stayed in The Hague working on various investment deals; José and Alves lunched in regal splendor at the Carlton after their meeting with Sir William and the next morning arrived at the Hook of Holland with the money. Five million dollars . . .

Don Simon had no trouble at all in getting the cases to Lisbon.

"Clockwork," José reported. "It went like clockwork."

And there were other things to be done in Lisbon. He concluded the outright purchase of two large Lisbon apartment buildings and gave them to Maria's father, who was about to retire from the English firm. "You will never need to concern yourself with money again, Father," he said. The older man was speechless. His wife, however, was not: she wanted to know why he would bestow such a huge gift. "There are many reasons," Alves said. "I have no father and mother of my own now. You allowed me the hand of your daughter . . . not without a struggle, I grant you." The old woman had tears in her eyes, but she was smiling. "And you may be sure that Alves Reis will never forget that you closed ranks and stood behind him when he returned from the Oporto jail. You might have done otherwise. . . ."

For his brother Alves bought a flourishing printing business and promised him a position in the Kreuger–Reis match monopoly when it came to that.

José decided to become a country squire. He bought three large estates: one from the Count of Guarda, which was called the Quinta da Musgueria and lay just outside of Lisbon; another from the Marquis de Sagres; and a third from the Marquis de Funchal. In Lisbon he bought a fleet of taxis and the city's leading shirtmaker, where he had traded even when he couldn't afford it. He also bought his favorite barbershop and had a free trim every day.

Alves explained to José that his friends at the Bank of Portugal had requested a new routine for the passing of the banknotes into the economy. The notes would have to be taken out of their numerical sequence. It was a time-consuming job, but the bank's word was law. "A small security measure," Alves said, "but an important one. New bills in numerical sequence might arouse suspicion in rural bankers who aren't used to such transactions. We must not have another counterfeit scare." Several hours each day were spent mixing the notes. It was tedious but not the sort of thing you could assign to a clerk in the Reis Limitado office.

José continued the agonizing process of buying Bank of Portugal shares, reporting each day to Alves as they laboriously worked their way through the two hundred thousand banknotes. For complete privacy they worked in the locked library of the Menino d'Ouro at night. They had even brought the Vuitton cases from Planas-Suarez's apartment by night in a paneled truck José had found in the garage of his taxi fleet. There had simply been no room in the Hispano-Suiza they had driven home from Paris.

In the late summer of 1925 there were ninety-seven thousand Bank of Portugal shares outstanding, representing one thousand seven hundred and thirty-four votes. Alves needed nine hundred of those votes to safely control the bank, and they were coming hard. He needed forty-five thousand shares, since two hundred and fifty shares provided one vote. There was no point in buying in other than two-hundred-fifty-share lots.

Some shares had been held for generations by Portugal's great families, and they would never be for sale. Such

holdings were looked upon by the families as their stake in
the power structure of the country. Governments could always change—and in fact frequently did—but the bank
was a rock, immutable.

By now Alves owned something over seven thousand
shares, about one sixth of what he needed for control, and
the price had risen from forty dollars a share to seventy.
Eventually, although the shares thus far were held in safe
names unlikely to be traced to him, his interest was bound
to become known. It wasn't the kind of thing that could
be kept quiet forever. And once it was known that a single
source was buying potential control of the bank the price
would go higher, and the bank itself would inevitably have
men sympathetic to their control begin buying shares to
deny the interlopers their aim.

"It would be so much easier," José complained one evening, "if I didn't have to find out for myself who owns the
stock. Why don't you simply have Camacho or Gomes
give you a list? What the hell, they're the ones we're buying it for. . . ."

"Ah, if only they could do it." Alves sighed. "But it's
too great a risk of showing their hand. . . . Naturally it
makes our job all the harder. With Arnaldo gone it puts an
even greater burden on you . . . but you have the shoulders
for it. I have complete faith in you."

That pleased José, and it was very nearly true. There
was no one left, it seemed, and Alves drew deeper into
himself. He didn't like it; he knew it was unhealthy. Frequently he was unable to fall asleep until exhaustion set
in and the sky over the Tagus was pink with dawn.

He did trust José, but trust was a matter of degrees. The
question was, did he trust him enough to tell him the truth,
as he had told Greta? He wasn't sure how else to impress
upon José the urgency behind buying control of the Bank
of Portugal. One sleepless morning he sat at his desk in the
library and wrote José a letter.

Meu Caro-José:
    *The time has come for me to speak more frankly
than I dared to you or any of our other colleagues.*
    *Surely by this time you know that the "contracts"
with the Bank of Portugal and Alves Reis are forged.
We have both been in jail and we surely do not have*

*to pretend to each other as we do with our more
hypocritical partners, Hennies and Marang.*

*I must tell you firmly that unless you apply your-
self with every energy and resource to the business of
buying the Bank of Portugal stock we will be defeated
—and jailed, of course. As you know, I am planning
a trip to Angola with Hennies to inspect our holdings.
While I am gone I must rely on you to carry this
through at the expense of everything else.*

He broke off there and read it through. It made sense.
He decided to sleep on it. When he awoke he returned directly to the library and read it again. How would José
react?

The fact was, José had become a wealthy and powerful
man. Such a frank confession on Alves' part might serve
to increase his diligence, to make sure he protected his
own newfound stature. . . . Or it might scare him to death.
In which case he might just transfer his assets abroad and
get out while there was still time. . . .

With a few hours of sleep behind him, Alves' own confidence had received a bit of a boost. Perhaps there was no
need to reveal his great secret. . . . After all, things had
gone well thus far.

No, he would not tell José. He crumpled the sheet of
paper and set fire to one corner, dropped it into the fireplace, sat watching it until it was ash.

*   *   *

There was so much to be done before the voyage to Angola, and the summer was running through his fingers.

As the most economically powerful man in Portugal, he
poured money into the colony. The fact was, he realized
late on the long, sleepless nights, he wanted simply to *own*
Angola. He saw it as fitting but spoke of it so baldly to no
one.

He signed a contract with the Aboim Company of
Angola, which owned large palm-oil plantations and a railroad. He issued a large loan with another to follow within
thirty days, and the loan was not only cheap; it was made
in rock-solid English pounds. It was now his company.

A similar deal was signed with Compania das Minas de

Cobre of Bembe, which operated huge copper mines. The Bank of Angola and Metropole would finance the building of a railroad from the mines to the port of Luanda.

A mammoth loan, which included an option-to-buy clause, was extended to Quessama Agriculture Ltd., a gigantic copra plantation.

The bank bought control of a large colonial trading firm, the Mercantile Company of Portugal and Angola.

The Graphic was Angola's leading newspaper. The Bank of Angola and Metropole bought it.

At a press conference Alves announced that the bank was opening several branches in the major trading cities of Angola, blanketing the colony. At the beginning of October, he further announced, he would personally return to Angola at the head of a party of technical and development experts to study a wide spectrum of Angola's problems, suggest solutions and then implement them. One key possibility, he stressed persuasively, was the settling of a thousand Portuguese families in the plateaus of Benguela and Macamedes. In this he had the complete and enthusiastic support of the Minister of Colonies.

His enthusiasm for what he now knew he could accomplish overflowed, touched everyone around him. He felt the power burgeoning within him. He worked at his office or in the library of the Menino d'Ouro twenty hours a day. The Hispano-Suiza was driven only by his chauffeur, carrying him to or from one meeting after another. There was no time left, not for himself, nor for Maria, Greta or the children.

One day a man he had known for years came to his office at the bank. He was crying. He needed seventy-five thousand escudos or he would go to jail for embezzlement. He worked for the government, didn't make enough money, had a wife and three children. Alves watched and listened until the story was done. Alves offered him the best cigar the man had ever seen and lit it for him.

"I have known desperation myself," he said, "and I have been afraid with no one to help me. You must not be ashamed of what you were driven to do . . . but you must try to better yourself." He squeezed the man's shoulder and scribbled something on a bank voucher. "Replace the money and use the remainder to get yourself back on your feet again." A teller outside gave the man twice the amount of the embezzlement.

By chance Alves discovered that a distant blood relative owed a very small debt of some six hundred escudos to none other than Camacho Rodrigues himself. He explained to a bewildered but delighted cousin that he, Alves Reis, absolutely insisted on making good. Alves then sent a note to the governor of the Bank of Portugal explaining that he wished to pay off an old debt owed by Luis Filippe Fernandes Reis, if the governor would be kind enough to send someone round with a receipt to collect it.

The governor was earning three thousand dollars a year, even though he was Portugal's most important banker, and even thirty dollars would come in handy. The receipt was sent round to Alves' office at the Bank of Angola and Metropole. Camacho also sent a warm personal letter of thanks on his own bank letterhead. Alves was amused at how much more elaborate the stationery he had designed for the forgeries was than the real thing. He put the governor's letter in his safe. Who knew when acknowledgment of a debt by the governor of the Bank of Portugal to Alves Reis might not be useful?

The newspapers both in Lisbon and Luanda were full of the activities of Alves Reis and the Bank of Angola and Metropole. A Lisbon reporter, Eduardo Fernandes, interviewed him at work. He wrote:

When Reis came into the room he immediately took charge. He always seemed to know what you were going to say before you said it. He always listened carefully, as if he were really interested in what anyone was saying. He always had a kind word, a pat on the back, a word of encouragement. And because he was so expert at remembering faces and names his popularity in the business community was unmatched. Undoubtedly he would have been a magnificent politician. In Lisbon today there are those who say without hesitation that we may well be entering what history will call the Age of Alves Reis!

That one he had framed. He sent copies to his various associates. He sent a copy to Greta. He couldn't resist sending one to Maria in Carlsbad.

Arnaldo wrote him a brief note of congratulation on the appearance of the article. "I always wish for you whatever you wish for yourself," he wrote, signing it, "Your faithful Arnaldo." Alves replied, thanking him, enclosing a check for thirty thousand dollars. "You earned it," Alves wrote. "If you for any reason fail to accept it, we are quits forever." The check was deposited.

Eduardo Fernandes, the reporter from Lisbon's largest and most influential newspaper, *Diario de Noticias,* saw Alves in the Baixa one afternoon and drew him away to have a cup of coffee. Fernandes was making a study of Reis's operations and Alves enjoyed the contact. "We can use each other," the reporter said. "I'll write about your great deeds, how you're the man who can save Portugal and Angola . . . and together we will become famous." They had laughed together. Today he was curious about Arnaldo.

"I ran into him the other day, bought him a drink. He told me he was no longer with you. I'd had the impression you two were inseparable. . . . How'd you let him get away? And why the hell would he want to get away now, of all times?"

"He's an intelligent man, he's a good judge of what he does best and wants from life. . . . He wants a smaller stage, less running about the world, less finance and more day-to-day business. You can't stand in a man's way." Alves sighed. "I shall miss him. He's irreplaceable. I didn't know a man could miss another man so much. . . ."

A week later Fernandes wrote a long piece in the *Diario de Noticias* in which he summed up the new ferment that had taken over the country since Alves Reis had thrown himself into the fray. He used Alves as an example of the new kind of leader Portugal needed, the dynamic man who shook things up, installed confidence in the financial community and generally left his mark wherever he turned his attention. He wrote:

The situation has changed remarkably in the past few years. There is more money around and it is harder money. And it is being used dynamically for the good of Portugal. Loans are easier to get. Jobs are more plentiful. Buildings are going up everywhere you look. Department-store sales are booming. Portugal seems to have emerged from a period of stagnation and is

once again on the move! And no one is more responsible for this rebirth than Alves Reis, a man possessed
of economic courage and vision far beyond his years.

No one knew better than Alves that every word was
true. He was leading Portugal into a new era, and at bottom what difference did the source of the money make?
If the bank's directors had seen what could be done with
the money, they would have had it printed with complete
legality. But they were not men of vision. They were
small, petty bureaucrats. Alves Reis was a genius, all right.
And his most ingenious maneuver of all had been the idea
of taking matters into his own hands. What was legal in
their hands was a crime in his, but he had gone ahead and
it had worked.

* * *

Alves would not have been honest with himself if he said
he didn't think about Maria. He did. She haunted him in
quirks and flashes, flickered through his mind unexpect-
edly. He remembered her as a woman, as she was, as she
had been. But he wasn't at all certain that he even wanted
her back. . . .

He wondered about what she might be doing in Carlsbad, wondered if she was fulfilling Greta's prophecy. He'd
thought he knew Maria, but he obviously hadn't. No, he
wasn't sure he wanted her back.

But she had anchored his life for a long time.

If he loved her now, through this, he supposed he'd always love her.

At dinner one evening with candles sputtering and the
breeze off the Tagus a pleasant relief from the heat,
Maria's mother resolved a hesitation Alves had noticed
from the moment of his arrival at their home.

"Alves, dear, I don't mean to intrude, but I must hear
what you have to say about Maria. . . . The children have
been without their mother for weeks. I just don't understand what's going on. . . ."

"It's not easy to explain, Mother."

"You see," Maria's father said, "I told you it was not
our concern. Alves, we shouldn't pry." He threw up his
hands.

"But she must have explained herself to you, dear," she said. "Is she unhappy?"

"How could she be unhappy? Her husband is the toast of Lisbon, she has all the money in the world and a wonderful family . . ." He shook the crumbs from his napkin and crumpled it impatiently on the table.

"Yes, she is unhappy," Alves said. "She was far happier when we were in Angola, when we were starting out—"

"Now she stays in Carlsbad and won't answer my letters." Her mother brushed at her eyes. "When is she coming back, Alves?"

"I don't know, Mother."

"Tell her that her mother is very concerned. She's always been very considerate—"

"She has changed," Alves said quietly. "Our lives have changed. I'm not altogether sure that Maria loves me anymore. . . ."

He heard the woman stifle a small cry.

"Now, listen to me, Alves," Maria's father said, tapping the tablecloth with his forefinger. "Women go through these things, they act peculiarly, they make no sense, they tell their husbands they don't love them anymore . . . and they don't mean a word of it! She wants you to show some interest, that's all, so tell her you need her."

It was time to go. At the doorway, the erect, white-mustached older man took Alves by the arm.

"Be honest with me, son," he whispered. "Man to man, is there another woman? Or another man?"

"I don't . . . no, that's not the problem. . . ."

They walked out toward the car. Her father leaned against the front fender and folded his arms. The nightbirds fluttered mysteriously.

"The problem between us is something else. . . ."

"Well, ask her to come back. She will or she won't, and when you have an answer to that, well, then we can worry about what happens next." He shook Alves' hand and stood waving as the huge gleaming car slid off through the night.

The next morning Alves composed a cable asking Maria to come back to Lisbon, to him and the children and the Menino d'Ouro. He would put all business matters out of his mind, and they would talk their problems through until they had reached a solution. He loved her and she should never forget that. He awaited her reply.

It was not long in coming. He received it before he left the office in the afternoon: I HAVE NO PLANS TO RETURN AT THE MOMENT. LOVE TO THE CHILDREN. M.

He was not altogether surprised. She was bound to come back eventually, but maybe it would be too late by then. In any case, he felt that he'd been pushed around long enough. Maria would just have to face the consequences of abandoning her husband and family. He lit an Upmann, rolled it on his tongue, enjoying the taste, and composed another cable, this one for Paris.

Greta Nordlund's arrival in Lisbon as the guest of Alves Reis went unnoticed by the press, but it was very nearly the last thing she did during her stay that went unchronicled. Alves was by this time such a celebrity that he was dogged in the streets by reporters from Lisbon's aggressive daily newspapers. Greta was also known, and it was inevitable that she would be recognized when she appeared in his company. He arranged for her to stay in the Avenida Palace's finest suite. José almost always accompanied them, *always* in the evening, and certain vague attempts were made to describe her as an old friend of that renowned patron of Lisbon's nightlife, José Bandeira.

She attended an opening night at the Ginasio Theater and Alves commemorated the event, welcoming her to the city, before the writers and photographers in the crowded lobby and announcing his personal gift of thirty thousand dollars for the modernization of the building itself. Their picture appeared the next day in every paper.

After publicly dining in any of Lisbon's finest restaurants she was delivered to the hotel, seen entering the elevator. An hour later the great Hispano-Suiza would appear at the rear service entrance, where she would quietly reappear, unobserved with the cooperation of the manager, and be whisked off to the Menino d'Ouro for the night.

"Well, my darling," she said after a week of such trysting, "what are we to do?" She had gone past the need to apply pressure, and Alves was grateful. "We meet, we laugh, you tell me about your scheme and I tell you about my film contracts and *Outward Bound* . . . and we ignore the subject of your wife. Is that what you want?"

"I want a life with you, knowing you're always there. . . . You leading your life, I leading mine, together when we can be."

"The point is, is that a dream? Can we make it happen?"

She soothed his temples with her fingers. He sighed. "I'm sometimes afraid that you cannot bring it all to an end, you and Maria. I'm not blaming you, you must believe that. You are the way you are and in my heart I know we ought never to have begun. . . . For your sake, not mine. If you put me behind you, you could quite possibly repair your marriage. . . . She'd come back to you." She smiled at him as he opened his eyes. The night outside was quiet, clouds across the moon. "You should try, Alves, one last time. . . ." She fumbled with a cigarette, lit it, flung the match at a cutglass ashtray on the bedside table.

"When she hears about my visiting Lisbon, she'll do something . . . you can be sure she'll hear. Listen to me, I'm more experienced in these things than you. . . ."

"Yes, I suppose you are," he said, producing a self-deprecating groan. "If she will come, I'll take her to Africa with me. That should give us enough time to see where we're going. . . ."

"Remember, you're not deciding if you love me or your wife. I know you love me, just as I know you love her. But Maria and I offer very different ways to live. . . . It's the rest of your life, that's what you're facing, the rest of my life and hers." He watched her stub out her cigarette and snap out the light.

The remainder of Greta's stay in Lisbon was spent driving out into the countryside for picnics, visiting the castle at Sintra, to Estoril, to Cascais. Alves knew he was being gossiped about; he didn't mind. The beautiful blond actress made heads turn wherever they went, and he enjoyed it.

Maria's father called. "Is it wise, Alves? Being seen with a woman who is not your wife?"

"My wife has abandoned me. The woman is visiting José. I cannot help seeing her. Frankly, I like her."

"But people are talking. You know that."

"You know what Maria replied when I asked her to come back. My being seen with Greta may bring her back."

"I hadn't thought of that. If she cares, she'll come back. It's a strategy. . . . You are a clever fellow!"

At last Greta had to return to Paris. Rehearsals were beginning.

"I shall miss you," Alves said self-consciously on the morning of her departure.

"You'll be back from Angola in no time. And think, by then your mind will be clear. . . . You'll know what you need, we'll all have had time to think."

"It seems too much like goodbye," Alves said. "I'm afraid. I don't want you to go." He kissed her. They were sitting in the back seat of the Hispano-Suiza. The glass was up. José and the chauffeur chatted silently.

She said, "Well, my darling, we've had a lovely time, haven't we?"

She pulled away, tears on her face. She licked them from the corner of her mouth. He pulled her close, tasted the saltiness. Then she pulled away for the last time, opened the door and was standing outside with José. She didn't look at Alves. She turned and went into Rossio Station, José following, the chauffeur directing the men with her bags.

* * *

Maria was back in Lisbon a week later. She had indeed read the Lisbon papers sent her by her friends. Their marriage was a farce. She was through with him and it. No, she had not had an affair, but she had not been without tempting suitors.

When she ran out of breath and energy, Alves began to talk. He talked for hours, about their years together, her parents' feelings, the pressures of business he'd been experiencing. He spoke of the beach at Cascais, the pride she'd felt in Luanda and the joy he'd taken in her, the beauty of their children, her loyalty to him during his agonies in Oporto. . . . He said that they could not smash all those years to pieces over the confused events of the past few months.

Would she consent to giving it one final try? They could return in triumph to Angola together. . . .

In the end she agreed. She still loved him, and she didn't understand what had gone wrong, only that it had happened. She cried. Alves comforted her. It would all turn out for the best.

* * *

Alves set sail for Luanda firm in the knowledge that everything he was leaving behind was going beautifully and in good hands. He felt as if the great plan were very nearly humming along under its own steam. José and Marang would be picking up another five million dollars from Sir William, and José was scheduled to push ahead with the purchasing of the Bank of Portugal shares.

The only cloud on his personal horizon was the question of what to do with Maria and Greta; the smell of the sea and the freshening tradewinds even brought him a new optimism on that front. The right solution would become apparent; he would recognize it and grasp it. And ahead of him lay what he knew would be a joyous return to Angola. He was at the top, the top of everything.

He even overcame his tendency to seasickness. He walked the sunny decks with Hennies, sent an occasional cable to his headquarters in Lisbon. Albano da Silva, one of the department heads at the Bank of Angola and Metropole, and Jaime Mendosa, his private secretary, completed the Reis party.

Maria harbored no overt bitterness; she was, in fact, calm and pleasant, even vivacious. She had learned to drive the Hispano-Suiza, which lay now in the hold of the ship. She had lost during these past months the girlishness, the dependence she had always felt toward her husband. She seemed to have made the passage to adulthood. Alves watched her, saw the changes in the seasons of her life. Now she was cooler, more reserved, less vulnerable. On balance, the changes struck him as beneficial, though he observed her from a distance, without the warmth they had once shared.

After dinner in the lounge one night she mentioned their prospects.

"I admit that I would rather have things the way they used to be. Life was very sweet then, when we were just ourselves. But it isn't possible now. . . ." The lamps glowed warmly on the brass fittings, the leather couches. A waiter brought coffee and bowed over them, fussing with silver cream and sugar dishes. Maria stirred the mixture with a tiny silver spoon, handed a cup to her husband. "We are different people now. How do people go backward in time?" The more he saw of her short, sleek hair the more he liked it. He watched her mouth on the rim of her cup.

"You can't go back and there are no guarantees about the future." Alves was enjoying the gentle roll of the ship,

the civility of the lounge and the stewards. The blood of
an admiral flowed in his veins.

He reached for her hand. "I feel as if we have been
tested. It's right that you should come back to Angola with
me."

"You always enjoy the grand gesture." She patted his
hand. "I learned more about you, just thinking by myself
in Carlsbad, than I ever knew before."

As the days passed a hint of the old warmth, a gentleness
grew between them. It was as if the greater the distance
from the shores of Europe, the greater the closeness between them. It took him by surprise.

"Perhaps one day," he said the night before they were
to reach Luanda, "we will come back to live out our days
in Angola, on a great plantation with old friends around
us, beautiful horses to ride. . . ." He laughed softly. "Maybe
even Arnaldo would come and settle nearby with his Silvia,
the three of us together again." He added self-consciously:
"Well, it could happen. . . ."

*   *   *

He was up early and walking the deck when he caught the
first sight of the Luanda harbor. He stood at the rail alone
as the Lower Town took shape and the cliffs with the
silhouettes of the buildings marching along emerged from
the morning fog. The sun painted the scene pink as it had
that first day, and Alves felt himself fighting off the impulse to weep. Maybe he should never have left. . . . Life
would have been so much simpler. But it had been only a
place to start. And it would make a fine place to finish
life's journey. But not now. . . . Still, he had never felt his
own roots so deeply. Maria slid her arm through his, said
nothing.

*   *   *

In London, Marang and José lunched at the Carlton with
Sir William and his two aides, Goodman and Springall.
Five million dollars in five-hundred-escudo notes changed
hands. Expressions of hope that they would all be getting
together again soon filled the air. It was a beautiful London
autumn, warm and sunswept.

It was raining in The Hague when they arrived. Antonio Bandeira, a worried look on his slender face, met them, gave them dinner at his home. Over coffee Antonio got it off his chest.

"Is it possible your man Hennies is not what he seems?"

José looked up, startled. "What does that mean? He's in Angola with Alves. . . ."

"Two weeks ago I learned that the Minister of Colonial Affairs in Lisbon applied to the Deuxieme Bureau in Paris for whatever information they had on Adolf. You don't drag counterintelligence into it out of mere curiosity." Antonio poured Napoleon brandy and passed it around.

"Are you saying Adolf is a spy?" José was fully roused from the lethargy the large meal had produced.

Antonio gave his brother a pitying look. "Once a spy, always a spy. . . ." He looked at Marang expectantly.

"Nonsense," Marang whispered, holding his brandy up to the candlelight. "Everybody was a spy in the old days. There was a war on. I can personally vouch for Adolf Hennies. I've worked hand in glove with the man for a decade! An international businessman, vast acumen and considerable resources. More to the point, he is a *friend*." He waggled a finger at Antonio. "You've been taken in by bureaucratic nonsense. . . . Those fanatics are always investigating somebody, justifying their own existence!"

"You will excuse me if I press this matter," Antonio said, frowning. The rain blew against the window and for a moment the electric lights dimmed. "I mentioned nothing about that kind of spying . . . the inquiry was made by the *colonial* people."

José grasped the point. "It's the old thing, then, German interest in our African holdings. . . ."

"Exactly," Antonio said. "Cigars, gentlemen?" He passed around a humidor.

"It's still nonsense," Marang said silkily.

"Nonsense or not, Karel," Antonio said, "there are, unfortunately, certain influential ministers and officials in Lisbon who are convinced that Hennies is a German agent *now*. They are convinced that his job is to get a big foothold in Angola by buying companies and plantations there through your Bank of Angola and Metropole. If Alves Reis had asked *me* I would certainly have advised him to leave Hennies in Lisbon. Instead, he takes him to Angola, giving

Hennies' enemies more ammunition. Most unwise, I must say. . . ."

"It's a straw man they've set up," José said. He clipped the end of his cigar with a gold cutter dangling from his key chain. "Believe me, all of our investments in Angola have been made *together* . . . as a group. Solely business and certainly not an international plot! It's absurd. Why should Alves Reis and I want to *give* Angola to the Germans? And who says the Germans would want it, even as a gift? The whole damned colony is bankrupt and all the Portuguese stuck there would give anything to get back to Portugal . . . but they can't get anyone to take over their investments. Hell, the reason we're putting money into Angola is because there are so many bargains."

Antonio shrugged. "You know best. But, remember, you have been warned. The whole thing is being taken very seriously in Lisbon. That alone makes it worth your attention."

Later at the Hotel des Indes Marang guided José into the bar for a nightcap.

"Don't let Antonio unsettle you," he said. "You know how diplomats are, worried every time a tree loses a leaf —they think it's a hurricane."

"Well, I'm sure he's exaggerating," José said.

"In any case, you didn't mention the key to the whole business, at least from our point of view. Our masters at the Bank of Portugal have *ordered* these investments in Angola. Alves has made that clear time and again. We are merely agents of the bank." He crossed his legs, arranged the crease, smiled calmly. "And the Bank of Portugal is not at the call of Germany."

Still, the problem raised by his brother nagged at him during the night. In the morning, having decided to take out some insurance, José went to Antonio's office in the Portuguese Ministry and withdrew from the safe the two original contracts between Alves Reis and the Bank of Portugal authorizing the issue of banknotes. He put them in a thick manila envelope and checked out of the Hotel des Indes.

Marang, for all his reassurances to José, also decided to exercise a measure of restraint. Before turning the latest shipment of banknotes over to Planas-Suarez, he placed a million dollars' worth in his office safe. He would store them until Reis returned from Angola and talked to their masters at the Bank of Portugal. It should be simple to find out at that end just what was behind this campaign against poor Adolf.

*   *   *

José stopped in Paris to see Greta. He escorted her to the party following the opening-night performance of *Outward Bound*.

"You were magnificent," he whispered in her ear. "As always."

"It is so good to see you," she said. "Like old times. . . ." She winked playfully. "Have you heard from Alves?"

"Of course. He seems to be enjoying himself."

"And well they might. Tell me, what is the situation between you two? Maria is back, of course. She's with him."

"Well, he must decide, mustn't he?"

"It would be an easy choice for me." José favored her with a wolfish grin. He leaned forward and kissed her cheek. "You must be very lonely."

"Of course I am."

"You needn't be lonely tonight. No one would ever know, just the two of us . . ."

"You should be ashamed of yourself," she said lightly.

"You never forget a lover, do you?"

She smiled, moved his hand from her thigh. "No one ever forgets a lover. I have certainly never forgotten you."

"You make no sound like yes."

"I am an actress, darling."

He took her back to her apartment but made no effort to accompany her inside.

"Will you grant me a small favor?"

"Of course," she said.

He handed her the folded manila envelope.

"Just keep this someplace safe. Forget you have it."

"What is it?"

"Insurance policy. Just put it away."

"All right." She kissed him for a while, then went upstairs. It was very pleasant, knowing that once again you were the toast of Paris. She dreamed of her own triumphs that night. In the end, that was what counted.

*   *   *

Arriving in Lisbon feeling as if he had taken a wise precautionary step, José was delighted by several editorials appearing in the newspapers. The general tone was that things were booming throughout the entire country. Several financial writers on the dailies were predicting that the coming Christmas season was certain to be the most prosperous Portugal had experienced in a long time—possibly, one writer enthused, "in living memory." The obvious prosperity and the jump in employment had impressed foreign-exchange dealers abroad. The embattled escudo was actually rising in value vis-à-vis the florin and that most sacred of all currencies, the British pound.

José could still not shake the slight sense of worry his brother had caused him about Hennies. He had been buying Bank of Portugal shares in the names of dummies, friends, relatives, even employees of the Bank of Angola and Metropole. The stock would be duly registered in their names on the rolls of the Bank of Portugal stockholders. But now that Hennies was being investigated, was it likely that the affairs of the Bank of Angola and Metropole would remain immune to the government's snoops? Surely they would realize the actual ownership of the shares. . . .

With this in mind he declared a moratorium on the purchase of any more shares. There was, he reasoned, no need to worry Alves. In his long cable detailing the news in the papers, all calculated to keep Alves happy and relaxed as he bought up as much of Angola as he found available, José resorted to a white lie. He told Alves that they now controlled twenty-two thousand shares. There was no sense worrying Alves, and they could always buy the shares when they wanted them.

*   *   *

Old Terreira hosted a dinner for Alves, Maria and Hennies the first night in Luanda. It had been a long day but an exciting one. Alves had been officially received by the city and colonial officials, some old friends and some strangers. There had been a ceremony in the central square of the Lower Town, a band had played enthusiastically, and there were placards hailing the return of the "Hero of Angola." He had received the cheers and the warm words with what he thought was a becoming humility. And after an hour of rest in the hotel's largest suite, they were ready for Terreira's dinner. Chaves, who had never believed Alves guilty of the accusations a year before, pumped his hand, hugged Maria, telling her how wonderful she looked. The editor and his blond wife were a little older; she kissed Alves' cheek, asked him to remember who brought Hennies to his party all those years before.

"Angola is at your feet!" Chaves said between courses. "They still talk about the High Bridge. . . . It's a legend now. By the way, I thought for sure you'd bring Arnaldo."

"He had business he couldn't leave in Lisbon," Alves said evasively.

The editor's wife, her cleavage deeper, her breasts fuller, leaned forward across the table. "It's the most excitement we've had in years. . . . You must be so proud, Maria."

Maria smiled at the faces watching her. "Yes, Alves seems to have become a great man."

"And it isn't only your friends!" the editor exclaimed. "It's even the people you rubbed the wrong way—the fact is they feel the strength of will you've brought to developing the potential wealth of the colony."

Over the amiable chuckles Terreira tugged at a mustache and said, "The thing is, man, nobody thinks of you as an impractical dreamer! By God, you've promised and you've delivered. You've put money into this country! You can't beat that for making them sit up and take notice. . . ." He grabbed his glass, splashing wine on the table, raised it. "To Alves and Maria," he cried, "may their fate and the fate of Angola be forever intertwined!"

"Hear, hear," Chaves bellowed.

"I can only say I wish it was my newspaper you'd bought!" the editor grinned. "Whoops, I'm drunk . . . don't tell the owner I said that. But read what I have to say tomorrow. All of you . . . you'll see how I feel about our guest of honor."

In the early hours of the morning Maria whispered, "Her breasts are bigger than before. I wouldn't have thought it possible." She laughed against the pillow.

"Yes, I noticed. . . . I'm only human. . . ."

"She'd give anything to have you in bed. . . ."

"Maria, you shock me!"

"Would you like to make love now?"

"It's been a long time."

"I doubt if you've forgotten how. You know what they say, it's like riding a bicycle. You never forget. . . ."

"Is this the way people talk in Carlsbad?"

"I'm afraid so."

An hour later she lay on her back, the bedclothes damp with their sweat, her hair plastered wetly across her forehead.

"Alves, this doesn't mean we've decided what to do."

"I understand that. We'll wait and see what happens."

"I was right, though, wasn't I? Just like riding a bicycle. . . ."

They laughed and then they went to sleep.

The next morning over breakfast they read *A Provincia de Angola,* the editor's paper:

> There is no need to introduce Engineer Alves Reis. Angola has for a long time owed him signal service, whether as a competent public servant with a magnificent record, whether as an enterprising colonialist, having set up, among others, the South Angola Mining Company to exploit the rich gold and copper deposits in the Mossâmedes interior. He is a man of action, with unusual vision, full of decision and initiative. He has unshakable faith in the great future that is in store for Angola, provided that the vast resources it contains are fully exploited.

Speaking for Alves Reis, Hennies announced that Engineer Reis, as the Angolans still liked to think of him, and his bank were interested in buying local properties for hard foreign currencies.

"My God, they'll lay siege to the hotel," Chaves growled happily. "The Banco Ultramarino has no facilities for transferring money abroad. My own lawyer tells me he's got half of his family in Lisbon—and they're starving because he can't get any money to them!" He shook his head in amazement at the predicaments people find themselves in, having managed it once or twice himself. "Why, you'll be able to buy as much of Angola as you wish. . . ." Alves smiled.

For days the lines of desperate businessmen and plantation owners clogged the lobby of the hotel. The electric fans revolved slowly overhead; damp handkerchiefs fluttered like flags of surrender before dripping, worried, hopeful faces. Smoke filled the air, the restaurant was always full, flies buzzed. Men in dark dust-covered suits arrived from the back country.

Alves and Hennies saw whom they could, offering welcome ice water, a shade-darkened room, brandy and cigars, fair offers for what they found suitable. Money changed hands, notes were signed, colonialists made ready to return to Lisbon with more money for the economy there, while Angola found itself being propped up as never before by one man.

Alves bought two enormous sugar plantations located on the right bank of the Quanza River, below Luanda. He was piecing together great parcels of land, building his own empire. Working on a map of Angola that covered an entire tabletop, he shaded in the areas he was acquiring. He used a pink pencil. "My own rose-colored map." Hennies blinked. "Never mind." Alves laughed. "Only a Portuguese would understand."

With his new acquisitions added to their heavy interests in the great Quissama plantation adjoining the Amboim Company estate, he owned a million and a quarter acres of the most fertile land on the planet. He was now free to build his own docks and ship on the Quanza, rather than depend entirely on the railway to Luanda.

In Mossâmedes he received a hero's welcome, which he was beginning to expect as his due, and received the news from Hennies that they were being kept under close surveillance.

"Why would anyone do that? We're hardly sneaking about . . . parades, official dinners, announcements in the press."

"No, I'm not joking. I noticed it early on and spoke with that old friend of yours, the police captain. He said I was right! Eagle-eye Hennies! He came to Mossâmedes. We're dining with him."

Curious but not overly concerned, Alves brought it up early in the evening.

"I only tell you this because of our long-standing friendship," explained the police captain, a slight, balding man who looked fragile but happened to be strong as two oxen. "Strictest confidence, Alves. . . . Officially I've said nothing.

There are two detectives and they are under orders from the Colonial Ministry—"

"The Colonial Ministry? What in the world are they about?" Alves gestured expansively, full of innocence.

"I don't know. But they have the authority to make copies of your cables."

"All the cables are coded. They must be having quite a time!" Hennies observed.

There was, Alves decided, no cause for alarm. Obviously his vigor in pursuing Angolan financial power was threatening someone with government connections, quite possibly the Banco Ultramarino itself. It must surely have been an uncomfortable assignment, since the detectives weren't among those invited to join the Reis party in the private railway car.

*   *   *

By mid-November they had returned from the countryside. Maria's spirits were high; she felt a oneness with Angola. They had tracked back over paths they had taken years before, spent evenings with old friends. At times she thought of Alves less as a new Ivar Kreuger and more as the man she had married. Her great eyes seemed to be evaluating him, and he found he didn't mind. He also found himself seeking her approval, making small jokes, flirting with her. Back in Luanda, there were a few press announcements he left to Hennies; the High Commissioner of Angola hosted a ceremonial farewell dinner on their last evening.

Flowers were everywhere, as were flags, men in white ties and ladies in their finest long gowns. Maria's diamonds reflected the candlelight; she glowed like a captive star at the head table. There were speeches, of course. The High Commissioner introduced the guest of honor, laying it on a bit thick in Alves' view, but then how often did the man have such a chance?

"It has been said of our old and dear friend that Engineer Reis is the savior of Angola," he said in a slightly trembling voice. "And I am certainly not the man to gainsay the opinion of the multitudes!"

The cries of approval rang around the hall, echoes from the past. Alves smiled to himself; he'd heard it all before. This time he would try not to spill his glass when he spoke.

Finally Alves held up his hands to quiet them down.

"You are all much too kind, my friends," he said. "After all, I am one of you, formed by Angola in my youth, now returned to repay my debt. . . . And how can I repay the debt? How I have wrestled with that question. With your help we undertake now nothing less than the creation of the Angola of tomorrow!"

That brought another tidal wave of applause and shouting. It occurred to him that he really should be running for something, but what was there? He had it all, more than any plebiscite could grant him.

"New communities will spring up and prosper. . . . Well-equipped ports will receive the ships that now despise and flee from Angolan waters . . . modern railroads will cut through virgin territory, bringing wealth to the interior of this vast land . . . jungles will be tamed to allow settlers to draw the maximum wealth from the rich land where healthy children will come with their parents to strengthen the name of Portugal in Angola!"

It was, he thought, a somewhat more polished piece of work than that other speech so long ago. The thrill he received from his audience, as they rose, their hands blurring with their faces as they applauded, was not quite so heady now, but it would do, yes, it would suffice. He put his arm around Maria's shoulders, drew her to him. He felt—he had to admit it—he felt like a king; and he felt as if he deserved it.

As the party boarded the German steamer *Adolf Woerman* they were cheered by the largest crowd Luanda had ever produced. The docks were seething, the streets leading to the harbor clogged. The Hispano-Suiza was driven up a ramp leading into the hold. They cheered the car.

Chaves and Terreira saw them on board. "You must return soon," Chaves said. Promises were made, hands shaken. Chaves and Terreira scuttled down the gangplank at the last moment.

"Your subjects," Adolf Hennies remarked. "I've never seen anything like it, Alves . . . not even Kaiser Bill."

"I've done well by Angola," Alves said. He saw the two men who had been following them clinging tiredly to the dockside railing.

"And by Portugal, by God. Who knows what kind of reception you'll get in Lisbon. What you've done for

Angola you've also done for Portugal," Hennies barked emphatically. "This is just the beginning."

The first night out Maria brought him a tiny leather bag with a drawstring pulled tight.

"A present," she said, watching him pull it open.

"Why, it's a gold chain."

"For your thunderbolt," she said. "The leather thong is frayed, almost worn through. Take it as a keepsake of your return to Angola."

"Thank you," he said. She came to him and he held her.

"Have we made any decisions about ourselves?" she asked, easing away. The ship's power throbbed faintly in the bulkheads.

"I don't know. Have we? It's as much your decision as mine." He fingered the chain, the gold warm to the touch.

"I've enjoyed being with you here, moving along through the past, remembering. But if you are in love with another woman . . ."

"I love you," he said. "But you are even newer to me than Greta is. You've become someone else since I met Greta. . . ."

"Because, not since. She made me see what a dependent child I'd been. I must continue to lead my own life. You'd have to accept that."

"One of those 'modern marriages' people keep talking about?"

"I'll still be your wife. And you can do as you wish about Greta. It will be no concern of mine."

"That's a little grim, isn't it? For us? It's not one thing or the other."

"It's quite common, I understand, among the very rich. Men with their mistresses, women with their lovers . . ."

"I'm not sure that will work for us." He slipped the amulet over his head and snapped the leather with a quick jerk. He began threading the gold chain through the tiny hole. He wondered what his grandmother would have thought about modern marriages.

"Well, what other answer is there?"

"To go back the way we were."

"You mean give away all the money, your newfound power, walk away from the house and come back to Angola and begin again?"

"No, of course I don't mean all that. I mean go back

just being happy the way we were . . . the two of us, the children, the way we were before it all got so complicated." He slipped the chain back over his head and glanced at the amulet, remembering his grandmother.

"We'll think of something." Maria smiled as he tucked the chain inside his shirt. "It's a long voyage home."

* * *

Smythe-Hancock had spent the year watching the rise of Alves Reis from his dark, nasty little office in the Baixa. The higher Reis's shooting star had climbed, the more of a worm's-eye view he'd had. He hated his perspective and he loathed the triumph of Alves Reis. To make matters considerably worse and to save his job, he had given up trying to warn Sir William off his dealings with Reis's syndicate. Many was the night he'd gone sleepless, sweating out his frustration in his narrow bed, wondering first how to save Waterlow the disaster and disgrace he was certain lurked ahead. . . . Then, he'd turned to thinking of Reis himself and the syndicate he headed—how might he bring it down, reveal it for the fraud it had to be. He had begun losing his hair early in the year; he noticed that his forehead seemed a good deal higher than it had ever been before. And he knew bloody damned well it was the fault of Alves Reis. In fact, almost everything in his life that wasn't going well could be laid at Reis's door.

Sir William had made it abundantly clear that he wanted to hear no more from his man in Lisbon. And without Sir William's ear there was little hope for advancement, for the final transfer to London, which had been Smythe-Hancock's ambition for years. He'd spent his years in the world's backwaters, he'd put in his time, he'd done a good job. Sir William had sent him letters of congratulations, and Alves Reis had made them worthless. Asking for a promotion was hopeless, ridiculous. . . .

Alves Reis! For an Englishman to be brought low by such an insignificant little man, a Portuguese confidence man! It was too much. . . . He'd always seen through Reis, always, even back there in that African hellhole. An Oxford man! The idea would have been laughable if it weren't so obscene. He could hear his hair falling out, strand after strand, floating through the air, clanking on the floor.

How had the man fooled so many important people for so long? He'd watched Reis in the hotel bar the night the word had gotten out about the stress tables. The man hadn't known a stress table from a road map. He'd seen that in Reis's eyes, and he'd bet a packet that the bloody damned locomotive would never make it across that bridge. The real engineers had assured him that it was an impossibility.

Yet the High Bridge had held.

The man was some sort of magician, obviously. He surely wasn't an Oxford man and he wasn't an engineer, either. At best he was some sort of tinkerer—a man who could make the odd contraption work, nothing more.

But in Angola Reis had been simply an irritant. In Lisbon he'd been revealed as a minor swindler and packed off to the Oporto jail. That should have been an end to it. A blot on the man's copybook that should have proved indelible. That was the English way, by God! When he thought about it his hands shook, his stomach hurt, his hair fell out, and he took the pills his doctor had prescribed.

The man had nine lives. How could he leave the Oporto jail, come back to Lisbon a known criminal and within a few weeks be an intimate business associate of men like Camacho Rodrigues and Mota Gomes? On the face of it, it was impossible.

Was there anyone in Portuguese financial circles more respected than Camacho? Hardly. But why would he have anything to do with a man like Alves Reis?

Yet, there it was. And he, Smythe-Hancock, Waterlow's man in Lisbon—he was forbidden to discuss Reis's enterprises with Camacho. Or with Sir William!

And the man's success was apparently limitless. Everyone was mesmerized. . . . But why? He couldn't pick up a newspaper without reading more pathetic drivel, praising Alves Reis and his new Bank of Angola and Metropole. The savior of Portugal, the hero of Angola. Madness!

But Smythe-Hancock had not let his personal feelings blunt his methodical intelligence. He had kept a file of newspaper clippings, rumors, his own random doubts, everything he could ferret out about Alves Reis. Friends in Angola kept him fortified with news from that end. Carefully piecing it all together, he reached several conclusions, two of which were that—incredible as it seemed—the presumptuous little bastard was out to buy control of both Angola and the Bank of Portugal.

Smythe-Hancock spent his days working out the best chances of bringing Portugal to its senses.

Finally, Smythe-Hancock was ready to act.

Alfredo da Silva was Portugal's leading vegetable-oils entrepreneur and, like most self-made men, he was jealous of his wealth and power. Smythe-Hancock made an appointment, pressing the urgency and importance of the meeting.

"I come to alert you," Smythe-Hancock said, sweating with the excitement of finally moving against Reis, "to warn you. Senhor Alves Reis and his Bank of Angola and Metropole are challenging your interests—buying up plantations in Angola. It's all beneath the surface, but I've made a study of Reis and his bank . . . they're acquiring the plantations through dummy companies they control. If you don't act soon, it could be too late. . . ."

"This is all very interesting," da Silva said, the leather chair beneath him creaking as he situated his great beefy backside, "but I must ask, what has it to do with you? You come to me with this urgent tip . . . but why? Long ago I gave up hope of ever finding the good Samaritan."

"A natural question, of course, and easy to answer. Alves Reis is a convicted criminal, a known swindler, and he is making fools out of the government, the Bank of Portugal and everyone else who cares about Portugal! I've known him for years and he'll never change. . . . May I confide in you, Senhor da Silva?"

"It seems to me you already have," da Silva said, tapping a gold pencil on the blotter before him. "Please continue."

"Reis, through his bank, is buying Angola. . . . Buying it!"

Da Silva's pencil stopped in mid-air. "Perhaps you had better go through this with me again. And let me have my secretary take it down." He pressed a button built into his desk. "If what you say is true, there are steps to be taken— the man is a menace. . . ."

Two hours later, having perused Smythe-Hancock's files at considerable length, da Silva personally called his close friend Pereira da Rosa, owner of Lisbon's most aggressive morning daily, *O Seculo,* the standard fare of which was scandalmongering and exposés. Fifteen minutes later

Smythe-Hancock and da Silva were in da Rosa's immense office with its heavy draperies, family portraits, glass-enclosed bookcases, heavy leather furniture. The newspaper owner was a compact, bouncy little man who dyed his gray hair jet black and wore a whalebone corset. He spoke in short bursts because the corset kept him perpetually breathless.

Da Silva made the introductions and told the story to da Rosa, turning it over at crucial moments to the Englishman, who had all the facts on call. Da Rosa listened carefully, puffing his way through an occasional interruption that kept him on the right track.

"This will make a great front-page story!" He bounded out from behind his desk, gesticulating, drawing the front page in the air before his visitors. " 'What's going on? *O Seculo* wants to know!' Say, you haven't gone to anyone else with this, I hope."

Da Silva looked hurt. "You ask me, your oldest friend?"

"My editor would have had to ask anyway. So, you've sold me on the idea. . . . There's skullduggery afoot, and *O Seculo* will dig it out. . . . Another chance to serve Portugal. . . ."

"You're a saint, Alfredo," da Silva cried, turning to Smythe-Hancock. "He's a saint! What did I tell you?"

"You're doing a great service to Portugal," Smythe-Hancock said.

"I'll get my two best men on it yet today. We'll start on the bank itself, dig into what's been going on. . . ." He was rubbing his hands together, hopping from one foot to the other. He reminded Smythe-Hancock of a pit bull aching to be set loose.

Four days later Smythe-Hancock read page one of *O Seculo* with a deep sense of satisfaction.

WHAT'S GOING ON?
O SECULO WANTS TO KNOW!

We are told that persons connected with a certain banking house that was greatly discussed even before its creation are seeking to acquire various businesses in Angola and Mozambique. Various landowners have refused to sell without first getting clear information about the object of the proposed deal so that they might be certain that such sales would not mean immediate or remote danger to national sovereignty. It is known that the group, through various intermediaries, has already purchased several thousand shares of the Bank of Portugal and that the shares have risen greatly in value as a result. . . . Persons, some of them in official places, have been acquiring buildings, some in the name of close relatives and others—when only weeks before they had no visible means of fortune! The expenditures in these acquisitions is believed to exceed $3,500,000. . . . And we ask how can such things be?

It even appears there are friends in the government who are interested in the organization of the mystery bank. On its Board of Directors are persons who if well known, as some of them, are visible in circles other than banking. . . . There is talk of their acquiring great newspapers here and abroad and launching new papers in the market! All this is suspicious and alarming, in a country such as ours with a vast and coveted colonial domain. What's going on? The nation must be told!

The hounds had indeed been set.

Two other papers joined in the sport the next day.

At government headquarters the Minister of Finance, who had grown increasingly concerned about the large purchases of Bank of Portugal stock by the new Bank of Angola and Metropole, called in the Inspector of Banking Commerce, Luis Viegas, and ordered him to find out discreetly what was going on out there in the financial jungle.

Viegas objected. He wanted to go slowly, let the matter develop naturally, but the Minister insisted, slamming his fist on the desk. Viegas swallowed his pride and set off to see José Bandeira, managing director of the Bank of Angola and Metropole.

The next day, at three o'clock in the afternoon, Managing Director Bandeira welcomed Viegas to his office at the bank's main office in the Rua do Crucifixo. It was a pleasant enough meeting, Viegas clouding his real purpose behind an official explanation implying that all Portuguese banks were undergoing a routine annual check. As a newly chartered bank, Viegas explained deferentially, the examination into the Bank of Angola and Metropole's investments would be a mere formality. Still, he would have to examine the books and the portfolio of investments himself.

José placed everything at Viegas' disposal, without giving it a second thought. After all, Viegas had gladly approved the bank's charter, and one of his relatives was a director of the bank.

What was bothering José were the newspaper attacks. He cabled Marang to inquire through any of his Dutch informants in Lisbon as to the financial condition of *O Seculo*. If the ownership was in any difficulty, they might consider selling the paper. Marang cabled back with a question of his own: Was the bank's board contemplating a libel suit against the newspapers? José replied that he felt it was better to wait and see how far they went. The fact was they hadn't mentioned any names yet.

On November 25, *O Seculo* named names:

The notorious Bank of Angola and Metropole has begun its maneuvering. Where has it obtained the millions with which it is flooding the country? Nobody knows. From Holland, say some. . . . From German banks, assure others. . . . None of the persons in the new organization is known in the financial world. But the public at large knows them, suspects them and has begun murmuring in protest. There is talk of Portuguese diplomats who have been intermediaries in the deal, and there is talk of the purchase of buildings for millions of escudos in the names of relatives. . . .

Names are being mentioned, and everything makes us believe that Portugal has fallen prey to a gang that is getting ready to devour the nation's heart. The Bank of Angola and Metropole is not wasting its time. It is maneuvering, intriguing and corrupting. . . . It has made a tiger's leap on colonial companies and seized some of them. . . . It has turned on the bank of Portugal and is harpooning its shares. . . . It wants to lead us first to the loss of our colonies and then to that of our independence!

Another instance. Someone came to *O Seculo* yesterday to obtain information on the paper's financial situation, which, we were told, was requested by an Amsterdam firm. What they wanted to know was whether we were in financial difficulties, if we wanted to issue stock or even if we were willing to give up our position as shareholders. Who was the instigator of this démarche?

The Bank of Angola and Metropole—there is a band of vultures hovering over the land, coveting every position of leadership and control of finances and of politics. And control of the press. It buys up everything that is for sale and that may be useful to it.

To be on the safe side José cabled Alves aboard the S. S. *Adolf Woerman* telling of the newspaper attacks, which still struck him as nothing more than sensation-mongering that would soon die down.

Only *O Seculo* persevered on November 26:

The plan of the A & M capitalists is obvious. Angola is on the brink of ruin. There could be no better time for a peaceful penetration. What was worth ten thousand a few years ago can now be bought for less than half that figure. . . .

Germany will be entering the League of Nations soon. It will certainly want colonies. Those she had before the war will not be restored to her. International public opinion is being prepared so that Germany may be quieted down and not be a spoilsport in the international concert—at the expense of Portuguese colonial dominion.

On November 27 *O Seculo* commented on the lack of normal activity at the Bank of Angola and Metropole:

It makes no discounts, receives no deposits and does not engage in operations peculiar to all banks. . . . Money here costs 12, 15 even 18%, yet a bank that seeks our market spurns this interest but uses 12 million escudos ($600,000) to buy and immobilize Bank of Portugal shares that fetch a mere 3%. . . . There is something rotten in this!

José responded by stepping up the conversion of the five-hundred-escudo notes into hard foreign currencies—pounds, florins and francs. His brother Antonio wired José on November 29 that the crisis was not only refusing to blow over but had in fact reached all the way to The Hague. The Ministry of Foreign Affairs had just recalled him to Lisbon for urgent consultation. It came through the wire that Antonio didn't like it a damned bit.

Throughout the *O Seculo* campaign there had run a thread of insinuations about a Portuguese diplomat who now drove a new sports car and hosted elaborate receptions abroad—even though only a year before he had complained bitterly in a letter to a Lisbon daily about the inadequate pay of a Portuguese diplomat abroad. There was no doubt as to the identity of the diplomat in question. The whole thing weighed heavily on José as he waited for Antonio's arrival on the Sud Express.

José met him, and they quickly retired to one of José's estates outside Lisbon.

"The situation is serious," Antonio said, composing himself over a fine cognac, "but in fact my position is strong. But the contracts—the magic documents between the Bank of Portugal and your syndicate—you have retained them, is that right?"

"Yes, they're quite safe. A friend is holding them for us in Paris." José smiled reassuringly.

"Well, those documents are the key to everything," Antonio said. "The ace in the hole, you might say. . . . It's odd," he mused, "that all this uproar stems directly from a struggle for power within the Bank of Portugal. You fellows—and me, for that matter—we're taking all the public abuse and it's Rodrigues and Gomes at the bank who are giving us all our orders." He cast a wary, appraising eye at José. "You fellows *are* agents of the bank?"

"Of course," José said. "Nothing has changed. The bank just wants to keep it all secret. What we're going through now is the price we pay for the advantages we've gained by our connections to the bank—inconvenience, nothing more."

Antonio nodded. "Well, that's good to know. Of course, my position is unassailable. The last thing I'm going to do is come whimpering to my Minister. . . . Outrage is a far more fitting response to all this nonsense."

At breakfast the next morning Antonio produced a letter he had just written. It was directed to the Ministry of Foreign Affairs. After noting that he was at the Minister's disposal, he concluded:

> *The campaign in* O Seculo *is even more scandalous in that it has brought in my name, too. Although the campaign is anonymous and does not cite a single charge, fact or document, I demand a complete inquiry into my activities in Holland, an inquiry designed to discover if I directly or indirectly ever intervened, informed or influenced anyone regarding the acquisition abroad of the capital for the Bank of Angola and Metropole or any other act related to that bank.*

"That, on the whole," Antonio remarked, "should get things in the proper perspective."

* * *

For almost two weeks Smythe-Hancock had awaited each day's newspapers with excitement. Over lunch, cocktails and dinners with business associates he kept his eyes and ears open to the slightest clue as to the Bank of Angola and Metropole situation. His role was always that of a listener, prodding his informants just enough to keep them talking. An unguarded moment of loquaciousness could easily set Sir William off again and cost him his job.

But his obsession persisted, growing. Alves Reis was a crook, a fraud; therefore, whatever he was doing had to be crooked. But Portuguese society was essentially corrupt, inferior, un-English; consequently the scoundrel had been allowed to rise again from the ashes of his own dishonesty. Along the way he was responsible for Sir William losing faith in one of his most faithful employees—namely, Smythe-Hancock. Now that Reis was obviously on the far side of the law once again one couldn't trust the newspaper attack to bring the man down. Everyone discounted much of what appeared in a press so dependent on scandal. No, the newspaper campaign was only the first step.

Obviously he had no *right* to the money printed for him. But the money was not counterfeit. So where was the crime? Where . . . ?

Unable to risk his own career by entering the matter publicly, Smythe-Hancock finally struck upon a plan. He would use someone else as his weapon.

Assis Camilo was a director of the Bank of Portugal who had steadfastly fought the Banking Council's granting of a charter to Alves Reis's new bank. Campos e Sa was a canny, naturally suspicious officer of the Bank of Portugal. Together they seemed to Smythe-Hancock just the right men for his plan. He called Camilo with an urgent request for a private meeting, requesting that Camilo's friend Campos e Sa might also wish to be present. The deeper he could draw the Bank of Portugal into the matter of Alves Reis, the more determined its officers would be to destroy him.

"The fact of the matter is simply this," Smythe-Hancock told them when they gathered in Camilo's locked office. Camilo, a reed-thin man with a long black cigar permanently protruding from his mouth, and Sa, dapper and cologned, with a tiny diamond stickpin centered in his black tie, leaned forward to hear the Englishman, who was almost whispering. "My most reliable sources have told me that there are possibly thousands of counterfeits in Oporto—the five-hundred-escudo notes, the da Gamas. Naturally you can understand my personal concern. . . . These alleged counterfeits are of Waterlow notes. There are even rumors that Reis is bringing them in from a Russian source!" He watched their mouths drop, Camilo's cigar wobbling dangerously on his pendulous lower lip. "As you will understand, I must remain most discreet and anonymous in all of this. Waterlow must not be mentioned."

"Of course," Camilo said. "Campo, get Pedroso. I want him to hear this."

"An excellent idea," Smythe-Hancock said. Pedroso was the bank's expert on counterfeits, the man who had during the summer pronounced the notes genuine during the first round of rumors. He was tireless and precise, proud of his expertise, just the sort of man Smythe-Hancock wanted digging around in Reis's business.

Once he had gone through the story again, Smythe-Hancock took Camilo aside. "There's no need to bring Rodrigues or Gomes into this yet, agreed?"

"By all means. We'll go to them when we've got ironclad evidence." Camilo gestured vaguely in the direction of Oporto to the north. "We'll go to Oporto tonight. I'd like you to come along. . . ."

"I'd be delighted, Director. Anonymously, of course."

"Don't worry. You'll be one of my aides, a lowly assistant." He smiled grimly.

* * *

When the Bank of Portugal deputation met at the station there was a cold wind whistling down the tracks. Smythe-Hancock wore his old Burberry with the collar turned up, a plaid muffler at his throat. Clustered beneath a yellow lamplight stood Camilo, Sa, Pedroso, Dr. Teixeira Direito, who was a Judge of Criminal Investigations and an Inspector of Commercial Banking, and a pair of bureaucratic aides who didn't have much to say. There was little idle chatter. It was a grim mission, fit to match the nasty weather. Smythe-Hancock had a sore throat and sucked alternately on lemon drops and digestive tablets.

On the morning of December 5, a Saturday, Oporto was not only cold but wet. A drenching rain had begun during the night and blew, wind-driven, across the gray city in solid sheets. The streets were puddled and empty and everyone had begun coughing. They went first to the central police station, where Camilo and Sa met with the Chief of Police, a middle-aged man with the face of a boxer and the physique of a weightlifter. Using his authority as a director of the Bank of Portugal, Camilo asked that a special police guard be placed around the Bank of Angola and Metropole, allowing no further transactions of any kind. He also suggested that Adriano Silva, the manager, be arrested.

"As you say," the Chief said, pinching his lower lip. He was not uninformed as to the power wielded by the Bank of Portugal, but he ventured a formal question. "With what crime do I charge Senhor Silva?"

Camilo stared coldly at the chief. "With complicity in the forgery of Portuguese banknotes. Do you think that is sufficient, Chief?"

Within the half hour the bank was ringed with uniformed police, and Senhor Silva, walking his dog a block from his home, was arrested and transported to the Oporto jail.

"Now, to da Cunha's, the money changer's." Camilo was taking over, Campos e Sa supporting his every move. "They are the biggest money-changing house in Oporto," Sa whispered to Smythe-Hancock. "We should find plenty of evidence there."

Alfred Pinta da Cunha, spending a leisurely Saturday morning in the office, was drinking a cup of hot coffee and complaining to his secretary about the weather when the bank deputation, led by Camilo puffing on his cigar and the huge Chief of Police sneezing into his fist, burst in on him. Before da Cunha could fully right himself to face the assault, Camilo identified himself and demanded access to the books for purposes of official verification. Before da Cunha was able to think of a good enough objection Camilo had gone on to demand of the Chief a complete and thorough search of the premises for all five-hundred-escudo notes. "Confiscate them," Sa barked at the Chief and his men, "all of them!" Smythe-Hancock leaned against a desk, smiling slightly, trying to fade into his surroundings.

The passage of another hour, filled with much door-slamming and glowering looks from Alfred Pinta da Cunha, revealed a great many of the da Gama notes, old and new. Pedroso had a long table cleared, and marked silence ensued. Da Cunha folded his arms across his chest, frowning at Pedroso, who took a magnifying glass from his briefcase and set about examining the newest of the notes. Pedroso moved methodically from note to note. Finally he carefully restored the magnifying glass to its suede pouch, removed his glasses and looked up at Camilo.

"These notes are genuine," he said. "That is, they are from the same plate as those issued by the Bank of Portugal."

Camilo looked at Smythe-Hancock, who frowned, shrugged. Of course, he had known the notes were good. Waterlow had printed them. But, still, the only thing to do was keep digging.

"You see," da Cunha bellowed, "you see! What do you and your goddam strong-arm men think you're doing? You've not heard the last of this!"

"Oh, shut up, you blowhard!" Camilo rose from a cloud of smoke, thumbs hooked in his suspenders.

He stormed out into the rainy street, followed by the entire battalion of bankers and policemen. They adjourned to the hotel, checked in and convened for lunch. Sa heaved a mighty sigh and pushed his plate away. The bank officials and Smythe-Hancock were at a table by themselves. Sa spoke to his tablemates.

"This could be somewhat embarrassing. We have—without a warrant or any evidence—imprisoned a bank manager who may very possibly be innocent as a newborn babe, and we have ransacked the offices of Oporto's most reputable money changer. . . ." He looked at Smythe-Hancock. "I suggest we compose ourselves and act less impetuously."

"Nonsense!" Camilo cried angrily. "We must take the slippery devils off guard!"

"Excuse me," Dr. Direito interjected mildly, "but we haven't found any forged banknotes."

"Weakhearted, Direito," Camilo said, "that's you. Somebody could steal the national treasury with you on guard. Smythe-Hancock says there are counterfeits in circulation here and by God I'm going to find them!"

"I was reporting only what I have been told," Smythe-Hancock said, "but my informants are reliable. There is definitely something going on here." His throat was getting worse, which took his mind off the pain in his stomach.

Direito took him by the arm as they were leaving the hotel restaurant. "Let's hope your informants are as reliable as you say they are, old fellow." He regarded the Englishman from small, deep-set eyes that gave away nothing of the inner man.

In the street Camilo saw a jewelry store next to the money changer's office: David Pinta da Cunha, Jeweler.

"That's it," he shouted at Sa. "It's the brother!" He broke into a run, crossing the rainswept street, the befuddled Chief of Police at his heels. Smythe-Hancock covered his eyes. My God, he'd turned a madman loose on the citizens of Oporto.

Camilo entered the shop, saw a younger version of Alfred, pointed him out and turned to the Chief. "Seize him! This is where they keep the counterfeits—I knew it was da Cunha, I knew it!" As it had threatened to do all day, the long black cigar slipped its mooring and plummeted to the floor, ashes flying.

David Pinta da Cunha, once he was assured that he had not been set upon by bandits, opened his safe, not wholly certain as to what the Chief intended to find. Camilo had neglected to identify himself, but the small shop was full of wet bankers and policemen: da Cunha had enough to worry about. Direito stood near the doorway with Smythe-Hancock.

"Aha! Da Gama notes!" Camilo was holding up a packet of fresh notes. "We've found them—Pedroso, Pedroso, where are you? Come here, man, get out your glass! Hurry. . . ."

Pedroso waited for calm in the shop, then peered at one note after another. The heat was growing oppressive. Camilo glistened, rain and sweat on his forehead. Smythe-Hancock tugged his muffler away from his throat. Finally Pedroso straightened up and surveyed the waiting faces sadly.

"Gentlemen, these notes are quite genuine. . . ." He waited for the bad news to sink in. "It is absolutely impossible to engrave a forged plate with the same perfection and evenness as the original . . . and these Da Gama notes were printed from the original. There are no exceptions to the rule, and there is no doubt about these notes."

"In this case, you must be mistaken," Camilo said vigorously. "Chief, this David Pinta da Cunha is in league with the forgers—"

"You are sure of this, Director?" the Chief said hesitantly.

"You question me? Arrest this man and confiscate the account books! Mark my words, we'll find our evidence here. . . ." Camilo looked around him. "And that little man over there, the bookkeeper—arrest him, too. We'll get to the bottom of this or my name isn't Assis Camilo, Director!"

Sa nervously caught Smythe-Hancock's eye, shook his head. Direito was already outside, standing out of the rain in the doorway. As Smythe-Hancock passed him, Direito remarked, "We'll be lucky to get out of here without being strung up from a tree. . . ."

They retired momentarily to the hotel lobby, where Camilo paced among the couches and antique chairs. He fixed the impassive Pedroso with a hard look. "You are *sure?* How can you be *sure?*"

"You could be wrong."

"He never has been, however." Sa stared glumly out at the rain.

"We have now sent three men to prison without evidence or warrant," Direito said, hands shoved deep in the pockets of his voluminous raincoat. "I imagine that Alves Reis, if he knew of our exploits since arriving in Oporto, might laugh himself to death. The Bank of Angola and Metropole, whether we like it or not, has exceedingly powerful friends. Let me suggest—before we have any more of Oporto's citizenry thrown into dungeons—that we consider for a moment the consequences of our failing to produce evidence of wrongdoing by the Bank of Angola and Metropole. Let's face it, this bank has most powerful allies in Lisbon. . . . Can you imagine the heights of invective oratory we're going to hear in the Chamber of Deputies? And imagine the editorials in the newspapers. They'll be clamoring about the dictatorial inequities of the Bank of Portugal and its police minions. And they'll completely forget about crucifying Reis and the Bank of Angola and Metropole."

Camilo muttered to himself, casting sour looks at Smythe-Hancock.

"What do you suggest we do, Doctor?" Sa spoke solemnly, looking for a way out. "What do you think?" he said, turning away from the doctor, who merely grinned, toward Smythe-Hancock.

"I'm thinking. My own feeling is that we're up against a kind of crime nobody has ever heard of before . . . but I'm sure it's there."

"Well, if there's nothing amiss here," Camilo said, "you are in a very difficult position. It's because of you we're here at all. That's the truth, gentlemen—it was Smythe-Hancock who came to us with this story." He spat out tobacco leaf and offered his comrades a defiant stare.

Campos e Sa had been quietly flipping through several packets of confiscated banknotes. He looked up, perplexed. "Say, this is strange . . . these notes aren't numbered consecutively, Pedroso, they're all mixed up. . . ." His eyebrows met above his small, pugged nose. "Look at this. Shouldn't they be consecutive since they've come straight from the bank in these neat little packets?"

Camilo was across the intervening distance in two bounds, yelping.

"Aha, let me see." He fumbled the notes out of Sa's hands. "Of course, Pedroso, you fool! Look at them, it's all a mess. . . . The bank never sent them out this way—these are the counterfeit notes! Oh, yes, the engraving is perfect, and why? Because," he crowed, jabbing the air with the cigar in one hand and a packet of banknotes in the other, "because the wily fiends have stolen the plates from Waterlow!"

Pedroso rose, slowly shaking his head. "Calm yourself. . . . I'll take another look."

"You don't understand," Camilo said, gloating, handing over the notes. "I'm telling you they *stole* the plates!"

Pedroso took the notes and went to a lamp, holding them up to the light, smelling them, snapping them tight.

"No, Assia, the notes are good. Stealing the plates wouldn't half do the job. They would also have to steal the exact paper . . . and they would need a machine to number the notes, a machine so rare and expensive that the Bank of Portugal itself has never been able to acquire its own!" He sighed heavily. "No, the notes are good."

"You're wrong," Sa cried, joining Camilo in the realm of pure desperation. "Well intentioned, José, but you are simply unaware of the incredible ingenuities these devils are capable of!"

"Right!" Camilo shouted as if sheer noise would see him through. "We've got to go to the Bank of Angola and Metropole and find the rest of these notes . . . right now!" Pedroso threw up his hands.

Camilo saw to it that the Chief of Police was found, and off they went to the bank, where the guards had been waiting since the morning. Moura Coutinha, the Oporto director of the bank's operations, was picked up at his home and delivered to his own office, having been informed that his manager was already in prison. The director's private safe was ordered opened. It was full of new da Gama notes, all in fresh packets. Camilo fell on them with rapture, throwing them into sacks.

Director Coutinha observed the goings-on with calm detachment. Obviously he had been set upon by maniacs. It would all come to nothing, and a suit for damages might prove immensely profitable.

"Take this man to prison," Sa said to the Chief, whose heart had obviously gone out of the entire enterprise. He did as he was told. Smythe-Hancock sat down in the director's chair, wiped his feverish brow. He knew the notes were good. What could he do next? Reis—the bastard was proving invincible again!

Matters grew worse at dinner. Pedroso gave Camilo and Sa a final warning that they had gone too far and staggered off to bed. At eleven o'clock, with the remainder of the deputation lounging wearily in the hotel bar, the Chief of Police returned. His demeanor as he entered the bar was distinctly menacing. Smythe-Hancock winced over his port.

"All right," he snapped, leaning over their table. "You've had me on a donkey's errand all day. I have arrested several innocent men on fraudulent grounds, looted the offices of a respected businessman and a leading bank. . . . I have just concluded my interrogation of Director Coutinha and that poor devil of a manager, Silva." He paused for effect. "These men are obviously innocent! Upstanding citizens . . . not forgers, not in league with forgers." His voice dropped abruptly to a whisper. "But you may be right about the presence of counterfeiters in Oporto . . . and it is my considered opinion that they may well be employees of the Bank of Portugal itself!"

"What the hell—"

"Shut up!" the Chief thundered at Camilo. "You heard me—I am halfway convinced that there is indeed a conspiracy afoot to deceive the Chief of Police, to imprison innocents and cast suspicion into every corner and a conspiracy of counterfeiters within the bank!" He straightened up, looked down his nose at them. "Now, sleep well. . . . The policemen in the lobby are for your protection, of course. They will remain through the night. And I expect you to have something worth saying tomorrow. We are not fools here, gentlemen, just because this isn't Lisbon!"

Smythe-Hancock felt his hair coming out by the handfuls and his stomach was a fiery furnace. He could feel their eyes turning on him, accusing him more seriously now that the Chief had gotten to the point of threatening them. He retired early, taking the packets of money with him. Something had gone wrong. He had not expected counterfeits, but he had been certain that the application of so much pressure would produce some cracks in the foundations of Reis's Oporto operation.

They watched him go with doleful, unhappy eyes. Dr. Direito alone smiled and nodded. Later, though, while he was shuffling the banknotes about on the bed, there was a knock at the door. It was Campos e Sa in his robe and pajamas, his spectacles sliding down the tiny nose. He was carrying a bottle of cognac.

They sat drinking, staring at the money on the bed.

They dozed in their chairs during the night, the rain falling noisily outside. Campos e Sa woke Smythe-Hancock with his snoring toward six o'clock. It was dark outside. The Englishman began shuffling through the banknotes again, picking them up, peering at them as if a secret was engraved upon each one. He sneezed, kept looking at them note after note.

"Campos! Campos! Wake up, man. . . ."

It was eight o'clock and the world was wet and gray. Smythe-Hancock was staring at two notes, his mouth going dry, his hand shaking.

"What's the matter?" Campos e Sa was coming dimly awake.

"We've got the little bastard!" The veins in Smythe-Hancock's neck were bulging. His head throbbed and his vision blurred. "Look at these notes. Do you see anything odd about them?"

Sa took the notes, adjusted his spectacles after rubbing sleep from his eyes. "Da Gama's face," he muttered, "same as always, little sailing ship, setting sun . . ."

"Look . . . at . . . the . . . numbers," Smythe-Hancock whispered, leaning over his shoulder.

There was a pause. The rain beat down. Smythe-Hancock's heart thudded in his breast.

"Why . . . no, it can't be," the banker said.

"Ah, but it can. The numbers . . . are the same. What we have here are duplicated notes! Proof—absolute proof—of forgery!" He was not quite certain of all the ramifications of what he was saying, but he knew the significance of his discovery.

"We'd better tell the others and call Camacho at once. . . ." Campos e Sa had come fully awake, a smile spreading across his small, neat features. He shook Smythe-Hancock's hand.

"We've got him," Smythe-Hancock whispered. "At last. . . ."

PART THREE

THE
AUTOBIOGRAPHY
OF ALVES
REIS 1966

Good manners required that I meet again with the young American journalist David Herschel in light of the effort he has put into this project of his. Which project, though I'm still amazed by it, is me. He is an enthusiastic young fellow, quite pleasant really, and intent on impressing me with the seriousness of his suggestions. He's succeeded, so far as that goes, but he cannot quite understand my hesitancy to leap in. I suppose he thinks it's a matter of age; and it's a delicate business conveying the vigor I still feel at seventy to a bustling young fellow of thirty or so.

It was a lovely soft October afternoon, and we were sitting outside on the terrace of the Ritz by the pool, with Eduard VII Park across the way, richly green at the top of the Avenue de Liberdade David Herschel had not, I think, been prepared for the gentle beauty of Lisbon, nor for the exceptional splendor of the Ritz. My own preference is still the Avenida Palace. But if I were Herschel's age I suppose I'd stay at the Ritz, too. In any case, it made an exceedingly pleasant spot for an afternoon libation. I took a sip of soda and lime, feeling the sunshine on my face, wishing I didn't have to disappoint him.

"I can't quite bring myself to say yes, I'm going to write the story of my life. . . ." I felt his eyes on me, sensed his frustration. "Forgive me, David, but I find it rather difficult to believe anyone will remember our little scheme—or care, for that matter."

"Nonsense, Alves! In Europe they remember—maybe not the specifics, but Christ, man, they remember the Portuguese banknote—" He stopped short, nervously.

"Ah, go ahead, say it . . . 'scandal.' There's certainly no denying it was a scandal." Ever since he'd arrived in Lisbon to talk with me, I'd been trying to put him at his ease. He saw me in a peculiar light, one I could barely understand, but he was so earnest.

He nodded. We'd spent several hours together and I'd told him most of the story; it had held his interest. Maybe he was right; maybe people would respond to the story. Life takes such ornate, ironic turns. Maybe that's why even now, nearing the end, I enjoy it so much. A slight breeze rippled the water in the pool, moved along the shadowed terrace. "Everybody's going to know the story of Alves Reis. . . ." His enthusiasm shone through each word.

"But it is all ancient history," I insisted one last time. "Forty years ago. We were all different people then. . . . Nobody cares now. That's the way it should be. What do people care about what happened in the Twenties?"

"Everybody I've talked to in Lisbon remembers. The story has been passed on from one generation to the next."

"You don't say," I said, laughing. "You talked with Arnaldo, did you?"

"Well, that estate of his—I damned near got lost looking for it."

"Yes, I know. Arnaldo bought it years ago from José, a very kind gesture. As usual, José needed money. . . . Poor José."

"This Arnaldo—he's the one who quit on you, right? He finally saw me, but he's not a very public man, is he?"

"Well, he's a very wealthy man. He was never a very gregarious sort, and money makes a person even less so, don't you think?"

"Well, he said he would not presume to speak for so great a man as Alves Reis. I would have to ask you."

"He was always a kind, loyal friend."

"And Salazar. . . . I saw him."

"Don't joke with me, David."

"I'm not joking. All it took was the mention of your name. Alves Reis! Doors opened, the Premier could see me after all."

"Incredible. What did he say?"

"He sort of croaked. Said I was wasting my time." Herschel made a face, shaking his head. "Called you a reprobate, a disgrace to the Church . . . licentious. He seemed to think that was the perfect word for you."

Once again I couldn't help laughing. The old man never forgives; he was always the same. How could a man be so sure he was right? If I took politics seriously, with my brilliance and determination, I'd have assassinated the man long ago ... but politics is a fool's game.

"You know, David," I mused, "there are certain scholars who say that Salazar owes everything to me. I'm sure that overstates the case. But there could have been no Salazar without an Alves Reis. Flattering but most regrettable in light of what he has done to Portugal. True or not, David, that has always amused me."

He was straining at the chair as if he wanted to leap about with excitement. "You, Alves Reis, are the heart of Portugal. . . . Mankind deserves to know your story! You've got to put your mind to writing the book. And we've prepared to do it any way you want to do it. You can use a tape recorder, or we can provide you with a full-time secretary. Alves," he said, "we'd be working together every step of the way. . . . What's it gonna be?" He had insisted his publisher had given him the okay, was waiting for word that he'd convinced me.

"I must think about it, David," I said. "I'll give you an answer as soon as I can. But this involves my entire family, many dear friends, and I have to ask myself certain questions. Will anyone be hurt by telling the story again? Will my sons be discomfited by the inevitable notoriety? Would it, in fact, be better to let the past simply swallow the story?"

He gave me a somewhat baleful look. We sat quietly a bit longer, the business part of our meeting clearly completed. Did I know what answer I would finally give him? Yes, I think maybe I did; but I wanted to be sure, to make certain that it truly reflected the way I felt.

We walked to the end of the terrace. Our footsteps echoed on the floor. In the main lobby I saw my son's car pulled up outside waiting for me. He was sitting behind the wheel intent on reading his book. I had finally succeeded in getting him to read P. G. Wodehouse.

Herschel saw me to the car, shook hands, and then, as we were pulling away, I heard his voice calling.

"Alves—one last question! Did you ever see her again?"

I leaned my head out the window; we were driving away. "Who, David?"

His voice sounded hoarse and distant.

"The actress, Greta Nordlund—did you ever see her again?"

I called back to him, couldn't be sure whether he heard me, and then he was gone, out of sight as we turned the corner and headed out along the park. My son was a good driver, and I leaned back, only half conscious of Lisbon passing. Herschel's questions had set me thinking, for better or worse. It was all coming back to me, echoes from across the gulf of time. . . .

* * *

When they came to get me at the harbor I was improvising an appropriate response and, all things considered, I don't regret the way I handled it. It was the sixth of December, 1925, a sad and rainy winter morning. The old S. S. *Adolf Woerman* was anchored in the bay at Cascais, awaiting the pilot boat. Through the fog and mist I saw that familiar stretch of beach that had been the setting for so many enjoyable moments. It was six in the morning. I was standing at the rail wondering what the future held for Maria and me when I noticed a boat coming toward us across the bay. As they drew closer I heard my name called. Some friends had come to warn me that handcuffs awaited me in Lisbon. They suggested I flee.

It all seemed so absurd, particularly in light of our recent triumphs in Angola. From that to this, well, it struck me as exceedingly unlikely. But the story they told had the ring of truth. An investigation into the affairs of my bank in Oporto had turned up counterfeits in the vaults. There was also a warrant for Hennies.

Once the boat had departed, Hennies, who had joined me on deck to hear the news, turned to me with a weary smile, adjusted his monocle and said, "Well, it was too good to last, old man. We'd better get out of here. Every great man knows when to make a strategic withdrawal."

"But, Adolf, I have committed no crime. I refuse to let myself become the sacrificial goat just because my friends at the Bank of Portugal lost to the other faction."

There was, I fancied, a twinkle of recognition in his eyes. I suspect it was dawning on him just how well I had laid my defenses.

"Wouldn't it be better to continue the fight and help your friends from abroad?"

"No, I must stay and fight," I said calmly. My mind, however, was racing. "I have photographic copies of the contracts and all the supporting evidence I need to prove that I was *ordered* to carry out the banknote issues by the governor and vice-governor of the Bank of Portugal."

"Alves, there isn't much time to sort this out. But you must listen to me. . . . Admiralty lawyers have an expression—peril point, when you pass the point at which you cannot recover from your own peril. Damn it, if you wait until they come and arrest you, you'll be bloody well past the peril point. . . . You'll have to prove your innocence from a jail cell! You can avoid the peril simply by coming away with me and fighting from Paris or Berlin."

I was adamant. Perhaps it was vanity. And anger, too. Here they were, coming to arrest me for no more than what the Bank of Portugal, with governmental approval, had been doing ever since the turn of the century—putting some new money into the economy. The only difference was that I knew what to do with it, for the betterment of both Portugal and Angola as well as for myself. But I wasn't one of them: I had to go to jail. Well, there was going to be a fight.

Hennies was in an altogether different position. It made good sense for him to get out. Once they had him in jail, God only knew what they would start digging up. He had a past of extraordinary complexity, and it wouldn't bear scrutiny. He wisely made a deal with the German ship's captain. For a small cash consideration he arranged to leave the ship on the pilot boat at seven. He had with him a large cash reserve, letters of credit and a very old passport. He was a remarkable man, old Adolf. I wished him luck and went to our cabin to tell Maria what was going on.

The new Maria took it well. We had grown closer again, but neither of us was clear about the future. I missed Greta, and Maria was not at all sure she wished to return to Lisbon in my shadow. She was no longer dependent on me to see her through. I thanked God just then that she was as she was. There were no tears. She listened carefully as I told her what she must say in the future—lies, yes, but crucial to the defense I was already planning in detail. She would have to attest at all times that Camacho Rodrigues and Mota Gomes had dined at our home, all the secret meetings they attended in my library at the Menino d'Ouro.

"And," I cautioned her, "you must recount these tales with conviction." She nodded. She understood.

At various times I've asked myself, when did she realize the fact of my crime? In Paris, when she found the fake stationery? On the S. S. *Adolf Woerman?* I never asked her.

In any case, I kissed her goodbye, told her to give the children my love and handed her over to Adolf for the trip to shore. I wasn't sure when I'd see her again, but I had no doubt that it would be soon. After all, there were limits in Portugal to holding a man, and with the case I had there really wasn't anything to worry about.

The police came on board at nine o'clock and I was waiting for them, trunks packed, freshly bathed, talcumed, cologned. I wished there was a fresh flower for my lapel. I was optimistic.

On shore they took me to a police car. There was no need for handcuffs, and they treated me with respect, as if they were embarrassed by what they were doing. I sat alone in the rear seat. The car moved slowly through the rain, passing the waterside cafés. Looking out through the streaked window, I saw Adolf sitting inconspicuously by himself, drinking coffee and reading a newspaper. The *Adolf Woerman* rode quietly past the quayside, a ghost ship in the fog. It wouldn't be leaving until its wealthy German traveler was back on board.

I didn't find out until later that I was arrested on purely trumped-up charges stemming from the Bank of Portugal idiots in Oporto calling the Lisbon police on Saturday! It wasn't until nearly noon on Sunday, three hours after my arrest, that Smythe-Hancock found the first counterfeit.

I was taken to the civil governor of Lisbon and then by order of Dr. Crispiniano da Fonseca, the head of the Criminal Investigation Department, I was transferred to the questioning cell of the Pampulaha precinct, where I would be questioned by Dr. Fonseca on the morrow.

My spirits took a resounding fall. It reminded me too much of the Oporto jail. The horrible hole I was thrust into poisoned every decent instinct in my heart. The damp, infected and morbid atmosphere of a cell with no light and no air revealed the inhumanity of the Republic. If such methods were to be used to wrench my secret from me . . . well, it stiffened my resolve not to surrender.

That was when I began to commit my greatest crime—

I would not give up. My blood was at the boil, sitting there in my best suit in that wretched stinkhole. How curious fate is! If they had treated me like the Hero of Angola, the greatest financial genius in Portugal, how much trouble everyone might have been saved. . . .

But life develops its own rhythms, as I have come to learn over these forty years. Scandal was going to be my revenge, and I coolly, quite calmly, began to conceive an all-out-attack—on innocent men, yes, innocent in this instance, but hardly innocent in any larger moral sense. The governor and vice-governor of the Bank of Portugal, the High Commissioner of Angola, the politicians—and I wanted to drag them all down in the wake of Alves Reis.

That is, *if* I were about to go under. . . . And if I were to survive, well, somebody else would have to pay up. It would have to be Camacho Rodrigues, Mota Gomes and their flunkies. In this manner, occupied with these less than uplifting thoughts, I passed the hours on my filthy cot.

It was late that afternoon that Campos e Sa got the word to Camacho. By then they had found several counterfeit notes.

The next day, Monday, the Bank of Portugal wired all their branches that all holders of the Vasco da Gama notes could exchange them for new notes of a different face. Camacho wired Sir William Waterlow that falsifications had been discovered; an expert from London was required. On Tuesday Sir William wired that a deputation from Waterlow was preparing to leave for Lisbon.

While people gathered at banks all over Portugal to wait in exchanging lines, the rumors flew in considerable profusion: the Bank of Portugal itself was involved in the counterfeiting scheme and several directors were already on their way to jail . . . or it had been a German plot to acquire Portugal's colonies . . . the notes were imported from Russia. . . . With each telling the rumors grew. In Lisbon and Oporto there were riots at the banks.

Incredibly enough, I had not yet begun my campaign.

* * *

Under the law I could be held under suspicion for a total of eight days; I might legally be held incommunicado only forty-eight hours. In my case the laws were a mockery, no better than a police state whether it was called a republic or not. I was held a week without recourse to a lawyer. I knew nothing of Maria or José. Had he been arrested? Were Hennies and Marang under arrest?

Most people have never spent time in prison. They do not know precisely what it is like, but for the clever and resourceful fellow, many things are possible. Once I was removed from the interrogation quarters, I found myself in a more commodious cell, still poorly ventilated but not entirely uninhabitable. I still had the contents of my trunk from the ship, and I made the best of it. Though I was being held without external communications, the quick arrests of Camacho and Mota Gomes cast me in a new, somewhat more favorable light. Thinking it possible I might indeed be innocent, my jailors made certain amenities available to me. Bearing my bank draft, one of them went shopping to furnish my cell as I wished. I was also allowed paper, pens and other normal office supplies.

I was so indignant at the complete disregard of my rights as a Portuguese citizen that I began to fight them on their own level. Given my office supplies and confidence, I falsified documents and letters, including receipts allegedly signed by Camacho and Mota Gomes. I knew their signatures as well as I knew my own. With a few well-placed bribes, I had some smuggled out to The Hague to convince Marang that my story was indeed a true one; others I used on the spot.

I wanted to revenge myself at all costs on a justice that sought the severest punishment for an Alves Reis, while others who had long held positions of power and influence were given *carte blanche* to do with Portuguese laws as they wished. Did I think I could win in the end? It was a very long time ago. . . .

* * *

Dr. Costa Santos, Attorney General of the Republic, was in charge of the investigation. In our interviews he was not a congenial fellow, not the chap you'd want investigating you if you'd pulled the greatest swindle since the invention of paper money. In a matter of a few minutes, secure in my little forgery factory, I created a receipt proving that he had once received a twenty-five-thousand-dollar gift from Alves Reis. When I bestowed it upon my captors poor

Dr. Costa Santos was at once removed from the case. A lunatic replaced him.

Dr. José Pinto Magalhaes and I got along famously. He interviewed me in my cell for several hours as soon as he was assigned the job—Chief Investigating Judge. A high-strung gentleman, he was wholly sympathetic to my unhappy plight. He kept telling me he knew an honest man when he saw one, that throughout his career he'd time and again been proven an infallible judge of character. "I've based my entire career on my instincts, young man!" he would say, puffing a great drooping briar, filling my cell with pungent latakia fumes. "Tell me your story. And before I walk out this door I'll tell you whether you're guilty or innocent. How's that for a bargain, eh?"

He was a large man, rotund, with a red rash on the back of his hands, and shoes that squeaked. I remember the rash because he was always picking at it, flaking off bits of dead skin. I remember the squeaking shoes because, as I talked, he was constantly leaping thunderously from his chair—yes, I'd had a pair of very nice club chairs installed in my cell—and pacing about the available space.

When the story was over he fixed me with a burning stare from beneath wild, bushy eyebrows.

"By God, man!" he bellowed, like a great animal rattling his cage. "You're the scapegoat. It's perfectly obvious. Only a madman would have tried what they say you did . . . and you're as sane as I am! Your story is obviously true." He charged about the cell, ashes dribbling from his pipe.

It was the first night I slept soundly.

In the morning—of the day Camacho and Mota Gomes were arrested—Judge Pinto Magalhaes returned to my cell, full of high spirits and eager to get to work on my behalf. Rather to my amazement he insisted on calling me "your excellency." He finally informed me about what was happening to my friends and family. Maria was worried, but he assured me that she would soon be visiting me—later in the day perhaps. José was under arrest, held only one floor away from me, and as a surprise he'd arranged for José to join me in my cell for lunch. He wondered if there were any other comforts he might provide me. I requested that he send over the newspapers dating from the time of my arrest and make sure that henceforth they be delivered daily.

My meetings with Maria and José were unproductive.

She was numb from the turn life had taken, and José was struck virtually dumb by the tidal wave of events. While José possessed a native shrewdness that occasionally served him well, the fact was he simply wasn't very bright. Dapper, handsome, stylish: a bit of a dim bulb, unfortunately. He thought he'd left all this prison stuff behind him, and he was frightened. He could hardly speak. I suppose I should have been thankful he didn't babble.

*   *   *

In the morning I read the *Diario de Noticias* with more than a little interest.

ACT OF INSANITY?

A serious occurrence took place yesterday which can only be attributed to a sudden disturbance in the mind of the Chief Investigating Judge, Dr. Pinto Magalhaes. During an exchange of conversation with a Foreign Ministry Official, the latter asked the judge what he believed was the consensus of opinion in the Bank of Portugal regarding the counterfeit note case. The judge grew suddenly excited and with wild gestures shouted to the Foreign Office official that he had naturally come to make insinuations on behalf of the government. "I am working hard to do my duty, and if I am not doing any more it's because I cannot." He then shouted very loudly that he couldn't stand it anymore. A crowd of people flocked into the room. The judge then dashed over to Dr. Camacho Rodrigues and Dr. Mota Gomes, who were also present, and, grabbing them by their coat lapels, he cried out in a voice that was heard all over the building: "You are under arrest! At my orders!" Then addressing a policeman who was there, the judge said: "Take them to a police station. Right away." The two bank officials were taken to a room next to the Civil Governor's office.

This rapid and unexpected scene left everyone astounded, and the judge's excitement continued. Questioned by some present who pointed out the gravity of his order, the judge said: "You are right! This is really serious. If there is nothing in the investigation that is against these men, I'll put a bullet in my brain."

The newspapers had become obsessed with me. Those sent to my cell included a complete set of *O Seculo*'s attacks on me while I was in Angola. The mere fact of my arrest and imprisonment had not satisfied them. Presumably the name of Alves Reis on the front page sold newspapers.

REIS: SPECIAL STATUS?
It is strange that the judge should have authorized Alves Reis to furnish in princely fashion the jail at the Lapa Police Station in which he is held and which already contains sofas, a dressing table, mirrors, rugs, etc. We don't know whether he installed central heating, but it seems nothing is missing for one who is used to the social amenities and receives frequent visitors. He enjoys a special status that softens imprisonment and encourages him to stand up to all endeavors to force him to speak the truth. Despite his incommunicability Reis knows all that goes on outside, reads the papers and receives the visits of his wife, who is in touch with his lawyer. In the Chief Investigator, Judge Pinto Magalhaes, Reis has found the ideal lawyer for his defense and his great protector. Were it not for him, the mystery of the A and M Bank would have been unraveled long ago.

There was a good deal of truth in the *O Seculo* piece. If anything they underestimated the extent to which the Chief Investigator had fallen under my spell. Shortly after I read of the arrest of Camacho and Mota Gomes the judge told me his version of the events of the previous afternoon and pleaded with me: "I've taken a great step in your behalf. Don't let me down, Alves."

"You are doing a magnificent job, Judge," I said. "Rest easy. You've got the two men who perpetrated this crime. In a few days there'll be irrefutable evidence."

While the judge was quite possibly a certifiable lunatic, he wasn't alone in his belief in me. All over Lisbon and throughout Portugal our cause had caught the fancy of the people. Rallies were held in cities, towns and villages. The people clearly believed I had been the tool of a real but utterly incredible plot concocted by the governor and vice-governor of the Bank of Portugal.

After a week of imprisonment, even with the surroundings I had arranged for myself, I was beginning to feel an immense loneliness. I could hear the shouts outside, at least in my mind, and I was growing acutely aware of the world I was missing and which I had grown to enjoy so much of late. Maria, what to do and feel about her? I was in a quandary. I was growing desperate, however, from want of word from Greta. But there was nothing.

* * *

The Waterlow party arrived on Sunday evening, the thirteenth of December. Normally I would have been limited to whatever was reported in the papers, but I had a special correspondent of my own, the judge himself, who spent the entire week questioning Sir William and his associates. Most of the week's events were carried off in a manner I had thought existed only in the novels of the immortal Wodehouse. Ridiculous confusion and missed appointments between the bank's board and Sir William, mistaken identities and the virtual arrest of Sir William by the judge. Most days he found time to stop by the cell and fill me in on Sir William's difficulties.

"He's all right, for an Englishman," he said one day. "Stuffed shirt, but I don't suppose he's used to dealing with slippery bastards like these bank fellows. The fact is, there are no honest trade practices in our country, and he just got caught in one of the biggest swindles of all. Would you care to join us tomorrow? You might help clear up a few points." I assented and he filled his pipe, settling in for another half hour. He sighed resignedly, laughing softly. "The reporters are waiting nervously each day. They don't want to be somewhere else when I shoot myself!"

My appearance was simple enough. Sir William and I shook hands soberly.

"Sorry to see you in this state, Senhor Reis," he said.

"These things happen," I said. "I have been used by these criminals at the bank, but it will all straighten itself out in the end. I thank you for your concern, Sir William." His face was terribly red. I had the feeling that he was a sick man, whether he knew it or not.

Under the judge's questioning I merely stated that the

contracts on which we had acted were genuine, given me by the governor of the Bank of Portugal. That seemed to satisfy everyone. Sir William's main concern was clearly how much he might be judged to owe the Bank of Portugal, if it came to that. How much was Waterlow going to have to make good on?

Very little was actually decided when the Waterlow party departed a week later. But their presence had caused a stir in the press, and the judge suggested that to avoid a scene in Rossio Station they make their exit under assumed names. Sir William used the name of "Smith," but the judge and some of his investigators saw them off, focusing attention on their much photographed faces and causing a huge onrush of the curious. My one greatest fear at that moment was that Judge Pinto Magalhaes would foul things up so badly that he would be removed from the case. That would be very bad luck for Alves Reis.

On the day Waterlow left Lisbon, *O Seculo* called all of Portugal to the barricades of outrage at the state of things.

THIS IS MORALITY?

We shall say it again: the Angola and Metropole Bank scandal could only be possible in a country such as ours, where misery prevails. In another country of sound morality, or even a less venal morality, the Reises and their ilk could never put into practice such a large-scale plan. This could only happen in a country where rottenness has corrupted all the fibers that make up the honor, the dignity and the prestige of a nation. All of the collective virtues have vanished. All of the basic qualities of the race, maintained by tradition through the centuries, through every calamity and sacrifice, have been throttled and despised by political gangs, greedy for money, no matter how acquired. Then there appeared Marang, a diplomat from a republic of blacks; Bandeira, the South African convict and then the Oporto thief, and then their trunks of 500-escudo notes. Everyone bowed low before them. The gang's success was complete.

Up in Coimbra at the university a pale, intense professor of economics was reading the accounts of the banknote case with more than routine interest. His doctoral thesis had dealt with the evolution of Portuguese currency; he was, at thirty-six, one of the country's leading economists. Not without political ambitions of his own, it had not struck him yet how my difficulties might involve him, Antonio de Oliveira Salazar, personally.

*   *   *

During my first weeks in prison I found the time going quickly, rather to my surprise. There was so much intrigue: the friendship and confidences extended me by Judge Pinto Magalhaes, the messages I was sending to Hennies and Marang in hopes that we might all buttress one another's defenses, the messages Maria would take out to my lawyer, the purchasing of furniture for my cell, the odd relationship developing between José and me, the longing I felt regarding Greta, who had vanished from my life, though I knew perfectly well she was in Paris performing in *Outward Bound*. I suppose at such moments I'd have given ten years of my life to spend whatever remained with her in Paris, having our picnics and walking by the bookstalls along the Seine and riding her horses on the cold, foggy mornings in the Bois de Boulogne. That was the life I wanted.

Maria remained in the Menino d'Ouro. Once again her parents were called on to comfort her. She was not the same helpless child they had always known, and that no doubt made their job easier, though I suppose they also found it sad, too.

One day under a bright, chilly sky José and I walked in the small exercise yard. We were allowed our own clothing, and he was surely the best-dressed prisoner in the world, though in my Parisian suits I was a good deal more stylish than I had once been. Regrettably there was a small round smudge on José's pearl-gray Borsalino.

"It's almost Christmas," he said glumly.

"Happy Christmas," I said.

"We're never going to get out of here. . . ." He was near tears. "Damn it, Alves, I'm so afraid. . . ."

"Of course we are. Trust me, José. Have I ever let you down?"

"No, but I've let you down in so many ways." He kicked

a stone that bounded against the high brick wall. "I never gave you back the money you sent me in Mozambique. . . ." I laughed shaking my head. "I've let you down in more ways than you know. . . ." He couldn't look me in the eye.

"Is that right, José? You want to get it off your chest? You can always confide in me. Remember that, José. Come on," I said, cuffing him on the shoulder. We were being watched by officers behind the glass, smoking cigarettes. "We've been down before and come back."

"Not this time," he said. "I'm going to die in here."

There was no consoling him.

* * *

Much of our finances were locked up tight, but I had taken precautions; there were other accounts elsewhere, under a variety of names. My agents made certain that Maria had plenty of money for the children's Christmas. I tried not to worry about them.

* * *

Judge Pinto Magalhaes visited me on Christmas Day, bringing with him an English plum pudding and hard sauce. Ceremoniously he stuck a candle in the center and lit it. I couldn't help shedding a tear. This man believed in me.

After I'd cut the plum pudding, he withdrew a fine port from his overcoat pocket and we toasted our Savior.

"It makes me think," he said, half to himself. "They're crucifying me, too." He laughed mirthlessly. "There's no doubt about it. They're out to get me."

I leaned back in my deep club chair, sinking a fork into the rich sweet as I listened to his story.

The directors of the bank had been threatening to resign for a week or so, blaming their persecution by the judge. Yesterday they had called a meeting in the directors' room at the bank making sure that the press and the judge were there. They began by steadfastly proclaiming their innocence of any wrongdoing of any kind.

After interjecting the suggestion that the Communists were probably behind it, they got to the real purpose of the meeting. They announced their joint resignations!

By now it was becoming apparent that this was indeed

the most dramatic moment in the bank's history. The group adjourned for the length of time it took to march to a larger meeting room, where a stockholders' meeting had been convened. Pandemonium. Our shares, officially owned by the Bank of Angola and Metropole, were now in the custody of the Liquidating Commission and would not be voted.

Vice-Governor Mota Gomes—both he and Camacho had been released from prison several days before, the Premier overruling the judge's orders—spoke first, sobbing openly as he described the insane judge's behavior. His chins quivered, enveloping his collar, the knot in his tie. His pudgy hands trembled as he fought to control himself.

"There gradually appeared in the press," Gomes said, voice choked with emotion, "and in the streets a campaign of discredit against this great institution. They accuse it of a crime of which it was the sole immediate victim. . . . Not only in our country but also abroad, newspapers with wide circulation have no hesitation in presenting the Bank of Portugal as swindlers. This was the result of a gesture by a magistrate absolutely unworthy of occupying such a position!"

The judge's eyes misted over as he revealed the calumny to which he had been subjected on Christmas Eve. Then came Governor Innocencio Camacho Rodrigues, and the applause that had rattled the room following Gomes' remarks was redoubled as the crowd spotted him. He cried, too. What a scene! The judge grimaced over his plum pudding, re-creating it for me. Camacho gathered his composure and began with an apology, babbled on in an excess of self-pity as the crowd cheered.

"Anyway," the judge said, preparing to take his leave, "there are other crowds in other places cheering your name, Alves." He looked at me in an almost fatherly way, this strange and inexplicable man. "Don't lose faith. You will be vindicated yet. . . ." At the door he whispered, "Merry Christmas."

His belief in me was touching.

*   *   *

In London Edgar Waterlow had successfully challenged Sir William's control of the firm over the issue of a company committee resolved to investigate the "facts and circumstances" surrounding their dealings with us. Sir William fought it, proposing instead that he have ten days to draw up his own complete report. The issue was joined, and Edgar's supporters carried the day, five votes to four. To all intents and purposes, Sir William's control of the company was finished. His bitterest enemy was now in effective command.

New Year's Eve was a low point. José came to my cell and we drank champagne. He was more talkative than he'd been lately. He wanted to reminisce, and we naturally turned to the New Year's Eve exactly a year before. The party at Greta's apartment, the snow drifting down through the glow of street lamps outside the cafés . . .

José chuckled. "God, how I misbehaved that night."

"You were a very bad boy," I agreed.

"I'd gladly go through it again if we could be back in Paris tonight." His grin faded. Reality was a little closer each day. "Those days are gone forever."

"No, no, we'll see Paris again."

"Tell me, Alves, did you forge the contracts? Was it all a swindle?"

"Of course," I said.

"By God! You really did it!" Life filled his face again.

He threw his arms around me, hugged me to him, kissed my cheeks like a French politician dispensing the Legion of Honor.

* * *

Late that night, as 1925 passed on into 1926, the year of my thirtieth birthday, I sat by myself. I'd been reading my dear Wodehouse. I was finally beginning to understand his books; perhaps I was going crazy myself. But I put the book aside and rubbed my tired eyes. Then I went to my small writing desk and took a sheet of stationery, uncapped my Big Red.

Dear Greta, I began. *It is 1926, my love, and I am beginning it with thoughts of you. . . .*

* * *

1926 did not begin well for any of us.

In The Hague the authorities celebrated New Year's

Day by arresting Marang. Up to the last minute Hennies had urged him to disappear into Germany with him, but Marang demurred. Thirty minutes before the police came for Karel, Adolf slipped away, resumed one of his previous identities, fading into the crowd.

The judge sent Antonio to The Hague to get the contracts from Marang, and that was another mess. José finally got word to him that Greta had the contracts in Paris. Antonio went to Paris to get them.

The Lisbon daily *ABC* had sent a reporter to Paris, and much to my surprise the copy that was delivered to my cell on January 3 featured a front-page interview with Greta.

When she was visiting in Lisbon last summer, the elegant actress was a woman of mystery. Her picture appeared regularly in the papers in the company of the notorious Reis and his partner in rascality, José Bandeira. She became a subject of gossip and speculation. Where was Senhora Reis? Who was the famous actress really visiting? There were stories that she left her hotel late at night for secret trysts. But with whom? All was forgiven her, then, however. She was daring, vivacious, world-famous. We expected excitement where she was involved.

But with the uncovering of Senhor Reis's unusual manipulations of the Portuguese economy, the gossip and rumor turned against Greta Nordlund. Praise in Lisbon became insults, admirers turned into accusers.

"Tell me, what will the future hold for Alves?" she asked when contacted by our reporter in Paris, where she is currently starring in a successful production of *Outward Bound.* "Is it true that he is being harshly treated? Has he done anything wrong? And poor *petit* José, what of him? They've told me what the Portuguese papers are saying about me—that I wasn't even an actress, had only walk-on parts. They called me a *cocotte* and said that everything I did was for their money, that I am responsible for wrecking Alves Reis's marriage, that I spent all his money. What nonsense!

"When I was in Lisbon they called me the Scandinavian Sarah Bernhardt! But from such people it was silly

praise! What did they know of my art, my class, my
position? And now they insult me. But I don't care.
What hurts me is not that they should doubt me as a
woman but as an actress. You've seen for yourself.
All Europe honors me. In the streets, in hotel lobbies,
in restaurants, wherever I go, people whisper about
me: 'It's Greta, it's Greta!' For them I mean nights of
emotion, tears and happiness. To think they consider
me in Lisbon a grasping, ambitious, wasteful woman. . . . They slander me. All I want to know is what
is to become of my dear friend Alves Reis."

It was very good to hear of her, and her concern buoyed
my spirits. Soon I would hear from her personally, obviously. I was amused by her question: has he done anything wrong? I could imagine the performance she gave
for the reporter, knowing the truth the whole time. What
a remarkable creature!

The worst news of all came the same day. Pressure from
the Bank of Portugal had led to the removal of Judge Pinto
Magalhaes from the case. My last, best ally was gone! His
replacement was Dr. Joaquim Augustes Alves Ferreira, an
Inspector of the Courts, a Judge of the Supreme Court—
an impressive fellow and distressingly sane. He forbade
Judge Magalhaes even to visit my cell to say farewell.

With Ferreira heading the investigation I began to feel
the full force of the state. I was cut off from the outside
world; the more they questioned me, the more implacable
my reserve became. Police Chief José Xavier stormed into
my cell one day to tell me that not only had Maria been
arrested but was being held in a filthy, rat-infested cell.
They had been questioning me—two teams working in re-
lays—for twenty hours. I was exhausted; finally I broke
down, sobbing. I told them that Maria was innocent, that
only I was guilty.

An hour later I was myself again. It had been a trick.
I was not at all sure they had even arrested Maria. I re-
tracted my confession. "Not another word," I told them,
"until I am brought to trial."

January 11 found Sir William and his Scottish attorneys
back in Lisbon at Dr. Ferreira's request. Sir William wanted
to make a settlement with the bank, but reaching a sum of
indemnity agreeable to both parties was a difficult task,

indeed. Both parties saw different animals. Waterlow saw a small skunk, not too dangerous but potentially awfully smelly. The bank looked about fearfully and saw an enormous monster, so big and dangerous they hadn't even been able to establish its measurements. They suspected that it might be getting bigger and more destructive all the time. Obviously Waterlow and the bank were on a collision course to litigation; in the meantime Waterlow would get no more business from Portugal.

Marang hired the best lawyers in Holland, and he remained utterly loyal to me. Although we were in jails hundreds of miles apart we managed to stay in contact by means of secret couriers. We prearranged our defenses. He cleverly guarded his money and its whereabouts. Unlike poor, foolish José, Marang never for a moment lost his head. Some of mine had been seized, but I had other accounts they simply could not find.

January passed into February, February into March. I learned that the international police were after Hennies. They knew he was in Berlin and were using an old mistress in their attempts to find him. I wrote to Marang, asking him somehow to get word to Hennies if he had a way to keep in touch. The Bank of Portugal also sent an agent to Berlin.

By now I knew for certain that Maria—my sweet little Maria, who had been through so much—was being held in Ajube Women's Prison. Through our courier system I had Marang give the messenger the money to stop in Paris for the purchase of six brassieres and matching vests in good crepe de Chine embroidered in pink from the Galeries Lafayette; also six boxes of Doge face powder, twelve pairs of silk stockings. . . . I was deeply concerned about keeping her spirits up.

The Bank of Portugal opposed her release, believing still that she was their only hope of getting a confession out of me. They knew of my love for her and the children; they were counting on my nature to collapse my resolve. Bravely Maria clung to the stories I had told her to tell the investigators. Not until late March did she break down and tell the truth, after being held almost ninety days.

Antonio Horta Osario, the Bank of Portugal's attorney, argued vehemently against her release.

*　　*　　*

The consequences of my acts against the Bank of Portugal kept spreading even wider. Even in my cell I could hear the mobs outside in the streets. From them I drew the strength to go on. I heard them chant my name, heard myself become a symbol, a rallying cry. . . . On May 28 the government was overthrown! The revolution was led by General Gomes da Costa, who issued a proclamation in the city of Braga, up in the northeast corner of Portugal, calling on his countrymen to join the struggle for national honor and dignity by throwing out the incumbent Democratic Party. It wasn't much of a revolution, nothing compared to what we experienced in Angola during the 1960s. But between May 28 and 31 the country did rise more or less in arms—at least most of the army garrisons mobilized and the government in Lisbon went down without a casualty. During the days of the revolution no one made the slightest effort to save the government! There was simply no will to survive. It was like a dead, hollow tree slowly toppling over in nothing more than a high wind. The woodsman's ax wasn't needed. What had been done to me —the Hero of Angola—had brought Portugal back to life. What had been done to me *and* what the people knew I had tried to do for Portugal. . . .

Coming down from Coimbra was the new Finance Minister, Professor Antonio de Oliveira Salazar.

My fame and the public support I received was growing. A novel was published stating the popular viewpoint, proclaiming me the potential—but thwarted—savior of the country. It was a fantasy, of course, but the people took it seriously. In their fervor, the fact that I was just a man never crossed their minds.

The night sky over Lisbon glowed with bonfire rallies in my behalf. The people sustained me as I realized that I was in fact being denied the opportunity to serve Portugal.

*   *   *

The Chamber of Deputies agreed with the populace at large on at least one point: I was no ordinary criminal. The Chamber passed a new law by which I would be tried not by a jury but by a panel of judges.

There were no laws in the Criminal Code to cover what I had done.

So they made some up.

If the state was going to convict me, it would have to be done with unconstitutional *ex post facto* laws.

* * *

Marang was tried in The Hague at the beginning of December 1926. My lawyers, however, had concluded that a speedy trial was bound to work against me. They undertook a series of delaying actions, hoping the case would grow cold with the passing of time, hoping that the passions would burn themselves out.

Marang's trial lasted six days. On December 10 the three judges found him guilty on one charge of receiving stolen property. The four trunks of Bank of Portugal notes that served as the evidence in the case were ordered destroyed. He was sentenced to eleven months.

Since he had already spent eleven months in jail awaiting trial, he was ordered released at once. Before the prosecution could get the matter before the Court of Appeals, Marang took his wife and four children to Brussels. Under Belgian law no extradition of criminals was possible for sentences of less than four years.

When I wasn't thinking about my own delicate situation I tried to distract myself with newspapers and books, much as I had done when confined in the Oporto jail. When I concerned myself with what was going on in the great world, I could almost feel part of it. Even now, in 1966, I can recall the great hum and buzz of the world beyond my cell.

Ibn Saud became King of Saudi Arabia, Pilsudski staged his coup in Poland, Abd-el-Krim's Riff war ended, everyone seemed to be singing the music from *The Desert Song*, and Dr. Paul Josef Goebbels was named Gauleiter of Berlin. Harry Houdini and Valentino died, and I read a brand-new book by one of Greta's friends, *The Sun Also Rises*. Germany was admitted to the League of Nations. On my radio I heard a new song that wouldn't leave my head: "I Found a Million Dollar Baby in the Five-and-Ten-Cent Store." I experienced it all, sitting in my club chair, having my meals brought in from Lisbon's best restaurants. Sometimes the unreality of it almost drove me mad.

In the summer I received the first letter from Greta.

My dearest Thunderbolt,

No, my darling, I have not forgotten you, nor have my feelings for you changed. I have followed your case as closely as possible. My tardiness in writing was planned—I knew you had a great deal on your mind and needed to concentrate fully on your difficulties. Now, you must have a plan of action to follow and I do not feel as if I am intruding.

Also, I had no idea what your trip to Angola with Maria had led to, in terms of your relationship. Well, I still don't know but I had to write to you—almost to remind myself as well as you of all that we have been to each other.

My work goes well. I will be making another film soon, possibly with a man named Fritz Lang directing. He is very good. A.H. turned up in Paris one day, incognito. We talked—all seems to be going quite well for him.

What to say, my darling? There is no other man in my life. How is poor little José? Give him my love. Write to me if you wish. Alves, my life is so much less without you.

Your Greta

I was overjoyed to hear from her. I had never accepted my feeling for her so completely as I did now that she was out of my reach.

She was the great love of my life: I admitted it now without a qualm.

It was not as easy for me to admit the truth about Maria and José. They had become lovers in Carlsbad, not, I think, out of any great attraction but from their own personal needs to revenge themselves on me. José saw himself closed out of Greta's affections; Maria . . . well, she took José as her lover out of loneliness and spite. If it had been an act of love, then she would have chosen Arnaldo.

No, I never spoke to either Maria or José about it. What good would it have done? I wasn't at all sure that I minded. What I was sure of was my feeling for Greta. I think the key is simply—December to December, 1924 to 1925—we were all becoming people we had not been before.

I wrote to Greta, a warm, friendly letter. I was afraid of expressing too much sentiment. It might frighten her off. After all, she was free and successful and well off.

There was no need to make her feel bound to me. If I were set free soon I would simply go to her; if my defense failed and I faced a lengthy imprisonment, she would be free to carry on with her own life. I was behaving as decently as I knew how.

We began a regular correspondence. We seldom touched on the future. We were waiting. She may have had lovers. I don't really know. I do know that her letters kept me alive.

As for Maria, the government kept our contact to a minimum. I saw her twice during the last half of 1926. Her moods would shift wildly even during the course of an hour's chat. One moment rational and stable, the next weeping over the wreckage of our lives. Our meetings did little to sustain either of us, I'm afraid.

I got a long letter from Arnaldo, as well. He was living with Silvia in Luanda, making a success of his business. He told me I should never hesitate to make any request of him. He told me to have faith, to remember my own resilience that had never let me down. He said that he loved me as only one man could love another. The letter made me cry.

In May 1927, still awaiting trial, I had a visit from a friend just returning from rural Germany who told me the story of Hennies' recent life, which was tied intimately to that part of his life that even our detectives had been unable to uncover.

He was forty-six now, well-to-do and lonely. His name was Johann Georg Adolf Doring, the name he was born with in Friedrichsbruck. He was the fifth of seven children born to a German peasant family of Huguenots, just as Sir William Waterlow's ancestor had been. Now Hennies had gone back to the Friedrichsbruck and Helsa area. He had been a bright boy, a voracious reader highly thought of by his teachers and the townspeople. But there was no future for him there since he was not interested in the family farm and there was no money. He had apprenticed himself to a cigar maker and moved to Helsa; he was nineteen. He married a local girl, Anna Schminke, in 1905; their first child, Anna Elizabeth, was born in 1907. Using his wife's small dowry, he opened a tobacco shop in Kassel that was not particularly successful. Then came the act of cowardice that changed his life and which he had hidden so well.

It was May 1909, and his wife was pregnant again. They

were just scraping along, and stretching ahead he saw dec-
ades of children and poverty. He deserted his family.
Frankfurt, Hamburg, a steamer to New York, working for
a cigar maker and saving his money, securing the Singer
Sewing Machine agency in Manaos, Brazil . . . Rio de
Janeiro in 1914. Selling everything from toothbrushes to
locomotives. The Great War. I pretty much knew that part
of the story, but the beginning—well, it was odd, placing
the Adolf I knew against that humble background.

Now his wife was dead and he had returned to Helsa.
He lavished money on his old friends and his daughters.
The reunion had been a happy one. When my friend the
salesman happened across him in a Helsa tavern, the
Goldener Anker, Hennies pretended not to know him. Well,
that was all right; it was the fellow's own business. Late
into the night my friend chatted with the tavern owner,
who had known Doring as a boy; thus, he heard the story.

Adolf was now living in a suite at the Hotel Schirmer in
Kassel. He was obviously rich. He was also restless, looking
about for a business opportunity.

In July 1927 Edgar Waterlow forced Sir William out of
the chairmanship of the firm and into the co-equal position
of joint managing director. The Bank of Portugal was still
insisting that only five million dollars would satisfy them;
Waterlow was thinking in terms of one hundred thousand.
There was no room for compromise. Obviously.

I read my newspapers, as many as six a day. The German economy collapsed on "Black Friday." The Socialists
rioted in Vienna, and a general strike took place following
the acquittal of Nazis for political murder. Trotsky was
expelled from the Communist Party. In America, a country
I increasingly wished I might someday visit, a grown man
called Babe Ruth hit sixty home runs in a game called base-
ball, and the papers from New York, which I frequently
perused, were full of accounts of the feat. Sacco and
Vanzetti were executed, and that was news in every newspaper I read. Lizzie Borden, whom I also read about in
the *New York Times,* died, as did the great dancer Isadora
Duncan. I suppose the most inspiring event of the year was
Colonel Lindbergh's flight across the Atlantic to Paris in
"The Spirit of St. Louis." He must, I reasoned, have been
a good deal like me. He would have understood what happened at the High Bridge.

Greta sent me Hemingway's *Men Without Women* with

a clever inscription relating to the title. She sent me several other new books: *Steppenwolf* and *The Bridge of San Luis Rey* and *Elmer Gantry* caught my imagination most thoroughly, as did an odd, ironic novel that struck me as a little too close to home—*The Treasure of Sierra Madre*. She told me about the first talking motion picture, *The Jazz Singer*, and wrote a capsule review of *Flesh and the Devil* with Garbo, to whom she bore a slight resemblance. How I wished I could be with her in the darkened movie palaces, holding her hand, knowing that life was better than any screen fantasy.

And so 1927 was gone.

* * *

The government that had been proclaimed in 1926 had hardly improved the state of the nation. Many sound fiscal heads acknowledged that there was only one way to get Portugal back on its feet . . . and *he* was in jail! Living costs in 1928 were thirty times what they had been in 1914.

In an attempt to get the country back on the path I'd set it on, General Oscar Carmona was proclaimed President of the Republic. On April 15 he made an announcement that would seal Portugal's fate for the next half century. The new Permanent Secretary of Finance would be "a man of the highest personal morality, a man of the most informed competence and deepest commitment, a man in whom the whole nation could have confidence."

When Salazar took the oath as Permanent Secretary of Finance he was forty-one; he wore the conventional sober black suit expected of our officials. He was thin, pallid; one of the papers of the day remarked that he looked like an "underpaid funeral parlor assistant who would bury Portugal's finances for good."

Carmona held the position of President from 1928 until his death fifteen years ago, in 1951—some twenty-three years. But even to the most naïve observer it was obvious almost from the beginning that Salazar was the complete, unquestioned dictator of Portugal. He retains the position as I write this, thirty-eight years after taking the job offered by Carmona.

Still in preventive detention, I went on laboring tirelessly to prove the iniquities of the Bank of Portugal. But, as my lawyers hoped, the whole thing was slowly losing the attention of the press and the public. Which was all well and good as far as their strategy was concerned, but it gave me a bit of a chill. I had always counted on the Robin Hood factor among the general public to see me through. If I were their hero, the man who had struck a blow for the common man, then all would finally come right. But the lawyers had told me that none of that public support would do me a bit of good before the tribunal that would judge me. "Time," they said, "is your only hope. The whole business shrinks as time goes on."

"Be calm, Alves," my lawyer said. They would playfully punch my arm; I would smile weakly. "The criminal always values delay." They would nod among themselves. "Witnesses die or disappear. Officials who remember the worst lose office. Prosecutors move on, to bigger jobs or the anonymity of retirement. As long as we can postpone the trial there is still hope!"

* * *

But my will was starving to death.

I was transferred to the Cadeia Penitenciaria de Lisboa, a fortress complete with battlements overlooking the Eduardo VII Park. I believed I had been abandoned by all. I had lost all hope and confidence in myself. I believed I had finally failed. I was through. . . .

For months I had been carrying an extremely active poison, stropine. When the cell door was locked at eleven o'clock on the night of May 31 I dissolved the poison in a glass of water. My mind wandered through the past; I composed myself. I thought of meeting Maria that day at the beach, of the first day in Luanda when I had been awash in my confidence. . . . I remembered the night I had walked the streets of Lisbon and found myself at the Castle of San Jorge and realized my destiny. . . . I thought of Greta with the lavender scarf blowing in the breeze at Biarritz, the first time I ever set eyes on her. . . .

At four o'clock I wrote a brief confession of my crimes, addressed to the Attorney General. I placed it in an envelope and put it in the desk next to my cot. I drank the potion and went to the washstand to rinse out the cup. I went back to the cot, lay down and closed my eyes. I was ready to die.

Incredibly enough I awoke on the afternoon of June 10,

bright sunshine streaming through the windows. Maria was sitting beside the bed, holding my hand. The light made a halo around her head. I thought for a moment she was an angel. . . .

She told me that on the first of June, at eight o'clock in the morning, they opened my cell door to deliver breakfast and found me stretched out on the floor wrapped in my own bedsheet.

They called the prison doctor, and my own physician came at ten o'clock. My condition grew worse. Only the strong body of a man of thirty-two wrenched me from the arms of death.

As I listened to Maria's account I was suddenly struck by what she was saying—no one realized it was a suicide attempt! The whole incident was attributed to a mysterious brain disease.

Once I was well enough to be returned to my cell, I opened the desk drawer. Thank God, there was the envelope containing my confession. I tore it to bits. I had been spared to keep up my fight.

I pulled myself together and launched a devilish plan to prove my innocence. I organized another full-scale attack on the Bank of Portugal.

I only wanted a great scandal, nothing less. I no longer even cared about the fates of my accomplices.

*   *   *

Almost three years to the day after my return from Luanda Sir William's departure from the family firm became final. The work of a lifetime had ended in defeat, humiliation, a shambles. Not even his son would enter the firm. In a way it had all been for nothing.

Sir William would become Lord Mayor in 1929. Customarily a man's firm bore the cost of that ceremonial and hugely expensive position. Sir William, however, would be paying for it himself. He had had to sell Whyte Ways, the family estate at Harrow Weald. I never had gotten to see it.

*   *   *

I heard from Marang in January 1929. He was living with his family in a pleasant Paris flat at 96 Boulevard Richard Lenoir. He was forty-five. He saw Greta every six months or so, said she seemed well and told him that she was in regular touch with me. Soon I would be out of prison and it was good to keep up one's old friendships.

As for himself, he had learned of a small electric chandelier manufacturing business that needed capital. He bought the business and soon had a modest plant at 34 Rue Brequet, not far from his flat. He walked to work.

He and his wife had just become members of the Dutch Reformed Church of Paris.

*   *   *

It was the late fall of 1929 when Manoel dos Santos came to see me. He was a pustule of hate and fitted my requirements perfectly.

Manoel had once been a messenger for the Bank of Portugal; he had been fired when he tried to get the proceeds of a winning lottery ticket that the owner had sent in to be collected. He had been unable to get another job; his children were hungry, he said, and his wife had turned to prostitution. He came to my cell to offer his services to me in my fight against the bank. He wanted no payment. He wanted only revenge. It was the saddest story imaginable.

After a few visits, however, his hatred and cynicism began to shock me. I was thrown off, gave him some fatherly advice—he was only twenty. He insisted that I hear him out when I'd finally said he must go. He took out his wallet, which contained a sheet bearing the signatures of several Bank of Portugal directors which he said he had forged.

Well, that caught my attention. I was astounded at the perfection of his work. I gave him my Big Red and asked him to reproduce the same signatures. He did so without a flaw! I decided to use him, personal distaste quite aside.

I planned a large-scale forgery establishing my own innocence and the directors' guilt beyond any imaginable question. This time I had a real Bank of Portugal letterhead, which I had obtained some months before through the bribery of a clerk.

I had fallen very heavily into a trap.

Manoel dos Santos had been sent to me as an *agent provocateur* through the disgusting and unethical connivance of a newspaperman and Antonio Horta Osorio, the bank's attorney. Naturally the story was spewed across the front pages of Lisbon's newspapers. In my cell I wept.

*   *   *

Everyone agreed that it was the strangest trial in the history of Portugal. The court had been specially constituted to deal with my case under laws which, since they had been written specifically to cover this one particular instance, were new both to accusers and accused. Being a special court, it had no regular meeting place. For some reason I was tried in the Hall of the Military Tribunal at Santa Clara, in Lisbon.

From the beginning our quarters were ridiculously crowded and hot. Batteries of electric fans kept blowing out the fuses. There was no place for any members of the public; it became quickly apparent that not even all the witnesses could be accommodated. The atmosphere in the room was wildly confused.

Dr. Simao was president of the court, and I felt sorry for him. What could he do to impose his will on the cramped room? José, Maria and I were represented by fifteen attorneys. There were six other defendants, all on minor counts, who were paying the price for merely having worked for us. But it was Alves Reis they were really after. José's fate was bound indivisibly to mine.

"Your Excellency," one of our counsel complained, his voice shaking with rage, "I have no place to sit! I demand a chair!"

Over the laughter the judge urged patience all around and himself left the room in search of more chairs.

Thirty-nine of Portugal's most distinguished judges packed the room. From among them seven, in addition to Dr. Simao, would be chosen to hear the case. The method of selection brought a smile to every face: Dr. Simao's son, nine years old, pulled the names out of a hat.

This procedure was followed by a roll call of the eighty-five witnesses. The room reeked of sweat, cologne, cigarette smoke. There was a steady jumble of conversation; insects buzzed steadily. Electric fans whirred in the corners. I was vaguely sick to my stomach. I had not been able to eat before we'd been called to order at noon. Late in the afternoon an Army major entered the room and explained that the space would be needed at once for a court-martial!

Judge Simao sighed patiently, nodded and announced that the court would stand adjourned until four o'clock on May 8. The twenty reporters leaped up and clogged the doorways.

Looking up, I saw Maria, her fingers knotted in a white handkerchief, her face gray, ravaged by the strain. Her eyes and hair had lost their luster, her face had lost its youth. I sat down beside her, just long enough to hold her hand and kiss her cheek. She looked at me blankly, then forced a smile. "Alves," she said softly, "are you all right?"

"Of course, my dear," I said. "Maria, listen to me carefully. Very soon, a couple of weeks at most, you will be free . . . out of prison. You must take care of yourself, use some makeup, have your hair done, have your parents ready to receive you . . . if you can hold on just a bit longer."

"Will you be free then, too?" Her eyes pleaded with me.

"I don't know." She wanted me to tell her yes, but I didn't know. I couldn't be sure. I kissed her cheek again.

There were twelve charges against me, only one against Maria. I was almost certain that even if she were found guilty Maria would be released, having already served more of a sentence than she would have received from the single guilty verdict.

Alves Reis, the indictment read, was charged with conspiracy, falsifying contracts, forgery of everything from letters to the Oxford diploma, to banknotes, bribery and fraud. . . .

Eight charges were leveled against José. Maria was charged only with having received stolen property.

Adolf Hennies had five of the charges read against him, but it was irrelevant: he no longer existed.

Since Marang had already been tried and convicted in a foreign court, he was not charged in Lisbon.

The prosecution was conducted on behalf of the public by Dr. Jeronimo de Sousa, on behalf of the bank by Antonio Osorio and Dr. Barbosa de Magalhaes.

I had two more days of waiting. I knew what I had to do. Not even my attorney was aware of my plans.

The trial went much as I expected. After all, they did have rather a weighty case to make, and they made the most of it. I couldn't blame them. This sort of opportunity came once in a lifetime. They took their time.

Dr. Nobrega Quintal defended me. He was not an eloquent man, but he made the best case possible while I sat and watched, almost certain of the result. I alone knew what I would say to the court at the end.

Dr. Quintal spoke with fervor, kept their attention.

"We are not dealing with merely a criminal, Your Excellencies." He nodded vigorously, agreeing with himself. He fanned himself with several sheets of his notes. "We are dealing with a great man . . . without offending anyone, I believe I can say he is the greatest man in this room! The man who has dreamed the greatest dreams, dared the greatest adventures and made for himself the largest place in Portugal's history. He is not unlike the greatest of our navigators, men who straddled the globe in the name of our country.

"But . . . but . . . Alves Reis, the Hero of Angola, was born in a smaller and entirely less heroic age. In another day great men saw obstacles and overcame them. But today such men are discouraged, brought to trial. . . .

"He saw no good reason for Portugal to grow poorer each day, drifting helplessly without leadership. And with his brilliant mind he created the means to scale the mountains again, to sweep power fully and with vision across the seas, to bring Portugal back from the brink of the abyss. . . . And we bring him to trial. . . .

"And he was right! You need only look back to the movement in Portugal during his heyday . . . the burgeoning prosperity, the optimism, the hope! Compare that to the Portugal of today—upon which I will not dwell. . . . And we bring such a man to trial!" He was trembling with emotion.

He summed up the points in my favor: my previous good character, the important services I had rendered to society, my intention of averting the economic and financial crisis that was bringing Angola into a desperate condition, the long imprisonment I had already undergone, my precarious economic circumstances.

"Oh, yes, by all means," Dr. Osorio snapped, outraged. "Reis seems to be in desperate straits, all right! But we know he has spent more than one hundred thousand dollars—that is two million escudos, Your Excellencies—in his own defense! We are still uncovering secret bank accounts all over Europe in the name of Alves Reis or his wife—and, frankly, I can't imagine that we'll ever find them all! No, not ever. . . ."

Dr. Quintal pressed on.

"In reality, Senhor Reis was an inflationist, not a counterfeiter, an inflationist who was merely carrying out unofficially the fixed policies of the Bank of Portugal . . . *at no cost to the bank!* Remember, Alves Reis and his associates had *paid* Waterlow's for printing the banknotes." He gave me a sidelong glance at the next point: "It is against the law to imitate the banknotes . . . but the law says nothing about actually *duplicating* the notes!"

Dr. Osorio rolled his eyes, smiting his forehead.

"And, finally," Dr. Quintal said, his voice beginning to give way, "may I remind Your Excellencies of the extraordinary measures taken by the Chamber of Deputies in passing retroactive laws solely for the purpose of covering Alves Reis—so that the crime of counterfeiting, which had been punishable by a maximum of three years' imprisonment, can now bring twenty-five years. . . ."

I remember him now, years after I last saw him. He did his best for me, and no man can do more than that. I listened to him with interest, but I was thinking about the next day when I would finally have my say.

*　　*　　*

When it came to my day in court Antonio Ferro recounted the events in *Diario de Noticias*. I had known Ferro in passing ever since we had been classmates as children. He had turned up again in Angola years later and had written about our final triumphant tour. Years after he covered my appearance in court in 1930, he wrote an enormously popular biography of Salazar. In 1930 he was covering his old schoolmate.

Everyone now knows Alves Reis is a criminal, the best of all. He has confessed it with unique pride, punishing himself publicly. There is no doubt Alves Reis succeeded in impressing—even overwhelming—the court yesterday. Perhaps he failed to convince it of his good intentions, but he unquestionably held all who heard him spellbound—with his intelligence, his eloquence, his ability and his admirable lawyer's temperament.

There was no defendant, no court, no jury. There was a free man before free men. A minister in the

Chamber of Deputies replying to a question, an orator at a rally, a captain of industry explaining his business. There was only admiration when he began speaking, and soon the court was his. Reis related his great adventure, with energy unbelievable in a man who has rotted in prison nearly five years, with a brilliant literary flavor at times—he dazzled everyone with articles and clauses, his overall knowledge of the law.

He related how he committed the fraud, how he discovered the numbers and series of the notes, how he forged the signatures, how he found out there was no "control" of the notes in the Bank of Portugal, explaining all this as an engineer might elucidate an intricate machine.

His sincerity astounded the court. The surprising thing was that a man who should appear beaten, timid, humiliated following his confession of a terrible crime instead stood with his head up, in a fighting mood, almost jovial, without any cynicism.

He dedicates himself with ardor to a new cause, the defense of his companions, whom he tries to clear of all guilt. This discredited and finished man suddenly became transformed into a terrible defender of his own victims. There is a certain moral grandeur in his attitude to the unfortunate men: "It was I who dragged them in here! Ruined five years of their lives. . . . Now I shall do everything to free them!" When a judge asked why he had changed his attitude so suddenly, Reis's answer was simple and moving: "You are here to judge only the men, not their souls!"

Yes, isn't it time to seek the human truth instead of the judicial truth? To give up the old clichés that a man who lies once is always a liar . . . 25,000 pages to find the truth! And has it been found? The Alves Reis of the Bank of Angola and Metropole has been tried and will be sentenced. . . . But this Reis, this great spirit who confronted us today as no judge in the nation's history has ever been confronted, does not this Alves Reis deserve our respect and our mercy? Our compassion?

Throw stones at him if you will. I cannot.

*　　*　　*

The days of waiting for the verdict of the judges were long and nervous. I was not in the least afraid of the result. I knew the Portuguese character, the role of law. As Greta wrote to me while I waited: "My love, remember what I've always told you. What will be will be. We are given our lines and we must say them." She still loved me; I wrote her long letters.

Ivar Kreuger had a courier bring me a handwritten note. *"Never forget that greatness is always under attack, Senhor Reis. It is a test of men such as ourselves, how far we rise above it. My thoughts are with you."*

It was, I thought, very kind of him.

The word reached us at midnight that the judges would deliver their verdicts at one o'clock on the morning of July 19. We were all taken to the same cramped room, and after a brief wait the Attorney General entered. The clerk followed and took his seat. The presiding judge was ushered in, followed by the other members of the tribunal. Our lawyers got the attention of the court, thanked the judges for their fairness in the conduct of the trial and retired from the room as the reporters buzzed among themselves, scribbling.

Dr. Simao calmly read the verdicts.

Maria Luisa Jacobetti Alves Reis was found guilty and sentenced to the time she had already served in prison. My wife was free.

Artur Virgilio Alves Reis, José dos Santos Bandeira and Adolf Hennies (in absentia) were found guilty on all counts, each to serve eight years in prison to be followed by twelve years of exile.

It was over.

*   *   *

Maria recovered her physical health; it was her mind that had suffered the real damage. She moved in with her parents and was allowed to visit me weekly, and more often than not she brought some or all of the children. Her eyes were often distracted, glazed, her face hollowed and wan, her hair dull and uncared for. Sometimes she barely spoke, searching my face with those empty eyes, looking for answers I didn't have. At other times she babbled uncontrollably about the minutiae of her daily life. Although the meetings were a strain, there was no alternative. Our lives were still bound together . . . and the children could not be left to forget their unfortunate father.

As her condition slowly improved, she needed to find a job, both for the money and her own state of mind. Left to spend her days lost in reflection, she had little hope for recovery. Jobs were hard to find now that Salazar had embarked on a course of drastic deflation. For the wife of Alves Reis matters were even more difficult. More than once she heard a prospective employer reason: "If I give you a job everyone will say I once got money from your husband." Eventually she did find work as a clerk in the government navy yard. The pay was twenty dollars a month. The money I had put away in foreign banks had either been found or couldn't be gotten out. Another irony in an absolute deluge.

* * *

The first three years of my sentence were spent in solitary confinement. There were constant rumors of my supporters planning dramatic escapes. To guard against that, an out-side spotlight was focused on my cell window every night. Finally I asked to see the warden.

"If I wanted to escape," I told him, "I would first speak to you. I'm not the type to scale walls. If I get out of here it will only be because I have bribed you. So please, re-move the searchlight so I can get some sleep. . . ."

It was removed.

* * *

The Bank of Portugal's case against Waterlow was heard in the late fall. On Monday, December 22, Justice Wright was ready with his judgment. He was sixty-one, a Trinity College man, a vastly successful King's counsel in his day. He had a dry sense of humor and a well-defined streak of irritability. He had heard the arguments with great care. Obviously a great deal was at stake, in terms of money, the impartiality of English law and the stature of a great London firm. He spent the morning outlining the case, and in the afternoon he was gathering steam.

"This crime is unique. *Unique.* . . . It is not a thing that will ever happen again. We may be sure of that. But we must decide this question—who was negligent, if anyone, and to what degree. . . .

"What damage was done by exchanging the da Gama notes for others? A very great loss, as I see it. These notes are currency in Portugal. They can purchase commodities, including gold; they can buy foreign exchange—and they can do this because they have behind them the credit of the Bank of Portugal.

"I cannot grant the bank interest on its claim. And the realizable assets of the liquidated Bank of Angola and Metropole—nearly half a million pounds—must be deducted from the claim. This leaves, if my arithmetic is correct, a balance of five hundred thirty-one thousand, eight hundred fifty-one pounds, or approximately two million six hundred thousand dollars, for which, in my view, there ought to be a judgment for the plaintiff."

The bank had won. Of course, Waterlow's would appeal, but their position was weak.

*   *   *

Greta was vastly amused by the verdict against Waterlow. "Bill was always a great one to overstep himself," she wrote, "and his natural greed finally got him. Well, my darling Alves, they say that we are each born with the seeds of our fate planted within us. Who are you and I to doubt it? Next month I am going all the way to Hollywood! How I long for your company . . . your touch, your strong arms around me, your lips—don't scold me, my love. I've not forgotten our pledge and I try not to write such things. But I think of them always and sometimes they flow from my pen onto the paper. . . . Remember that I am yours forever. . . . I will write from California."

*   *   *

Early in July 1931 Sir William was stricken by severe abdominal pains. Following surgery, peritonitis set in. On July 6 he was dead. That great pink-faced Englishman who had found us all such odd little foreigners . . . Sir William Waterlow was sixty at the time of his death.

His death represented one more remove into the past from what had come to seem in my mind's eye glorious, disreputable, exciting days. . . .

The Times carried a full account of the funeral of the onetime Lord Mayor. St. Paul's Cathedral, great pomp, a personal condolence from the Royal Family; *The Times*'s guest list was more than a column long. Waterlow and Sons was represented by a very junior chap called Smith. *The Times* called Sir William's reign as Lord Mayor "one of the most brilliant of modern times." He was buried in the Harrow Weald Churchyard, not far from the great house he had once owned.

When I close my eyes now and try to bring him back in my mind the picture I summon is the first. He comes forward, hand extended, booming, "I am Waterlow!" For me he is there, frozen in time. Forever.

*   *   *

In 1932 I also noticed with a kind of wistfulness that is not my custom that with the crash of his economic colossus Ivar Kreuger shot himself to death in his apartment in Paris. I can see him even now, leaning toward me, the large, pale face beaming. "Do you know, Reis, that a hundred million matches are struck every hour. . . ." Maria still has the jeweled matchstick he gave her, diamonds with rubies at the tip. It was one trinket that somehow survived.

*   *   *

Salazar officially became Premier in 1932, an absolute dictator. His new constitution was full of Fascistlike bits and pieces cribbed from the vile Mussolini. In January 1934 the General Confederation of Labor and the Communists staged a revolution that Salazar ground out in a manner so brutal and bloody that it drew warm approval from Adolf Hitler. At the next elections there were candidates only from the National Union Party, Salazar's party.

The tyrant did balance Portugal's budget, and the inflation of the escudo was brought to a halt; but the cost was very high unemployment.

Maria was now visiting me several times each week. She was getting along well enough, though she was never really able to understand how the glories that were ours that one incredible year could vanish so quickly. Her father had died, leaving a decent estate, and now she and her mother and the children lived in a modest but pleasant apartment on the outskirts of Lisbon. We were growing closer again, now that her reason had returned. They allowed her to enter my cell so that we eventually came to embrace rather shyly. We walked in the sunny exercise yard, holding hands, almost with the innocence of our first meeting on the beach at Cascais. I began to see again why I had fallen in love with her. . . . Her gentle goodness, which I believed I had killed, had returned. She brought tenderness with her to the prison. . . .

One day she told me a popular joke.

Salazar was upset by the sad condition of Portugal's economy. An old friend said: "It's no problem at all. I can solve it for ten escudos." How? asked Salazar. "We just spend it on cab fare," his old friend replied. "We go to the prison by cab, take out Alves Reis . . . put you in his place and him in yours!"

Maria smiled. Salazar was said not to be amused.

* * *

Time remained abstract for me, at least for the most part. Salazar's personal attitude toward me was utterly unforgiving. There were too many people in Portugal who still felt that I had been better for the country's economy than he. As repression and depression increased, he increasingly viewed my very existence as a slap in the face to him, to his authority. Driven by this hatred and a desire for revenge, he decreed that there could be no exile for Alves Reis, despite the suggestion of the sentencing.

I would serve my full twenty years. In prison. At such moments time was less abstract, but in prison you accustom yourself, you adapt.

* * *

When I looked back on the past, as I inevitably did, it seemed to have been a kind of glorious celebration, a long party illuminated by the people around me. Waterlow presiding over the first delivery of banknotes, the New Year's Eve in the streets of Paris, Kreuger treating me as an equal, the cars and the jewels and the Menino d'Ouro . . . but it was the people who made it real, who provided the candlepower, who made it a life lived within a coruscating, glittering chandelier.

Now, as the years were passing and I was being preserved, almost like a specimen in a laboratory or a zoo, I was struck by the growing shadows. The lights, like lanterns on a receding pier, were growing dim, flickering out one at a time.

Sir William. Ivar Kreuger. Both before their time, victims of themselves, their own flaws.

Chaves, the Angolan railway man, was stricken appropriately enough on a train outside Luanda and expired before reaching the city. Terreira, he of the vast white mustaches, died peacefully, having spent his retirement in the Azores. So it went. . . .

Hennies—I could never think of him as Doring—suffered a series of business reverses during the Thirties. He tried to make use of his old espionage contacts from the Great War: little aid there. He then ingratiated himself with the Nazis, who found certain not very important uses for a shady old rascal who didn't ask questions. On one occasion, having worked a small confidence trick, his Nazi friends saved him from jail.

But, in the end, they couldn't save him from his Byzantine past. Out of the night came a man in a raincoat, never identified, with a score to settle. He settled it with a knife, and no one ever knew for sure who had been murdered— Hennies or Doring or someone else who at one time or another had occupied that body, looked at life through that monocle.

When I think of him now the images blur together. I see him the night we met in the courtyard of our house in Luanda. He was a rascal, God knows, but I think of him fondly. I liked the man. . . .

The lights kept going out, the shadows reaching out like lengthening fingers, seductive, promising the final rest.

*   *   *

My years in prison came to an end on May 7, 1945, at four o'clock in the afternoon. The sun was shining brightly, the sky a transparent blue. The past five years I had been a trustee, and the warden had become very much like an old friend. We bade each other farewell in his office. There were tears in our eyes.

"They are celebrating in the streets, Alves," he said. "Bands are playing, Rossio Square is alive with people, dancing. . . . It's the day Alves Reis is coming out of jail."

"You are pulling my leg, my friend. The war has ended today—that's a real reason for celebration."

We laughed together.

Maria and the boys met me. We had not stood together outside prison walls, in the sunshine, in nearly twenty years. I held her in my arms, my full-grown sons watching. She closed her eyes, squeezing them shut against the tears, clinging to me.

"There's someone else who wants to see you," Maria said at last, wiping her cheeks with a frail lace handkerchief while I kissed my boys. Her hair was quite gray. But there was the glaze of innocence in her eyes that had been lost for a time but was back now, her nature asserting itself. Oh, she was not a child, but neither had the hardness of the bad times remained. She pointed out, "See . . ."

I looked down the street where a black Rolls-Royce shone like ebony in the sun. Slowly the door swung open, a man in a black business suit, a tycoon, stood before me, a shy smile on his face. He held out his arms.

"Arnaldo," I said.

* * *

The years since then have not been unkind. I have done some writing, helped Arnaldo—out of the goodness of *his* heart. I have assisted my sons in their various small business enterprises. We have managed to live.

Arnaldo and I have been close friends, almost like brothers. His wife Silvia passed away during the war, leaving him with a son and a daughter. He has prospered beyond imagining. He has given us free run of his estates, and he remains in robust good health. We have discussed the banknote business in detail, almost academically, and he has expressed wonder more than anything else.

Many an evening the three of us—Maria, Arnaldo and I—have sat around the dining-room table with the photograph albums I so assiduously filled in the old days. Then for an evening the room is full of people and there is no pain for us, not anymore. There Arnaldo and I stand again before the giant locomotive at the High Bridge, Maria sits so elegantly atop the white horse, Greta stands languidly between Marang and me at the Longchamps races. . . . No, there is no pain anymore.

The three of us laugh at remembered moments, and sometimes the laughter fades into wistful silences. But Maria will point at a picture of José with his wolfish grin and we will find ourselves on the snow-slick Paris streets, the crowd gathering, the headlamps of the taxis making it daylight in the middle of the night as José and I punch each other.

Maria, Arnaldo and I, now almost at the end, still inseparable. Perhaps the French are right: the more things change, the more they stay the same. . . .

There is little to say of José, who drifted off into his own circle. He bought a small bar, lost it, and the new owners hired him as a greeter. He became something of a figure in Lisbon's nightlife, with his reputation and ornate tales from his past.

In March 1960 he had a bad fall, broke his hip and thigh. I went to visit him in the hospital. He looked like what he was, an elderly white-haired man who had lived a full and somewhat exhausting life.

"Alves Reis," he said, as if he hadn't spoken my name in years. "I've been meaning to call you, have you to the club. . . ." He shrugged. I remembered him kicking a stone in the Luxembourg Gardens when he'd capitulated to me, given up Greta. I remembered him as a young man, telling me about women and drinking too much wine. . . .

"How are you?"

"How do I look?" He laughed harshly, but his face softened when he looked up. "I understand these things happen when you get old, eh? Look at the present I got today." He pointed to a handsome Grundig radio on the stand near his bed. "Greta sent it to me."

"That's very nice," I said. "She is quite a woman, our Greta."

"Do you write to her?"

"Oh, yes, sometimes. . . . Yes, we write. She called on New Year's Eve. I've seen some of her movies. . . . She's very famous, isn't she, José?"

"More famous even than Alves Reis," he said. "You really loved her, didn't you?"

"Why, yes, I did," I said. "It was all very romantic."

"I never loved her," José said with a small shrug. "Love . . . I hardly know what it is." Then his face brightened. "But I liked her more than any other woman I ever knew."

I don't know if his body had just worn out, or if there was some complication I never heard about. But José died on March 29. Under his hospital pillow they found a tattered, dog-eared memento—a photograph of Greta Nordlund standing in riding clothes beside one of her horses in the Bois de Boulogne.

He left a scribbled note. He wanted me to have the Grundig radio. Another light had gone out.

*   *   *

About the same time I learned, by an odd chance, that Smythe-Hancock had perished long, long ago. The Blitz, London . . . Friends and enemies, time was making them all equal.

*   *   *

A week after José's passing I got word of Marang. Business had been good: he was a multimillionaire, retired for many years to the Riviera, where he and Madame Marang lived regally at Cannes.

Now I received a clipping from *Le Figaro*, sent by Greta.

Mme. Karel Marang, Mr. & Mrs. Karel Marang, Mr. and Mrs. Florent Marang, Mr. and Mrs. R. H. MacDonald and Mr. and Mrs. Ido Marang and his twelve grandchildren announce with great sorrow the death of Mr. Karel Marang, who died at his home, 8 rue du Canada, on February 13 after a long illness. He was 76.

Greta's note was typical: ironic, amused, loving.

Hold on, Thunderbolt! There aren't many survivors. I still love you. Greta.

Along the way, Waterlow and Sons had ceased to exist.

*   *   *

Greta called one night in 1965. She was well past seventy by then, but her voice was strong, still husky and remarkably sensual. She had never married, not since we had met. . . . Maria answered the telephone, and I heard a cry of delight: "Greta!" They must have chatted for half an hour, Paris to Lisbon. A fortune, but Greta can no doubt afford it. She still appears in films regularly, the *grande dame*. Maria handed me the telephone, smiled, her fingers lingering on mine for an instant.

Greta was full of life, making small jokes. She teased me, called me Thunderbolt, wished me a happy birthday. I had completely forgotten. It was September 8. I had embarked on my own seventieth year.

She made me promise we would come to Paris for a reunion at Christmas. "Even better, New Year's Eve." Her voice dropped to a whisper, the joking gone. We were young again for a moment. "We became lovers on New Year's Eve," she said, "forty-one years ago. Come to see me."

I said we would try.

But Greta and I belonged to the past. I had my memories. I didn't have to see her again. I loved her, and that would never change.

EPILOGUE

Salazar was finally dead. Officially dead at last. For two years he'd been very little more than a vegetable, hadn't even known he'd been replaced by Caetano during the coma following his brain hemorrhage. When he came to, his doctors had believed the news that he was no longer Premier would kill him. So for two years the charade was carried on. His advisers and cabinet ministers would appear regularly in his bedchamber, nod their heads at his rambling orders, go away. He was not allowed to have newspapers, radios or television. He was dead, but he didn't know it.

On April 28, 1970, he made his last address to the people of Portugal on the occasion of his eighty-first birthday. Alves, almost seventy-four himself, watched the speech at his son's house on the new television set. Maria found the Premier an awful bore and had gone instead to the country estate of a friend. Then, in late May, Salazar had gone to the zoo in Lisbon, God only knew why. In mid-July he was stricken with a kidney infection that finally carried him off on the twenty-seventh.

Alves Reis might have been expected to feel a certain satisfaction, but it didn't amount to much. Oh, surely, he'd outlived another of his enemies, another relic from the old days, but at seventy-three it cannot be counted a major triumph. Salazar had had a good run for his money. And you had to give him credit for saying what he meant, standing by it. "The Portuguese must be treated as children," he was fond of saying. And "The business of government is simply too important to be left to the governed" —that was another favorite. Dean Acheson, the American, had once said of Salazar: "This remarkable man is the nearest approach in our time to Plato's philosopher-king." That sort of thing was a little hard to swallow. What the man had been was an intellectually rigorous, mean-minded little Jesuit who stayed a bachelor all his life and believed that the key to ruling was simply to keep the people dumb and poor. He had not trusted the twentieth century. He'd done as much as anyone to deny its existence.

Such were the thoughts of Alves Reis, white-haired now, dapper in a white suit sitting in the bar of the Avenida Palace, looking out at the crowds in Lisbon's Rossio Square. The bar was dim and quiet, a friendly spot where he dropped in almost every day for a glass or two of port. He'd gone forty years without a drink of anything alcoholic, but his physician had suggested a couple of years before that a port or two would be wonderfully restorative.

The funeral service that morning, which he had attended through the intercession of an enormously wealthy friend, had been held in the very grand sixteenth-century Jeronimos Monastery, where Vasco da Gama is buried. Vasco da Gama. Alves couldn't but smile at Da Gama. He always pictured Da Gama as the face on the five-hundred-escudo banknote that had not been in use for years. Fortunately Salazar was being buried at Santa Comba Dao, his hometown. The thought of him resting near the great explorer was too much.

Caetano led the mourners, of course. Members of the armed forces carried the coffin, draped with the red, green and gold flag, to a special train. Caetano and four hundred dignitaries accompanied the body on its five-hour ride. It was a very hot day, the poor devils. Brazil had sent Augusto Rademaker, the Vice President. Germany had sent Karl Schmidt, also Vice President. Thank God the Americans hadn't sent the Agnew fellow. They did send a person named Maurice Stans, Secretary of Commerce, obviously not an important figure.

The eulogy he'd sat through had been ridiculous, but then if you couldn't say ridiculous things about a man when he died, when could you? Monsignor Moreira das

Neves had actually compared Salazar to Henry the Navigator.

Alves sipped his port, looked up, caught his reflection in the large gilt-framed mirror over the bar. Here I am, he thought, just an elderly old fellow having a drink waiting for my son, reflecting on the death of a dictator. Portugal must be full of us this afternoon. But none quite like me, he thought. How many men have been called the cause of Salazar's rise to power? Not many, he supposed. None, actually, that he could remember, other than himself.

The crowds in Rossio Square were milling about as if they didn't quite know how to top off the day of the funeral itself. There was a haze of dust hanging over the square. In the dim bar the shapes of men grew like toadstools, out of the sun's blast. Fans rotated slowly The bartender came over and stood beside the polished table. He was carrying a small glass of port for himself.

"It's a good day for a toast, Senhor Reis," he said softly, leaning over and replacing the ashtray with a clean one. Alves nodded, smiling crookedly.

"To you, sir," the bartender said. "The man who stole Portugal. . . ." It was said quietly, an almost silent toast between the two of them. Alves mimed a demurral.

"Sit down, Marco," he said. He removed his dark horn-rimmed spectacles and wiped away the day's dust with his handkerchief. The bartender sat down. The bar was very quiet. It was the middle of the afternoon.

"The last of Salazar," Marco remarked blandly. There was no visible emotion. In all probability he was a Communist, and so far as Alves was concerned, that was Marco's business. Alves had never really gotten involved in politics. Politics was a waste of time in Portugal. He had learned a very long time ago that money was what made the difference, not politics.

"The last of Salazar," Alves repeated. "The mighty Salazar."

"You knew him, didn't you? In the old days? People say that you and Salazar were great friends at one time. . . ." The bartender's eyes flickered with rare curiosity.

"Marco, history teaches us one great lesson—namely, that history cannot be trusted. You know me. And you should know you mustn't believe too much of what you hear about me. I am the most lied-about man in the long, noble history of our troubled land. As for my friendship

with Salazar . . . let me say that it has been widely mis-
interpreted. And exaggerated."

Marco winked at him. People who knew him, or met
him and realized who he was, were always winking at him.

"Has my son been here yet?"

"Not yet, Senhor Reis."

"Well, he'll be here soon. We're on our way, you know.
Brazil. Three months in Brazil . . . a new adventure." He
smiled.

"A long way," Marco reflected.

"Indeed. But what are time and distance? Only dimensions, infinite, forever. Not of much consequence to a man
my age. . . ."

The bartender went to answer a call. Alves watched the
doorway for a few minutes. Brazil, he thought. Brazil, of
all places. You'd have thought a man of his age, who'd
seen what he had, would have walked away from any more
adventures. But the inclination never died. It reminded him
of his grandmother. She had always said something to the
effect that a dog couldn't change his nature. It seemed
quite reasonable at the time, and time hadn't done it much
damage.

"Alves Reis . . ."

He heard the scrap of conversation in the dim stillness.
He couldn't see who had spoken. It didn't matter. It happened from time to time. You could hardly blame people.
Curiosity wasn't a crime. He smiled slowly to himself,
knowing he was being watched. He took a cigar from a
leather case in his suit pocket, fished a lighter from another pocket. Solid gold, a Dunhill, cost the earth at today's prices. It was, however, almost half a century old,
softly burnished. The inscription engraved on the side was
almost obliterated, but it didn't matter; there wasn't much
chance he'd ever forget it. It had been given to him by the
most beautiful woman he'd ever seen, had marked the most
remarkably romantic moment of his life.

He was smoking and staring at the chunk of gold, slowly
revolving it in his hand, watching it catch the faint light
from the window, when he felt his son's hand on his shoulder.

"Papa, the taxi is waiting." My son Virgilio, he thought,
is fifty. Good Lord, what next? "The bags are all packed.
Mama is going to see us off at the airport. I have the
tickets. . . ." He is a nervous fellow, Alves Reis reflected,

but he has always had to live with the shadow of his father.
A good boy.

He flipped his hand jauntily at the bartender.

Marco said, "Give my regards to Brazil."

Alves nodded. He hated goodbyes.